Naughty Bits

Joey W. Hill

B

BERKLEY BOOKS, NEW YORK

THE BERKLEY PUBLISHING GROUP
Published by the Penguin Group
Penguin Group (USA) LLC
375 Hudson Street, New York, New York 10014

USA • Canada • UK • Ireland • Australia • New Zealand • India • South Africa • China

penguin.com

A Penguin Random House Company

This book is an original publication of The Berkley Publishing Group.

Library of Congress Cataloging-in-Publication Data

Hill, Joey W.
Naughty bits / Joey W. Hill.—Berkley trade paperback edition.
pages ; cm
ISBN 978-0-425-27643-3 (softcover)
1. Man-woman relationships—Fiction.   2. Sexual dominance and submission—Fiction.   I. Title.
PS3608.I4343N38 2015
813'.6—dc23
2014041313

PUBLISHING HISTORY
InterMix eBook editions / April–July 2014
Berkley trade paperback edition / January 2015

PRINTED IN THE UNITED STATES OF AMERICA

10 9 8 7 6 5 4 3 2 1

Cover design by George Long.
Woman © Maksim Shmeljov/Shutterstock; *Lace* © Incomible/Shutterstock; *Flowers* © april70/Shutterstock.
Interior text design by Kristin del Rosario.

Praise for the novels of Joey W. Hill

"Joey W. Hill is one of the best authors of erotica for a reason—her exceptional ability to bring together . . . complex characters along with gripping romances that revolve around the world of BDSM . . . When Ms. Hill writes a love scene she brings all of the senses to life." —*Risqué Reviews*

"This is a scorcher! It's one of those books that keeps the sexual tension on superstrength and leaves you squirming for a resolution." —*The Forbidden Bookshelf*

"Joey W. Hill blends the erotic and emotional perfectly . . . providing readers with a gorgeous romance." —*Joyfully Reviewed*

"Joey W. Hill's books are nigh on impossible to define as each has to be read for itself and each offers the reader something uniquely theirs to relate to. Not only are they great books, they also pick at your soul." —*TwoLips Reviews*

"I do not expect many erotic romance novels to be full of literary depth or to leave a lasting impression . . . Ms. Hill's beautiful way with words, impressive plot, and evocative characters managed to reach inside my heart." —*Colorful Reviews*

"Stripping away the emotions and layers . . . Joey W. Hill demonstrates her fantastic ability to develop characters and bring them to life on the pages of her story." —*Just Erotic Romance Reviews*

"Fans of Ms. Hill will devour this story and start all over again once the journey is completed. The characters are more than mere sums of parts on paper; they are people who live, breathe, hurt, crave, and love." —*Long and Short Reviews*

ACKNOWLEDGMENTS

My tremendous thanks to my three critique partners: Sheri Fogarty, Ann Jacobs, and Angela Knight for going above and beyond to help me with the initial release of this series as four separate novellas. As many of my readers know, writing novellas is not easy for me. I love writing long, involved stories! Fortunately, my CPs have much more expertise with novellas, and they kept me from total disaster. They not only helped me tear down and rebuild The Lingerie Shop (Part I) to make it FAR better, but gave me invaluable advice and direction on the other three parts. I don't know what I'd do without you three.

With respect to Part II, The Training Session, special thanks to Dotty—avid reader, expert hairdresser, and all round lovely person—who helped make sure that Madison cut Logan's hair properly. Logan particularly thanks you for that, Dotty! As always, I deeply appreciate your support and enthusiasm for my work. You're a treasure, as well as a reassurance—if my stories attract great folks like you, I must be doing something right (grin). Looking forward to the next time we get to hang out . . .

As always, any remaining shortcomings in *Naughty Bits* are the fault of this thickheaded author, not the exceptional talent of these very patient ladies. Thank you all for taking the journey with Logan and Madison.

PART I

The
Lingerie Shop

"I've got you. You're all fucking mine."

He had his hand wrapped in her hair, holding so tight her scalp ached. He moved his mouth against her throat, against a vital artery pulsing with adrenaline. Pressed up against her back the way he was, he allowed her no personal space. His thigh was thrust between her legs, his cock a bar of steel branding itself on her buttock, even through his jeans. When she sucked in a breath, it was all him. Spiced aftershave, heated male. She wanted to turn, put her face right against his throat, nestle in that scent, in his strength.

He controlled everything, and she felt safe. For the first time in her life. If only he wasn't a dream. But in her mind was the only place where she could give him control.

"You're thinking again. You get punished when you think."

As he stepped back, she wanted to reach for him, but she couldn't. He had her bound against a cool cinder-block wall. Embedded manacles held her wrists and ankles, and dozens of taut, thin lines crisscrossed her body from shoulders to feet. The bindings were threaded through two vertical columns of hooks, outlining her against the stone. When he released her, until normal, mundane movement restored her skin, she'd bear the impressions of those lines. And other marks as well.

She yelped as the flogger hit her buttocks. The rough, braided strips bit into skin, left marks like a bird's sharp toes.

"Beg for punishment."

"Please . . . hurt me."

"No."

She moaned as he threaded his hand through the crisscrossed lines to push between the wall and her body. He caressed her navel, then dropped down to probe her clit, work it with a single firm fingertip, an excruciating and pleasurable tease. "It's not about hurting you. It's about you letting go. Ssshhh . . ."

He soothed, even as he tormented. She struggled like a moth in a web, made tiny cries as he kept flicking and tweaking. The orgasm was as close as the prayer for mercy when he stepped back.

"I don't care what you *think*. Tell me how you feel. The first word that comes to mind."

The flogger struck and she jumped. "Afraid."

He did it again, and she gasped. "Wet."

He gave a dangerous chuckle. "Trying to get me to play with your pussy again, aren't you? You'll have to earn that."

Whap!

"Hot . . ." "Alive . . ." "Need you" . . . "Aches . . ." "Stop . . ." "Don't Stop . . ."

"Free." She said that one several times. Each stroke made the feeling more real. The flogger cut into her, but instead of cringing, she was arching, trying to lift her hips, spread her arms wider, a swan taking flight, fighting what held her to the ground. She licked her lips. "Master. Please."

He kept punishing her until she was a quivering mess, then he closed in on her again, took hold of her hair in that tight hold she loved. He bit her neck and she trembled more. "Say it."

"I'm yours, Master." She believed it. There was no doubt. No fear. No thinking. She heard that delicious sound of him unbuckling his belt, unzipping his jeans, then she let out a sigh of relief as his cock probed between her spread legs. He rubbed the head in her overflowing juices, getting himself slick before he started to push up inside her.

He'd fuck her like this, while she was helpless against the wall. She'd come so hard her flesh would be scraped by the cinder block, because she'd writhe against it like a snake shedding a skin. He'd take her home, rub soft lotions into her flesh, make her sleep naked next to him so he could play with her body whenever, however, he wished, all night long. His long, strong fingers would stroke those whip marks, the scrapes, push inside her. Anything he wanted, she'd give him, because she trusted him with everything. At least in this moment.

Dawn would come and dread would return. Along with a hundred other emotions wrapping her up like those crisscrossed lines, only these imprisoned her mind and denied her heart.

Only by being his was she truly free.

"Madison, are you ready to go? Earth to Madison?"

Alice's voice, pulling her out of the fantasy. Or memory. The man and the dungeon wall were fantasy; Alice's voice a memory, because Alice was dead. It was Madison's subconscious, recalling her to the present.

Madison blinked through the car windshield. She was parked in the alley behind Naughty Bits, looking at cobblestone pavement, a set of Dumpsters and an early morning sky, the clouds made smoky and gold-edged by the sun starting to come up somewhere beyond the row of buildings. Why'd she get out of bed this morning?

Because it was time to get moving, do what needed to be done. After weeks of being closed to the public, Naughty Bits needed to be reopened, but she didn't have to face that this morning. She was here to clean, evaluate inventory. Surely she could handle that.

Taking her purse and coffee cup with her, she locked the car. As she moved toward the back door, she fished out the key. So focused on getting the door open, she didn't understand why the lock turned easily but the door resisted, until she looked down.

A UPS package was propped against the door. It was the size of a cinder block, and obviously weighed the same. As she lugged it inside, precariously balancing her coffee, Madison wondered what kind of item with that poundage would belong in a lingerie store, but then Naughty Bits was far more than a lingerie store. The BDSM section had plenty of things that belonged in a medieval dungeon. Maybe it was an engraved ball and chain. A special-order gift for the Master who had everything.

Hefting the box through the stockroom, she took it up front. It'd be easier to have it sitting behind the counter, ready for whomever had to be contacted to pick it up. She left it there as she went to unlock the front door. No, she wasn't opening today, but she didn't expect customers this early in the morning and she didn't like the trapped feeling of a bolted door. Turning back toward the display counter, she saw the envelope.

Everything else vanished.

To MadGirl was written on the outside. It looked like it had been placed in its current location weeks ago, bearing a light layer of dust, same as the display counter glass beneath it.

Leave it to Alice to think of doing something like this. Fishing out a letter opener from the drawer beneath the cash register, Madison slit the envelope. She ran tense fingers over her face, a reassuring hard stroke, then unfolded the pages.

Sell doesn't have to be a four-letter word. You used to know that.

Madison blinked. Now, of all times, her sister would choose to be snide? Alice had great hook lines, though. She never started a letter with the traditional "Dear Madison." Her handwritten script had flourishes like Thomas Jefferson's. She'd done cursive that way since the eighth grade.

I'm not being snide. Sell connects to two other really important four-letter words. Want. Need. But I think the word that best describes it is provide.

Did you ever look that one up in the Encarta dictionary? The legal term means to require something in advance as a condition or as part of a contract. The non-legal term is to supply somebody with something, or be a source of something wanted or needed by somebody. Sets off something in your gut, doesn't it?

Madison swallowed. "Stop it, Alice," she muttered.

Fuck is another four-letter word, and it gets a bad rap. Cock, cunt, come . . . Do you think God and the Devil were playing a word game that day? "See how many naughty words can start with C, and whoever wins gets to handle everything connected to sex. Go!"

You know the Devil won that one, hands down. God's still pissed about it. Probably why He started the rumor sex was a sin.

Madison choked on a laugh.

Getting tired, so have to cut to the chase. Here's the thing, MadGirl. Great selling isn't about tricking someone into buying crap. It's about helping them get something they truly need that adds value to their lives.

"Oh, Alice." The ache in her throat increased as her voice echoed in the waiting silence of the store. Waiting for a mistress who would never return, who'd known how to turn a lingerie store into an adult Disneyland, complete with the enchantment, promise of princes and happily-ever-afters. She'd told Alice that once, only then she'd had derision dripping off every word. Now she thought it simply as it was. Truth.

I'm leaving you my store. You know that, but what you're going to find out from my executor when you call him about this letter is that I set aside enough money for you to run the store for the next several years. If you don't want to keep it after a year, sell the inventory and seek another path. But promise me you'll give it a year. I'm betting you'll find it easier to leave your life in Boston than you expect.

How right she was about that would have been unsettling, except the subsequent paragraphs left Madison even more flummoxed.

This next bit is the awkward part. My passion was getting people in touch with their sexual selves, but we're sisters, so talking about sex beyond jokes and generalities has a certain Eww factor, right? Before you turn red as a tomato, think how bad this would be if I were your brother!

Madison snorted, but then her fingers tightened on the page.

I know you're a sub, sis. I knew it even before I dragged you to that first BDSM club in Chicago. I made it sound like a silly adventure to get you there, but I thought it might help you come to terms with it, stop repressing it. You were so mesmerized: barely moving, clutching your drink, hypnotized by everything you saw.

It came back in perfect clarity. Madison's eyes had clung to the female submissives. The one who knelt at her Master's feet. The one who'd been restrained, her cries of pain and pleasure drawn forth by the slap of the flogger, a male hand, the paddle. The one who passed within three feet of her, wearing a collar and leash her Master had wrapped around his hand, his other palm intimately low on her hip, guiding her.

She'd stared and yearned for a language she understood but couldn't speak herself.

As a teenager, Madison had devoured the old bodice rippers on her mother's bookshelves. The more contemporary romances left her detached and, in the dark corners of her mind, Madison knew why. When she masturbated, she'd see the pirate captain tying her to his bunk, the king using his strong hands to push open her thighs, a cop forcing her to her knees with an insistent tap of his baton and feeding his cock between her lips. She'd gush around her fingers, driven to climax by those imaginings.

Sitting in the club booth, surrounded by all the sensory input of Dominance and submission, the mantra of "at last, at last" had pounded inside her heart. She'd wanted to be every woman there embracing submissive pleasures.

What Alice hadn't known was that Madison had agreed to go that night because she'd been nursing the hope that a garish, stark reality would drive the need away, a need that had become worse over the years with each failed relationship. No matter how hard she worked at each one, the man she tried to love still left. She always fell short.

Choosing the wrong guy is different from being wrong about yourself,

MadGirl. Madison focused on the letter again. *Stop trying to prove you could do something to make Dad love us more. I loved her, but Mom was weak. She destroyed herself because she thought it was her fault Dad was an asshole who wanted younger women. Don't be her. Stop trying to be what every guy, Master or not, wants you to be. Embrace who you are for* you. *Anything else is a pointless soul-suck.*

"Goddamn you," Madison murmured. This was why she'd distanced herself from her sister during the last two years. Alice had been a hammer, relentlessly pounding on the idea that Madison kept making the wrong decisions when it came to relationships. But none of that mattered anymore, did it? A point underscored by the last paragraph.

Dominance and submission isn't one-size-fits-all. You have to make choices. Giving yourself to a Master is an incredibly special gift. I loved you more than anyone, MadGirl. Given how many cool, amazing people I met in my absurdly short life, that's saying quite a lot. You always did underestimate what kind of gem you are. Maybe you'll get a chance to shine here and see what I always saw in you.

Be good, sweet sis. But not too good. Remember me by showing your "naughty bits" once in a while.

Shit. Madison put the letter on the counter and slid down the wall behind it, giving in to the hard sobs.

Madison had been up in Boston, selling stocks and bonds, managing people's investments. Alice had called once a week and Madison always answered, but she'd stayed passive-aggressive, cordial, distant. As a result, she hadn't caught the vital clues. Alice's allergy attacks that came more frequently, the colds and flu bugs. Her sister had been getting weaker and sicker.

Then, a couple months ago, Alice had called on a Thursday, not their usual day. In her matter-of-fact way, she'd said if Madison could come home that weekend, she'd really like to give her a quick last hug. She also wanted Madison to go through her collection of high-end, well-sterilized sex toys to see if she wanted any of them before they had to be boxed up and dumped. Incredibly enough, the Senior

Citizens' Auxiliary at the hospital wouldn't accept them as donations for their thrift shop. *You'd think they'd realize there's nothing better for cardiovascular health than a good daily orgasm . . .*

Her lips twitched at Alice's acid observation now. During that call, Madison had simply been stunned. She'd said something absurd like, "Okay, let me check my schedule, I have this meeting, but I know I can get out of that . . ."

Alice had always known her so well, no matter how much Madison hated that. She'd merely listened. "No worries, MadGirl. Come if you can."

Once off the phone that day, Madison's brain had cleared. She'd called her boss, told Barbara what was happening. Barbara said she had to at least come in Friday and handle her scheduled client meetings, because Barbara had a tee time with board members. Madison refused. Barbara told her she'd be fired, and Madison retorted if she was that replaceable, Barbara could keep the damn job.

Just like that, she'd walked away from a career she'd excelled at for five years. Crazy, right? But it was as if she'd been treading water in a pool, blinded to the fact dry land was as close as the nearest ladder. Until Alice had arranged a wake-up call in the form of a simple deathbed request.

Come give me a quick hug.

If the memory had theme music, it would be something sad, wistful. Instead, the overtly erotic strains of "Boléro" injected Dudley Moore and a running Bo Derek into Madison's brain, jarring her fully into the present.

She'd forgotten that music played when someone came into the store. Alice had the classics like "Boléro," "Somewhere in Time" and "Claire de Lune" on the playlist, as well as sultry Latin numbers by Enrique Iglesias and pure fuck-me-now Barry White and Boyz II Men songs. She'd also thrown Rod Stewart's "Do Ya Think I'm Sexy" and "Tonight's the Night" into the mix because, well, why not?

Once the door triggered the music, the whole song would play unless someone else came in. Each time the door opened or closed, a new song started, letting Alice know she had a customer arriving or departing. If there were no new customers after a song played in its entirety, there would be silence. Madison had asked Alice why she didn't set it up so the music played constantly, and her sister said there was value in silence as well.

Honest to God, Alice's choices gave the store a personality all its own. Madison wouldn't be surprised if she could hear the store breathing.

She yanked her attention back to the more important issue. She wasn't alone, and she was hiding behind the register counter. She hadn't expected lingerie shopping to be popular at seven a.m. Jesus, she hadn't even flipped the OPEN sign over or turned on lights, but having worked sales before, she knew customers were as bad as kindergarteners when it came to paying attention to details like those.

She should pop up from behind the counter like a macabre cartoon. *"Yes, how may I help you?"* Instead, she wiped her eyes and rose into view in a way that made it look as though she'd been bending below the counter to get something out of the cabinet, rather than pushing herself up the wall as if her weight had tripled since she'd landed there. "I'm sorry, we're not open yet."

She said that before she took a look at her first customer. A good thing, since she might have stammered. He wasn't the type of client she'd expected, and not merely because he was a "he."

In his early to mid-twenties, this guy looked like he'd escaped the cover shoot for a romance novel. His stonewashed jeans, belted at his lean waist, defined a superior tight ass, well displayed because he was turned away from her, examining the merchandise on the rounder closest to him. The rolled-up sleeves of his denim shirt exposed tanned forearms. He had good shoulders—wide enough for his age. As he grew older and muscle weight thickened, they'd probably get even nicer. She expected beneath those clothes his body would be well sculpted by the gym. Guys who worked out hard moved like wild animals, with easy grace and strength.

His sandy brown hair brushed his collar and brow, and when he glanced toward her beneath an attractive scattering of strands, his blue eyes reminded her of the sky. "Hi. I'm Troy. I work next door."

"Oh." Not a customer, then, even though he'd been perusing a rack of bras, fingering a lacy D-cup with speculative interest and no self-consciousness. Cross-dresser? Before their falling-out, she'd spent plenty of time in Alice's world, brushing shoulders with everyone from transgender to cross-dressers. As a result, she didn't think he fit the type. He wore his clothes without any excessive fashion sense. Simple, basic guy clothes, blues and denims, work shoes. Though a cross-dressing straight guy was possible, his gaze marked her with typical unoffensive hetero interest. Interest in what she looked like out of her clothes, not *how* she wore them.

"Nice to meet you." She regretted her wooden tone, but he didn't seem fazed by it, approaching the counter to extend his hand. She suppressed the urge to take another swipe at her face. Yeah, that would be nice. Wipe her nose, then offer her hand.

In Boston, her client list had included exacting millionaires and powerful corporate businessmen. She could handle an employee from . . . what was next door? A hardware store. In this artsy downtown area of Matthews, a quaint municipality on the outskirts of the much bigger city of Charlotte, all the stores were kitschy, boutique-type ventures. The hardware store, the brief glimpse she'd had of it, was a historic leftover from eighty years ago, maintaining the original brick façade in front. It was still run like one of the old-timey general stores, advertising horse feed and strawberries in season, as well as small engine repair.

Alice had relocated here from a Charlotte strip mall a few years ago. Because of their falling-out, Madison hadn't had a chance to meet her new neighbors.

"When we heard you knocking around, Mr. Scott told me to come over and see if you need anything."

Troy still had his hand out, and she was staring at him as if he'd sprung out of the walls. With a jerk, she lifted her hand to clasp his. He closed his fingers over hers, held them. He had a rough palm, a warm grip, and those eyes never left her face. "We're so sorry about Alice. She was an incredible person, and she loved you so much."

Wow. He zeroed right in on the personal, leaving her nowhere to hide. Madison blinked, hard, and unconsciously squeezed his hand, to find her own squeezed right back. She'd been dealing with lawyers, city clerks, real estate people, all of whom talked about Alice in distant niceties. This man was as much a stranger as they were, but his obvious personal connection to Alice, physical and emotional, made her hungry to maintain the contact. She didn't want to make a fool of herself, but Troy saved her from that. He covered her hand with his other one, holding hers sandwiched between them and giving her an excuse to keep it in that position.

"She left me this place," Madison said. "I'm not sure how to run it. I mean, I know how to run it. I've been in sales, but . . ."

Good grief, Madison. She shrugged to get him to let her go and put both hands on the counter, pressing her palms against the cool glass. Beneath it was an array of nipple clamps and clit jewelry, displayed as elegantly as any New York diamond district's offerings. She was pretty sure some of them had actual diamonds, since one had a four-figure price tag. For nipple jewelry? In contrast, on top of the counter, Alice had a basket of plastic hopping penises, breasts and bright red lips. Madison took a closer look. Okay, those weren't lips. At least not the mouth kind. A cheerful yellow bow on the basket drew attention to the contents.

Alice. God, I'm going to miss you.

Troy picked up one of the toys, wound it up, let it hop across the counter. "She was crazy," he said. "Crazy, wonderful, beautiful, sexy."

She glanced up at him. Had they been lovers? Somehow she didn't think so. Yet his tone was intimate. It was impossible not to focus on his mouth, those eyes. She liked hearing his Southern accent after all the Boston ones. The drawl, the slower pace of talking. Feeling, living, everything. She could imagine him uttering an endearment in that sexy drawl.

When she realized it was obvious she was staring, she flushed. He straightened to his six-foot height and broke eye contact.

"Sorry. Mr. Scott says I need to be careful about doing that. I tend to be distracting." He said it without ego, giving her a half smile. "He says there's nothing wrong with looking the way I do, as long as I give as much pleasure as I take. But since I love giving it, it gets kind of confusing, because that's a form of taking, you know?"

Fortunately, he didn't seem to expect an answer to such a complex question. "Anyhow," he continued, "I better get back. Come by later if you want to check out our store. You're always welcome. Mr. Scott wanted to give you time to settle in, but remember to call if you need us. We're here for you."

With a nod, he moved back to the front door. "Boléro" was on its finale. As he opened the door, "Twinkle, Twinkle, Little Star" started, done as a poignant piano instrumental. Alice used to sing it to her when Madison was five and she was ten. She'd called her Little Star.

Christ, how was she going to do this?

Madison locked the front door and retreated into the stockroom. Throwing herself into practical things, she spent most of the morning going through the inventory and reviewing Alice's accounts on her laptop. The business had been doing very well, no surprise. Alice blended class with whimsy, sensual with the blatantly sexual, easing her clientele into the offerings of her store and daring them to expand their boundaries.

It was evident in the store's layout. The display window to the left of the door included art nouveau–style mannequins posed in dramatic, interactive ways, a natural flow from scene to scene. One mannequin lounged in a gorgeous peignoir. A veil was caught beneath her, a rhinestone wedding set on her finger. Another wore a provocative teddy coupled with sleek stilettos and classy pearls, a sheer scarf tied at the waist.

On the other side of the door, Alice showed off a set of her role-playing costumes. A French maid sat on the lap of a male mannequin dressed in a Victorian suit, his hand resting high on her thigh. When Madison flipped the switch on the lighting, a holographic fireplace came to life behind the couple, suggesting they were in his study. She pictured the gentleman flipping the maid over, pulling down her ruffled panties and giving her several smart slaps for not dusting the upper shelves. She felt the tingle in her own buttocks, could too easily see herself in that costume.

Only in her rich fantasy world, it was no costume. It was the real thing—she was a real maid, and her boss had piercing eyes that always watched her, the stern mouth promising all sorts of dark, sinful pleasures in his service . . .

Madison leaned her temple against the display frame, forcing her gaze back to the wedding set. The spotlight made the pearls gleam and tiny sequins in the peignoir glitter. It didn't evoke any fantasies for her. Not unless that Victorian Master was the prospective groom. For their wedding night, he'd wrap her wrists with the pearls and lace her into a white corset, make her hold on to the bedpost as he drew the laces tight, binding her so that she felt dizzy.

She'd had seven serious relationships since college, and Gerald was the first of those who'd made her think of marriage. He was a psychologist who seemed to understand so many things about her that she'd trusted him with a glimpse of her fantasies. A little spanking, a little being tied with scarves to the bed rail? He was okay with it. After all, in the movies and TV, they kinked things up like that. But when Madison had gotten carried away with it, wanted more pain, wanted him to demand she call him Master, that had changed.

She cringed, remembering the look on his face. Anything more than the mildest of BDSM play had been freak-flag territory for him, so she'd developed the discipline and willpower to stay the hell away from it before she lost him. And lost him anyway.

Through all her relationships, she'd played hopscotch with her sub cravings. Tried to make it work with one guy, completely shut it away in a box with another. She'd never been able to trust any of them enough to make the full leap. No matter what Alice said, that was why the failure rested with her.

She'd gotten so tangled up about it that, after her last relationship ended two years ago, she'd decided to quit all of it. Her heart was too battered, her mind too confused. Maybe she'd take up dating when she was past menopause. Sure she'd have to wait a couple decades, but women at that age seemed like they had stuff figured out. Maybe the hormones drove the stupid shit out of the brain and only left what was important.

Stop thinking about this.

She turned her attention back to the layout of the store, making inventory notes as she went. Clothing choices were in the front, but as a customer moved toward the back, Alice had tasteful displays of vibrators, a wall of erotica DVDs and novels catering to women and couples. Over that section a silver-framed, black-and-white print showed a couple in bed, the woman secure in the man's arms as she read to him. He cupped her bare breast, his palm discreetly concealing the nipple, his mouth on her throat. She had glasses perched on her nose.

Such quaint, erotic details were everywhere, making a stroll through the store a sensory experience. Alice had even done her own product presentation. She designed velvet display boxes, mesh bags and other containers, discarding tacky, porno-type packaging.

Steeling herself, Madison moved to the very back corner. The archway there led to the Dungeon Room. It held all the BDSM toys, furniture and more hard-core pieces related to fetish lifestyles. To help

her customers explore their wilder side, Alice had strategically placed
a refreshment kiosk in this room. As Madison looked at the empty
table, a hard lump formed in her throat. She could almost smell the
freshly brewed coffee, tea and homemade baked goods Alice had
served her customers.

Why was seeing a mundane reminder of someone's existence
almost harder to bear than other, more dramatic events surrounding
her loss? Probably because it felt like a mockery, God's cruel game.
Look, she was here, just yesterday, baking a cake, and now, *poof*, she's
gone. Forever.

Troy. Now she remembered. Alice had mentioned him in the
handwritten letters she sent at least every couple of weeks. Madison
wished she'd kept them all.

*Troy, a treasure and treat who works next door, regularly comes in to
pilfer lemon muffins. Mom's recipes never fail to attract men, lol.*

Madison had no doubt plenty of women would let Troy devour
their muffins. She tried to log the room's inventory with her peripheral vision, thinking of them as nameless objects. Not padded cuffs,
spreader bars, soft floggers, bamboo canes and blindfolds. Framed
photos on the walls showed both Masters and Mistresses in various
poses with their submissives. One of them took the window display
to its natural conclusion. A severe, darkly handsome Victorian gentleman clamped his hand over his maid's wrist as she flailed on his
lap, his other palm raised to give her bottom a disciplinary slap. The
young woman's lips were parted. Though she was struggling, the
aroused expression on her face was unmistakable.

Madison breathed in through her nose, released it through her
mouth. Alice had taught her the stress technique years ago, to manage
panic attacks during college finals. *You are way too type A, MadGirl.
Yes, success matters, but what matters more is why excelling is so important to
you. You're not responsible for running the whole world. It won't fall apart
if you have some fun or think about what you want once in a while.*

Maybe you think you understand, Alice, but you don't get it.

She was a control freak who had one wish—to lose control. The contradiction of that was enough to tear a soul apart and leave the heart forever aching. Alice had wanted Madison to unleash her submissive desires. She'd never realized Madison wanted nothing more than to hand over control to someone and trust that everything wouldn't be lost or fall apart. But to do that, she had to believe he *wanted* to be that safety net, as much as she wanted to be wrapped up in it and care for him like no one else ever would. From her painful relationship experience, finding a man who wanted to step into that role—and that she trusted to do so—was more of a fantasy than any of her lurid imaginings.

She didn't want to be the discarded Barbie strung out on Prozac her mother had become. So yeah, the parent thing was part of it, she didn't deny it, but it was merely icing to the dysfunction cake. 0–7 stats didn't lie, right? She'd researched enough about submissives to know her need for it was nature not nurture, something that had always been a part of her. It wasn't just a manageable spice-up-the-relationship kind of urge. Based on that, she supposed that it shouldn't surprise her Alice had realized how deep it ran for her sister.

Sighing, she returned to the cash register. If she was going to give running Naughty Bits a try, she needed to get rid of the Dungeon Room, for her own sanity. But that was something Alice would never do, and since this still felt like Alice's store, Madison was reluctant to make such a big change.

At a loss, she looked down to find her hand resting on the letter. She also noticed she'd missed a postscript on the back of the last page.

P.S. You can trust Logan with anything. Don't forget that, MadGirl. You can trust him like you trust me, like family. No, even more. Like a soul mate. He took care of me until you came.

Who the hell was Logan? Alice had never mentioned him.

Madison was all alone now, a quicksand feeling she tried to keep at bay whenever it crossed her mind. Mom, the Prozac zombie, had crashed her car into a tree when Madison was in college. Dad now lived in Ecuador with wife number three, even younger than the last one. Alice had been her family, and yet she was saying Madison could trust this invisible Logan person more than she'd trusted her sister, the only person she'd ever trusted?

Her sister was probably on really heavy meds when she wrote that part. With another sigh, Madison set the paper down. As she shifted, she bumped that heavy package, a reminder that it was still there. Squatting to take a closer look, she let out a mildly irritated oath. It wasn't hers. It was supposed to go next door, to A Different Time Hardware. Damn it, she'd had Troy right here.

Well, she could use the break. The quiet of the place was getting to her. It was as though Alice was standing there, waiting, watching, yet separated from her by a veil that couldn't be penetrated. Madison's head hurt.

She also hadn't brought a soda, and she bet they had some over there. With the times-gone-by theme, maybe an orange-cream one. And a Mallo Cup. She'd pass out from sugar shock and discover this was all a bad, crazy dream, her sister gone, leaving Madison to run Naughty Bits.

When the store had been in its planning stages, Madison had been the first to call it that. *"My sister, selling naughty bits . . ."* Next thing she knew, "Naughty Bits" had its Christmas grand opening, with the catchphrase "Where naughty *is* nice . . ." She'd helped Alice decorate a tree, giggling as they adorned it with everything from filmy, sparkly thong panties to crystal snowflakes and tiny bullet vibrators in gleaming colors of blue and silver. At the top, they'd put a porcelain angel dressed as a dominatrix, complete with wings that looked like two fanned-out floggers, tipped with gold. Alice had teased Madison when she caught her experimenting with it, *thwapping* her arm with their ineffectual length.

Hey, when we were little, you could have used Barbie dolls as floggers, all that long hair. Ooh, remember the Tiffany doll? The one with ten inches of reversible blonde or black hair? The black hair could be her evil pain side, braided with beads and sharp stuff, and the blond . . .

Madison shook her head, biting back a painful smile, and picked up the package. Given the weight, the clanking she'd mistaken for chain was probably nails or some kind of fastener. Exiting the front door of her store and locking it behind her, she walked down the sidewalk. According to the hours printed on the hardware store window, they opened at seven a.m. Tuesday through Saturday, explaining why Troy had been able to show up in her store so early.

The humid air suggested it was building toward a hot June day, but enough of a breeze stirred the crepe myrtles planted along the sidewalk to keep things pleasant. Around the entrance to the hardware store, hanging baskets spilled out lush falls of petunias, tempting pedestrians to buy.

The door was already propped open with an iron boot brush. A chalkboard sandwich sign had been placed beside it with the day's specials: TOMATO PLANTS, $3, ALL GARDEN TOOLS 20% OFF, FRESH BAKED APPLE PIE AND COFFEE, $1.50.

Heated apple pie was one of her favorite breakfast foods, and she smelled it as she stepped into the shop, past the fan that was angled at the open door to minimize its negative effect on the air conditioning. The next refreshing thing to hit her senses was Troy.

He was stocking shelves. The fact he was perched on a ladder gave his ass a nice taut lift and conjured a visual of him sprawled facedown across a bed. He'd be sleeping, wearing nothing but a very artfully arranged sheet. A hint of pale buttocks above it, firm thighs exposed below. His fine toes would be curled against the cotton. One sandy lock of hair draped in his eyes, his lips parted, inviting a lover to press her lips to his, tease his tongue, wake him in all ways. A nice, normal fantasy.

"He's beautiful, isn't he? I've seen women's hands curl into fists at their sides, as if they're restraining an overwhelming urge to touch him."

She jumped, not only because she had company, but because her private thoughts had been intruded upon so accurately. When she turned, she discovered something even more disconcerting.

Her tongue had tangled at the sight of Troy. What she was looking at now stole all words and left only incoherent need, strong enough to close her throat entirely, take her breath.

Yes, Troy was beautiful. Everything a virile young man should be. What was standing behind her was what such a young man could aspire to be, even though she expected few achieved it. It wasn't merely this man's looks. It was everything she sensed beneath them, the inside creating the outside.

Like Troy, he was six feet tall or better, with a breadth of shoulders like she'd expected to happen to Troy with maturity. He wore jeans and work boots as well. The cotton shirt unbuttoned at his throat gave her a glimpse of curling chest hair. She saw Anglo-Saxon in the solid bones of his face, a large man with large hands, a commanding presence. The warm brown eyes that focused on her face held complex things. It would be impossible for a woman to experience anything bad standing inside that gaze. No heartache would dare intrude while she was under his spell. All she needed was to have him nearby.

Red alert! Red alert! Jesus, hadn't she made this mistake enough times already? *Rein back crazy and return to reality.* He was close to forty, with gleaming, thick brown hair brushed back from that masculine face. She couldn't see how far it fell down his back, but the fact he had it tied back suggested it went past his shoulders. Though she'd always thought grown men who wore their hair long looked ridiculous, as though they were attempting to hold on to vanishing youth, the look seemed right on him. It only enhanced his masculinity, the way it did a desert sheikh, fierce Viking, kilted Scots laird . . . or pirate captain.

Stop. It. She'd told Alice she loved that look in men—just not many men could pull it off.

He did.

For the second time today, she was staring, not responding like an articulate adult. Realizing it, she struggled to recall his remarkable statement about Troy's beauty. Not the usual thing for a straight male to point out. *Please God, let him be gay as a maypole.*

"Are you two . . . together?"

The word trailed off as his gaze sharpened on her. Christ, even if Matthews was an annex of the urban Charlotte area, she was still technically in a small town, not Boston. "I'm sorry. That was rude."

"Not where you're from, obviously." His amusement relaxed her, on that point at least. He had a voice that could narrate books. Whether they were romances with quiet whispers in the dark, seafaring adventures that called for commanding roars, or English mysteries needing a sexy, cultured tone with the right pauses for emphasis, his voice would hold attention, making ears strain to catch every intonation.

He crossed his arms and hooked his thumbs under his armpits. "No, we're not together. And not just because you're my preference. I'm training him for someone else, in exchange for blatant exploitation. Home Depot has fifty thousand square feet, but I have Troy. The local ladies turned out in record numbers for my spring gardening sale." He winked. "I even lured some of the males interested in that sort of thing away from the Depot's home décor offerings."

"Do you offer to let everyone touch him?" she asked.

"I wasn't offering that. Just observing how tempting it is to do so."

"Sounds like entrapment."

"A suspicious, intelligent woman. Just my type." His gaze got warmer, warming her inside. Even if flirting with this kind of man was like walking a minefield, it improved her mood. But the ache in her arms reminded her she was holding his package. God help her, she flushed at the unintended mental entendre, and felt as foolish as a teenager.

"Oh, I brought this. UPS left it at my place by mistake."

His fingers brushed hers as he claimed the package. "Sorry, I should have had you put this down right off. It's like a pile of bricks."

Twisting that excellent upper torso, he put the box on the counter. Being solid wood, it looked far more capable of handling the weight than her glass display case. "Clarence—that's our delivery guy—used to leave our stuff over there all the time, though he was usually considerate enough only to leave the lighter parcels."

"Did he have a problem delivering them here?"

"Yes. Alice was far prettier than we were, and she had cookies."

When he smiled, Madison decided it wasn't only Troy who lured women here. The younger women might gravitate to Troy, but any woman who'd graduated past teen crushes would head for this one like a fly toward a bug zapper. This had to be the hardware store's owner, Mr. Scott.

"As her illness progressed," he continued, "Clarence got in the habit of checking in with her first. He'd tell me what kind of day she was having, whether I should check on her. Since she'd get after us if we hovered too much, it was how we kept an eye on her without taking away her sense of independence."

All while her closest relative stayed in Boston, not doing a damn thing for her. It didn't matter that she hadn't known Alice was sick. Madison still had to squelch the overwhelming guilt, as well as the need to listen for condemnation in his voice, look for it in his expression.

"Even after she'd closed the store for good, he'd still occasionally leave a delivery at her door. He knew we'd see it." He regarded the box on his counter. "I think he kept doing it because letting go of the habit is letting go of the person."

She rubbed her temple, a nervous tic she usually tried to control, but today was proving a little too much. He and Troy could drive small-talkers to suicide. "You and Troy don't do chitchat, do you?"

His eyes met hers. "Given our relationship with Alice, we're already past that, don't you think?"

So he and Troy had been pretty involved in Alice's life. Enough to make "Mr. Scott" assume he could be overly familiar with a family member he'd just met. She was starting to get a worrisome premonition. The authoritative vibes that emanated from him, the fact he knew Alice . . .

Alice, if I'm right, I'm going to kill you. I don't care if you're already dead.

"Troy tells me you're a little nervous about running the store."

"It's not something I've ever sold before, but selling is selling. I worked on a used car lot when I was sixteen, moved on to Sears' appliances, and eventually into stocks and bonds after I earned my accounting degree. I'll get a handle on it."

The same way she was going to get a handle on this conversation. She wasn't going to be driven by hormones, groundless fantasies or shared grief to encourage this beyond a friendly-but-not-too-friendly, neighborly relationship. She needed to figure out a way to make that clear.

As he moved around the counter with a noncommittal grunt, she tried not to notice how the shirt strained over his broad shoulders. The temptation to reach out and touch the curls of coarse hair at his throat was making her fingertips tingle. What would he do? Would his hand close over hers, stop her, those eyes centering on her face, an unspoken command to keep her hands to herself . . . until she was given permission to touch?

Shit, shit, shit. Seeing the perfect opening to change the subject, she seized it. "I figured someone had sent you a cinder block."

Those attractive lips curved as he fished a box cutter out of a drawer and slit the box open. "Lead. I have customers who pour their own bullets for hunting, self-defense and historical reenactments, so I keep a supply on hand, along with primers, powder and the like. But there should be something else." His expression brightened. "Right here on top."

He freed the item with remarkable gentleness, revealing a set of antique brass metal hinges. "The supply house for bullet lead also does metalwork?" she asked.

"They're an eclectic enterprise. A mom-and-pop place in Missouri. They even have a blacksmith who shoes horses and makes swords for Renaissance Faires. I've been out there." He glanced up, gave her a distracting wink. "Almost bought an Excalibur replica, but decided on a good wood lathe. The lathe was cheaper."

When he extended the hinges so she could take a closer look, she studied the engraved design. It showed a vine of thorns, interspersed with tiny leaves and loops. "You don't usually see thorns without a rose."

"No, you don't. The potential of the thorns is often overlooked." He set them aside and extended a palm. "Give me your hand and I'll show you."

She curled her fingers, uncertain. This guy was doing weird things to her. She needed to get back to her store. "We haven't even been officially introduced."

"I'm Logan Scott."

She took a step back from the counter before she could stop herself. This was Logan? *Trust Logan. Like you'd trust me. Or a soul mate . . . He took care of me until you came.*

He'd cared for her sister, all except those last three days? The hospice nurse hadn't mentioned another caregiver, but maybe Alice had told her not to do so.

Goddamn it. She bit her lip. *If I hadn't scattered your ashes over the river already, I would mix them in some random cat's litter box, I swear to God.*

"Are you all right?"

Tuning back in, she saw nothing in his face that said he knew the contents of that letter. He'd left his hand out, and it would be rude and stupid to act like a frightened deer because of a mysterious reference about him from her sister. But it was way more than that. He had that submissive side of her on its knees, all senses on alert toward his every action. His every desire or demand. *Give me your hand.*

In the past, it was her own inner yearnings that had led her down unwise paths with men. But this compulsion seemed to be originating from him, a distinct, dangerous difference. She told herself to get a grip. He was going to think she was a freak if she didn't start acting normal.

She put her hand out. Her fingers whispered across his palm as his own closed over them. She'd never thought of a man's touch as unforgettable, but she drew in a breath at the way it felt. Reassuring. Firm and strong. Something that would become a permanent craving if taken away.

"At last," he murmured. "We meet."

The simple statement underlined his close history with Alice, close enough that Alice had talked about her. A courtesy she hadn't offered Madison. Her anger about that couldn't hold, though, not when she saw their contact unlock the abiding pain of deep loss behind his gaze, a pain she understood.

Before that could freak her out—any more than the whole situation was doing—he loosened his grip and turned her hand over. He pressed his thumb against her palm so her fingers half closed over it. With the other hand, he brought the tip of the box cutter to her skin. He paused, watching her adjust to what he was about to do, giving her the chance to draw back. Her pulse was beating higher in her throat, but she didn't pull back. That sent a message so significant, she wasn't surprised to see his eyes darken, his mouth tighten. She relished the reaction.

He pricked her with the point, along the lifeline. He didn't do it hard enough to draw blood.

"A tiny hurt, like the bite of a thorn," he said. "Your fingers twitched, like you might pull away, but when you realized it was bearable, you stilled again." He lifted her hand to his mouth then, brushed his lips over the spot. "Now a reward, a mix of pleasure with pain. It makes you crave a little more of both. Or maybe more than a little."

Giving her a half smile, which didn't lessen the intensity of his gaze, the import of what they'd just both communicated without words, he squeezed her hand before letting her go.

This wasn't flirting, but something way more hazardous. She closed her hand around that touch, put it to her side to hide the tremor in her fingers. "What are the hinges for?" She had to blurt it out, but fortunately it didn't sound as strident as she feared.

"A commissioned piece I'm making. I have a woodworking shop here on the premises. I'll show it to you sometime, if you'd like."

"Okay. Maybe. If it's no trouble."

"Maybe" was an escape hatch, but in truth, she needed a reprieve from all the empty spaces where Alice was supposed to be. She was antsy for human contact, no matter how unsettling. Though she obviously couldn't afford a lot of one-on-one exposure with Logan, she couldn't deny she wanted to find out more about the man Alice had said she could trust.

"You're no trouble. Though I expect if you chose to be, you'd be the kind of trouble that a certain type of man would relish."

Okay, time to start putting *him* off-balance before she teetered right off this seesaw. She cleared her throat. "Were you and my sister ever . . ."

Given that everything coming out of his mouth was like a shovel thrust into the bottom of her emotional well, flinging muck out over the top, it seemed a little pointless to be tactful, but she found she couldn't say it outright. Fortunately, he understood what she meant.

"No. Her interests lay elsewhere, as did mine." His gaze did that sharpening thing again, spearing the fluttery place beneath her rib cage.

"I think we should choose another subject for now." Though she really had no idea what subject they were talking about, her instincts told her the topic was fraught with peril. "You said you were training Troy. Does he work at another store?"

"No. I'm a training Master at the local dungeon. Being under my tutelage is a requirement of his Mistress."

Bull's-eye, direct arrow. She'd been right about the fraught-with-peril thing. It took a Herculean effort not to leap all the way back to the door, the way she had the day she almost stepped on a snake sunning on the top step of their family's back deck. His gaze remained on hers, steady. He was waiting for her reaction, like a damn scientist studying a hapless rat in a glass box. On top of that, he'd done it right in the middle of the mainstream public.

She stole a flustered glance around the store. A couple of men, apparently contractors, seemed engrossed with selecting parts down one aisle, while a pair of women were having pie and coffee over in the refreshments area. None of them seemed to be staring, but then, maybe it only seemed to her like a herald bellowing an announcement in the public square. In fact, only one person other than herself seemed to have picked up on the discussion.

"Those nails aren't going to stock themselves, Troy," Logan said. "You're not part of this conversation."

As he spoke, Logan never shifted his attention from her face. Yet despite the apparent mildness of the comment, the undercurrent had the effect of a cattle prod. "No sir," Troy said immediately. In her peripheral vision, she saw him busy himself with the stock, acting as if he'd donned supersonic noise-canceling headphones.

Logan's tone of command affected Madison as well, holding her in place like a hooked fish. But hearing he was a training Master brought forth another memory, something that hurt. *It doesn't mean anything. It's not real to him.*

"It's all right," he said quietly. "I wasn't trying to shock you."

She knew that. She was well attuned to people trying to manipulate her emotions, and he wasn't setting off that alarm. Alice might have told Logan about Madison's cravings, but it didn't mean he was privy to her sister's posthumous plottings. Alice was gone and Madison could set him straight about all that, right here, right now.

She summoned a hard smile. "Sorry. You took me by surprise. This is still new to me. I'm not as knowledgeable about these things as Alice was. I don't have her instincts."

"We all have an instinct for Dominance and submission, Madison." He nodded toward Troy. "But if you'd like to expand your knowledge, you're welcome to come help me with Troy's next training session."

Very matter-of-fact, and helpful. It made sense, right? With a BDSM section in the store Alice had left her to run, the obvious assumption would be she had at least a business-level comfort with it. However, going anywhere with Logan that involved restraints and whips screamed *bad idea*. The last time she'd been to a club, she'd been with her sister, not a charismatic male sexual Dominant.

"I don't know." She glanced back at Troy, considering all the things that "training" might mean. "I'm not into hurting anyone."

He looked down at her hand, the one he'd pricked. "Pain and pleasure are often interchangeable. Regardless, every step is consensual. He lets go of as much control as he desires. Under the right conditions, the more control is relinquished, the more freedom is found. You're welcome to simply watch, Madison. Friday at eight."

"We'll see. I have a lot to do, and if I'm tired that evening . . ."

Those coffee-colored eyes came back to her face. He wasn't staring. Staring would have been less unsettling. She felt like a book he was reading, every word a page full of information about her. He let her run down before he spoke again, courteously. "Understood. If you do come that night, use the interior door between our storerooms. It's always unlocked."

"You do the training here?" She tried not to let her voice squeak. Right close by, where she could hear the slap of a flogger on flesh, cries of pain and pleasure . . .

"I have a couple rooms in the back, one for the training, one for the woodworking."

He might have equipment in there. Cuffs, chains . . . like the things in her store inventory, only these would be worn from use, scratches in the wood of the St. Andrew's Cross, rendered silky smooth by sweat . . .

"I'll be adding those hinges tonight if you want to come see the woodworking part of things," he added. "I know it must be hard, hanging around Alice's house at night."

That was going to be the danger, wasn't it? He had more than one road past her shields, and his understanding of the loss she was dealing with could be a four-lane highway. Under ordinary circumstances, she'd be restrained by common sense. Going into a back room after business hours with a guy she didn't even know wasn't a good idea. However, thanks to Alice's note, Madison's uppermost fear was that he was her own personal Pied Piper of Hamelin, the tune he was offering one she longed to follow.

"Okay. I'll think about it." As if she was considering an offer to come over for tea. *Jesus.* "Thanks. It was . . . nice to meet you. I'd better get back to the store."

She would have fled if it she could have, but she maintained her dignity with a decorous pace. As a result, she had time for a few thousand thoughts before she reached the doorway. She stopped, bit her lip. "Logan . . . when you said, 'At last we meet,' it felt significant. What did my sister say about me?"

"She gave you to me."

Her face must have conveyed her startled jolt, because his lips twisted in wry response. He lifted a hand, staying her *what the fuck* reaction.

"She said . . ." He paused, his expression serious. " 'I'm giving her to you, Logan, but you might just give yourself to her, too. For the first time in your life.' What man could resist a challenge like that?"

"Was she on a lot of meds when you had that conversation?" Madison asked weakly.

His laugh, deep and rich, literally aroused her. Her body tightened, the flesh between her legs swelling. When her hand curled into a tense ball at her side, the humor disappeared from his expression, his mouth firming. "Go back to your store, Madison," he said softly. "We'll talk later."

She turned and went.

• • •

Not because he told her to do so, but because she had obviously stepped into the deep-ass end of the pool. Her sister had been capable of some odd things, but this? *She fricking* gave *me to a guy?* What the hell did that mean? Under other circumstances, Madison would have considered a restraining order. It still wasn't out of the question.

Okay, slow down and breathe. Think this through. Madison thought back to another time Alice had dragged her into a club, this time when they were vacationing. Since it was there she'd had the experience which caused the sharp pain under her ribs when Logan said he was a training Master, it was a good reminder that the cons of her going down that road far outweighed the pros.

Alice had said visiting clubs while they were on vacation was a good way for her to deduct a portion of the trip as a business expense. Madison had feigned reluctant indifference, but she'd gone, her stomach flopping with butterflies, her palms damp. Once again, she found a secluded corner table, nursed a drink while Alice flitted here and there, making contacts, asking questions. Leaving Madison alone with her fantasies.

Then she'd seen the Master and his female submissive. More importantly, he'd seen her.

"*Come* closer."

He'd helped the woman onto a table and she was lying on her back, naked. Madison didn't realize he was speaking to her, not the woman, until he turned, met her gaze. He wasn't handsome, but he was charismatic. His dark hair, peppered with gray, was trimmed neatly and his blue eyes were direct. He had the type of body that looked decent in the surprising choice of a suit, the kind a man would wear for business.

He didn't repeat the command. It was implied in his straightforward glance, the way the contact arrowed hard through Madison's center.

The music in the club was pounding drums, a New Age tribal beat interspersed with silvery flute, loud enough to mix with the environment and get the blood humming, impair judgment. Madison rose, leaving her soda. Did he need her help? Was he going to lay her down on the table right next to the woman? Shouldn't he be asking her if she wanted to play? She knew there were rules.

"You can't see as well from over there," he said, pointing her to a stool pulled up near the woman's head. He leaned over, placing a blindfold on the supine woman. Her lips pressed together, their fullness more noticeable as her eyes disappeared beneath the fabric. The middle-aged, short-haired brunette didn't have a model's figure, but in her few club experiences, Madison had noted a general acceptance of any size or age. Dominance and submission weren't about those things. While this woman had some fleshy padding, it was decently toned and her breasts were a nice size. The Dom tweaked her nipple after he blindfolded her, making her jump. And smile, though it had an anxious, anticipating quality to it. "Play with yourself while I get ready," he commanded.

Obediently, the woman moved her hand down her body, finding her clit and labia to tease them with her fingers. Madison shifted, swallowing. The Master glanced up at her. "Feel free to do the same if you like."

His grin was playful enough not to scare her, to win a wary smile back, but she noticed the intensity of his gaze didn't lessen. He was confident, in control of this situation. Did he realize how nervous she was? How uncertain? Thank God Alice was somewhere else. There were a few other people coming in and out of this section, but right now she was his main audience.

Pulling a handkerchief from his jacket pocket, the Master left it on the table as he removed the coat, hung it up on a wall hook. Madison watched him roll up his sleeves. Why was it so sexy when men did that? He loosened the tie and removed it, carelessly opened a couple of the top buttons of the shirt. She saw he was wearing a silver cross beneath the fabric.

"You're going to hold my tie, baby," he said to the woman on the table, wrapping the silk around her wrists in a figure eight, then doing another wrap around that, securing it so her wrists were loosely bound. Lifting her hands to his mouth, he sucked on the fingers she'd used on herself, then rubbed them dry with the handkerchief. "But if you get it dirty, you know you'll be in bad trouble. Put your arms over your head. I want your wrists resting on the knees of the woman behind you."

Madison stared down at the woman's lacquered nails. She had a good manicure. Her fingers were making little flexing motions, rubbing her knuckles erratically against Madison's thighs. Her body was quivering as her erotic tension built. Madison felt like they were sharing that same energy. When she dared a glance at the Master again, she found his eyes upon her.

"Put your hands on the joining point of the tie, between her wrists," he said.

Madison did it. "I'm not . . . I don't want to do anything wrong."

His lips curved and he reached out, caressed her jaw as if it was the most natural thing to touch a stranger that way. And calm her with that touch. "You can't possibly, sweetheart. I won't let you. Vanessa, I want you to hold her wrists."

Madison's grip tightened on the tie. When the woman's fingers curved around hers, holding Madison's wrists, an unexpected hard quiver shook her, as if she'd been bound with a set of flesh-and-blood manacles. She told herself not to get carried away. This was simple, straightforward. Safe. Even better, Alice would be pleased that Madison had indulged herself, and lay off a little.

The Master pulled a variety of items out of his bag. Candles, bowls, burners. It might have taken ten minutes for him to set up, but time had no meaning. This was the first time Madison had been this close to, this involved in, something that felt exactly like what she'd hoped it could be. A ripple of panic went through her. She was going to lose her mind, beg him to take her home. Make a total ass out of herself.

She would have bolted, but Vanessa was holding on to her. Though Madison's fantasy-laden brain had wanted to interpret his command to Vanessa as a way to restrain *her*, her rational mind knew the real intent was to give Vanessa an anchor. In the woman's touch she felt the need for that contact. If she drew back, she'd be abandoning her. She couldn't do that.

"Let's keep me entertained while the wax is melting." He withdrew a clit stimulator from the bag and fitted it on Vanessa, strapping it around her thighs to hold it in place. "There you go."

The hum reached Madison's ears as Vanessa jerked, gasped. Her fingers tightened on Madison's wrists, while her own grip on the tie constricted, a wordless bond and communication between them. *I'm here. We're together in this, what he's doing to us.*

As he waited, he propped his hips on the table holding the burners. The typical dim light of the club, intended to promote a mysterious, erotic environment, was enhanced by the flickering light of the candles and burners. The drum-and-flute music was like a male-female counterpoint. From other parts of the club, Madison could occasionally hear a cry, loud enough to be heard over the music. She inhaled the fragrance of the wax burning, the scent of fire itself.

She'd become part of some sensuous, pagan ritual. The Master was a Druid priest, preparing Vanessa for sexual initiation where she'd belong to a circle of Druids, her sexual energy used over and over for their mystic purposes. Vanessa's body moved in sinuous response to the vibrator. Her hips lifted, pressed down, her legs shifting restlessly, toes curling. Her toenails were painted a silver-pink, like her fingernails. A tattoo of a vine twined around her left ankle, punctuated by tiny pink flowers.

Madison swallowed as Vanessa's grip got brutal. The stimulator must be bringing her close to peak. Her lips parted on a moan. "Master," she breathed.

The man appeared absorbed in her erotic response, yet detached from the plea in a way that was indescribably arousing. He was feeding his own pleasure off of her denied need.

"He's watching you," Madison said in a thick voice. "He can't take his eyes off you." She would sell her soul to be looked at like that, to feel whatever it was Vanessa was feeling, under his control.

She'd said it because she couldn't seem to stop herself, and the panic returned. She thought she might have committed an embarrassing faux pas. Though the Master didn't lift his gaze from Vanessa, his lips curved, eyes sparking, telling Madison she hadn't done anything wrong. Vanessa's response proved it. Her hands convulsed on Madison and her body gave an all-over shudder. She repeated the word, with need and reverence both.

"Master."

He picked up one of the burning candles, and Madison was once again reminded of a Druid ritual, the way his back straightened and his focus increased. Standing over Vanessa, he balanced the candle in his hand so it wouldn't tip and spill the accumulation of wax burning in the pit below the flame. Not until he was ready.

Vanessa cried out as the drops landed on her upper abdomen, twitching as he made his way slowly down her center, leaving a trail of pale ivory wax that hit her skin, rolled in different directions and quickly solidified. Madison's gaze clung to every inch of progress he made toward that juncture between her legs. Her own pussy was throbbing, anticipating, and her thighs pressed together beneath Vanessa's knuckles.

"Please . . . tell me . . . when . . ." Vanessa was gasping.

The Master's eyes cut toward Madison. Anything she might have said froze in her throat. That look of pure command was as arousing as anything she'd yet witnessed. Ironically, what added to its potency was how it contrasted to the earlier smile, his gentle touch on her cheek. To know that beneath all that, this side of him could surge to the forefront, his true core, taking control of everything around him, made a woman quiver and want to be on her knees to him.

She found her voice, though it was a rasp of sound among the drums. "He says no."

The Master gave a slight nod, his eyes glittering on her a diamond moment before he turned back to what he was doing. Vanessa sighed, helpless acceptance. Several drops later she let out a piercing, needy cry as the wax splashed on her clit, her smooth mound. He'd saved the bulk of what was melted on the candle for that area. As he drizzled it in a spiraling motion, she writhed, called for him again, arched, and her nails bit into Madison's hand.

For her part, Madison was motionless, mesmerized, her throat dry. Inside she was quivering as hard as Vanessa, but on the outside she was still as a mouse in a corner. The Master set the candle back on the table, watched Vanessa twist, her hips rolling, tongue darting out to lick her lips. Madison thought he saw everything happening to his sub, head to toe, even if his eyes weren't on every part of her anatomy. It was as though he was inside her mind, absorbing her every reaction like a form of magical energy in truth.

"Be still," he said. Even the music couldn't compete with the steel command in his low voice. Vanessa obeyed with tremendous effort and little whimpers. She clutched Madison's wrists.

He poured some of the liquid wax from the burner into a bowl, stirred it with a brush. Bending over Vanessa, he ran the brush along the outside of her right breast, then her left one. This type of wax didn't seem to have that first moment of searing heat the other did, because Vanessa didn't make the involuntary jerk. Instead, under the brush strokes she seemed to melt like the wax. A murmur caught in her throat as he passed over her nipples.

"Would you like to see what it's like?"

Madison looked up, met the Master's gaze. Did he mean? She couldn't . . .

"Turn your palm up so I can put it on your forearm. Vanessa, let go of her right wrist."

Vanessa immediately complied. The Master gave Madison a courteous, encouraging nod. The man had as many faces as the moon. His pleasant tone now wasn't like the demanding, pure-sex demeanor he displayed when interacting directly with Vanessa. It was as if he stepped out of one room and into another to speak to Madison now. Whereas she'd felt like she was in that room with them for a few, blissful minutes. She wanted back there, but that was a limited invitation, wasn't it? She held out her arm.

Oh . . . wow. It was like a heated, damp tongue, the brush running a few inches up her arm before he pulled it away. "Paraffin," he told her. "It does wonderful things to the mind."

Giving her a wink, he returned his attention to Vanessa. He used several different types and colors of wax, alternating between the candle drippings and the paraffin, decorating Vanessa's thighs, her navel, her breasts. Though he'd left it in place, he'd dialed down the vibrator during all that. Now he turned it off, put it aside and replaced its stimulation with his own fingers.

"A nice, wet pussy. All wet for your Master, isn't it?"

"Yes sir," Vanessa gasped. "Please . . ."

"Please, what?"

"I want to come."

"Whose wants are important, Vanessa?" His eyes and voice had gone back to flint sharpness. Madison was on the edge of that cliff with Vanessa. *Please let her come.* She couldn't take her eyes away from his long fingers, manipulating the fragile flesh between Vanessa's legs, his knuckles worrying the clit, stroking the labia. From a flex of his arm and Vanessa's guttural cry, she knew a couple of those digits had disappeared inside her. Madison's pussy contracted in sympathetic response and need.

"Yours, Master," Vanessa said.

"So what do you want?"

"I want . . ." Vanessa swallowed noisily. "I want you to want me to come, Master."

His smile went feral. "Lucky for you, that's exactly what I want. Right now. Come for me."

It happened that fast. He'd kept her balanced on that pinnacle like a maestro, only a twitch of his wrist needed to send the orchestra into full crescendo. He kept stroking her labia and clit with thumb and forefinger, thrusting inside her with the other fingers, showing off an expert precision and rhythm that said he knew how this woman's body worked.

Vanessa flushed beneath the wax, the blush spreading from her sternum up her throat as she arced off the table like a rainbow and began to scream out her release. Madison clung to her as the woman rocked, thrust up against his hand. Her eyes were shut tight, mouth opened wide, her nipples tight points, embellished by the layers of wax painted across them. Some of the larger pieces on her skin cracked as she transformed into ocean movement, rolling and cresting, crashing and rising again.

When she finally wound down, he was moving his hand in a slower rhythm, stroking her, giving her light pinches that had her shaking with aftershocks. At length, he bent, pressed a single, chaste kiss right on her pussy. Madison glimpsed the tip of his tongue, taking a brief sample of her climax before he lifted his head, pressing his lips together.

"That's my baby," he murmured. "There you go. Slow it down, watch your breathing." He stroked her hip, his gaze fixed on her for another few moments before he eventually raised his attention to Madison.

"Thank you," he said.

"Sure," she managed, and earned that smile. She wondered if he would touch her face again and ask her to strip and take Vanessa's place on the table. She wondered what she would do if he did.

He stepped closer to her, put his hand over hers, a purely reassuring touch. "Let go of her, Vanessa," he said, a quiet command.

When Vanessa complied, he closed his hands over both of Madison's and brought them to his lips. He brushed his warm, firm mouth over her knuckles.

"You were like a wide-eyed sprite, there in the corner," he said, smiling at her. "Irresistible. The day you decide to stop watching and start playing, some Master will be very lucky. Now, if you'll excuse us, I need to take care of Vanessa."

She nodded, scrambled off the stool and almost pitched herself on the floor at his feet. Fortunately, he anticipated her disorientation and steadied her, with caressing hands and a knowing glance. Then he stepped back, breaking the spell that had bound her to them. She was now outside the circle again.

She retreated, but not to her booth. Somehow she found her way to the bathroom, locked herself in a stall and leaned against the wall, closing her eyes. Trying to breathe as well. She'd thought it had to be whips and restraints, things she wasn't sure she could trust any man to do except in her fantasies. But this Master had merely brought her into the fringes of that world, let her have a taste, and suddenly she'd felt braver, ready for more. And flooded with so many cravings and desires, she thought she might be drowning. It scared her. *Breathe. Breathe.*

Looking down at her hands where he'd kissed her knuckles, she saw Vanessa's grip had left red bands on her wrists. The bite of her nails had made crescent impressions on her hands and forearms. Would Vanessa look at the impression of the tie on her own wrists, the redness of her skin when the wax was removed? Of course she would.

When she left the bathroom and paused at the bar, Madison saw the Master in the public sitting room. He was on a couch, cradling Vanessa in his lap, giving her water, stroking her hair, tucking a blanket around her as she came down from the euphoria the session had brought her. Madison wondered if he'd removed all the wax from her skin as tenderly as he was treating her now.

"I hear he's a really good Dom, if you're looking to try one out."

She jumped, turning to see Alice at her shoulder. Nothing in Alice's face suggested she'd witnessed anything that had happened though, which was a relief. Her next words confirmed it.

"Sorry, I got hung up in the lounge area with some guys who make custom floggers." Her sister put a hand on her shoulder. "Seriously, why don't you give him a try? No strings attached. If you can believe it, he's gay. His partner's not into the scene, but is okay with him doing his thing with women. Apparently he's awesome at it. I hear newbies are his specialty."

Madison blinked. Yes, she already knew enough about this world to know that many BDSM sessions were compartmentalized, only-in-the-club-type things, but he and Vanessa . . . she'd been sure they were together. How could they get so intensely intimate with one another and . . . it mean nothing? Not really. It wasn't what she'd hoped, imagined . . . or wanted.

"So it's not real."

Alice gave her an odd look. "I wouldn't say that. Within the session, it's real enough to give everyone something. It might be a safe way for you to explore it. I know you're worried about losing control, and I don't blame you. This type of thing, it's such a high, you could think you're in love with the first Dom who trips your trigger the right way. You know?"

Madison dragged herself back to the here and now. Her panties were damp, her breath shallow, and there was a hard ache behind her heart. She had an overwhelming urge to lock herself in the store's bathroom again, only this time she wanted to bring herself to climax. The only thing that held her back was she knew how empty she'd be left afterward. Sometimes it was like being a paraplegic with virtual goggles that made her think she was walking. When she took them off, she'd still be trapped in the chair and her heart would explode.

She heard her sister needling her as clearly as if Alice were standing at her side. *You've tallied up a handful of assholes who betrayed your trust, walked out on you when you needed them, battered your self-esteem in a hundred different ways. Isn't it time to follow a different set of instincts?*

What had Logan said? *We all have an instinct for Dominance and submission . . .*

Usually Alice knew when to back off, but that night with the Master and Vanessa, Madison had felt too fragile and Alice pushed too hard, until Madison was in tears. Her sister had apologized, hugging Madison and telling her she was trying to help. It hadn't made Madison's growing resentment with her sister's confidence about what was best for her any less poisonous. They'd had their two-year falling out soon thereafter.

You need to let me pick your next guy, MadGirl. You're bad at it.

Had her sister decided to force her hand through a last wish? She wasn't surprised Alice would do such a galling thing to her, but why would an intriguing, self-possessed male like Logan agree to it?

She'd lied to him about the knowledge stuff to get him to back off. Unfortunately, by claiming ignorance, she'd probably just encouraged Logan to help "educate her." God save her. He and Troy obviously had that compartmentalized, structured-session kind of D/s relationship. Between relationships, she'd thought about sticking her toe in those waters, but the idea of approaching it like a gym workout depressed her. On the flip side, anything she'd tried involving emotional commitment had gone disastrously.

God bless the Internet, the anonymity of chat rooms, video sites, forums. She limited herself on them, so she didn't turn into the BDSM version of a crack addict, but it didn't mean she didn't soak it up like a sponge during her short forays, using it with a vibrator to assuage simple sexual frustration and keep it all under control. When it came to her desire to submit, she didn't know how to do anything in moderation. She'd learned her lesson. At least she thought she had.

Brownstone's "If You Love Me" started playing, making her bite back an oath. She hadn't locked the door after her trip to the hardware store. She'd tell whoever it was that she was closed. She hadn't even set up the register to take a sale.

But as she emerged from the stockroom and saw the one lone customer, she decided to test her sales skills instead, see how it went.

The tall girl with long brown hair and a delicate face like Liv Tyler was idly browsing through the selections along the wall, so Madison cleared her throat. "Good afternoon. Can I help you find anything?"

"Uh . . . well, no. Yes." Looking over her shoulder, the young woman gave a half laugh. "Guess you get that a lot in here, right?"

"I'm still fairly new to running a lingerie store, but that's how I'd be about it if I was a customer. Kind of out of place, like I needed to keep the exit door close."

It was meant as a joke, but even Madison could hear the acid in her tone, fueled by an unexpected surge of bitterness. Suddenly she was back in the Boston lingerie store she'd visited while still trapped in a relationship with Leroy. She'd felt like a fraud, trying to plug a hole in the Titanic with crotchless panties.

Her brittle smile made it worse. The woman shot her an odd look, cleared her throat. "Thanks . . . er . . . I'll let you know if I need any help."

Madison tried to salvage the attempt. "Is it for a special occasion?"

"No. Not really. Not in that way." The woman gave her a nod, headed for the door. "Thanks."

"Come back and see us."

She gave that absent, *probably not* kind of nod, and then she was gone. The song changed to Boyz II Men's "I'll Make Love to You." Madison gave serious thought to ripping the speaker wires out of the wall.

Yes, it was only her first attempt, but if she couldn't keep her personal baggage out of it, she might as well quit before she started.

Who was she kidding? Her mind wasn't in the right place to do this. Maybe she should hire someone to do it, even though she knew that wouldn't be honoring Alice's request the way she'd intended.

Well, damn you. Her fists closed on the counter. *That kind of pushy meddling was why I didn't visit you for two years and you fucking know it.*

Shit. She passed a hand over her face, felt the faint tremor in her fingers. *I'm sorry, Alice.* It didn't matter if it was true. She'd do anything to have her back. Anything. She thought about what Logan had said about the UPS man. Maybe honoring a loved one's last request was the same thing as keeping up a habit. Holding on to them as long as you could.

A trio of women had slipped in as the other woman left, so she had no choice but to try again. And fail again. Unfortunately, for the next hour, she had a slow trickle of impulse shoppers, no chance to tactfully lock the door and turn off the light. She tried asking questions but, as before, it was always the wrong question, the wrong attitude projected. She fell back on the tactics she'd used to sell cars and discovered there was a big difference between asking people if they were looking for a family vehicle or a four-inch-diameter dildo. Ouch, by the way. Hadn't Alice worried about liability issues if people actually used that thing?

Long and short, struggling to find the right approach with customers while fighting her own emotional debris about the main reason to be in a store like this—to enhance a relationship—meant the only thing she accomplished was embarrassment, for both herself and the customers. A couple of them exited the store as if a fire alarm had been set off.

Eventually she resigned herself to staying behind the counter, no better than a passive, hired employee, available if the customer initiated contact. She sold a bra and a three-set of filmy panties, and Naughty Bits made no more of an impression than any generic clothing store.

As soon as the opportunity presented itself, she lunged to lock the door, though her relief only frustrated her more. She punished herself by going through Alice's hard-copy files in her little side office, organizing things for taxes that wouldn't be filed for months.

Why was she doing this to herself? Because Alice had asked her to do it. But surely she could put it off another month or two, right? She'd said she'd left her enough money to live on, and Madison had her own savings as well.

"Putting it off's not going to make it any better," she told herself. Gritting her teeth, she designed the grand reopening ads on the laptop, uploaded them to the local online and paper circulars. There. She'd officially set into motion what felt like a forced march into hell.

Okay, even Alice would say that was a little over dramatic. Maybe she needed to close her eyes, indulge in a safe little pleasure trip where she imagined herself under Logan's tutelage like Troy . . .

She stopped in her mental tracks. Oh God. Of course. Maybe her wayward emotions had fucked up her grasp of that situation as well. Yes, Alice wanted Madison to embrace her submissive side, but she also would have wanted to help Madison successfully run the store. Alice knew she'd need to learn how to connect to her customers, understand how to make their fantasies come to life. Nothing was farther on the deep end of the sexual fantasy world than BDSM. So by "giving her to Logan," Alice was offering Madison the chance to get in the right mind-set. Logan could help her learn how to do it. He'd said he was a training Master.

The strategy made a weird kind of sense, more practical and reassuring than the idea of her sister giving her to Logan like a mail-order bride. And Logan had said she could *help* with Troy's training. That was far different from being tied up or flogged herself. Maybe . . .

Sighing, Madison shook her head, deciding to give it a rest. It was time to call it a day.

A glance at the clock told her "calling it a night" would be more accurate. It was a little past seven. She cocked her head, only mildly alarmed when she heard movement in the back. The hardware store closed at five, but the same pickup truck from this morning was in the back next to her car, suggesting Logan or Troy was still around. Then she heard a mild curse and recognized the voice, though she wasn't sure if that didn't make her more alarmed, albeit in a different way.

Logan was shifting boxes in her storeroom. Looking beyond him, she saw the connecting door he'd mentioned, open now to show the full shelves in his own storage area. He straightened. "Good evening."

"Can I help you pilfer something? Perhaps a teddy and pair of stilettos in your size?" Her gaze coursed over his work shoes. "We might have a thirteen. I think the teddy's more flexible, due to the thong style."

He chuckled at that, but his brow creased as he gazed at the three tiers of shelves. "Alice let me keep things in here when I had overflow, because her inventory fits in a smaller space than mine. I was looking for a case of screws. I always tell Troy to put our stuff in this corner over here, but maybe Alice rearranged it. Or Troy forgot and I'll have to make him drink motor oil to help him remember in the future."

Her side of that connecting door had been locked, which meant he had a key to it. She wondered if she needed to set polite but firm new boundaries, but she'd wait until she was sure she wasn't being pissy because of her first non-event of customers.

"I haven't had a chance to go through all the dusty back corners yet, but I covered most of the rest of the stock." She came to stand at his side, bending to look deeper into the lower shelf. "Wait, see behind the pink box? Is that it?"

He bent with her, laying a hand on her back as he did so, a casual gesture that nevertheless spread heat from the point of contact. When he smiled, that heat increased. "Yep, that's it." He pushed her gently aside to stretch his longer frame over the wide board, treating her to a view of denim straining over an excellent ass. His broad shoulders shifted as he pulled the box forward and ducked his head to come back out, the thick tail of his hair falling over his shoulder. "Good eye. So, are you done for the day? If you want, you can have that tour of the woodworking area now. I'll even throw in a quick tour of the hardware store. Alice had a free pass to grab anything she needed whenever. You're welcome to do the same."

"Is this your version of a pickup line? Come check out my woodshop?"

His easy smile kept that liquid heat curling around her vitals, but she noticed his brown eyes became more serious. Something dark and pleasurable lay behind that considering expression when he looked at her. She didn't know what it was, but like earlier, her subconscious responded to it like metal to a magnet. Fish, hook, metal, magnet. Oh yeah. Being around him was going to be a metaphor grab bag.

"Would it work?" he asked.

"I've fallen for worse lines."

The smile disappeared then. He curled his other hand around her elbow, bringing her with him as they moved out of her room and into his. "I'll never use a line on you, Madison. I don't believe in them."

He put the box down in an empty space in his storeroom, and then took her hand in his, again simple and easy. "Troy will put those out when he gets here tomorrow morning."

She noticed his shelves were piled much higher than hers, underscoring his need for overflow room. "Did you pay Alice a fee for use of her storage space?"

He sent her an amused look. "No, but I have a feeling her sister the accountant is going to change that."

"Well, Alice tended to let people take advantage of her."

He came to a full stop at that, dropping her hand. "Excuse me?"

Jesus, that was uncalled-for. Cursing her tongue and her temperament, she blew out a breath. "I'm really sorry. That was unbelievably rude."

"Yeah, it was." He paused a moment, then spoke in a mild tone some part of her recognized as anything but. It stabbed her conscience, making her want to squirm. "I get that you have trust issues with men, Madison. But until I specifically deserve it, I'd prefer you not lash out at me because of what someone else has done."

A resentful part of her wanted to answer that with another snap. But he wasn't saying anything more than the truth, right? She'd behaved badly, and he deserved the return volley. Even if it hit a little too close to home. She wasn't used to a man grabbing the bull by the horns so directly. He demanded respect up front and gave her the same. She was all too aware that clarity of communication was very much a Dom trait.

"I said I'm sorry." She managed it with cool dignity, then sighed. "Hell, it was a rough day. I'm out of sorts and taking it out on you. Listen, I'll just go back to my store and we'll start fresh tomorrow, all right?"

That expression eased, which made things better, but he recaptured her hand, keeping her in place. "Or, you can hang out with me and get in a better mood. In my experience, nursing a bad mood by yourself just moves you into melancholy."

"Yeah, but you keep more friends nursing it alone." Not that she had a lot of those. She hadn't left much in Boston, all in all. Three more failed relationships and a job she'd aced but that had been safe, not fulfilling.

He squeezed her hand, as if sensing the additional punch she'd swung at her mood. "Just as an fyi, I've found a good spanking cures most pissy moods."

"I'll find my paddle if you get pissy," she said dryly.

She was pretty sure her *yeah right* tone didn't cover how her hand twitched in his at the provocative suggestion. The moment he said it, she saw him putting her over his knee and giving her a sound spanking for mouthing off in such a rude manner. She could even cast him in that photograph on her store wall, the severe Victorian gentleman, so proper and powerful. He'd walk with his wife in a landscaped park every evening, using his silver-handled walking cane with easy grace to clear any debris from her path, so she didn't snag her skirt or soil her slippers. Yet when they got home, he'd yank down her perfectly arranged hair, spread and bind her to their bed. As she gasped under the demands of his hands, mouth, he'd drive away any inhibitions, all vestiges of propriety out the window as she begged him to take her, as he stroked her between her spread, bound thighs with the smooth head of that cane . . .

Her free hand curled, finding dampness in the creases of her palm.

"I'd give one of Troy's testicles to know what's going through your mind right now."

She snapped back out of it. Her other hand was tight on his. He was waiting on her, studying her face. It was as though she was stepping in and out of two different dimensions in his presence. He didn't act as if there was anything strange about her pauses, her distraction, making it seem like he was right next to her on that journey.

She rallied. "One of Troy's testicles? Not your own?"

"I have use for both of mine."

Before she could figure out how to reply to what couldn't be anything less than a delicious threat, especially when he coupled it with a frank look at her flushed face and parted lips, he tugged her across his storeroom, taking her to a door on the far side with a keypad. As he punched in the code, she thought about the way their buildings looked from the street outside. "So the empty building on the other side of your store is yours?" she asked.

"Not empty. Just not open to the public."

She recalled that building's windows were papered with advertising for his store's wares and others in the district, as well as flyers for community events. The mural of advertising would allow him to screen the potential eyesore of a woodworking shop, but when she stepped into the space, she saw there was a far more vital reason he preferred privacy for it.

She thought she'd be safe looking at his creations. Sawdust, power tools, nice furniture. What she was looking at was a workshop for custom-made BDSM equipment. Her sister had probably brought him business, arranged orders for her own customers. The closest piece looked like a picnic table, only it was about half the traditional length and the space between the benches and table was too narrow to slide one's legs between them. The benches were padded, as was the table itself, with beautifully tooled red upholstery secured with antique gold tacks. The wood was a dark cherry, polished and finished. The quality was excellent, the type that fetishists paid four figures to own.

She thought of Logan's hands, the calluses and rough palms, and knew where he'd acquired them.

Her gaze moved to a St. Andrew's Cross not yet stained, and the hand sander next to it that said it was still being prepped. No scratches from bound, straining hands yet. She tried to clear the thickness out of her throat. "Wouldn't a power sander be faster?"

"Electronics have their place." Logan braced a hand on the door, hooking his thumb in his jeans pocket as he followed her gaze around the room. "They make things happen faster. But being in direct contact with the grain opens it up, lets the wood talk to you, tell you what it needs to become. Which is a lot like what happens to the people who use the finished product."

She folded her arms, a defensive movement. *I can't be here. I can't.* She was suddenly aware of how alone they were. When he touched her face, she jumped.

"You keep looking at me like that," he said quietly, "you're going to make me think I should have made that spanking a promise instead of a tease."

Here he had his choice of equipment to make that happen. "Don't," she managed, and he took his hand away.

Fortunately, he left her at the door, as if nothing unusual had happened. It gave her room to breathe, to steady herself. As he moved to the far side of the room, she saw a long wooden chest. It had carved feet, allowing a few inches of space beneath it. The piece was done in a golden pine, and the carved embellishments on it reminded her of the hinges she'd seen this morning, suggesting that was their intended place. As she drew closer she saw she was right, because he'd already screwed them in place.

She really needed to get out of here. Instead she came to Logan's side. He'd squatted next to the chest and unlatched the top. The front of the chest became two doors that folded back like wings along the short sides, with the help of the ornate hinges.

"This piece is for Troy's Mistress."

The chest walls were a facade for . . . a cage. A human-sized cage, if the human stayed on all fours or lay down. He or she could sit up, if the head stayed bowed.

"She plans to put it at the foot of her bed," Logan explained. "At the base corners are cutouts for air, so if she decides to close him in darkness, to punish or deny him the ability to see her changing clothes, she can."

She should act appalled, shocked, but his tone as he spoke of Troy and his Mistress, the way he passed his hand over the top with such pride in his handiwork, killed the impulse before it could form. Instead, she had an image of herself in the cage, Logan reclining in some manly chair, reading or watching cable. He'd have his ankles crossed and beer in hand while he glanced casually at her, watching her become more and more aroused, awaiting his pleasure.

A weird flutter moved up to her throat.

"Troy's doing the sanding, the hardest work on a piece like this. Once it's smooth enough, I'll stain and finish it. It's not ready for the hinges yet, or even the bars, but I put the pieces together tonight to make sure it's coming together properly. And to impress you." He gave her a disarming smile, so potent it had the opposite effect.

"He'd sleep in a cage for her?" She was proud of her note of cynical incredulity, even if it wasn't an accurate reflection of what was happening inside her. When Logan glanced up at her, she had a feeling he saw it, because his eyes did that delve-into-her-soul thing as he replied.

"For some submissives, that total ownership is a deep craving. When she locks him into this cage, she's underscoring he's her possession. It gives him a sense of safety and reassurance as well."

"He doesn't seem the timid sort."

Logan snorted. "Not in the least. Last year they were on a road trip and a couple of junkies tried to shake them down at a rest area. He jumped in front of her, fought both of them while she dialed 911 and grabbed her gun from the car. She shot one of them in the leg, the other in the stomach. Between Troy's beating and that, the police pretty much only had to do cleanup. It scared her to death, though, the thought of losing him. That's when I met them. She was punishing him at a public club session."

"Punishing him. For protecting her?"

"For not protecting what was hers. Himself. The punishment wasn't really a punishment, just a way for her to vent. But she branded him that night, made him hers permanently, which I think he considered the best of all outcomes. She really hadn't committed to him before then. She'd treated their relationship as more of a temporary situation, denying her feelings."

So Troy had the toothpaste-in-the-sink relationship, the pot of gold at the end of the rainbow. But Madison already knew it worked for some people. Just not her. She couldn't figure out the right formula, the secret code to it all.

She shook her head. "To most people, this isn't a normal conversation. Not in the least."

"How about to you?"

"You're making assumptions about me." She set her jaw. "I don't know what Alice told you . . ."

He didn't say anything as she trailed off. When he rose, and she started to step back, he spoke the same word she had, with a very different meaning, his voice brusque, eyes direct. "Don't."

She stilled, even though a quiver ran through her, telling her to run, run, run. But her mind was drowned out by emotions she couldn't explain.

"Better. You don't need to run from me, Madison. Whatever Alice told me about you, it doesn't change the fact you and I have just met, which means I'm learning everything about you from the source. You can be what you want with me, as long as you're true to yourself."

Though he wasn't touching her, less than a foot separated them and the impact of those words was more potent than a passionate kiss. She shifted her gaze to his chest. "It's not normal," she said.

"Deep inside all of us are vulnerabilities," Logan said, low. "Things we only reveal to the person capable of stripping us bare and yet cherishing the nakedness they find, not exploiting it. That's a common thread beneath a lot of the Dominant and submission sexual fantasies people have, whether or not they're actual Dominants or submissives."

She lifted her lashes, met his gaze, and earned a look of approval. "Good," he said. "I like it when you look me in the eye."

"Is this how you teach people? As a training Master?"

Despite her earlier aversion to the idea, she decided—with a spurt of bravado—maybe it was time to toughen up. He was practically giving her an engraved invitation to explore things with him, and he wouldn't judge, right? It wouldn't get personal. At least as far as he knew. It was always personal to her.

He shrugged. "Depends on the person. I do one-on-ones, like with Troy, but I also do talks about BDSM to interested groups, and orientation for club newcomers. I've even addressed a group of erotic romance authors. They asked a lot of interesting questions."

"I'll bet." At her nervous chuckle, he smiled at her. His expression shifted then, becoming more practical.

"Earlier today, you implied selling at Naughty Bits would be like selling cars or appliances. But you're selling a fantasy, a wish, an emotion realized, a hope or a dream. So that makes a difference in how you sell it." His gaze met hers. "Most importantly, you have to believe in what you're selling."

"You don't think I believe in it?" she asked, stiffening.

His brown eyes kindled with . . . interest, challenge? "I think it's hard to believe in it when you've dealt with men who've made you believe it's a scam, not a fantasy. A fantasy connects to your reality in a way that gives the fantasy wings, but it always returns to your heart, to who *you* are. Madison."

The man could overcome a woman's senses with nothing but words. The way he said her name, like punctuation at the end, made her want to hear him say it again. Each time he did, she'd be bound to him even further, as if he were a sorcerer.

She'd tried to become a pragmatist, and in business, she'd succeeded. Most of the people who knew her in Boston would agree that was one of her strongest traits. But Alice had never bought it as more than a skin-deep act. *You're a romantic, MadGirl. Jesus, it's obvious in every decision you've made. You can't change who you are by putting on a different coat of paint. It's always the same house beneath.*

He tilted his head toward the cage. "Would you like to try it out, see what it feels like?"

"Sorry. I try not to let men I barely know lock me into cages. Especially in windowless rooms. Falls under the whole *only if I've lost my freaking mind* category."

He grinned at that. It helped dial back her discomfort, yet her gaze lingered on the cage. The hinges and carved embellishments gave a feminine touch to the piece, making it a proper fit for a woman's bedroom, even though it was built to hold a strong, tall man like Troy.

"I made one last year for a tester bed," Logan said, leaning against the St. Andrew's Cross. "Since the bed sits up so high, it was easy to build it to fit beneath. The customer had a live-in sub, but wanted a detachable cell wall that could be added to divide the cage in case she ever had a second, additional sub staying over. She could watch her pets play with each other through the bars, if she ordered them to do so. She called her subs her pets," he added, as if she needed that clarification.

What a Master could require two submissives to do to one another through those bars was whirling around in her head like leaves on a fall day. Encouraging her to jump into the raked piles. "What do you call *your* subs?" she asked with a note of desperation. "Pets? Slaves?"

"Mine." His attention slid over her face. "Though I have none right now. What would you want to be called, if you belonged to a Master?"

"I wouldn't . . ." She tried to scoff, cleared her throat instead. "I've never given it thought."

"But now you will. Let me know what you come up with."

She gave him a quelling glance, an attempt to convey that she had no interest in being part of such a conversation. "What's the picnic bench?"

He looked puzzled, then he followed her gesture toward it. "It's a modified spanking bench. The sub lies down on her stomach on the platform and her legs are folded beneath her, shins resting on the side pieces. That one over in that opposite corner"—he nodded toward it—"is another version of it. It has two different levels, so the submissive can brace herself at different angles, depending on what the Dom desires."

She moved to touch the wood of the "picnic" bench, as well as the upholstery covering the side pieces. The wood felt like silk. "It's beautiful work," she allowed. "I've been in Boston furniture galleries where designer pieces aren't as well made as this. It must take hours to sand properly."

"It does. But it's a meditative process. You get into a rhythm and your mind goes into good places. You work out problems, come up with new ideas, defuse from a stressful day. I can show you the proper way to sand if you'd like to give it a try sometime."

"Does anyone actually fall for that? To help you get out of sanding?"

He chuckled. "It's the truth, but it does occasionally result in some help. I'm very particular about how it's done, however. Troy's gotten his knuckles rapped more than once."

And of course that converted Logan into a stern schoolteacher in her mind, the next page of the fantasy volume she was building around him. She tried to suppress the resulting ridiculous tingle at the base of her spine. Her praise had obviously pleased him, and that made their discussion feel less one-sided. She wasn't totally a wide-eyed newbie. She was in control here.

"What did you do before the hardware store?" she asked. She stepped away from the piece, winding her way through the different items with a flick of her glance here and there, neutral interest. It put space between the two of them.

Logan let her get away with it, bracing his very fine ass on a sawhorse, crossing his arms. "I went into the Army from high school. I've done woodworking and construction all my life, so after my tour was up, I worked as a building inspector. Then I became a private contractor, building houses on a resort island. That's where I pulled together the money for the hardware store. Once I had the hardware store up and running, I started this as a hobby."

He nodded to one of the pieces. "As to the quality of the furniture, it has to be well made. There's risk involved in BDSM, so a good Dom's top priority is safety. Making sure the equipment's sound is a big part of that."

"Did Alice send you business from her customers?"

"She did." Logan gave her an even look. "But that's not why I'm showing it to you."

"Though it's a nice side benefit," she pointed out. He didn't smile, and she turned away to study the item in the last corner, not able to meet his penetrating gaze. She swallowed as he came up behind her, his fingers wrapping around her elbow again, only this time it wasn't to guide her. Their bodies overlapped, his upper thigh brushing her buttock where he stood behind her and to her left. She didn't pull away.

When his other hand came to rest on her hip, her breath started shortening. He was about half a foot taller than her, so he bent his head, close enough she felt his breath pass over her temple. "What are you doing?"

"Learning you. Watching you react. Watching the wheels spin in your fascinating mind. What do you think of this one?"

It was a short-legged, three-foot-long rectangular bench, with two round cutouts a third of the way along the horizontal surface. Beneath the center of the bench was a crescent-shaped support piece.

"The Master who wanted this specified the two round cutouts so when his slave is lying on her stomach on the bench, her breasts fit through the holes. It's low enough to the ground, her knees and palms can reach the floor. She has pierced nipples, so he'll run a chain between them so she's bound to the bench. The crescent piece beneath is high enough he can also have her lie on the floor on her back, and he can position the arch of that piece over her throat, without it pressing on her windpipe. We've designed a track system so he can lock the bench to the floor of the playroom. She won't be able to shift it or accidentally turn it over."

"Of course," she said. When she swayed, his hand tightened on her hip. He continued as if he hadn't noticed.

"Anything involving the throat requires critical safety precautions. I made this stool capable of holding over three hundred pounds. But no matter what I do, he has to care for her as well. Locked beneath it, she has no way to protect her face, making her very vulnerable."

Madison had a wholly different view of that vulnerability. She visualized herself beneath that bench, staring up into Logan's face, through his spread knees. He might blindfold her. Or perhaps he'd take his cock in hand and masturbate over her face until he came.

The lock system would hold her there when he decided to get up, kneel between her legs, scoop up her hips and fuck her. Or eat her pussy. Or take her to climax over and over with a vibrator.

"Why would anyone trust someone that much?" she said, trying to pull herself out of her head.

"Perhaps they need to believe they can."

So many of her conversations with Alice about this type of thing had been about her, not Alice. Yet Alice had to have had a certain affinity for it, to sell BDSM materials as well as she did. "How did Alice . . . feel about things like this?"

"She wasn't in the lifestyle, if that's what you're asking. However, she was one of the few I was able to get to help me sand, and who did it properly."

When she glanced up at Logan, she saw that fond sadness, a ghost of a smile around his lips. "She did send me some business, but only a select few, because of how particular I am about it. I want to know my clientele. I don't do cash or anonymous. Nothing I spend hours creating is going to be used by some irresponsible novice or worse, a deranged sociopath who doesn't understand what Domination and submission is all about."

"And what *is* it all about?" She wanted to hear it from him, because it was different for everyone. "I'm not her, you know."

Suddenly that seemed not only a very important point, but *the* point, the one that had made this day take a turn for the worse and now made her wonder exactly why she was here, what Logan was seeking from her.

"I know you're not her, Madison." His countenance suggested he could tell everything she was thinking, which was too reassuring. She feared that familiarity. It could pull her under, take her where she'd fought going for so long. "Just as I know that you, even better than your sister, know what Domination and submission is all about. She knew it, too. No, wait. Don't withdraw. Just listen. It's not the technical stuff or the jargon, knowing whether this is a picnic table or spanking bench. It's an internal recognition, a call to something inside yourself you can't deny or shut down, not when faced with it like this."

"This is the conversation Alice always tried to have with me. I don't want to have it with you."

"Maybe she thought if you had the chance to have it with a more neutral party, you could figure some things out for yourself, at your own pace, rather than feeling like a trapped animal, being force-fed things."

She eyed him warily. "Are you offering to be my teacher? Is that what this is all about?"

He held her gaze. "That's one of the things I can be."

"What if it's the only thing I want from you? Or if I don't want anything at all."

"That will be your choice." He nodded. "But once you stop trying to shut it out, you'll find a wide range of things to explore. Endless spaces, like a honeycomb."

He didn't move any closer, but it felt that way, in how he looked at her. His tone became gentler once again. "What it's not about is harming someone. Not the absence of pain; there are good kinds of pain. I'm talking about damaging someone emotionally by betraying their trust, by not caring for them at the same time you demand their utter surrender."

He knew all the right things to say, all the right buttons to push. "Have you ever heard the best con man is the one who believes what he's saying?"

"Why do you need what I say to be a lie, Madison?"

"If you don't mind," she said tightly, "I'd like to skip the psych evaluation. We can do the store tour another time."

She turned away without waiting for his response and moved to the door. She was being rude again, but in all her relationships, she'd tried to be so accommodating, so pleasant. After lucky number seven, she'd finally decided her best dating strategy was not giving a shit about what was expected of her. Which, given that was almost physically impossible for her, meant not dating at all. She was reminded of that now, because a big part of her didn't want him to let her blow it off. Or let her go.

"I'd prefer to give you the full tour now."

Looking over her shoulder, she saw he was replacing the sides of the cage, transforming it into a chest again. When he straightened and turned toward her, he didn't look irritated. She wondered what it would take to rile him up, and whether she really wanted to go down that road. A part of her did. A very dangerous part.

He strode across the room to join her. She moved out of range, a pointed message that she didn't want to be touched. He respected it, though when he opened the door for her, he slid his fingertips along her lower back, an incidental touch that set off nerve receptors all around it. What was it about that guiding, protective hand that could wake up so many things inside a woman?

As they exited the room, he left the door cracked, suggesting he planned to do some work later. How many evenings did he spend here? If she worked late hours, it was likely he would be nearby. He and all his creations. Another hazardous thought.

"Do you listen to music while you do the building and sanding?" she asked, shoving that away.

"Sometimes. Depends on my mood. Usually the local oldies station. They play everything from Motown through the eighties."

"You're showing your age."

"Closing in on forty fast, and proud of it, baby." Giving her a wink, he pulled back the curtain that separated the storeroom from the main floor. "The center aisle here has fasteners, hooks, tie-downs and rope. It's the one Alice needed most often when she was running short on things for her displays. She'd nip in here, grab something and disappear through the curtain, waving at me with what she was taking."

It coaxed a small smile from her, especially when he gave her hair a quick, playful tug. She wanted to apologize for how defensive she'd become in the other room, but she bit it back. He'd been pricking things she'd rather not explore, and maybe her brusque responses would keep him from revisiting that territory. For her part, she knew it was best she steer clear of that room in the future, and show only a distant politeness if he brought up other projects.

Yeah right. Because so far she'd passed that test with flying colors. *Not.*

"Do you offer discounts to the local dungeon members?"

He nodded, not taking it as the joke she'd intended. "If they show me their membership card, I give them ten percent off for bringing their business here instead of 'Dom Depot'." He fingered a length of chain on a spool, and she found herself caught by how the silver links looked, twined around his knuckles. "D/s equipment is expensive and practitioners are creative. We're always looking for new ways to restrain, to punish."

"Not pleasure?"

"It's all about pleasure, Madison." He met her gaze. "Give me your hand again."

She thought about saying no. Instead she laid her hand in his, curiously docile. When his grip closed over it, he used the other hand to pull off a length of blue nylon rope. He wrapped the silken cord around her wrist. Once, twice . . . three times. Then he held the end of the rope under his thumb over her pulse, his other fingers wrapped around her forearm.

"Breathe," he reminded her. "When I did that, your eyes glazed and your lips parted. Something inside you focused and got still, waiting."

"What am I waiting for?" she asked, hearing a whispery note to her voice. She cleared her throat.

"To see what I'll do next. What I'll demand from you." Slow and easy, but confident—the way she suspected he'd deal with a shy wild animal—he shifted behind her, his chest pressed against her back.

Sliding his free hand onto her shoulder, he gripped it briefly before he moved to her throat, his fingers settling over it in a firm collar.

"Ah . . ." Her mind flailed for an appropriate response, but every other part of her got even more still, as if waiting for the answer to a question.

"When I place my hand over a submissive's neck like this, she might be keyed up, anxious, or aroused, but there's a subtle give, a relaxing of tension. In this position, where I hold all the power, there's nothing she can do. Nothing she needs to do. I've got her, on every level."

Oh God. It was just like her fantasy. *I've got you. You're all fucking mine.*

"Like a rabbit in the jaws of a wolf?" She forced out the comment, all too aware she was leaning against him, not pulling away, when she should have jumped back like he'd hit her with electrodes.

"You know how they say magic is just unexplained science? In D/s, chains are magic. Binding the body frees the soul, lets it fly. A woman stops thinking. She just feels."

"You're thinking again. You get punished when you think." More of the same fantasy.

He stroked her carotid with light fingertips and she barely suppressed a moan. She expected he felt the vibration beneath his hold, though.

"Think about Naughty Bits," he murmured. "Some women walk by it with those ugly-assed rectangular glasses and their overeducated noses in the air, and see it as frivolous or worse, a disgrace, where women do things to please men, serve their baser desires."

"Alice would talk about that. She knew it wasn't true."

"So do you. Deep down, you know the opposite is true. It's where a woman can explore a different, powerful side of herself, unleash it for mutual pleasure."

His thumb holding the rope lifted, and she watched it loosen and uncoil, dropping away as she lowered her arm and he stepped back from her. He kept a hand at her waist, not removing that support until she was steady on her feet.

Just as she'd thought, he was teaching her. He probably did demonstrations at his club. That was why he could draw her into something as captivating as any stage performance. It wasn't personal. She could tell him to back off if she thought he was going overboard, if he was using it as an excuse to feel her up, but this didn't feel like that.

Alice had told her to trust him so he could make her see Naughty Bits in a way that would help her continue its success. All this was merely an unusual on-the-job training program. Thinking about the customer earlier in the day, versus this moment, Madison could see the connection, a hint of the possibilities. She wasn't supposed to be a clerk, telling her clientele which aisle held nipple clamps. She was a travel agent, helping plan a memorable experience. It made her wish she could turn the clock back to the morning and do it over.

But if she could do that, she'd turn the clock back for far more important things.

"Alice used to say, if time travel were possible, people shouldn't go back in time to stop huge catastrophes. They should change small things, because a pebble has the best effect. Ripples on the pond."

She wasn't sure why she'd said that out loud. She turned to face him, putting more space between them.

"Sounds like her," he said.

"Hmm. 'A woman stops thinking.' So you're saying nothing gets in the way of a woman's desires like her mind?" Madison arched a brow. "So sad for you men, that females can't be lobotomized for *our* mutual pleasure."

He shook his head. "When a woman gets out of the way of her instincts, and doesn't let the baggage she brings from her day-to-day life drag her down, she's the one who leads. As her Master, I put her in touch with those instincts; she's the one who uses them to take us both to a deeper level of connection."

As her Master . . . The way he said it, it was so painfully straight-forward. The way his gaze stayed trained on her, waiting for something, made her shift uncomfortably, look elsewhere. "I think it's time for me to go home. It's getting late."

"All right," he said at last. "But I have something for you up front. Based on what I overheard today, I think it will help you with the store."

After today's disaster, she thought only a miracle would do that, but she was willing to give anything a try. Then she registered his words. "What do you mean, 'overheard'?"

He held up a placating hand. "Patrons tend to talk about their shopping experiences elsewhere on the street when they're in the store."

Her first impetus was to tell him to mind his own business, go to hell, but he was only telling her what she already knew, right? What good would it do to jump in his face about it? But it still rankled.

"They talk about you, too. One of the women said you had a really poor selection of wood chippers. Nothing the right size to dispose of her husband's body."

"I'll work on that. I do like to satisfy a woman." Giving her a wink, he moved toward the counter while she thought about whacking him with one of his hammers. Seeing its price tag brought her to a stop.

"Over a hundred dollars? For a hammer?"

"There are five-dollar ones as well. That's titanium, perfectly balanced, guaranteed for life." He came back to her and picked it up, handing it to her to examine. "The tool you choose should fit the job. To a craftsman, or a person who makes his living building, it's essential to pick the right one."

"What about the guy with more money than sense who wants to have the best in his garage, even if he hires out all his handiwork?" That had been Henry, relationship number four.

Logan acknowledged the truth of that with a half chuckle. "They're a good revenue source, but most men take their tools seriously. I know I do."

He picked up one of the tool belts. "In the box stores, you'll find plenty of tool belts made in China that can handle a year of wear, if you're lucky. I don't carry much stuff like that. People don't come to me when they're looking for cheap and disposable. This one costs far more, but it will last a good long time. The material is supple but strong, double-stitched around the buckle and edges."

He wrapped it around his own wrist to show her, his knuckles curled into a fist, his forearm flexing below the rolled-up cuff of his shirt. "I depend on my tools to hold up to what I require of them. In return, I take very good care of them."

Hanging the belt back up, he guided her onward, that broad palm resting on her lower back again, and her moving slow enough to feel its pressure. At checkout, he had an antique cash register with metal keys and a pull-down arm. Since a computer system was next to it, she assumed the antique was for show, but he'd used the metal sides to display magnets like "if I can't fix it, it ain't broke" and other appropriate sentiments for a hardware store.

He had to lift his hand from her back to stretch over the counter, reach beneath it for whatever he wanted to give her. While that was a pleasure to watch, she felt the loss of his touch. While she'd learned to be hellishly good at repressing her desires, he was way too immediate, too strong an impact on her senses. She reminded herself she was going home in a few moments. It was all right. She could hold it together until then.

Logan revealed a carved wooden box that matched the workmanship she'd seen in the back, clearly another of his creations. Placing it on the counter and opening it, he withdrew a pair of police handcuffs, a key and what appeared to be a tarot deck, contained in a transparent gauze bag. The cuffs made her stiffen, but he put the three things down before her in a precise line.

"I thought a little experiment might help you understand how Alice ran her store so successfully. You'll be alone when you do it. It's a self-test."

That made her feel a little better, but even so, she wasn't giving an unconditional response to anything. "What kind of test?"

He put his finger on the key and met her gaze. "Freeze this in an ice tray. Change into something that makes you feel sexy. I'm think-ing you go for the simple and devastating. A black lace thong and nothing else, except a necklace. A pretty choker."

She had a jet bead choker. It was one of her favorites, reminiscent of the 1940s. Maybe because of the close fit around her neck, the caress of the beads, it always made her feel supremely feminine and sexy. She'd had an all-too-similar sensation when he'd closed his fingers around her throat.

She didn't say anything, waiting for him to continue. She wasn't going to tell him about the choker, and she definitely wasn't going to get in an in-depth discussion about her underwear choices. But she didn't tell him to stop.

"After the key is frozen in the ice, put on the cuffs. Take the ice and this deck of cards to an open space on your floor. Kneel."

When he spoke the one word, her knees weakened. She thanked the gods she was wearing slacks that covered the reaction. With that penetrating scrutiny, Logan could probably discern an elevation in heart rate, let alone a visible quiver in her knees. "Fan them out in a circle around you," he said, "and flip thirteen of them randomly. When you look at the images, think of them like breadcrumbs, leading you to your own fantasies. Then think about the type of breadcrumbs your store can offer people coming through your door, helping them reach their own."

He was an expert in his field, so to speak. This was his milieu, and he was simply trying to be helpful. Being entranced by how he put the items back in the box, and how his fingers felt brushing hers when he handed over the box was incidental.

The carving on the top was the triskelion. As her fingers slid over it, he nodded to the symbol. "Do you know its meaning?"

"I know it represents BDSM somehow."

"It can represent a lot of things. The three sections"—he placed a finger on one of them—"can symbolize safe, sane and consensual, the core mantra of BDSM. Or the three types of practitioners: Doms, subs and switches. A lot of important things in life connect to a trinity." He shifted his hand, touching her knuckle as he did so. She didn't move it away. Acknowledging it, he lingered there, teasing the soft, thin skin between two of her knuckles. She realized she was holding her breath again. She felt his eyes on her, but kept her own on their hands.

"The small hole in each section represents how the need for Dominance or submission can't be satisfied alone."

He touched her chin, lifting it so that her eyes met his. He'd said he liked that. "No one figures everything out the first day, Madison," he said mildly. "Alice said you were a type A personality, a perfectionist. You have to give yourself time to learn."

Alice was never afraid of making mistakes. Of course, why would she have been? Alice's mistakes had a way of turning into successes, whereas even Madison's successes often turned out to be failures in disguise. She was afraid of doing the same to the store Alice had loved.

"Thanks for the box." Hugging it to her, she stepped back. "I might do it. It beats surfing cable."

Or dreading another day of the polite, get-away-from-me looks from her customers. If this could help her feel better about that, it might be worth it. But she wasn't going to make him any promises about doing it. "Thanks for all the lessons. Professor."

He didn't say anything and she frowned, looking down at the counter again. "You make me uncomfortable when you stare like that."

"I don't think making you comfortable is what you need from me, Madison. But I do like to see you smile." Pulling a magnet off the antique cash register, he handed it to her. "On the house."

"Think of all the women on the Titanic who passed up dessert." She couldn't help it; she smiled, and it stayed there when his expression eased into the same.

"That's better. I'll walk you out." He took her elbow. "When you stay late, you should move your car to the front, or let me know when you're leaving, so Troy or I can escort you. It's a safe area, but a deserted alley is still a deserted alley. Best not to take risks."

Yet he and her dead sister had no problem pushing her to risk her sanity, with his not-so-subtle offers to unleash his Dominant side on her senses. Hell, he was already doing it, as if it was such an intrinsic part of him, he couldn't help himself when he was around a submissive.

She flinched inwardly. *Stop thinking of yourself that way.* "It's nice of you to do this, but I'm sure it's fine."

"I'm sure it is. I'm still walking you to your car."

He was moving her down the center aisle, back past the fasteners, hooks, ropes. She tried not to think of all the ways they could be used. Dom Depot, indeed. But the danger was never the sword, but who was wielding it. *Nice phallic entendre there, Madison. Alice would be smirking.*

She set her jaw and stopped, pivoting toward him. "Even if I say no?"

She'd put the box under an arm and held out her other hand to bring him to a halt, which brought her palm in contact with his chest. He was solid muscle, and distracting curls of gleaming chest hair, revealed by the open collar of his shirt, tempted touch. They were only a few inches above where her fingers rested. She pressed them against his flesh, an attempt to quell the urge, and realized she'd conveyed something else.

He closed his hand over her wrist, then he closed the space between them. It was a gradual but inexorable movement, like tides rising. The words she intended to say went away as he held her gaze, a restraint as effective as the ropes behind her. Which kind of proved her point about the sword, but she wasn't opening her mouth to make it.

Keeping his attention on her face, tracking her every reaction in a way that couldn't help but make a woman feel like the center of the universe, he lowered her arm to her side. His grip shifted, and now that same arm was being slowly twisted behind her, her knuckles brushing her ass, then the small of her back. His knuckles pressed against the top of her buttocks as he held her hand. The position arched her body so the tips of her breasts almost touched his chest.

"*No* means nothing to me when it conflicts with your well-being, Madison."

Her swallow was audible. "Let go of me," she whispered.

"That's not what you want me to do."

"No, but . . . please."

He did it with kindness, caressing her wrist before stepping back. "I'm walking you to your car," he said firmly. When he gestured her to precede him, she turned back in that direction, trying to scrape up her shattered composure. As they moved toward the exit, he thankfully stayed quiet, though his hand settled on her back again. The gesture was so easy for him he couldn't possibly know how raw and exposed it left her.

They were approaching her back door. He'd open it for her, and she'd get in her car like some dutiful puppet whose strings he'd managed to pull all the right ways, making him think he could do that tomorrow, and the next day.

She spun around and faced him, holding the box between them to ensure she didn't make any unwise contact this time. "I get it. You think you're some Master-Dom-guru who can bring people to the light through whips and chains. Well, that's awesome for you. Go and start a cult somewhere. But I'm not signing up. As for what Alice told you, about giving me to you, that's more of her bullshit. The type of things that made people think she was this amazing, quirky person who everyone wanted to be around, who everyone loved, who never had her heart broken . . ."

Her voice was shaking. She thrust the box at him. "You were her friend. You don't have to be mine."

He closed his hands over hers on the box and took it, but only to set it aside on one of her shelves. "I have no intention of being your friend, Madison. Not that way." Then he curled his strong fingers over her nape, exerted pressure. "Come here."

"I don't want this. I don't want to do it. I don't want to do any of this." She didn't jerk away, just resisted him with counterweight, futile against a man who was twice her weight and at least half a foot taller. He put his other arm around her waist, using it like a lasso to bring her to him, one reluctant step at a time.

"Come here," he repeated quietly. She'd never had a man talk like that to her, equal doses of irresistible command and compassion, gentle strength and authority, which had her body throbbing as much as her aching heart.

Once his chest took up her vision, he wrapped both arms around her, her hands curled tense against her sternum, mashed between them. "Just breathe. I'm sorry. That was too much, too soon."

She stood in his embrace, rigid. But not withdrawing.

"I wanted too much, too quickly," he said. "You have that effect on a man."

"Yeah, right." But she didn't have the courage to look for the truth. Not right now. His arms felt too good. She should pull away. Instead, she leaned, a little bit.

"Did she . . . did she have a lot of bad days?" The words were muffled against his chest.

He sighed. "She said the good days always outnumbered the bad, until the end. That was when she called you. She loved you, Madison. You were the only thing she wanted, at the last."

"Shit." She closed her eyes tight, pressing her forehead against his chest. "I loved her, Logan."

"I know that. So did she."

"I don't understand any of this. Especially what you felt about her, and how that relates to me. How that can be a good thing. I'm not her."

He straightened, holding her away from him to give her a look that had an edge to it. "I told you I know that already."

"Yeah, but what people say and what they understand about themselves are pretty different. For a long time I told people I wasn't anal and I actually believed it."

His lips twitched at that. Then his expression sobered and she suspected he was considering his next words carefully, a shift in the air that brought the tension back between them. She still didn't move out of his grasp. The touch of his hands was something she couldn't resist.

"At one time," he said, "I found Alice very intriguing. Fascinating. I even entertained the idea of a romantic relationship. But as colorful and passionate as she was, she was really quite grounded." He shook his head. "She explained she genuinely loved everyone so she didn't have to risk her heart on loving someone. She told me *you* were the brave one. Despite having your heart broken, shattered and stomped upon, you kept looking for the right person to care for it. She said if you ever found the person you could trust enough to let go—the person who deserved your trust—you would finally find that."

He cleared his throat. "She knew me better than anyone, Madison. She told me I didn't want her. I wanted you."

She didn't know how to deal with that, but tears were brimming, a response to hearing what her sister had thought of her. He took the hem of his shirt and dabbed her eyes with it, making her choke on a half chuckle. One nervous hand landed on his bare abdomen. Her fingers pressed into the hard ridges as his head lifted, a different awareness in both their eyes now.

"I need to get home," she said, pulling back from him. She didn't wait for his reply. Instead she grabbed the box off the shelf and pushed out the back door, aware of him standing in the entrance, watching her until she got into her car and drove away.

She felt as though she were fleeing the scene of an accident.

Hearing Alice's perspective of her floored her. She'd never really thought about it, because Alice had always seemed to have a lover . . . or two. But she'd never talked about marriage or commitment. Had she ever?

Madison was still pondering that when she fell asleep. She slept better than she had thus far, alone in Alice's house. She'd slept in her clothes, Logan's sawdust and aftershave scent lingering in her nose. When she woke, she found her arms wrapped around herself, and recalled a dream of strong male arms surrounding her, the way he'd held her at the store.

Usually when she had such dreams, the arms constricted, choking the life out of her. Alice had called them her emotional claustrophobia dreams.

She decided to stay at the house today. Thinking about Logan's overly developed sense of personal responsibility, she realized she'd better call or he or Troy might show up on her doorstep. It was too early for them to be open, which relieved her of the possible chance of talking to him. If yesterday was an example of what being next door to him every day would be like, she wasn't sure how she was going to cope. Or stay away.

As she listened to his voice on the answering machine, she told herself she would *not* call during off hours to hear that sexy timbre encouraging her to leave a message, telling him what she needed.

"Uh, hi, this is Madison. I'm going to work at the house today. I figured you'd wonder where I was if I wasn't there, and I didn't want you to worry." The words sounded wrong to her, like yesterday had been a far deeper connection than it was, but there was no way to take it back, so she added, awkwardly, "I mean, I know you feel a responsibility toward me because of Alice. So that's why I thought I'd better call. Bye."

God, she was an idiot. Turning off her phone, she considered what she could do at the house, now that she'd committed her day to it. She didn't have to hang out here. She could go into Charlotte, go shopping, go to a museum. She honestly didn't want to pack up more of Alice's belongings, decide what to keep and what to donate to the local charities.

Going upstairs, she stood outside the one room whose threshold she hadn't yet crossed. It was the spare guest room Alice had converted into what she called Wonderland, a quirky play on her name. Madison cracked the door, saw a glimpse of color and sparkles, and closed it again.

They'd loved playing dress-up as little girls. The fact they never gave it up had been their shared secret. Every time she came to visit Alice, they would spend at least one night in that room, with a great deal of wine and a full one-hundred-count box of Russell Stover's, playing dress-up with the vast array of costumes. Alice had started the collection with what she kept from her college theater days. The role-playing costumes she bought for the shop had augmented it considerably, things she'd liked enough to buy an extra in her own size. Fortunately it was the size she and Madison shared as adults.

They'd often been mistaken for twins, another reason Madison was so wary of Logan's fascination with her. It wouldn't be the first time one of Alice's cast-off boyfriends thought Madison was a suitable second.

She leaned against the guest room door, remembering the last time they'd spent an evening in that room. She'd been twenty-six, on soon-to-crash-and-burn relationship number three. God, what she'd give to have that night back again.

"*There* are like two hundred outfits in here," Madison teased her sister. "You're a hoarder."

Alice gave her a lofty look from the other side of the room. She was wearing a Marie Antoinette costume, complete with corset and long white-blond wig. The skirt stuck out on either side like a broomstick was beneath it. "This from a hooker."

"I'm not a hooker. I'm a high-class escort, versed in every form of sexual pleasure, called to service the world's most powerful men.

They give me diamonds." Madison stretched out an arm loaded up with sparkly bangle bracelets, and crossed her legs in the microminiskirt that showed off the mesh stockings and stiletto heels. "I earn ten thousand dollars an hour."

"Great. You can take care of us both when we're old and gray and our boobs sag."

"I'll buy us plastic surgery so we'll never look older. We'll never get old and gray."

Sighing, Madison left the room behind and descended the stairs. A shower seemed the most neutral decision. She stayed in there awhile, leaning against the wall, letting the spray roll over her. When at last she reached for the soap, lathered it up and ran it over her skin, her mind went to Logan's hands. Resting on her lower back, closed over her wrist . . . her throat. She laid her fingers in the same place and closed her eyes. With the water drumming in her ears, it seemed safe, isolated, to think about it. To want his hands on her again. He surrounded a woman with his presence, his strength, those penetrating eyes. All the things she'd sampled from the Master with Vanessa, Logan offered as a full course meal.

She thought about the box she'd left on the kitchen table. In an uncertain mood when she arrived last night, she'd lifted the lid only long enough to fish out the key and drop it in a filled ice tray, telling herself that didn't commit her to anything. Would he ask her about it, next time she came into the shop? She didn't like feeling obligated. But he'd offered it to her as a way to help her. What else was she going to do today?

Dressed in a terry cloth robe, running her hands through her damp hair, she went to the kitchen to get a cup of coffee. As she added sugar and cream, she studied the box, then propped her hips against the counter, sipping from the mug. After a few moments, she sidled over to the box and folded back the lid. The cuffs were on top of the card deck. Noticing a folded note in between the two, she put her cup down.

Opening it, she saw what she assumed was Logan's unexpectedly neat, even handwriting. Just like an old-fashioned schoolmaster. It was insanely easy to envision him with queued hair, tight breeches and a long coat. Take away the fancy computer at the front of his store, and she could see him standing in the same spot three hundred years ago, behind an antique register and a carved wooden counter. His woodworking shop had possessed power tools, but also a lot of hand tools, so she thought he wouldn't feel out of place at all.

She'd be the student sneaking glances at his groin in the snug breeches and getting her knuckles rapped. Or kept after school and held firmly around the waist, clinging to his side as he applied that ruler to her backside. He'd make her pull up her skirt so it marked her skin through the thin drawers . . .

Thinking of her room upstairs, she wondered if Logan liked to play dress-up. Did he wear leather and chains at his club? A pirate shirt and boots? The ridiculous thought intrigued her far more than it should. She turned her attention to the note.

Relinquish control—on your own terms.

Relinquishing control made her feel like she was trapped in a bucket, waiting for the bottom to drop out. A counselor who treated her for depression in her teens suggested she try to make a B instead of an A, saying she needed to stop trying to control everything, be a perfectionist in all she did. Fortunately, her mother had decided that was an asinine idea, but in this case, Logan wasn't advising loss of control through a lower level of performance. He was presenting her with a way to see the store differently, help her excel with it. A pretty unorthodox way, granted, but as she'd realized yesterday, her traditional sales experience didn't mean squat there. It was an erotica shop, not RadioShack.

Still, she hedged. She should return the box to him, say thanks but no thanks.

She left it there and went into Alice's home office. For the next few minutes, she riffled through some estate paperwork. The idea of doing that repulsed her, so she wandered back into the bedroom.

She'd returned to Boston after Alice's death long enough to hire a company to pack up her belongings and ship them here. Now she stared at some of those boxes, stacked against the lavender-painted wall. Most of what she'd brought here had remained unopened, except for her clothes and essentials. What was in the bulk of them was impersonal to her, stuff she was likely to donate anyhow. Alice had a fully stocked kitchen of brightly colored, mismatched dishes. Why would Madison unpack her practical designer china, a set of six she'd never used, since she mostly ate out of reusable plastic frozen-food trays?

Even with the logical explanations for it all, it was still surreal to her, how she'd simply walked away from everything. It was as if Alice's summons had been the completion of one book of her life and the opening of this new one. Perhaps she'd been ready for a huge change, everything in Boston a reminder of what she didn't have. Or what she'd been there.

Now she found the box with her few pieces of intimate wear and jewelry. Sure enough, she found the choker. And a black lace thong.

She'd never worn them together for a lover, but what was interesting was how often she'd imagined doing so. She'd envision the faceless male hooking his finger under the choker to pull her up off her knees and capture her mouth in a kiss. His hands would drop to grip her bare breasts, squeeze and pinch as she writhed under his commanding touch. She was always on her knees when he did that. He would blindfold her, so she could feel everything even more intensely.

She'd never had a lover she'd trusted enough to blindfold her, or restrain her in a way she couldn't remove herself. Her spotty Dom/sub attempts with lovers had been very low-key. Even when she'd dared to invite one of her relationship partners, like Gerald, into that dark part of her head, she hadn't trusted any of them to treat her like one of the submissives she'd seen on her adventures with Alice. But that hunger when she watched them be blindfolded, chained, was a dragon, gnawing on her soul.

A form of magic. Chains on the body become a way to free the soul . . .

For heaven's sake, it was just her alone here. Dropping the robe on the bed, she stepped into the lace thong. The friction of the back strap against her rim, the way the rest hugged the labia, made her aware she wore a garment that only had two purposes—arousing herself and a lover. When she lifted the choker in front of the mirror and put it on, she watched her nipples tighten, felt a similar reaction between her legs.

She hadn't opened the curtains in the living area, so she didn't have to don the robe to move back through the house. It felt decadent, walking down the hallways and through the rooms that way. She pretended her Master had commanded her to wear only this until he came home from work. Such secret 24/7 Dom/sub fantasies usually featured her Master as a man in a suit, his clean-shaven jaw strong, his lips firm with authoritative resolve. She'd kneel by the door, her eyes down as he came home from a day at the office.

Now instead of seeing creased slacks and shiny shoes in her mind's eye, she saw heavy work shoes beneath the cuffs of jeans. When Logan squatted, tipped up her chin to give her a heated, approving kiss, his warm brown eyes took her over, the rasp of his five o'clock shadow a welcome abrasion to her fair skin.

Okay, Logan could be today's fantasy. That didn't mean anything. Logan was a charismatic man and very self-assured. Dominant. Master. She rolled the words over in her mind. She'd always told herself it was a title those in the D/s community gave themselves, like an adult calling himself Captain Kirk because he donned a Star Trek uniform for a sci-fi con. It didn't translate outside the mass delusion of that exclusive community. Logan was the first Dom she'd met who clearly emanated what he was outside a club environment. He'd affect a ninety-year-old grandmother, let alone her.

Since she didn't care to dwell on the fantasies he likely inspired in all those female gardening customers, ninety-year-olds or otherwise, she retrieved the box from the table and the ice tray from the freezer. Snagging a dish towel to fold beneath it, she brought all of it back into the living room.

First the cuffs. When she fitted one around her wrist, latching it with that ticking *click* noise, she remembered Logan's fingers circling her wrist. When she secured the other cuff, a tiny expulsion of cream bloomed against the crotch of her thong, dampening her flesh. Nerves tingled across her breasts as if his fingertips had teased the flesh there.

She'd gotten into the habit of treating a self-inflicted climax like the impulse decision to eat a cookie. Empty calories but instant gratification, no matter the shame or regret afterward. It was easy enough to do, whether by manual or electronic means. As such, she thought about lying down on the floor right now to masturbate. Given how the cuffs were affecting her, she expected it wouldn't take long. More empty calories, but the impulse was strong. Really strong.

If Logan was here, he'd order her to go through with the whole experiment first, denying her. Building her response, much like the very thought of him making her do his bidding did now. More dampness between her thighs, a hard contraction that made it even more difficult to resist that masturbation urge. If the mere idea of Logan bending her to his will could result in that reaction, how dangerous would the reality be?

Gerald had told her BDSM was deviant behavior, something that could quickly become a sex addiction if she indulged it. Since he'd treated patients who'd gotten lost in that world, he'd unnerved her with the half-assed diagnosis. Probably the only thing that had saved her from being fully sucked in was Alice's reaction to the comment when she'd told her about it. *What a fucking idiot.* The other thing that had kept her from being swayed was his delivery, more a resentful accusation than the honest concern of a lover.

This was just her in her living room. No accusations against, no persuasive suggestions for. Just her own mind and her own reactions to face.

Alice had always kept the living area clear to do her yoga, which made it the best area to do it. Logan had been here, tending Alice, so he knew the layout of her house. At his store today, would he be thinking about Madison doing this, in the thong and choker? If she invited him to dinner at some point, would he stand in the doorway to this room and visualize her kneeling here?

Of course he would. For all his Master-of-the-Universe routine, he was a guy. The moment he'd said *thong* to her, he'd probably stripped off all her clothes in his mind. From here forward, if she wore a parka to work, he'd still see her as a naked paper doll.

He'd probably chuckle at her cynical observation, making her nerve endings ripple with the masculine sound. Hell, just hearing it in her head, they danced. Kneeling on the carpet, she shifted into a seated position on her hip and reached into the box with her bound hands to remove the deck. She loosened the drawstring bag so the cards could slide out. The backs displayed a brilliant blue color with detailed gold edging. A note had been slipped under the band holding the cards, the folded top showing more of his neat handwriting.

Read this. Don't look at cards first.

She opened up the note and found a repeat of the instructions he'd given her. Had he given these out before? And to whom? It didn't matter. She could hear his voice, his calm, authoritative way of talking as she read the words.

Fan out the cards in a circle around you, facedown. Choose thirteen at random to turn over. Whatever is on the card, consider how that picture or word makes you feel. Does your pulse elevate? Are you afraid? Intrigued? Aroused? If it's a body part, touch yourself there. Think about someone else touching you there. Let the cards create a fantasy for you.

She laid out the cards around her. In the center of that blue field on the back of each card was a single gold star, something that had been obscured by his note. While it was pretty, eye-catching, the face sides were works of art.

Her first card showed a fecund goddess with heavy, bare breasts lying amid lush red flowers. In the top left corner, in bold calligraphy, was the word *Breast*. At the bottom right corner was a smaller word, the ink more refined. *Heart*.

She thought about the direction on the note. *Touch yourself.* The goddess in the picture was doing it, supporting one breast in a hand. Madison cupped her own breast, ran her fingers over it. She imagined herself as that goddess, drawing a male like Troy to her, an earth mother offering sustenance and pleasure. Bringing his mouth to her nipple, she'd cup his head, twine her fingers idly through his sandy hair as he pulled on her breast and desire swirled in her loins like planets orbiting a sun.

Her mind twitched impatiently away from that, toward far more dangerous imagery. Logan's hand closing over her breast, possessing it, thumb passing over the nipple, his other hand at her waist, holding her still as he bent. He didn't intend to suckle her like a child of her universe. He was here to conquer a goddess, so he captured the nipple in his heated mouth, nipping and pulling on it in a way she felt all the way to her womb, making her thighs loosen for him . . .

She turned over another card, the next word sending an arrow of sensation directly to the subject. *Cunt.* It was in white letters against a black cavernous circle, around which were twined black and red roses. A snake made a circle around all of it. A smaller word was printed in the lower right corner, against a tiny blood red heart. *Soul.*

Curious, she chose three more cards and discovered the same pairing pattern: *Possession/surrender. Pain/release. Blindfold/trust.*

She stared at that last card for a while. It showed a man and woman twined together, bound by red rope so they couldn't move, but they didn't look as if they desired to do so. His arms were wrapped over her shoulders, hers threaded beneath his to cling to

his waist and back, her face pressed into his chest. She was the one
blindfolded.

Two more cards. *Collar/belonging. Whip/flight.*

Her reaction was climbing at an exponential rate, the flesh between
her legs throbbing, her neck pulse thumping. With every restless shift
of her body, she was reminded she wore the cuffs, the choker, the
thong. She looked like a submissive, a sex slave, kneeling on the floor
and playing sensual games with herself until her Master came home.

Unnerved by the thought, she forced the focus from herself to
Logan's training of Troy. She imagined the male submissive in nothing but a collar, kneeling in an aisle of the store while customers
moved around him, unconcerned, knowing he was waiting for his
Master . . . Was he waiting for his command? His punishment?

He would be staring at the floor. She couldn't see herself in the
same position, surrounded by people like that. Or could she?

As her mind's wheels turned, she flipped six more cards, taking
her to the thirteen. Then she kept going, until she'd turned over all
of them. They ran the gamut of sexual play, from positions, to role-
playing, to toys . . .

She slid from her hip down onto her back, the slick cards pressing
against her skin. She stretched her cuffed hands over her head, her
body elongating, arching up, as if she were displaying herself for a
lover. She wanted to spread her thighs, wanted to be commanded to
spread them. She wanted his hands gripping her, pushing them apart,
making her do his will. She closed her eyes, not wanting the reality
of her surroundings judging her.

She rotated her hips, taunting him. Yes, she was bound to his
will, but she would do all she could with her body to beg him to
come to her, to touch her. He would stand back in the shadows and
watch, letting the moments stretch out, her body getting more and
more excited as she lifted her hips, lowered them as if he was already
inside her. Fucking her. He wouldn't let her demand, wouldn't let

her take control. He would let her keep doing what she was doing for *his* pleasure, *his* enjoyment, and that would just make her hotter.

Now at last he would speak. *Touch yourself, Madison. Rub your cunt for me.*

She shuddered at the thought of his whisper, his fiery eyes burning her. She lowered her hands, and when the cool metal of the cuffs pressed against her pelvis, her fingers reaching her clit, her body bucked up, ass and shoulders pressed into the floor. A gasp broke from her lips. "Yeeess . . . please . . ."

He liked her begging, enough to make her do it for all eternity. He was a sadist, and she craved that, didn't want him to give in to her. She wanted to know he held the power, the decisions. That she, the ultimate control freak, controlled nothing. Her only choice was to belong to him.

Sliding her fingers beneath the thong, she found her labia silky slick with her juices. She tweaked her clit, stroked the tender inner crevices that had so many nerve endings. She pushed up beneath the clit hood, increasing the intensity there, and then slipped her fingers inside herself. Watching her fuck herself with her fingers would make him harder, maybe make him take a step out of the shadows. That powerful body getting closer . . . She thought of his muscled chest beneath her hand, fingers twining and tugging on his chest hair.

She rose and fell, her hips twisting and grinding against her touch and the floor. The cuffs pressed into her lower abdomen, her thighs, and the fingers of the hand she wasn't using dug into soft flesh. "Please . . . may I . . . let me . . ." She whispered it, and heard—at long, long last—the order.

Go over for me. Only for me.

She tightened up all over, forcing her thighs to remain open to increase the intensity of it, even as she wanted to curl into a ball around that hand and contain all those spasming nerves into one prolonged wave. She cried out, the sound echoing in the spacious room, and she rode the feeling until it ebbed away under her fingers, leaving her twitching and trembling there on the living room floor.

She turned onto her side, curling around that core. When she brought her trembling hands back up to her face, she smelled herself as she tucked her fingers under her cheek.

The ice cube tray had turned to water, the key floating at the top. She could unlock herself at any time. She didn't move toward it. She didn't want to leave this feeling behind. Somehow, the cuffs were vital to holding on to it. She preferred to think of herself as waiting for him to remove them. She'd wait as long as he required. Days if necessary.

It made her think of that scene in *Secretary*, Maggie at the desk in her wedding dress. A lot of people hadn't understood that scene. Probably, like Gerald, they assumed it was a sickness. But it was no different from the knight who swore an oath of fealty to a king and went into a hopeless battle for him. The test wasn't the battle. It was proving his oath was more binding upon him than anything else, that his devotion and loyalty to his king, his Master, couldn't be swayed.

It was a fantasy, yes, because you couldn't trust another human being that much, could you? But you could pretend for a little while.

The cards beneath her were sticking to her perspiring flesh. When she moved the one beneath her cheek, she discovered it was the *Possession/surrender* one. The graphic was a woman kneeling, a collar on her throat, a tether wound around the hand of the male lover who stood over her. She looked up at him, and he touched her face. Even as an illustration, the bond between them was unmistakable.

In her last few relationships, the crap had taken over such that sex wasn't a conduit to deeper emotions—it was a way to avoid them. Here she was surrounded by cards that spoke of sexual things. If the designer had left it there, she might have remained more detached. But adding that one provocative, emotional word to each, as well as the incredible detail of the illustrations, spoke of the far deeper things the physical were *supposed* to mean. Things she'd shut herself away from, because if the basics of the relationship were missing—trust, belonging, laughter . . . love—what was the rest, but a hollow illusion?

She'd never chosen her relationships based on her craving for a Dominant. She'd run from that, because the choice meant relinquishing control, and no one could be trusted that much.

But a woman could only let fear and repressed desire run at cross-purposes for so long. Gazing at the thirteen cards she'd turned over, she realized how many of them were about the world of Dominance and submission. There were as many cards in the deck not about that type of sexuality, so what did it say, that she'd picked those at random?

Coincidence. Accident. She wasn't going to get maudlin here.

When it came down to it, her personal shit wasn't important. What was important about tonight was that it had clarified how she could connect with her customers. She hadn't failed yesterday because she couldn't sell. She'd failed because, in order to connect, the conduit had to be as open on her side as on the customers'. She was going to have to embrace things she'd kept at bay, face what kind of sexual being she was in order to coax the same to life in those who walked through her door.

It was a useful revelation, but the idea of actualizing it brought the same overwhelming anxiety it always did. She curled into a tighter ball, trying to stave off the despair that started to spiral in her lower belly, spoiling the same track desire had taken only a few moments before.

Then she thought of Logan. His touch, his eyes, the understanding that lay in both, reaching as deep inside of her as the fear and desire combined.

Damn it, she wasn't backing away from this. Even if she was a screw-up in her personal life, she'd never been a screw-up when it came to business, school, or anywhere the public stood in judgment of her performance. She was going to do what was needed to make this work.

Which meant she was going to go on Friday. She would watch Logan train Troy, would learn more about relinquishing control . . . at a safe distance.

Even as she had that thought, her mind scoffed at her. Looking at the cards, the cuffs and the key, she knew one thing for certain.

The words "safe" and "Logan" would never be paired on a card together.

PART II

The
Training Session

What did one wear to help a modern-day Master train a sex slave? Was it black tie, or like going to a Habitat for Humanity worksite, where one expected to get sweaty and dirty?

In the end, she did what a woman did when she was going to be around a handsome man. In this case, two of them. She dressed up, but toned it down enough to make it look like the effort was a casual afterthought. The off-one-shoulder tunic top was belted at the waist so it formed a short skirt over black jeans. The shirt clung to her breasts without being slutty, reinforcing her intent to support the mood but not become part of the performance. No matter that her damp palms and elevated pulse rate seemed to indicate otherwise. After brushing out her hair so it was a silken ripple over her bared shoulder, she slid into a pair of heeled boots and was ready to go.

She hadn't returned to Naughty Bits this week, instead focusing on the grand-opening details from home. A side benefit of that was she didn't have to worry about Logan cornering her to find out if she'd done what he suggested with that wooden box.

It had been a gift from him, the box containing a set of suggestive tarot cards and a pair of cuffs. He'd given her a solitary exercise to do with them, something intended to help her get in touch with her own sensuality. She'd ended up wearing the cuffs and masturbating to climax, imagining him as she lay upon those fanned-out cards.

The next morning, when he'd called the house, responding to her message that she wouldn't be back to the store this week, she'd still been too flummoxed by that experience to talk to him directly. Instead, she'd listened to him on her voice mail. He'd thanked her for letting him know her schedule and told her to give him a call if she needed anything. Very cordial.

"Don't forget about Friday. I could use an assistant. The boy can be a handful."

She'd spent the interim days doing this and that, but she still couldn't bring herself to do much in Wonderland, Alice's second-floor bedroom that was chock-full of costumes and dress-up clothes. She did have her coffee in there Friday morning, looking at the assortment of outfits like a museum display as she thought about the past . . . the future.

Truth, all of it had helped harden her resolve about tonight's plans. If she couldn't go through the contents of that room, how could she possibly figure out what would work best with Naughty Bits' customers? Joining Logan for Troy's training session would help her. She'd face it like a dental appointment. It was a necessary cleaning of plaque buildup, a mental block preventing her from shining the way she could. *Focus. No sentiment. No Alice memories. Just sex, whips and chains tonight.*

It wasn't quite dark when she pulled into the alley behind her store, but twilight was settling in, the time of possibilities. She unlocked the back door and slipped into her storeroom, letting the door close behind her. Putting her purse on one of the shelves, she saw the connecting door between her storeroom and Logan's was open, underscoring the invitation. She stepped across that threshold and moved to the curtained pass-through to the main area of his store. Everything was quiet and dark, only the dim security lights providing illumination. "Hello?"

"Sorry. Here I am." At the muffled bump, muttered curse, she relaxed, hearing Troy's voice, his feet hurrying toward her down one of the aisles. When he turned the corner, she was confronted with a lot of firm male flesh. All he was wearing was a pair of drawstring pants. A light sheen of sweat made his muscles above them gleam.

"I'm so sorry, Madison. I was finishing up my workout in the glass-cutting area and time got away from me. Master Logan told me to be at the storeroom door so you wouldn't think you were walking onto a horror movie set."

"The one where two charismatic men lure an unsuspecting woman into their shop after hours to chop up her body with power tools and compost her?"

"You have Alice's sense of humor. A bit more dry and edgy, but still." Troy grinned. Taking her hand like a high school kid latching on to his girlfriend, he drew her through the storeroom, toward the annex door. She didn't mind him holding her hand.

Why couldn't she be like other women her age? The ones who said, "Who needs them?" when it came to men. The self-sufficient females who were content to have their girls' night out with wine and lots of male bashing. She couldn't seem to stop wanting a man. *The* man. The one she was always hoping she'd find, but who apparently didn't exist for her.

Two years ago she thought she'd overcome the weakness. After seven failed relationships, it was clear she needed to focus on her career and stay away from temptation. She'd chosen a career that paid well but didn't engage her passions. Staying on an even keel had seemed safer, at all levels of her life.

Alice had called it self-euthanizing. Making herself numb. Madison had hung up on her during that phone call.

Stay away from men. It was a simple enough rule. Yet here she was. She was an idiot.

"What kind of workout do you do around sharp glass?"

"Yoga. I used to be a gym freak, and then Shale, that's my Mistress, showed me yoga is just as strenuous, but less hard on the joints. My first session made me a believer. I couldn't walk the next day." That quick grin again. "And the glass-cutting area has pretty clear floor space, so it's good for doing the positions. No chance of being cut, unless I don't sweep it the way I should."

She could imagine that was part of Logan's incentive to make sure his assistant did his job. "So what is this training going to involve?"

Please God, let it not be me putting Troy over my knee for a spanking while he sucks his thumb and calls me Mommy. She wouldn't joke about such a thing, in case that was his deal, but she fervently hoped it wasn't.

"Master Logan will have to tell you that." Troy's tone was apologetic.

Not "Mr. Scott," making it clear that their relationship had a very different cast tonight. Was she expected to call him "Master Logan"? Did she want to do so?

Troy escorted her to the woodworking area. Light spilled in from an open door on the left wall, one that had been closed the night Logan showed her this room. She'd assumed it was a supply closet, and that the training area Logan used was the same as his woodworking area.

The other room was definitely not a supply closet. This space was the same size as the woodworking area, the annex building bisected to accommodate it. The whole place was a fun house, each door revealing another wonder.

The room was unfinished, setting the proper ambiance for its purpose. The open beams above showed the electrical wiring, and the concrete floor was marked with a wild spatter of paints and whitewall compound. There was no drywall, the insulation tucked in and sealed with plastic, pegboards attached to the framing over it. The boards were occupied by an array of paddles, floggers, whips, chains, fasteners, coils of rope. Promising pain, pleasure, bondage.

A pair of chains with shackles hung from the main support beam. A cushioned work mat was placed on the floor beneath them, and over that a large clear plastic tarp was spread, like the kind used for painting. Catching fluids.

"Where is Ma—Logan?"

"Here." He came out from a bathroom, drying his hands. Wearing a dark button-down shirt loose over his jeans and the heavy-tread work shoes, he was as distracting and appealing as other men would be in a tuxedo. She saw his gaze turn to a workbench where an array of coiled ropes in different colors and thicknesses had been laid out. His critical glance suggested it had been Troy's job to arrange what Logan desired to have at hand. She wondered what the consequences would be if Troy had missed anything. As her gaze returned to the chains, the plastic, her stomach tied itself neatly into a knot.

"I'm not really sure what I'm doing here." She blurted it out, then colored. He nodded, unperturbed.

"You can leave at any time, Madison, but I'm hoping you'll stay with us throughout the entire session. We'll start with something simple. Troy, go to the shackles. Madison, put them on his wrists."

Just like that. No chitchat, no time for her to get more nervous than she already was. In a way it was helpful, being treated like the assistant she expected to be, something functional and not the center of attention. Though that knot still tightened another notch at the way he told her to do it. It wasn't a *please, would you mind* kind of tone. It was an order.

Troy obediently moved to the mat. Logan was studying the ropes on the workbench, but she wasn't fooled by the inattention. She knew he was tracking her responses, because he emanated that Master-of-the-Universe vibe she'd accused him of having, primarily because it turned her on so much.

She made her feet move, followed Troy. When she reached the mat, she closed her hand around one manacle, dangling near Troy's shoulder. As he raised a hand so she could put the cuff around it, she noticed a new tension to his face. Not fear. Anticipation. She could feel it increase as she locked the cuff around his wrist. As she did it, her own increased as well. Needing to reassure herself of his well-being, she murmured, "Okay?"

The young man nodded. His focus seemed to be turning inward as she completed the task, as if putting on the cuffs transported him to a different plane. She remembered the way her own state of mind had shifted when she'd locked the cuffs on to herself at home, knowing the key was behind the ice, temporarily inaccessible.

Because of the lack of floor or ceiling cover, the hollow room echoed every noise, including the metallic sound of the shackles being fitted into place. Troy's wrists had a light dusting of pale blond hairs over them. She slid a fingertip over them, petting them like a cat's fur. When she glanced up at his face, she saw those blue eyes had shifted to hers.

"Finish the task, Madison."

Logan's tone held a slight reproof. If he did prescribe a punishment for her transgression, would running be an option?

She stepped back.

"Lift your arms above your head, Troy. Eyes down. She's lovely, but you haven't earned the right or my permission to look at her."

The young man cast his gaze downward, though she noticed his line of sight remained on her legs. Logan noticed it, too, because his lips twitched. "So it's going to be that kind of night, is it?"

He pushed a button embedded in a wall plate. At the sound of gears engaging, she glanced up to see the chains were attached to a track. The concept was similar to a garage-door opener, only this motor drew up the slack in the chains until Troy's arms were pulled taut over his head. The greater the stretch of his torso, the more lost Troy's expression became in that inward focus. The abdomen muscles elongated, the chest and rib cage arching as his heels left the ground. Logan stopped him there, only the balls of his feet still touching.

As captivating a picture as Troy was, she found herself trying to

watch them both. Logan's full attention was on Troy, apparently gauging the tension he was placing on his muscles, studying the arches of
his bare feet. From his rear position he had the enviable view of Troy's
ass, all tight and tilted. Then he caught *her* attention fully.

"You wanted to touch him, Madison. You can touch him now.
Touch him however you wish with your body, but only above the
waist with your hands. Until I say stop, he's your possession to enjoy."

Logan stepped forward, leading by example. He ran a palm down
Troy's back, then gripped his nape. Troy's lips parted, the tip of his
tongue coming out to lick them like a nervous animal. Logan pressed
himself against his back, his hand shifting to curl around Troy's
throat. The look in Logan's eyes shifted as well, to dangerous and
feral.

"You have no control now, Troy. I can do whatever I want to you."

"Yes, Master." Troy gasped as Logan gripped his hair, jerked his
head back.

"I didn't say you could talk, did I?"

Troy shook his head, the best he could against that powerful hold.
"I'll let it pass, since you were polite." Logan's touch eased, his knuckles sliding down the valley of Troy's spine, then he stepped back,
looked at Madison.

"Think of how you felt when you saw him stocking the shelves,
Madison. You wanted to touch him, didn't you? Only yes or no
answers."

She swallowed. "Yes."

Logan nodded. "It's nice, isn't it? Touching something this beautiful without having to play games, to excuse yourself or apologize?
You see a rose and you touch it, smell it. You don't explain yourself
to the rose, figure out the right approach. You don't stop touching
it because you think you've overstayed your welcome or you're wondering how the rose is feeling about it all. You could tear the petals
off if you wanted to do so, but instead you find yourself cherishing
it all the more because of your power over it."

He slid his hand up to Troy's nape again, his large fingers stroking through the thick, sandy hair. Troy's eyes closed, another shudder passing through his body. "You cup it in your hand," Logan continued, "appreciate and cherish it through that touch, through your attention. It makes that moment all the more powerful. He's a rose, Madison. A rose with some thorns, but the chains neutralize those. He's pure pleasure, all for you to touch and savor."

Madison made a mental note to have bottled water on hand to wet a dry throat when she was around Logan. She may have only known him for a day, but he generated an erotic charge in her that she'd never experienced, even in her longest-term relationship.

Her feet were moving, bringing her closer to Troy. Her hand was already out. Troy's eyes were open again, but his gaze was lowered, per Logan's order. When she was standing before him, she found she wanted something different.

"I want to see his eyes. May I?"

Logan had moved, too. His hips were propped against the workbench, arms crossed over the broad chest. He was looking at her as if she were an ocean sunset. Okay, maybe that was a womanly interpretation. He was looking at her as if she were naked and holding a beer. As well as a universal remote to an eighty-inch flat screen, programmed only with sports channels. Then something flickered and the gaze was toned down, neutral. But the brief intensity still shook her up.

"Since you asked nicely." He showed his teeth, and she had to remember to breathe. "Troy, you heard the lady. She wants you to look at her as she's touching you."

"Yes, Master."

She found it difficult to pull her gaze away from Logan's, so she didn't, not right away. His words about the rose made it okay to keep looking at him, holding eye contact. Despite her anxiety about this whole situation, the longer she looked at him, the more something loosened inside her, producing a whole different reaction to her surroundings and the scenario. Something that might make her commit perilous mistakes, mistakes she'd made before.

At that thought, she tore her gaze away. Troy's attention was pleasurable and far less intimidating. Safer. That was the key that had made her unlock this door, wasn't it? Troy had a demeanor that made a woman feel as if it was okay to come to an isolated, private room equipped with chains and weapons. Logan was no serial killer, but her moth-to-the-flame attraction to him said she should be running. Instead, she reached out to touch Troy.

Her fingers settled on his sternum, finding another fine layer of blond down. It was harder to see than Logan's coarse, dark chest hair, but still a nice reminder that what she was touching was all male. And a lot of raised muscle tone, especially with his heels off the ground this way. Sliding up to his shoulder, she felt the tension there. Maybe this was why he'd done yoga first, to loosen up, be even more flexible, aware of the demands that would be placed on his body. The faint anxiety that emanated from him suggested he never knew the paces Logan would put him through.

He was impossible to stop touching, once she started. Especially like this, where nothing would stop her but Logan. As she was touching Troy, it was as if she was sending a message to Logan as well, and that made her bolder. She let her hand drop back to Troy's chest, followed that terrain down to the rib cage, the transition to the upper abdomen. Then around, her circling Troy and turning her hand over so her knuckles trailed low along his lower back, so low she grazed the upper buttocks. It was there, on the small of the back, that she found the brand Logan had talked about, that Troy's Mistress had put upon him. Had she done it herself, or stood to the side, watching while the brand was applied to his skin?

Her fingers slid over it, making him quiver. It was an S, she assumed for Shale, his mistress. Such a crazy symbol of devotion made her throat tight, so she left it alone, lifting her hands to lay both palms on his back.

Logan had said she could touch him with her whole body, so as her hands glided over that expanse, she leaned forward, put her mouth between his shoulder blades, tasting sweat, soap, Troy. He quivered, a reaction that sent a sweet shiver through her. Her hands parted, sliding down his sides, her body against his back, the curve of his ass against her upper abdomen. Her palms molded to his waist. In this position, the pants rode pretty low, such that in the fronts his hipbones were revealed. Logan had said nothing below the waist, but according to the companies that made women's jeans, the "natural" waist was at the hipbones. She was willing to let that piece of utter nonsense work to her benefit now.

She let her fingers creep down, touch his hipbones, and then she shifted under his arm, faced him again, keeping her mouth close, breathing heated air on his flesh, watching his nipple crinkle underneath the effect.

"Fuck," Troy muttered.

His cock had become fully erect during her stimulus, that shaft jutting against her. She hadn't had direct contact with anything of that shape not run on batteries in quite some time. As a result, it was startling, but she managed to keep herself from either leaping back—or pressing forward shamelessly. She made herself stay still an extra moment, just feeling. When at last she drew back, keeping her hands at his waist, she looked down to study the look of it beneath the cotton. No, Troy had no deficiencies in any department. When she wet her lips, he stifled a groan, which told her she'd been right to ask him to watch her. It was sweet like cake, knowing how much she was arousing him.

Logan was also right. Knowing Troy couldn't require anything from her, while she indulged herself fully, made enjoying this rose all the more pleasurable. Yet she found herself wondering if what Troy was experiencing was even sweeter. His arousal seemed to be intensified by his helplessness, Logan's commands. Nothing was required of him except obedience to Logan's will, allowing him to get lost in all of his body and mind's natural responses to those demands.

When she shifted her grip, her fingertips slid beneath the waistband of the pants. In a blink, a much larger hand closed over her wrist. Her startled gaze flew up to Logan's face. He was standing next to her.

"No touching below the waist," he reminded her. "Not with hands. That's a special privilege."

She turned her hand so she could curl her fingers around his, her middle finger able to graze his knuckle, a shy caress. "How does one earn such a privilege? *Master* Logan?"

She'd intended to make light of it, a step back from the intensity, since his touch had recalled her to the reality of the situation, but her voice didn't cooperate. It was barely past a whisper and held the weight of need.

He let her go to touch her temple, stroke her hair back over her ear. From there, his palm slid under the weight of her thick locks, cupped her nape the way he'd cupped Troy's, making it clear the man was irrevocably under his control.

"I'll let you know. Take off his pants, fold them up and put them on the workbench. Troy, eyes back down."

He left her then, moving to the coils of rope. When she turned back to Troy, the loss of his gaze was a tangible thing, but the heat emanating from his bound form had not diminished.

She tugged at the drawstring. Hooking her thumbs in the sides, his smooth skin beneath her knuckles, she worked the pants down, adjusting them to get the fabric clear of Troy's erection. He had a nice thick, stiff organ, fluid smearing the tip. It had probably dampened the inside of the pants, which he'd worn without underwear. Pushing the pants to his ankles, she squatted and pulled the garment free, unsuccessfully trying to ignore how close she was to his erect member. It would be so easy to taste that fluid, the salty musk to it.

She loved going down on a guy. The way they reacted to it, how it felt to her. She liked doing it on her knees, liked servicing him that way, as if she was . . . his.

She wasn't sure she'd ever told anyone that, even voiced it to herself, but this environment was translating what she'd considered a foreign language into plain English, unearthing things in her subconscious.

Folding up the pants, she put them on the workbench as directed. Logan moved back to the controls for the chains. With a whir of the mechanism, he gave the chains enough slack to take the strain off Troy's shoulders, put him solidly on his feet while keeping his arms above his head. Moving behind his captive, Logan gripped his shoulders, kneading them, checking for strain. Troy's eyes closed in pure bliss while Madison stood stock-still, watching the ruggedly handsome man, fully clothed, cosset the beautiful and naked Troy. It made her wish for a camera.

"Madison, come here."

Logan left Troy to pick up a coil of rope from the workbench. He gave her a thoughtful perusal as she came to him, his eyes passing over her upper torso. "Watch him. Keep an eye on his breathing, how comfortable he seems to be, joints, muscle cramps. You saw how I lowered the chains. They can go all the way down to the ground if needed. Troy, if there's a problem, you tell her. Otherwise, you stay silent and keep your eyes on the ground. Not on any part of her. Acknowledge me."

"Yes, Master."

He was good at concise, clipped orders. Maybe because he'd been in the military, where there was no unnecessary chatter or superfluous words. Logan waited until she nodded, then he disappeared out the door. From the sound of his footsteps and doors opening, she thought he'd gone into the hardware store.

He hadn't told her she couldn't talk, but she didn't want to taunt Troy with a one-sided conversation. Plus she liked the fact that silence was an option. She settled on a stool, choosing to watch his profile, since that allowed her to keep an eye on all the things Logan mentioned, as well as drink in the sight of a restrained, aroused, naked male, his cock so high it brushed his belly. She imagined gripping his ass in both hands, kneading, rubbing her mound against the luscious cheeks. Troy had no tattoos. She found that unexpected, in these days when all young men seemed to have them. Did Logan have any?

She imagined him with a heart on his butt, just to defuse the tension inside her, but it didn't really work. She wanted him to come back, because whatever spell this was would lift if he stayed away too long, and she didn't want reality to intrude. Fortunately, he was back within five minutes. He was carrying one of the baby-doll T-shirts from a rack up front. The shirt had the store's logo printed in a small circular design on the left breast side. He put it into her hand.

"As pretty as your top is, for this next bit, you need to wear something a little less flowing." Answering her unspoken wish, he slid one finger from her collarbone to the point of her shoulder. Her nipple stiffened beneath her strapless bra, and she barely contained her shameless desire to straighten her posture, draw his attention to her breasts. It made her think of how she'd touched herself earlier in the week, the way the images on the tarot cards had made her feel.

"Change into this. The size is right."

He turned and moved away, providing her privacy with his averted body and Troy's requirement to keep his eyes down. She slid off the tunic top, pulled the baby-doll over her head. Not letting herself think about what can of worms she might be opening, she released the clasp on the bra, got rid of it.

She re-thought the idea once she pulled the baby-doll down. It was snug. Very snug. And she was quite obviously aroused. But she looked at Troy, naked and vulnerable, and then Logan's broad back. He was totally in control of everything and everyone in this room, no question. Some perverse part of her wanted to see what happened if that control was tested with the unexpected.

Yeah, she knew she was playing with fire, but it was hard to be in this combustible environment and not want to stoke the flames. She put her top and bra in a neat fold next to Troy's pants.

"I'm dressed," she said.

Logan pivoted with a handful of coiled nylon. His attention went right where she'd expected. His gaze turned heavy-lidded, making her stomach leap up and give her lungs a jolt. She might have just stepped over the line between "guest helping with Troy" and something far more involved.

"Come here."

No question—that was definitely an order. She moved to him, her body prickling under the heat of his regard. Three steps and her nerve deserted her. What was she doing? She'd done it without thinking, pure impulse, but clearly it sent a message of what she was willing to do. And she had no idea if she really was willing to do anything. She wasn't a tease, not normally, and she felt ashamed of being one now. This wasn't really her. Hadn't seven relationships taught her she was no good at this?

She'd stopped halfway to him. "I'm sorry. I—"

"Madison." Logan extended a hand. "It's all right. Come here."

The tone of his voice still brooked no disobedience, but the modulation, from stern sergeant to something gentler, made her take those last three steps, put an uncertain hand in his.

"I told you that you would be helping me with Troy tonight. I don't change the terms of what I require, even if the environment, what you feel, compels you to send me messages that push for more. Do you understand? You're safe here. I said that from the beginning, and it will be true until the end. You be whatever you desire. I will keep you safe, even from yourself."

She digested that. "Do you have a tattoo of a heart on your ass?"

Troy gave a strangled half chuckle. Logan lifted a brow, put his warm palm against the side of her neck, drawing her a step closer.

Troy was a healthy-sized male, but standing next to Logan was like standing in the shade of a brick building.

"Actually, it's a pink unicorn, but I don't talk about it. Now hush."

A mild reproof, but one that made her fall silent. He dropped his touch, but only to unwrap the coil, shake out the line. "Troy, turn around and watch what I'm doing. Madison, you keep your eyes on me."

Troy obeyed, pivoting so that the chains above him twisted. Logan had given him enough slack to permit that without taking him off his feet. She saw that in the corner of her eye, since not keeping her eyes on Logan would have been impossible, regardless. He formed a loop out of the rope, something that looked like a noose, only with a different kind of knot, the resulting two lengths of line falling below it to his feet.

"Japanese rope tying is one of the things I'll be doing to Troy tonight. Would you like to experience an upper body harness? I can do it over your clothes."

Yes. She'd nodded before she even gave it thought. He stepped closer, putting the noose over her head. If he'd hesitated a mere second, she would have chickened out, but what she'd seen in Troy's eyes when the shackles closed over his wrists she experienced now, a curious stillness that made her breathing more shallow.

He put evenly spaced knots into the two lengths of rope, and continued with that past her waist. Then he adjusted her so she faced Troy, less than two feet between them. Logan retrieved another coil of rope from the bench and moved behind her. When he clasped her hand, her fingers squeezed his. He guided her arm so it was bent behind her, then he did the same to the other, gently changing her grasp so she held her forearms.

"This is called a boxed arm position." He wrapped her forearms in the rope. Troy was keeping his eyes down, but she detected tiny flickers as he fought his own desire to look. It was a heady combination, being bound by one man and compressed between the heat of desire from both. Logan shifted to work the ends of the rope into the lines between the knots in front. It opened up the parallel lines of knotted rope, creating a diamond pattern down her front. He used another line to create a similar pattern over her breasts, two diamonds framing them, and then cinched the lines snug by working the ends into the wrapping of her boxed arms. His fingers brushed her breasts, her collarbone, her upper body, in dozens of small functional ways.

When Logan moved behind her, tightened the ropes, it lifted her breasts and her posture, displaying her more provocatively. Desire speared straight to her core.

Should she tell him to stop? That this was more than she'd anticipated? She couldn't find words to speak, too lost in this. When he'd said "harness," she'd expected something like a halter top made of rope. Instead, he'd bound her arms, ensnared her in a net. A net she had no desire to escape.

Troy's breath got shorter; so did hers. She'd never been tied up like this in her life, and the way Logan did it, so efficient, no hesitation but no hurry either, made it all feel like it should. Everywhere he touched her to test the hold of the ropes, the way the knots lay against her skin, kept her nerves sizzling. Yet she was also paralyzed. She thought of how Troy had looked, somewhat hypnotized as he was restrained, and knew the same feeling. Everything sensitive, hyperalert, but caught in a sensual haze.

Just as she'd been mesmerized in the clubs where Alice had taken her. She felt like she'd stepped into a world that had merely been waiting to welcome her back, knowing she was finally ready to embrace what it had to offer. How was that possible?

Earlier she'd torn her gaze away from Logan. She'd been evading that direct look because the answer to the question was in his brown eyes. Eyes that had embers in their depths, capable of immolating her and her fragile, false reality with their flame. She swayed.

"Master—" Troy spoke.

"Got it." Logan's hands were on her shoulders, holding her steady. "Breathe, Madison. Don't forget to breathe."

She took a shaky breath, then another. He stroked her hair, waiting for her to settle. It took some time, but a blink after she realized she was okay again, so did he, and it was reinforced by Troy's quick nod, showing how closely aligned the two men were, even with Troy in his own restrained state. For a brief moment, the young man held her gaze, a lifeline between them, both of them tied up at Logan's behest.

Then his lashes fanned his cheeks again. Was she imagining that he'd lowered his gaze at a more leisurely pace this time? Her breasts constricted by the harness made them highly provocative, especially in the thin T-shirt. When Troy did the lip-wetting thing, she was pretty sure her nipples hardened further. A reaction that only increased when Logan adjusted the ropes once more. She made a noise that sounded suspiciously like a quiet moan.

"Keep an eye on her, Troy," he ordered. "Her breathing and balance, not just her breasts."

"Yes, Master." The strained note of amusement in Troy's voice was matched by the wryness of Logan's.

Picking up another rope off the bench, Logan moved behind Troy. "What are you supposed to be doing, Madison?"

"Breathing," she said, a little breathlessly.

"Good. Talk to me, prove you're doing it. A customer comes in. She wants to get the fires going again with her husband. What would you recommend? What's in your inventory that will do the trick?"

She'd been that route personally, and had had a recent reminder of it, in her first disastrous interaction with her customers. With failures number one and four in the relationship track, she'd tried lingerie to generate excitement again. Jonas had smirked and Henry had given her a resigned, indulgent look, like she was a child he had to entertain before going to do more preferable, adult things.

Her nails dug into her forearms. Even when she'd donned the

lingerie alone, she hadn't felt comfortable in it, as if she already knew it was a pathetic attempt to save a relationship going south. She couldn't blame Henry. She'd probably come off like a kid putting on her mom's work clothes and pearls. The clothes had been no different than they'd be on a mannequin. She hadn't worn them; they'd worn her.

"I'm not the best one to suggest that," she said. The bonds were restrictive in the wrong way now. She should tell him to take them off.

"Look at Troy, Madison. He's worked up over you, wants like hell to disobey and take a good long look, not just steal those quick glimpses I'm going to take out of his hide. He wants to stare at your breasts, how gorgeous and swollen they are, tied up in the rope, your nipples stiff and wanting to be sucked. Imagine you're going to pick something out to wear for him in your bedroom later tonight, when he's not tied up, when he has the chance to seduce you. He wants to put his mouth on you, his cock inside you. What would you wear to make him even crazier? You're driving what's already there, not coaxing it out. Any man you have to talk into getting hard for you is the wrong guy. Plus he's fucking blind and too stupid to live."

She choked on a laugh, but she had a crazy quiver happening, too, the husky timbre of his voice emphasizing the male power he could unleash. It wasn't Troy she was seeing in her bedroom. When she lifted her gaze to Logan, she wondered if he saw the hunger, what she couldn't voice. Then she didn't have to wonder.

His jaw relaxed, those fathomless eyes flickering. "All right then," he murmured. "What would you wear for me? For yourself, to make yourself feel beautiful, seductive, capable of bringing even a Master to his knees? Bringing this Master to his knees."

That did steal her breath. But she responded. "Nothing but a T-shirt like this and a thong. All cotton. I think you'd like that best."

When she saw the curve of Troy's lips, pleasure surged through her. She must have guessed correctly. She also learned that Logan's brown eyes transformed to a tawny hue, the more aroused he became.

Obeying some instinct of her own—and the unspoken message of his intense regard—she swept her own gaze down.

"You're doing a hell of a job distracting me from training Troy."

"You were the one who asked the question," she pointed out.

He snorted. "Keep that up, and Troy won't be the only one who gets his ass blistered tonight."

He slid between them, giving her hair a tug. She imagined him bending her over one of his beautiful carved benches, blistering her ass with hand or paddle and then ramming into her, holding on to her hair as he thrusted.

It was a full-blown, no-holds-barred domination fantasy. She closed her eyes, scrambling for some type of sanity, some type of anchor. But her mind refused. It wanted her to stay right here, and it made her open her eyes.

He'd turned toward Troy. There was enough space for him between their bodies, but with one more step she'd be up against him. She wanted to put her cheek against his back, see if his heart was thundering the way hers was. Only his display of a Master's authority and her own fear kept her in place, though the former ironically made her long to do it even more. As if she was seeking that punishment.

He did the same upper-body harness on Troy, only he took it lower. When Logan moved behind Troy, no longer obscuring her view of his front, her eyes widened. The rope wrapped around the base of his cock and looped his testicles, the two ends passing between his thighs and disappearing around back, loose enough there was a small space between his balls and the slack. Troy adjusted at his Master's grunt, spreading his thighs wider. When that slack disappeared, Troy's jaw snapped closed and his cock jumped. Every muscle in his body stiffened, as if he battled an irresistible need to move.

"I'm putting knots in the rope and running the line of them along the crack of his ass," Logan explained to her absently, his head down as he focused on what he was doing. "One right up against the rim.

Put the proper pressure there . . ." Troy grunted, body tautening further. "And the results make it impossible for him to think of anything but wanting to come. But you're not going to do that, or I'll ream your ass with a jackhammer. Got it?"

He gave the young man a slap on the buttock, hard enough Troy jumped. "Yes sir."

Constricted like her breasts, Troy's cock and testicles were an eye-catching display. His fingers flexed against the chains, the metal making tiny clinks. Semen dripped from his slit, creating a small pool on the floor. The fluid that clung to his cock head made it glisten.

"You'll be scrubbing that tarp with a toothbrush, boy."

She heard Troy's muttered oath, a groan as Logan did something else behind him. Though she couldn't see, she suspected Logan had pushed that knot deeper against his rim, was massaging it. He caught Troy's throat and shoulder in one big hand as he kept up the manipulation.

"You want to push it with me? I tie a sexy woman up in front of you and your dick gets hard, makes you think you can be a badass. I'll rip you a new one, you don't get in line right now."

Logan sounded as menacing as she'd ever heard a man be. And instead of being terrified, she was caught in that erotic stasis. His eyes were pinned on Troy and she had no doubt Troy could feel them like a blade at his throat.

"No sir. I'm sorry. Please . . ." Troy's lips stretched back, teeth baring as he fought the climax she could tell Logan was building. "I don't want to disappoint my Mistress. Or you."

"Yeah. That's better."

Logan stepped back, and Troy let out a relieved breath, swaying in his bonds. As Logan came back around Troy, she knew her pussy was as drenched as Troy's cock head. When he shifted to stand behind her, put his hands at her waist, she shivered. "You want to help me really torture him?" he said against her ear.

Pretending that she was still somehow his assistant instead of his willing victim, she nodded.

He eased her forward, as if knowing she might startle like a deer if he moved too fast. Her breasts mashed against Troy's chest. With her heeled boots giving her some extra height, that constrained cock pushed against her lower abdomen, above her mound. If she lifted onto her toes, she could rub the crotch of her jeans against it. Logan did say she could help, right?

When Logan was retrieving something else, probably more rope, she couldn't resist testing the theory. Leaning against Troy for balance, she rose on her toes to grind herself against him. Mischievous pleasure surged at the answering flash in Troy's gaze, the further constriction of his jaw. The quiver of a man's restrained lust—while his body was likewise restrained—was a heady combination. Add her own restraint to it, and it was indescribable.

Troy shifted enough to rub himself against her, a skillful stroke against her clit. She gasped as his lips firmed. Logan had warned her when he warned Troy, hadn't he? Tie a woman up in front of him, get his dick hard, and the need to re-assert himself was there. Being a submissive didn't obliterate Troy's innate male desire to conquer female flesh.

Then she gasped for another reason. The heavy leather slapper caught Troy squarely across his hindquarters. If the noise didn't tell her the impact it delivered, Troy's snarl, the flare of pain in his gaze, certainly did. Logan's hand holding the slapper clamped over Troy's shoulder, fingers digging in as he gripped Troy's hair with the other hand. He yanked his head back while the young man was still quivering from the strike. As scary as he'd been a moment ago, the words he spoke against Troy's ear were nothing less than a sure promise of violence. "She's mine, the way you're mine right now. So you don't have the fucking right to look at her, to touch her, to even have a wet dream about her, without my say-so. I'll come into your dreams and rip your dick right off, you so much as consider it. Got it?"

"Yes sir. I'm sorry, sir."

Logan kept his eyes on hers, an even more captivating lock than the chains holding Troy. "You're not sorry enough. But you will be."

"I'm sorry," Madison stammered. "Logan, it was me. I misunderstood what you told me. I—"

He moved behind her again, his hand on her shoulder. The grip was firm, but not punitive. "You've done nothing wrong, Madison. I didn't put any limits on your behavior. Only his. He's the one being trained to restrain himself at his Mistress's behest."

The easy shift to a calm tone, the squeeze of his hand, told her this was all part of it. The anger wasn't true anger, only a response calculated to have an impact on Troy. Even so, the way Logan had looked at her as he spoke to Troy, it was as if he meant every word. *She's mine.*

She sensed Logan waiting, wanting to be sure she was all right before they continued. She could end it here, say she'd had enough, was in over her head, but pride held her back. He'd made it clear her role was helping him create the atmosphere for Troy. He wasn't intending to make her submit like Troy, no matter where her imagination was trying to take her.

So she nodded, and then Logan threw her further off her axis. He proceeded to bind the two of them together. She tried to remember how many lengths of rope were on that workbench, how many he'd used thus far, but her brain was far too clouded with lust to figure it out.

Chest to breast, waists, then a wrap beneath the curve of her buttocks in the jeans, cinching her up against Troy, pressing her clit against his rigid muscles and aroused reaction, making her moan again. Did all assistants act like this?

At the beginning of the evening, she'd assumed a training Master's assistant would be an arm's-length thing, where she was standing shoulder to shoulder with Logan, a partnership. Could he possibly use her like this, compartmentalize it, and still see it that way? There was no way in hell she could. She'd anticipated a little voyeurism, some nervous speculation, but in no way had she anticipated this full immersion. She was being swept along in an irresistible current. If he was intending to take her deeper, it was a diabolically clever way to do it, disarming her with Troy, seducing her with the possibilities, so nothing felt too frightening. Logan knew how to mix the emotional with the physical, keeping a woman compliant.

The ironic thing was she could have all these cynical thoughts and still not want to be doing anything different from what she was doing right now.

"Put your cheek against his shoulder, Madison. You'll be more comfortable, and it will relax your body into his." He gave her hair that tug again. "If you were my sub, you would have earned a punishment as severe as his tonight, with that little bump and grind of yours."

The idea sent a startling thrill through her vitals. Troy's body twitched against hers. When she laid her cheek on his chest, his breath stirred her hair.

"No sir," Troy said quietly. "I'd take both of our punishments."

"Protecting her, hmm? Just what I'd expect of you. Don't tighten up on me, boy, or I'll make it worse."

In this position, she couldn't see Logan, but she could certainly feel the results of his presence. When that slapper hit again, Troy's body became as rigid as a plank, but he made a visible effort to relax, to do as Logan commanded. Her fingers curled, and she closed her eyes as the next strike came.

She'd witnessed the close relationship between pleasure and pain in the dungeons. Now Troy's cock convulsed against her, hips jerking as he tried his best not to let his increasing arousal earn another response from Logan like before. Her heart was clutching at what sounded like a totally awful punishment, while her body was liquefying against his, in more ways than one.

"Stop," she whispered. "Don't hurt him anymore."

Troy's lips brushed the top of her head, and he groaned as Logan landed another blow, the hardest yet. His body shuddered with each strike. She realized she was rubbing against him, her stiff nipples, her mound, her thighs, unable to stop herself. With every blow she absorbed through his body, she was getting more and more excited. Too excited.

"You're thinking you'd like the same kind of punishment, Madison, aren't you?" Logan grunted, not slackening the rhythm. "Only maybe you'd like it even rougher. You need the punishment to let go. You crave the release."

She might have been able to stop her reaction if the only stimulus was physical, but Logan's words took the choice out of her hands. The friction she was creating against Troy, the vibration of his body against her with those blows, the power of Logan watching them, was too much. The orgasm rose up fast, unstoppable. Though she fought against it, made a desperate attempt to claw it back, desire won out. She bit Troy's chest to muffle her cries, her hips jerking against him.

Hard, quick and intense, the way such an unplanned response could be. Troy risked further punishment by shifting his engorged cock against her clit, increasing the sensation when Logan kept striking him. Because of the repetitive impact, she imagined Troy thrusting into her. It prolonged the overwhelming sensations an extra few sweet seconds.

The sudden wave, here and gone, left her light-headed and tingling. Her soaked panties clung to her, a wet friction.

The blows stopped, Troy panting against her. Logan's fingers wrapped over his hips. "Easy, boy," he said. "Give her a moment. You hold back until I say otherwise."

"Yes, Master." At the desperate note in Troy's voice, she looked up at him, saw the strain in his face. It brought Logan's face into view, over Troy's shoulder. She couldn't hide the flush of her skin, the mussed hair, her moist lips. Though a part of her wanted to duck her face, she couldn't turn away from the magnetism of that forceful glance.

"Fucking beautiful," Logan said. "You want to bring him home, Madison? Has he earned it?"

Jesus, yes. When she managed a jerky nod, Logan cocked his head. "Since you like rubbing that hot little body against him, make him come that way. I'd free you, but you'd want to do it with your mouth then, and I won't permit that. Your mouth is mine."

She saw herself on her knees, her arms still boxed behind her, Logan's hand fisted in her hair as she worked his cock in her mouth. Servicing her lover, possessed by him. Her knees quivered, her body reacting to the idea like an aftershock to her climax. Fortunately, she was still tied to Troy, keeping her from collapsing.

Logan leaned away, pulled a condom out of a drawer of a rolling table he'd drawn close to hold the slapper or various ends of the rope he'd cut. Tearing open the protection, he reached around Troy, rolled it onto his cock. He'd tied them so closely together, his knuckles pressed against her mound, easing her back the scant amount possible as he rolled the condom onto Troy. She shuddered, another aftershock passing through her, and his brown eyes passed briefly over her face, a visual caress.

He put on Troy's condom with the same efficiency he'd done everything else. Though she felt nothing but straight vibes off Logan, he obviously didn't have any hetero hang-ups about touching another male as a Master to a sub. In fact, she could well imagine him fucking Troy's brains out as a way to exercise Dominance, not as a sexual preference.

The idea made her hot all over.

"Don't want him to mark your clothes any more than he already has. He's going to go off like a rocket." Logan moved away from them both, pulling up a stool so he was seated a few feet away. Thinking of what he'd told her to do in the aftermath of her climax, she found herself self-conscious, even though her body was still vibrating.

"You know why men love lap dances?" Logan asked casually. "All those curves moving over their body, squirming and wiggling. The way a woman can rub herself against his cock—tits, ass, cunt—is indescribable. He's on the edge of begging for it. Aren't you, Troy?"

"Yes, Master. Please . . . Madison."

The husky voice, the plea in it, got her started, though mainly it was Logan, his ability to know what to say and when.

She crowded closer and was gratified by how eagerly Troy thrust his cock against the damp denim. She squirmed against his chest, dragging her nipples against his bare flesh once more. Growing more confident, she nibbled at the pocket of his collarbone, using her tongue to taste the perspiration there. His hips worked against her as she increased the movements of her own, dragging her clit up and down his cock, the condom fortunately lubricated enough to make that work against the fabric. Logan was right, though. Between the punishment and her teasing of him, he was ready to go over. His heart was thundering in his chest and his breath was hot puffs against her, his jaw against her temple.

"Fuck . . . God . . . Master . . ."

"You have to ask me, Troy."

"Please, Master. May I come?"

She caught Logan in the corner of her eye. He'd leaned up against the workbench again, had unscrewed the top of a water bottle and was taking a sip. His eyes remained on them, his mouth a firm, unrelenting line. "Keep rubbing against her while I think about it. Feel how hard her nipples are. She's soaked with her climax. If those jeans weren't in the way, you could be greasing yourself between her thighs, her cunt rubbing against your cock."

Troy let out a desperate noise, but he obeyed, not slacking up in the least.

"You come without my say-so, Troy, you'll get a beating twice as bad as the first."

"Yes . . . Master."

She was getting aroused all over again by the wealth of need pouring off of Troy, the incredible effort he was exercising, holding back. She nestled her cheek harder against him, her fingers clasping her forearms behind her back. Her gaze lifted to Logan.

He'd moved, was standing next to them again. He touched her face, sliding a knuckle along her cheek. Turning her head, she caught his finger in her teeth, sucked it in, needing to taste him, wanting his mouth, his flesh, anything she could get. His other fingers fanned out along her jaw, lightly stroking her throat. The sensation made her close her eyes. His breath, his lips, brushed her brow, but when she tilted her head up, he drew back, not giving her the taste of his mouth she wanted.

"You can thank Madison for that delay, Troy. She distracted me. You can come."

Troy let go with a groan, humping hard against her body, only the ropes helping her keep her feet as he spurted into the condom, though she was sure some would run down to bathe his testicles and dampen her jeans further. The scent of it, of herself, of male and female perspiration, of sex and heat, kept her just as wet beneath the denim.

During sex, time could get eaten up by the things she felt obligated to do. Movement of hips, whispered encouragement, contracting muscles. However, tied the way she was to Troy, both of them under Logan's command, she had the luxury of savoring. Through sight, sound, scent and every vibrant nerve, she relished Troy's climax, but not just as a spectator. Since she was tied against him, it was a fully immersive experience. She never wanted it to end.

But at length, of course it did. As Troy started to come down, Logan set the water bottle aside and stepped in close. He laid his hand on the young man's shoulder, idly rubbing him there, a soothing touch as he studied Madison. When his gaze lighted on her parted lips, she couldn't move.

"The things I could do with that mouth," he observed in a low voice. "Would you like that, Madison? Would you like to see the things I could make you do?"

She had enough brain cells left not to respond to that. This was way over the top of what she'd expected. She wasn't throwing herself off the whole cliff. But fortunately, he didn't push her for an answer. Instead, he moved to the wall controls and gave Troy enough slack he could lower his arms.

"Hold on to her, Troy. She's not steady on her feet."

Troy's lips brushed her temple and then his arms dropped around her, surrounding her with his strength as Logan loosened the ropes tying them to each other. He unboxed her arms and removed the harness, making her breasts tingle from the increased blood flow where they were mashed pleasantly against Troy. As that subsided, she was able to straighten and hold on to Troy as well, because he wasn't entirely steady on his feet, either. His rueful chuckle against her ear, acknowledging it, gave her a soft smile as well. She increased her hold on him, inhaled the scent of replete male and was content to be and do whatever she was directed to do. No thought was required for this. It was all feeling.

Eventually, though, Logan separated them, guiding them both to sit on a bench. As he kneaded Troy's shoulder muscles again and gave him a thorough examination, she summoned enough brain cells to analyze what he was doing. Perhaps gauging the color of Troy's skin where he'd been bound, how he was moving. Whether he was showing any evidence of residual pain, other than the wince when he first sat down on those paddle marks. Confirming it, Logan retrieved a cushion, bade him rise and shoved it under him before pushing him back down. He brought Troy and her both a bottle of water. Logan made sure Troy could hold it and sip it on his own, then he took a seat between them and offered her the same.

As she closed her hand on the bottle her fingers overlapped his. He held on to it an extra moment, gave her cheek a quick touch.

"Next time you open the store," he said, "remember this. Hold

on to the feelings you had here tonight. Believe in what you're selling. It's a fantasy, but it's real, too. It's not a game, not in the traditional, negative sense."

He passed a hand over her hair, a casual stroke, though the look
in his eyes was anything but casual. "Thanks for helping tonight."

"Sure. Anytime." She coughed on a chuckle to cover the pang. It
really had been all about the scene, hadn't it?

She'd had this problem in every freaking relationship, assuming
things that weren't there, turning wishful thinking into reality. But
he was so deliberate in how he used language and gestures. She
couldn't help thinking about it. *She's mine . . . Alice gave you to me . . .*

She rose, setting the water aside and retrieving her bra and tunic
top. "Restroom?"

Logan nodded toward it, and she responded with a tight smile. It
only took a couple minutes to change back into the top. She left the
bra off, since for the quick trip home she didn't really need it. The
tunic wasn't as revealing as the snug T-shirt. She'd take the T-shirt
home and pay him for it. She certainly wouldn't mind wearing it
again to promote his business. It was the neighborly thing to do.

When she came back out, Troy had pulled on his drawstring
pants. Everything was civilized again, if the eye didn't stray to the
shackles dangling loose in the middle of the room, the tarp marked
with the small puddle of Troy's precum.

"Well, I'd better head home." Her casual expression was going to
break her face, but she'd lost her dignity plenty of times in relationship missteps. She wasn't going to screw this up. Logan was helping
her learn how to get in touch with her inner sex goddess to make the
lingerie store more profitable. End of story. "I really appreciate you
giving me the experience," she told him, including Troy in the look
of pleasant gratitude. "Please thank Shale . . . your Mistress, for me
as well."

Troy gave her a tentative smile, still fuzzy on the edges, but he
was studying her a little too closely, like Logan. In a minute, one of

them was going to ask her if everything was okay and her dignity was going to topple from its pedestal like a one-legged statue.

Troy's lips parted, as if he were about to speak, but Logan stood, cutting off whatever he was going to say. "You're good?" Logan asked. The young man nodded, giving him a thumbs-up and touching the bottle to his nose in a parody of a sobriety test. Snorting at him, Logan stepped closer to Madison to curl his fingers around her elbow. "Let me take you to your car."

She allowed herself to be directed. Right now, a numbness was keeping the embarrassment at bay. As they moved into his storeroom, she made herself say the expected things. "I've seen sessions in dungeons, but that's the first time I've participated. It's a lot different from the inside."

She'd talk about it like it was a vacation experience, not an emotional connection. That was the way to handle it. There was a lot of intensity inside the walls, an outlet for deeper needs expressed in a safe way, but outside, everybody put on their day-to-day faces. She'd be as mature about it as he was. As Troy was.

Logan made a noncommittal noise as he guided her through his back storeroom. It was dark but he didn't turn on any lights, letting the faint lights from the exit signs and fire detectors guide the way. When they reached the dividing door to her storeroom, she turned toward him. "You don't have to walk me all the way. I can—"

Catching her under the arms, he lifted and shoved her back against the wall, putting himself solidly between her thighs. In less than a frantic heartbeat, he'd captured her erratic breath in his own mouth. Fisting his hand in her hair, he held her in place as he plundered that moist cavern, tongue locking over hers, lips demanding everything.

Oh God. He had her pinned with every inch of his hard body. His erection pressed with unmistakable demand against the cross-seam of her jeans. She'd been so distracted by Troy's naked cock, how had she missed Logan's very sizeable reaction? Her damp tissues contracted. If he wanted her right here, up against this wall, she'd let him do it. He was too overwhelming to resist, and her defenses were already shattered.

"Lift the shirt," he ordered against her mouth.

She groped for it, pulled it up, baring her breasts, and then she cried out as his powerful back curled and he hiked her up further so that he could clamp damp heat around her nipple, sucking it into his mouth. It reminded her of the tarot card that had shown a lush Goddess figure. When she'd gazed at it, trying to imagine herself as a dominant Goddess suckling Troy at her breast, commanding a man's submissive devotion, instead she'd fantasized about Logan taking her over entirely.

She'd been right about that. This was a man who might cherish female power, but he'd never kneel to it.

He pulled on her nipple such that coils of need awoke anew in her lower belly. When his hands dropped to cradle her ass, knead and squeeze, she was squirming, trying to get closer, trying to push her breast farther into his mouth. He switched, giving the other one the same thorough attention.

When he finally raised his head, let her feet touch the floor, he didn't let her go. Yanking open the button of her jeans, he put his fingers down into her panties, capturing her clit and slick lips between two strong fingers, another finger stroking the compressed flesh so she was instantly working herself against him, as frenetically as Troy.

"Logan," she pleaded. "I can't . . . Don't . . ."

"Come for me. Prove you're mine."

I already did. She knew it had been his presence, his command, even more than Troy's physical contact, which had brought that first climax. Now he swept her away with a second one.

She screamed this time, unable to stop it, but he put his mouth over hers, absorbing the cries, working her. No fast spin this time. He kept her going until he'd milked the full measure of her climax from her. When he was done, she was holding on to his rigid biceps and panting, her forehead against his pectoral.

"Wow," she said, a rasp in her throat. "You know, if you wanted to thank me for helping, that was overkill. A fruit basket would have been fine."

He chuckled against her ear, and it made her nerves tingle, even as her heart broke a little. *Don't make a mistake, Madison. Don't believe this is more than it is.*

But then he tipped her chin up, and she saw the gleam of his eyes in the darkness, the serious set of his mouth. With Logan, it was very hard to separate fantasy from reality.

When she arrived home she made herself a cup of hot chocolate, the best way she could think of to deal with what had happened. She paced the kitchen a few times, then collapsed in a chair.

Tonight had been incredible, amazing. Surreal. How could she handle the next workday, being around the two of them? *Hi guys, awesome night. We should do that again sometime. Next time I'll bring the rope.*

The unsettling thing was she had less of a problem laughing off what had happened with Troy and all the D/s stuff than what had happened with Logan in the back room. She'd never been so overwhelmed by a man so quickly, though she'd certainly fallen hard before . . . and paid the price.

She put her fingers on the deck of cards she'd left stacked in the center of the table. She'd gotten into the habit of idly plucking from the top when she passed through to grab a snack. Now she turned one over. It showed a redheaded girl teetering in her mother's heels on the upper panel. On the lower one, the same redheaded girl was grown-up and in a sexy nurse outfit, complete with stilettos no nurse in her right mind would wear. Along with that really short hemline. This card didn't have a pairing of words like most of the others did, but there was script on the bottom.

Let make-believe change your reality.

She considered the card. Maybe she was trying to be too much of

who she'd been in Boston. She'd left her job, her life there, behind,
so why was she clinging to old habits and fears? What if she tried
really getting into the spirit of her store? She pursed her lips, thinking about the Wonderland room upstairs. Maybe she wouldn't go as
extreme as the naughty nurse, but there were other, appealing options.

Tonight, Logan had unlocked a door inside her. Somehow, tying
her up had released her inhibitions, and she'd embraced a deeper side
of herself that had always seemed too overwhelming to let free. Yet
she'd let it free under his restraints. She'd trusted him.

A startling idea and perplexing contradiction, but one couldn't
argue with success. She looked at the naughty nurse, and felt a weird
combination of laughter, intrigue, anticipation, excitement . . . She
wanted to follow the feelings that had been unleashed tonight, and
she wanted to use them for the store. She didn't want to dread tomorrow. She wanted to anticipate it.

She'd just let herself be tied up and brought to climax with a guy
she barely knew, after all. Trying out a new fashion would be far less
nerve-wracking.

*Go to bed, Madison. Turn it off for one night. Tomorrow's a new day.
Yeah, yeah, same shit, different . . . oh, the hell with it.*

Leaving the kitchen, she headed for the second level, carting her
hot chocolate with her.

That morning, she turned the store sign from CLOSED to OPEN.
She'd borrowed some of Alice's clothes, but given the style her own
spin, donning a gauzy lavender top over a short, pale green camisole,
one that bared her midriff. She coupled it with her own earring
choices and a pair of stonewashed jeans that revealed the navel piercing she'd had done with Alice when they were in their early twenties,
never realizing that a decade later one of them would be gone. She
brushed her hair out until it shone and then caught it in a clip at
her shoulders.

Glimpsing herself in one of the display mirrors, she was pleased to see Bohemian sensuality that was approachable, not scary. She might be channeling Alice, but she was going to roll with it, focus on the state of mind that had lingered with her since last night and see where it all took her. Maybe she'd try a different outfit each day, a different style. One day she'd even cross-dress, go Victorian male with trousers, cravat and crisp white shirt. Have a sale on anything in the store with a *Man with a Maid* theme. Do latex another day, have *Mad Max* playing on the flat screen up on the wall. Be creative, have fun with it. This didn't have to be about all the other shit.

She propped the door open with the iron doorstop, since it was a pretty enough day to invite in the breeze and sunshine. Troy was making a change to the chalkboard sign out in front of Logan's store. Apparently this week's sale was on manual push mowers. At the sight of her, he grinned, gave her a leer that was more playful than aggressive, making her roll her eyes at him. She was relieved at the lack of awkwardness. But why should there be? For him, it was a training session to benefit him and his Mistress, that was all. It would only be awkward if there was more to it than that for one of the participants, right?

New look, new state of mind. Even so, she thought about that kiss with Logan in the back room. *Mental note: stay clear of Logan for a few days.*

"Glad to see you open for business," Troy said. "You look great."

It was amazing, how a sincere, appreciative male compliment could affect a woman's ego. "Thanks. I'll have to work on getting the coffee and baked goods started up."

"Praise the gods." He winked.

"I'm not as generous as Alice. There will probably be a charge."

"Maybe we can arrange a barter." The young man leaned on the sandwich board sign. "You know, if you need any maintenance done around Alice's house or here."

"Serious?"

"Serious." He nodded. "I'm buried under student loans. I'd do anything for money, including selling my body, if my Mistress would allow it."

Madison glanced around. "You talk about her so openly."

"Just us here, and you already know about her. I'd talk about Shale all the time if I could."

The S of the brand flashed through her mind. She'd been right about the significance. The way his countenance softened, simply from saying Shale's name, made his feelings clear. It was so easy when you were younger. Of course, he wasn't that much younger than her. Just less scarred. She decided to ignore resentment in favor of curiosity. With Troy, she could consider it market research.

"Isn't she possessive? What Logan did with you last night, that doesn't bug her?"

"Oh yeah. Shale can be mean as a snake if she thinks someone going after what she considers hers. But it's different with Logan. For one thing, he's straight as they come. For another, he gets off on being a Master, no matter if he's topping male or female. You picked up on that?" He gave her a grin, not realizing how directly the arrow hit the sore spot. "Logan's like a really strict football coach. Really strict."

He did a furtive rub of his backside, winked. "Looks like you have a customer."

She pivoted, seeing a woman had stepped into the store while she and Troy were talking. Giving Troy a nod, she shook herself mentally. *Different look, different day, different outcome. Go, team!*

Crap. It was the pretty girl with dark hair and expressive gray eyes from earlier in the week. The Liv Tyler look-alike. Last time, Madison had inspired nothing in her but a desire to escape. But she'd returned, right? What better opportunity to prove she could do this than to win back a customer?

Her long fingers were caressing the filmy fabric of a baby-doll nightgown, but she had a crease on her brow.

"Anything I can help you with, I'm right here," Madison said warmly. She moved toward her counter. She'd make herself busy with

122 Joey W. Hill

some jewelry rearranging, giving the customer that necessary sense of privacy, rather than projecting a buy expectation, a sure way to run her out of the store. Studying her beneath her lashes, she recalled how Logan had watched Troy, registering every shift in expression, how close he was getting to climax, his wants, his needs. He'd never turned his attention from Troy's mental and physical state, and so now she did the same, judging the girl's body language. What she saw had her ambling out from behind the counter.

"Special occasion, or are you playing with an idea?"

The girl responded with a half laugh. "I think I'm looking for a miracle. A friend of mine came here last year, and she said that you really helped point her in the right direction. I came earlier, last week, and didn't get that vibe, but then I thought . . . well, it felt like you had more to give and I should give you another chance. Understand?"

She turned, and met Madison's gaze. Her melodious voice went with her quiet movements, such that Madison saw her as a willow tree, whispering on the banks of a slow-moving creek. Yet what caught Madison was her note of uncertainty, a touch of despair mixed with exasperation. And that note opened a new door inside herself.

Madison suddenly saw her customer, not as an obstacle to surmount, a goal to reach, but as a unique soul like herself, with needs she was having difficulty articulating, possibly because of how deep her desires ran. Just like Madison. But different, too.

Selling wasn't about the seller. This exchange wasn't supposed to be about Madison's experiences and needs, about how great a salesperson she was, how much she could impress herself. It had to be about the buyer, figuring out what she wanted and needed.

Almost exactly the words Alice had used in the final letter she'd left her, the letter Madison had found the day she came back to the store. She took a breath.

"Your friend would have been dealing with my sister, but let me give it a try. What's your name?"

"Samantha. Sam."

"All right, Sam. What's the situation?" She was a pragmatist, after all, and she saw no reason to beat around the bush, now that the shot had been fired. Sam seemed to agree, because her attitude toward Madison became less guarded.

"Two friends. Close friends. Guys. They both like me, and they like each other. They don't know what to do about it, and I thought . . ." She sighed, visibly summoning up the courage to look toward the back archway, at the stenciled pair of handcuffs beneath the flourished "Dungeon Room" label. "One of them, I think he's like that."

She colored a little, but at Madison's neutral reaction, she elaborated. "Sometimes, the way he looks at us, the way he acts, I think he'd like to tie us both up and have his way with us. And I think Chris really wants that, too, though he can't say it. There, I said it out loud. Are you horrified? I mean, how much more taboo can we get? Threesome, bondage, and two guys who probably want to touch each other as much as they want to touch me. Maybe I'm crazy."

Before last night, Madison might have gone wide-eyed and fumble-tongued. Even up until this moment, she'd been mostly focused on her own baggage regarding last night's session, but it had apparently accomplished what Alice had hoped it would. Madison felt an almost audible click as she connected to what Sam was feeling.

"Are they with you now?" Madison nodded toward the door. "In the car, I mean?"

"They're in the hardware store. I think they wanted to come in with me, but you know, lingerie store, they figured it would be all these women . . . actually I think they're being shy."

"What's the other one's name? Chris and . . ."

"Geoff."

"Okay. We should invite them in to shop with you. I'll give them some ideas that will help you figure out if you're right or not. What do you think? Are you feeling brave? Say yes, quick, before I decide I'm not as brave as I think *I* am today."

Sam's eyes widened, then she chuckled. Pleasure surged in Madison as the smile brightened, Sam making that small step of trust in herself and in the absent men. And in Madison. "Okay, yeah. Why not?"

"Good. I'll get them. You stay here."

Sam looked surprised, but stayed put as Madison pushed out the door and strode toward the hardware-store entrance. Would Logan be there? The very thought had her pulse tapping urgently against her throat.

Stepping into the hardware store, she saw he wasn't in view, which was kind of a relief. She couldn't afford to get distracted, even though her body was already warm all over.

"Chris, Geoff?" She raised her voice enough to carry through the store without shrieking like a fishwife.

A dark-haired man looked up from the shovels. She expected he wasn't really looking, but planted in a half doze, because he had stubble on his attractive jaw, and he held a generous-sized cup of coffee, despite the mid-morning hour. A late-shift job, maybe, such that mid-morning was early for him. His burly build suggested he did a lot of manual labor, perhaps construction work. Or maybe bar bouncer. She was going to assume this one was Chris.

The other man who looked toward her was in the rope aisle, fingering a length of twine with an entirely familiar absorption. She suppressed a smile. His clean-shaven and sharp-eyed appearance suggested young professional, possibly a lawyer. He didn't have Chris's bulk, but his body was lean and toned. Both men would catch female attention.

"Sam needs your opinion on some things next door," she told them. "Don't worry, she's my only client right now. No gaggles of women to scare you off."

Chris grinned. Geoff, though eying her speculatively, gave her a serious smile. They moved toward her, joining up at the top of their respective aisles. She noticed Geoff let Chris slide in front of him.

The man Sam thought was a Dominant watched his friend, his gaze sliding over his nape, down the broad back. Since it reminded her of Logan's attention to her or Troy, just far less actualized and confident, she experienced another tiny thrill. Sam might be on the right track.

So was Madison. She knew it. It was all in noticing cues. That was the same, no matter what kind of sales she was doing, but this was more complicated. It was like discovering a story, and once the story was uncovered, she could help with the happy ending. Or beginning, as it were.

As she stepped aside to let them pass, she said, "I'll be over to help you in a moment."

The heat along her skin had increased exponentially, telling her for certain Logan was now behind the front counter. After they stepped out of his store, she let her gaze travel there, a flush rising in her cheeks. It was probably in full bloom by the time she met his gold-brown eyes.

He had his palms braced on the counter, his head cocked as he considered her from head to toe. He took his time about it, no matter the generous scattering of customers throughout the store. She could hear Troy's voice down an aisle, where he was helping someone.

"That's customer poaching," Logan said lazily.

"It's quid pro quo." She sniffed. "All you have to do to cause a stampede from every store on the street is announce Troy is doing a demonstration of . . . anything. How to hammer a nail."

If Troy was shirtless and wearing a tool belt, Logan would probably have to have EMTs on standby for swooning. She didn't add that, but there were a couple female patrons who obviously filled in the blanks, their eyes sparkling their appreciation of her. Which meant two new potential customers might come check out her store, just to see what the cheeky proprietor had to offer.

Logan straightened, sauntering to the end of the counter. The second he started to move she remembered that over-the-top, heated kiss against the wall of his storeroom, his hands on her, his whispered command to come in her ear.

It was hormones. That was all.

"Don't worry," she added, glancing down the rope and fastener aisle. "I'm sure I'll be sending them back your way. We don't have any of that at my place."

"Alice knew it was right next door. Whenever she needed it."

His slow smile made her narrow her gaze. "I have a store to run," she said primly. "I don't have time for you."

The attractive lines around his eyes crinkled. "How about a movie tonight? We can do it at your house, if you're more comfortable there. About eight? Just you and me."

"I'm not sure. Let me think about it." She guessed it was her house now, though she still thought of it as Alice's. That wasn't the source of her hesitation, though. She wasn't imagining them watching a movie. In her mind, he was pushing her onto her back in the bed, holding her wrists to the pillows, his mouth at her throat, his body between her legs . . .

"Remember what I said last night, about me setting the parameters?" He leaned across the counter, dropped his voice down low. "No sex on our second date, Madison. Nothing but two adults watching a movie, getting to know each other better. All right?"

"Maybe. I'll let you know at the end of the day. Though maybe . . . I'd rather wait a few days, all right? A few days."

She backed away and slipped out of the store, catching her toe on the threshold in her haste. As she hurried back to her own store, her whole body was vibrating. She'd wanted him to touch her then and there, in front of people buying bedding plants, lawn implements and power tools.

It was good she returned when she did, though. Chris and Geoff had joined Sam, but she was still at the rounder of nightwear, looking at loose ends about how to proceed. Examining their body language, Madison could see the problem right off.

Geoff.

They both deferred to him, probably responding to that sub-liminal thing Logan emanated like a neon sign. Logan was near forty; Geoff was in his mid-twenties. Logan had fully embraced that side of himself some time ago, perhaps exploring it at the age Geoff was now. Geoff might still be struggling with it, about how two people he cared about would react to the shape and form of his desires.

An electric current connected the three of them, the charged power of unrealized fantasies and desires. She wondered how strong that current had looked between her and Logan a moment ago.

"So . . . there are some pretty things over here I'm thinking you'd like, Sam." She eased her away from the lingerie and toward more of the role-playing clothes. Following intuition, she plucked out a Cath-olic schoolgirl ensemble. The willowy figure and doelike eyes would be a perfect match for it, down to the frilly panties that barely hid under the short plaid skirt. Geoff sharpened on her choice like a spear, and suddenly Chris seemed far more awake.

"And for Chris . . . hmm." All professional shopkeeper, she perused his serviceable T-shirt and jeans, the woman in her approv-ing of the build the shirt strained to cover. She glanced at Geoff. "What do you think? I'm thinking he doesn't really need a special outfit. Maybe he's the yard boy who can't keep his eyes off of her as she's coming home from school."

"Well, he does mow the grass at our rental house," Sam teased her roommate, laying her hand on the arm holding the coffee. "Even does the weed eating and edging. He needs to start his own landscape business, rather than working for one."

"Then I'd never have time to mow *our* grass," he pointed out, giving her a nudge.

"So he already has his costume," Madison mused. "All he needs to do is take off the shirt, work up a bit of a sweat, and there you go."

She gave them a wink, even as she noted Geoff's silent regard, watching Sam and Chris flirt with one another. "Why don't you two look at the options, consider the possibilities? Have fun with it, like playing dress-up when you're kids. Nothing's off-limits. I'm going to show Geoff something a little more appropriate for him."

At his surprised look, she guided him away from them with a light touch on his arm. As it became clear she was moving into the Dungeon Room, he paused, his gaze flicking to Chris and Sam as if he wasn't sure if he wanted them to see him headed there. Madison moved smoothly into the room ahead of him and lifted a soft flogger from the wall. "Now, this might be good to punish a naughty school-girl, but this"—she lifted a heavier slapper, like what Logan had used on Troy—"might be just the thing to keep your yard boy thinking about what you pay him to do, not ogling her."

That got his full attention. The way he moistened his lips, stud-ied the slapper ends sliding over her fingers, told her she was on the right track. He had enough of those Dom vibes that when he raised his steady gaze, the sub inside of her, the one that Logan had coaxed out, shivered, recognizing his potential. Lucky Sam and Chris, if he embraced that side of himself.

Directing him to the shelf of books on the wall, she removed one that had an instructional DVD for Japanese rope tying. She showed him the photographs of restraint designs. He studied one of a man and woman tied together, the Master standing behind them, holding another rope. He was so absorbed in the picture, it gave her time to do the same, remembering last night vividly.

"Imagine doing something like this." She tilted the page toward him. "His genitals are tied down so he can't 'accidentally' get inside her. But she's squirming, excited, rubbing against him. You'd have to spank her to get her to behave. But Chris, being so chivalrous, he wouldn't like that. He'd tell you he'd take the punishment." Just as Troy had done. She gave Geoff a wicked smile. "And you'd be too happy to oblige."

She didn't expect that Geoff, Sam and Chris's needs would be an exact match of her adventure with Troy and Logan, but right now that experience was her best guide for this. She wasn't Alice, after all.

No, she wasn't. But she hadn't been Alice last night. Yet it had all felt familiar to her, despite never having been in that situation before. She expected it was the same for Geoff, because his eyes had sparked at the images she was painting.

"This kind of erotic binding dates from the days of the samurai." She flipped the pages, let him see some more possibilities. The book was nearly fifty dollars. If they bought floggers and a few outfits, she'd be making quite a tidy sum. Chris might work for a landscaper, but Sam's jewelry said she worked in a higher-paying profession. Geoff was young enough to have a lot of student loans, but if he was already working for a firm he'd have some discretionary spending power.

Stop. What was she doing?

She closed the book abruptly, set it back on the shelf. "Will you follow me back to your friends?"

His brow creased, puzzled, but he nodded, following her back to Sam and Chris, who were teasing one another, pointing out the outfit choices. Cop, vampire, clown . . .

"You'd be sooooo irresistible with a red-rubber-ball nose." Sam rolled her eyes. "Like you need help looking like a clown." She reached out to Geoff, taking his hand and drawing him closer. Madison suspected she'd seen his speculative look at her casual touch on Chris's arm, and was balancing it by touching him, trying to send them both a message. *This isn't a competition, you idiots. I want* both *of you.* "You'll have to help us choose, Geoff," she complained. "I can't get Chris to be serious."

"I have a suggestion," Madison said. Glancing at Geoff's face, she took her cue from his conflicted expression and hoped she wasn't losing her mind. "Sam has opened a door that I suspect you all have thought about, but maybe not in as much detail as she has."

"Sam, overthinking things? With her OCD personality? Not a chance." Chris said it with a straight face, earning a shove from Geoff and a mock scowl from the young woman.

Madison chuckled. "Men aren't great at asking directions, so someone has to be willing to get out of the car and ask before things get too frustrating." She gestured around the store. "I'm not going anywhere. Why don't you all go down the street to the sandwich shop? They have great breakfast bagels and outdoor seating, and it's a lovely place to relax and chat. You can talk about it. Talk about what each of you really wants."

As she met their eyes in turn, she realized they were listening to her as if she knew what she was talking about. More amazingly, she felt as though she did.

Nothing more dangerous than a little knowledge, she reminded herself dryly, and tried to rein it back, keep it in safe parameters. "I think Sam knows what she wants, but she's afraid of losing or offending either of you by saying it. I also think Geoff knows what he wants, but he's not sure how both of you feel about it. And Chris . . ." She turned her gaze to him, thought of Troy, and couldn't help smiling. "You're the easygoing one of the group. You'll be the one who boils it down to what it is, keeps them both from overthinking it."

He grinned at that, but he had a thoughtful look of his own. With her serious talking points, he'd realized more was happening here than awkward doublespeak and playful costume choices.

"So go talk about it. Go home and play with the idea, play with each other. And then come back to me when you're ready."

"You're not going to sell us anything?" Sam's brow furrowed. "We're interested in—"

"No, she's not going to sell us anything," Geoff cut in, met Madison's gaze. "Not right now. But later."

"Yes, later." She put her hand on Sam's arm. "I could load you up with several hundred dollars' worth of merchandise. But you'd take it home, play with it, then set it aside like a gimmick, vaguely unsatisfied, because you played with the wrapping, not the present. Not what lies beneath the surface. Figure that part out, then you can come back and decide how you want to wrap up the gift."

Sam considered that, then nodded. Impulsively, she covered Madison's hand, squeezed it. "I'm so glad I followed my intuition and came back here. I don't know about your sister, but you seem exactly as my friend described her to me."

The words lanced her heart, painful but not necessarily wrong or bad. "I learned a lot about this kind of thing from her." *I just have to open myself to listen. And please, God, let Alice be guiding me now so I don't run these three nice people down the wrong path and ruin their lives.*

"When you come back, if you come back, I'll be delighted to put you on my frequent buyer reward program," Madison said. "Here, take my card. You can call me if you want to check my inventory from home. We'll have a website running again soon, though I'm always happy to have you come here to see me."

Chris and Sam both looked toward Geoff. Geoff put his hand on Sam's lower back and touched Chris's arm, holding it briefly in a way that had the man giving him a bemused look. "Bagels sound good," he said. "Thank you, ma'am. We appreciate it. We'll be back."

"I hope so." She sent them off with another smile and wave. When the door closed, a sultry Latin tune winding to a finale over the store speakers, she drew a shuddering breath. "Oh my God. Did I really just do that?"

She'd taken over, guiding them toward actualizing their fantasies and improving their sex lives, maybe their very relationship. While in that zone, she'd felt like she'd been doing it for the past ten years, not for these past few minutes. Her first real sale. Nearly. If they came back.

She gave the ceiling a suspicious look. "You're not possessing me, are you, Alice? Because that would really piss me off. I'm not sure about this whole selling-something-by-not-selling-it. It seems like exactly the kind of thing you would do."

But it seemed right to Madison as well.

"She doesn't strike me as the possession type. Though I can arrange for a priest if you need it."

She twisted around to see Logan standing at the opening to her storeroom. "I need to change the locks. The people next door have no respect for privacy."

He chuckled. "Sorry. I was putting something else in my overflow storage and couldn't help overhearing. Well played."

It bolstered her more than she wanted to admit. Riding the feeling, she decided to act on another impulse, with a far greater potential for disaster.

"Okay," she said. "About the movie. My place. A week from Friday. And no sex. Like you said."

Because if she stated the term, he'd honor it, as he had last night. On Friday, when he crossed her threshold with all that out-front sexuality that promised he could leave a woman as satisfied as a cat with a bowl of cream, she'd regret it, but another part of her liked knowing she could trust him like that.

Giving her a nod, his eat-you-with-a-spoon smile, he disappeared. She listened to his steps, taking him back to his store. For the first time in a long time, she felt the excitement of the unexpected, the thrill of . . . infatuation. It was terrifying.

Fortunately, the strains of "Boléro" began, telling her she had more customers. That was exciting as well. She hoped she'd see Geoff, Sam and Chris again, and not just because she needed to pay the rent. She wanted to see how the story turned out . . . or continued . . . or began.

"*What* kind of oil would you prefer, Mrs. Grady? This one has a touch of vanilla, but more importantly, the chemical blend comes closest to replicating your own natural lubricants, working with your body, and helps with the pH balance so you're not as susceptible to infection. Here, I have sample bottles, if you'd like to take one with you rather than committing to a purchase right away."

Madison added the sample bottle to the fifty-something woman's pink bag of merchandise, which included several pairs of stockings for her excellent legs, a remote-controlled, multisetting bullet vibe and the special panties with the insert to hold it.

"Your husband will never look at ballroom dancing the same way," she promised. "But remember what I said. Men tend to think the highest setting is the best one right away. Tell him it's like a dance. You ease into it, twirl and spin, and work up to the crescendo."

Mrs. Grady chuckled. "You and Mr. Scott must be working as a team. He keeps the men busy buying tools and manly things while we ladies come over here and decide how to reward them for an afternoon of home improvement."

"Nothing stokes a woman's libido like a man who can fix things," Madison agreed, knowing her eyes were twinkling. "As far as my arrangement with Mr. Scott, we can't disclose the details of our frequent buyer reward program."

"I've seen Mr. Scott," Mrs. Grady responded. "Lucky you."

Madison had to laugh at that. When Mrs. Grady entered the shop, she'd been standoffish and stiff, killing time rather than seriously shopping. But now she held a bag full of items and a warm smile, and was teasing Madison in a scandalous way she wouldn't have expected from the woman at all.

Alice had once said the more she gave her customers, the more they gave back. Madison hadn't been sure of her meaning, but she was starting to get it. On that same note, Sam, Geoff and Chris had returned earlier in the week. It was clear they'd made substantial strides together, from the easy, sensual touches they exchanged when they were looking at things. Geoff had taken the reins in more ways than one, and Chris and Sam's eyes clung to his every movement as he went to the Dungeon Room and picked out the soft flogger, eight sets of Velcro cuffs and one of the Build-It-Yourself bondage equipment books that sent him directly to the hardware store afterward. She'd already accused Logan of having Alice plant those there specifically to drum up business for him, and he hadn't denied it.

Sam had given her a big smile and a mouthed *thank you* as her two lovers escorted her out of Madison's store, carrying armloads of merchandise. Things they truly wanted, not something bought on the spur of the moment, based on wishful thinking and unrealized fantasies.

As Mrs. Grady departed to recover Mr. Grady from Logan's store, Madison glanced at the clock. Not that it was really necessary. Tonight was movie night, and the anticipation that had been tingling under her breastbone since breakfast grew stronger with every passing hour.

She was glad she'd let some time pass, wanting to slow things down, see how things evened out after their first volatile night together. Troy had remained flirtatious and friendly. Logan was attentive and helpful as well, both of them touching base with her at least once during each workday. They'd come over after hours one night to help her stabilize a shelf when she discovered its anchors were loose in the wall. The two men had worked together with distracting casualness, all flexing muscle and haunch, exchanging the typical male banter as they moved in sync with each other.

When they were done, Troy had to get to an evening class and Logan had excused himself as well, saying he had a demonstration to do at the local dungeon. He hadn't extended the invitation to her to attend. Maybe because he was respecting her need for space. He picked up on cues better than any male she'd ever met. That didn't mean he was easily swayed from his own desires, however. She already knew if he wanted his own way, a woman would have to have superhuman fortitude to back him down. It was part of the reason she'd taken the week, to marshal her defenses, give herself half a chance to hold her own. The way his gaze lingered on her suggested he was anything but detached from the idea of pursuit; merely biding his time.

It was closing time. She locked the front door, closed out the register. When she emerged from the back entrance, she discovered Logan was bringing out the trash. The chance encounter gave her a surge of foolish pleasure. As he straightened, he smiled at her, making her think he reciprocated that.

"Mrs. Grady gave her husband a glimpse into her pink shopping bag. He almost bought flooring nails instead of wood screws."

"A sure sign of male distraction," she agreed, lips twitching. When he leaned against the wall, hooking a finger into his jeans pocket, she eased a little closer. "So how was the demonstration the other night?"

"It went well. It was about the proper use and care of whips."

"Who did you use as your victim, if Troy wasn't there to eagerly volunteer?"

His lazy gaze slid over her face, to her throat, her breasts, her hips. He didn't make any pretense of not looking where he wanted to look, any time he wanted to do so. Rather than finding it offensive, she found it incredibly stimulating. "Stop that," she said for form's sake. "You're trying to make me forget the question."

"Nope. I just don't divide my attention when I'm enjoying a good long look at you. That's a new outfit."

She'd decided to borrow from her inventory today, wearing a pleather zippered vest that molded to her upper body and offered deep cleavage. Each day she was a little more confident and daring in her clothing choices. She'd put the vest together with latex leggings and calf boots. To ensure she didn't scare away the Mrs. Gradys of the world, she'd worn a ruffled scarf that screened the cleavage and a short skirt that didn't show how the latex molded her ass and the crease of her sex. As a result of being the live model, she'd sold a couple versions of the outfit today. She was already planning future ensembles to inspire more sales.

"You like it?"

"I like anything you wear. But I'd like it better without the scarf and the skirt." His gaze swept over them, as if he already knew how revealing the vest and latex were without the outer layers. "A private viewing. It's hard enough hearing how the men talk about you after they leave their wives or girlfriends at your store."

"Jealous?"

"Make a move toward any of them and you'll find out," he said. Her heart pattered a little higher in her throat. "Take off the scarf."

Even out here, in the late afternoon sunshine, he could make her feel as if the walls closed in, holding her still for him. "You still haven't answered my question," she hedged, to see if she could resist him. Or what he would do if she did.

"What was the question?"

He was teasing her. Even so, she sniffed, indulged him. "Who helped you do the demo at the club?"

"One of the staff subs. A pretty blonde, all naked and oiled up so she was slippery to the touch." He caught the ends of the scarf before she could draw back. "And she still didn't make me half as hard as you did, showing up all big-eyed and unsure, wondering what I might do to Troy . . . and you."

"You're too overwhelming," she complained. Thanks to the tug on the scarf, their bodies had barely a hand's span between them. "Overwhelming men tend to be unreliable."

"No. The men you've known tend to be unreliable. I'm different. Take it off."

He could take it off himself, but her obeying was part of what was spiraling between them. She didn't want to analyze how she understood that or why she removed it the way she did, pulling it slowly from her throat, lifting her chin as the silk-cotton blend caressed her skin. When she had it in both hands, lowered to her waist, he hooked the tab of the zipper in the vest, tugged it down enough so the cleavage became deeper, revealing the lace joining point of the black bra beneath. He slid his knuckles into that valley, then up to follow her throat, tip up her chin. His face was close enough to make the possibility of being kissed excruciatingly inevitable. She played with a strand of his hair that had come loose from where he'd tied it back. "Have you always worn it long?"

"No." His breath smelled like the free wintergreen mints he kept by his cash register. "Alice wanted me to grow it out long for you. She said you thought only a certain man could carry that off, but when he did, you really liked it. She convinced me I could carry it off. When it was too short to be tied back, but long enough to be in my way, she'd come over, have me sit on a stool and brush it back, run her fingers through it, tell me it was a crime for a man to have hair like that."

The man's eyes were like swimming in brandy, rich and potent. "That's why you're overwhelming. You say things like that to me, as if you've known me for a long time, and I've only known you for a little while."

"Yet it doesn't feel that way, does it?"

No. She didn't say it, but the answer was in her eyes. How was it possible? Probably because he brought her hormones to full raging, and that was easily mistaken for an emotional response. She eased back, putting some space between them.

"Why didn't you invite me to the whip demonstration? You would have, if you'd wanted me there."

She'd never been this forthright in any of her previous relationships. Maybe she'd reached the *fuck it, I've nothing to lose* stage, where relationship guessing games exhausted her. She was interested in different games. The kind Logan played.

"Because it wasn't time for that." He leaned against the wall again. "BDSM is often a rigidly structured arrangement between the players. Like me and Troy. Once the session ends, that's it. Even if you have a regard for one another outside of it, you don't have a relationship."

"But Troy responds to you as a sub, even when he's not in session."

"When he's under my training, he's always in session. Shale wants 24/7. Troy has the right makeup for that, but training with me was a way of proving that to himself."

"He's staying with you?"

"Mm-hmm. Sleeping on a mattress on my bedroom floor, like a good pet."

She arched a brow. "He's never tried to get into the bed with you? Most dogs will."

His eyes kindled, acknowledging her teasing. "He might try that with Shale. Not with me. There's only room in my bed for the pet I intend to keep."

She decided to let that one go, but kept needling. "No cage? I figured you'd have one of your own at home. For the occasional overnight stray."

"Easy now," he chided. Hooking a finger in the plunging neckline of the vest, he tugged her a step closer again, so they were leaning against the brick wall together. As his body shadowed hers, she found her back against the brick. If he put up his other arm, he'd have her trapped against the unyielding surface.

"I don't need a cage to make my pet obey me," he said, glancing meaningfully at the open space he'd left her for escape. "But I liked how your pupils got bigger and you stopped breathing when you were looking at the one in my workshop. Since then I've thought a lot about what you would have done if I had ordered you into it, rather than just offered you the chance to try it out."

She reminded herself to inflate her lungs, which only made his gaze slide down, watching the rise of her breasts. At this angle, he could see a great deal of their shape beneath the vest, almost to the areola. But she wasn't drawing away from his heat or challenge.

"I still don't understand why you didn't invite me," she said, holding on to her resolve with both hands. *I am in control of this. It's just aggressive flirting.*

"Yeah, you do. You want me to say it, to be sure. Which is why I won't. When you're sure, it'll be because my actions have left no doubt in your mind, Madison. You've had too many pretty words and lies."

Had Alice told him *everything* about her? It was like one-sided computer dating. She could be resentful of it, but so far, he hadn't been wrong in any assumption he'd made. That took more than just being fed facts. He'd deduced things deeper than what Alice could have told him, because some were things Madison herself hadn't even articulated. She really needed some quid pro quo so she could be less in the deep end with him. It was time to start studying him as carefully as he studied her.

Avoiding a direct comment, she touched that loose strand of his hair again. The rest of it lay in a thick, glossy tail between his shoulder blades. "She was right. It is a crime for a man to have hair this beautiful."

"It's a pain in the ass," he grunted. "You better appreciate it every day, or off it all comes."

"Whatever you wish, Master," she teased him.

His eyes flashed, fingers digging into her hip. "Say it again," he demanded.

She shook her head, put a quivering hand on his chest, the only defense she could manage. "I know how to cut hair," she said. "I'll cut it for you tonight. I don't want you to be different for me."

As much as she loved how he looked with long hair, short hair suited his face, his profile. She wanted him to look like who he truly was.

"I intend to be different for you, Madison," he promised. Shifting away from her, he held on to her scarf. "I'll see you tonight."

"Don't lose that," she warned. "It's thirty-five dollars plus tax."

Putting it to his nose, he inhaled as he gave her a roguish look. "I'll buy it. So I can hold on to your scent until tonight."

How could she trust something that sprang to life so quickly when, fast or slow, her relationships always ended up crashing and burning? Maybe by merely having fun with it, not making too much of it. Which was probably all he was doing, and she needed to follow suit. He was headed back into his store, but the door hadn't quite closed behind him yet. She cleared her throat. "No sex, right?"

The door caught as he stopped it with his palm, peered over his shoulder. She raised an innocent brow. "Just wanting to know how firm you are on that. The terms of tonight's date, that is."

His lips twitched at the double entendre. "You wanted to take it slow. We're taking it slow."

"And you never change your mind about a session, once the parameters are set at the beginning."

"No. I don't. You have a good memory."

"Okay. Just checking." His speculative look almost made her laugh. Then he nodded past her. "UPS, with a late afternoon delivery. You'll want to get that. Be sure you open it first thing when you get home." He turned and disappeared back into his own store.

She watched the truck trundle up. Clarence disembarked with a flat dress box from her regular costumer supplier. She hadn't remembered placing a new order, though she needed to do so, since she was starting to know which outfits turned over more frequently than others.

"All good today, Ms. Fine?"

"Yes, Clarence." She'd told him he didn't need to call her Ms. Fine, but she suspected he'd called Alice that. Maybe it reminded him of her, to keep doing it.

He smiled at her when she took the package and told him she'd have chocolate chip cookies next week. Those were his favorites. Maybe she should expand, buy the empty storefront across the street, hire some help and run a bakery. She and Logan could take over the whole block, their own little empire.

She chuckled at the thought and went to her car, opening it up and putting her keys and purse in the front seat. Laying the box on the hood, she slit it open with her penknife, too curious to wait to see what it was.

On top of the folded tissue paper was a typewritten note.

Wear this tonight.—L

Pulling back the tissue paper, she saw he'd ordered a replacement for the Catholic schoolgirl uniform Sam had bought, only this one was in her size. Or at least as much as size was relevant for two scraps of cloth; a white shirt that tied between the breasts and a plaid skirt the width of a curtain topper. He'd gone all out on the accessories, though, including the long white stockings, black patent shoes and a white cotton thong, which he apparently preferred to the frilly panties.

The day he'd helped stabilize the shelf, he'd been wearing a gray T-shirt that molded to his upper body. With his size, it had to be an X-Large. That night, she'd lain in bed and imagined herself in the cotton thong panties he preferred and that shirt, surrounded by his scent and body heat, the cotton fabric slightly damp from his sweat so it would cling to her skin.

Even as far back as grade school, she couldn't remember having a crush this strong and fast. It was terrifying. She thought of Sam in the Catholic schoolgirl outfit, Chris on his knees, kissing his way up the inside of those long legs. Geoff "discovering" their transgression and devising a punishment that resulted in all three of them together in bed, sweaty and replete, limbs twined together.

Except for the Bohemian outfit she'd worn that first day, most of her clothes had come from the shop. It was a good sales approach, but part of it was avoiding digging deeper in Wonderland. However, on the dresser in Wonderland was a cameo on a black silk ribbon. It would tie snugly around the throat and be a nice addition to the schoolgirl outfit. There was also a black garter with satin ribbon clips she could use to hold up the white stockings.

She fingered the fabric. Was it ridiculous, a woman in her thirties wearing something a girl Sam's age could pull off so much better?

Apparently Logan didn't think so.

The thought gave her self-confidence a boost, brought the doubts down to a quiet roar. If she wore this, she might test his resolve about the no-sex thing. A lot. She liked that idea.

She got dressed at seven o'clock. He hadn't provided a bra, though she had several very sexy ones in Wonderland. Alice had obviously added some things since they'd last "played" in there. Madison even found a latex catsuit. Holding it up in front of the mirror, she thought, with her long brown hair, she might look a little bit like Catwoman. She remembered playing Batman and Catwoman when she was little, wanting Batman to come rescue her. She'd liked how "bad" Catwoman was, and how stern Batman was with her. Madison snorted at herself. If she searched the Internet, she was sure she'd find fan fiction where Catwoman received that spanking she'd deserved from her nemesis. The web was a wealth of such dark yearnings.

She decided against the bra, concluding Logan's omission was intentional. The shirt was thin enough that her nipples were displayed prominently. After donning the cotton thong, she added the garter belt with black ribbon straps, clipping the ends to the long stockings, which came up to midthigh. She also tied the cameo around her throat, feeling the rapid beat of her pulse beneath it. She closed her eyes as she tightened the ribbon, imagining Logan doing it.

She'd planned to make *him* crazy, but by the time she'd added the last piece, the panel of the thong pressed against her noticeably wet crotch. Turning, she verified that yes, the lower curves of her ass cheeks were visible right beneath the pleated hem.

He'd said firmly, adamantly, *no sex*. Yet he'd dressed her as if she had one purpose in life, and that was to be fucked.

He was a sadist.

She went downstairs to the kitchen. She'd set out clippers, scissors and cape to cut his hair, and she had beer and wine in the fridge. Alice had a movie popcorn popper, and she had that loaded in case he wanted to share a bowl during the movie. She wondered what he would bring for them to watch.

As she drew a bowl out from the lower cabinet, the cool air of the kitchen caressed her ass, making the damp cotton against her pussy more noticeable. Her reaction to that forced her to steady herself against the counter. It was no use. No matter how she tried to distract herself, every movement of her body reminded her of what she was wearing, how she looked . . . how aroused she was.

When the doorbell rang, she struggled to compose herself. She wanted to torture *him*. Surely she could have enough self-control to do that, given how much satisfaction it would give her to see him unbalanced. She sauntered down the hallway with a lot of hip action. Though she knew he could see through the window panel of the front door, she didn't look through it, not brave enough to make eye contact.

Opening the door, she saw he'd worn a sports coat, dress jeans and nice shirt. He'd even brought flowers, yellow daisies, and a bottle of wine.

At her amazed look, he lifted a shoulder. "It's our first official date, after all."

"I'm underdressed."

His gaze coursed over her. She'd opened the door but stepped back from it, letting him open the storm door so she wouldn't be glimpsed by the neighbors. As he shouldered in, a big man filling her foyer, he took her hand, setting the flowers and wine on the side table. His scrutiny was thorough and avid, making her skin heat under his attention. "You wore it."

"You told me to."

She cast her eyes down when she said it. Part of it was an involuntary reaction to his proximity, but she made the conscious decision to keep her gaze down, trying to battle down the butterflies as she did so. D/s permeated his life—training Troy in his store, doing demonstrations in the evening. Was she crazy to try her hand at giving him such an overt submissive cue?

She thought of Sam, how brave she'd had to be to initiate things. But Madison didn't need to take the lead as Sam had with Geoff. Logan lived and breathed Dominant. It wasn't play for him at all, which probably meant she shouldn't be encouraging it.

However, as she tried to bring her gaze back up, she found herself unable to do so, as if her subconscious was stubbornly insisting on the message, inviting his next reaction. He stepped closer and she let herself be backed up against the wall. His hand settled on her waist, the other under her hair, holding her still.

"I put out all the things to cut your hair," she said, apropos of nothing. "If you'd like to do that before the movie."

"You were serious about that."

"Yes." She managed to lift her gaze briefly to his and was held there, breath catching in her throat. "I can tell you prefer it short. I want you to be . . . you."

"All right," he said. A woman with hair that beautiful would have agonized over it, at least a moment. It meant no more to him than shearing a sheep. She rolled her eyes at him.

"But you'll cut my hair without this." Giving her a wicked look, he tugged on the knot between her breasts. When he grazed her nipple with his thumb, she caught her lip between her teeth. "Nothing better than a topless female barber."

"Sounds like another business opportunity."

"Probably been done, but yeah, we could use one around here. Though I'm not suggesting you sign up. I want you as my private hairdresser."

She chuckled at that, but stayed still as he came even closer. She let out a little moan as he imprinted his erection on her thigh, then shifted his stance so it rubbed against that nothing skirt and panties. "You're hot and eager, aren't you?" He nuzzled her hair, ran his hand down her shoulder, her upper arm. "God, you test a Master to the limits. Show me where you're going to cut my hair."

She needed his supportive hand to straighten from the wall. She wanted him, right there, right now. For the first time, she noticed he was carrying a tote slung over his shoulder. Her mind went in a dozen different directions, imagining what he'd brought.

"Where's Troy tonight?"

"Somewhere else."

She bit back a smile. Guiding him to the kitchen, she put the wine on the counter and retrieved a vase from the cabinet. Adding some water before she arranged the flowers in them, she made a note to trim the stems a little later to keep them fresh. It wasn't one of those cheap mashed-together grocery store bundles, but a bouquet that looked arranged by a florist. Amid the grouping of daisies and black-eyed Susans were several pale pink rosebuds. She'd have the pleasure of seeing them open up over the next few days.

Turning, she found he'd dropped the tote in a chair and was surveying the kitchen, the trio of "kitchen witch" puppets Alice had kept hung over the sink, the stained glass ornaments that caught the sunlight in the morning. "You haven't changed much yet."

"No. Having it the way she had it makes me feel like she's still here." She fussed with the flowers, fluffing them out, keeping her attention on them. "You were here a lot? I mean, even before she was sick?"

"Yeah. We were friends." His hands closed over her waist, the bare flesh so accessible above the tiny skirt. His thumb slid along the waistband, caught the edge of the thong beneath. "Just friends," he reminded her.

She believed him. Alice had never mentioned him in her letters. Alice always mentioned her lovers. Of course, she often mentioned acquaintances or friends, and she hadn't done that with him, either.

He set his jaw alongside her temple, his arms coming around her front, over her chest, as he suddenly held her against him. Not in a sexual manner, but in a way that had her putting her hands over his strong forearms.

"It still smells like her in here," he said.

"I know." She closed her eyes, held on, and realized they were holding each other. "Why didn't she ever tell me about you?"

He was silent a moment. "The first time we met was when Clarence brought her one of our packages. It was the day she opened the store. She brought me the delivery and cake. We talked a few moments about nothing in particular. But when she headed back to her store, she stopped in my doorway, turned and said: 'Madison.'"

He gave a pained half chuckle. "I said something brilliant, like 'What?' or 'Hunh?'"

She could see a faint reflection of his face in the splash guard that ran beneath the upper cabinets. It looked like impressionist art; something that appeared nebulous but held the eye, conveying significant meaning to deeper parts of the psyche. She almost reached out to touch that impression, run her fingers along the wavering lines of his jaw, his hair, but instead closed her hand on his forearm.

"She asked me if her saying the word made me feel anything. Anything at all." Logan chuckled, a deep rumble that vibrated against her shoulder blades. "I assumed she was one of those harmless, hippie-gypsy, New Age types. I was going to say something casual, like Madison Square Garden, but the way she was looking at me . . . it made me look inside for a real answer to her question. She had a gift that way."

"Yeah, she did." It was sad, how one could say to a stranger what had grated like hell to say directly to the family member in question. An offering of love met with resentment merely because familiarity—or family—bred contempt. "So what did you say? Unless it's part of some secret code she made you promise to take to your grave."

"No." His arms constricted, as if he knew the uncomfortable swells her boat of memory was experiencing. "I said, 'It sounds like a place I'd like to visit and never leave.' Her eyes lit up as if I'd given her the key to the universe. But she didn't explain why she'd asked the question. Not then."

She dropped her hands to the counter, ran her fingers over the sandy-colored granite pattern. He shifted his arms away from her but gripped her waist again briefly, squeezing. "You ready to cut off this mop?"

"It's hardly a mop. You can take a seat in one of the kitchen chairs."

When he withdrew, she appreciated the time he gave her to collect herself before she turned and put the vase of flowers on the table. He was shrugging out of the sports coat, and she took it from him, disappearing into the back guest room to retrieve a rack and hang

it up, place it by the door. When she returned, she saw he was looking at the wooden card box she'd left in the center of the table.

"I've been meaning to get that back to you," she said

"You're welcome to keep it, especially if you're finding it beneficial.
Did you use it?"

"You know I did."

"Do I?"

"Yes."

His gaze on her sharpened, and he spoke softly, causing another
shiver across her skin. "Where?"

It was uncanny that she'd known his main interest would be
where in this house she'd followed those directions. She made herself
meet his gaze, a Master's eyes.

"In the living room. On the floor." Emboldened by what was
swirling through her and since he hadn't yet sat down, she sidled up
to him, fingering the button on his shirt. "If I'm supposed to take
mine off, seems only fair you do the same."

He caught her finger, bit it with a teasing touch of his heated
tongue. "The pleasure of being a Master. I don't have to be the slightest bit fair. Stop flirting and cut my hair, woman."

"Brave words for a man letting me get close to him with scissors."
She tossed her hair. "Didn't Alice tell you I gave her a Mohawk when
she was fourteen? Including a purple dye job? Our mother about
murdered us both."

"I'll take my chances." He eyed her. "If you're angling for a spanking, you'll get far more than you bargained for. I'd beat you with a
knotted rope end. It wouldn't be pleasant in the least."

On the contrary, she expected he could make it equally pleasurable and painful. Though now she was wondering how a girl went
about angling for a spanking. The idea of bending over his lap made
her hot all over.

She decided she'd better behave. For the moment. When he took
a seat in the chair, she tucked the small hand towel under his collar

and then picked up the cape and settled it around him, enjoying the act of smoothing the fabric over his broad shoulders. "Your female patrons aren't going to thank me for this. One of them calls you Fabio."

He gave her a mildly horrified look. "If I'd known that, I would have chopped it off much sooner, no matter how much Alice said you'd like it."

"She meant it as a compliment. I get a lot of interesting conversations about you in my store."

"Same goes. Want to compare?"

"Let me guess. A few suggestive grunts about my rack? An academic analysis of how much they'd like to grab my ass?"

"It's like you're reading my mind."

She chuckled. "The women are more articulate. Somewhat. It's fascinating, how so many of them pick up on your 'Master' vibe. Especially when most of them are very much beginners in that area. More feelings than knowledge."

"It's about feelings far more than knowledge," Logan reminded her.

She wasn't going to analyze that, not when she was already aroused and overwhelmed by his proximity. She decided to make a sharp right turn before the subject took her to the deep end.

"When they're shopping with other women, they're braver. They'll talk about you and Troy pretty openly. A couple of them have some interesting male/male fantasies about you."

He gave her a pained look. "You don't have to go into detail on those."

She laughed. "Why are straight men so funny about that? When you care for Troy, you don't seem to have the slightest problem touching him."

"It's like being a doctor, caring for a patient. I'm pretty sure my doctor has no fantasies when he's asking me to cough. If he does, I'm switching health care providers."

"That's different, and you know it." She paused, considering. "Troy says it arouses you, dominating anyone, man or woman. It really doesn't matter who, does it?"

"You're fishing. We've had a discussion about that." Reaching back, he caught her wrist, drew her around to his side. "You've started working on my hair, but you're not dressed for it." He gave the white top a meaningful look.

"It's not concealing much as it is," she hedged.

"No, it's not. I approve fervently. Take it off."

The words came with a wash of heat, direct from the cinders in his brown eyes. His grip on her wrist stayed there as her lashes lowered. She heard the slide of his breath, like the sound of steam escaping a dragon's nostrils.

She untied the knot between her breasts. She kept her eyes on the task, because she couldn't hold his gaze when he had that look, or when she was obeying such an astounding command.

Take it off.

She slid out of the shirt, her nipples peaking further in the open air, and draped it on another kitchen chair. Though she kept her gaze down, she could feel the heat of that dangerous dragon as Logan studied her breasts. He was right. With him sitting and her standing, her curves, the jutting nipples, were pretty much there at his eye level. She hoped she didn't mess up his hair because of lack of coordination.

"Are you trying to distract me from discussing my customers' male/male fantasies?" she asked.

"How am I doing?" He tugged the edge of her skirt, a playful move, but then straightened and faced forward so she could proceed. Taking a steadying breath, she freed his hair from the clip, spreading it out on his shoulders. Though his hair *was* beautiful, she could already imagine how a shorter style would enhance the severe planes of his face, the intensity of those brown eyes. He'd look even more intimidating and tempting at once.

"Buzz cut, right?"

He gave her a sidelong look. "Haven't had one since the military, but I can do that, if it's easiest."

"I think I can give you a little more style than that, never fear." She started combing it out, following the comb with her fingers. When her lingering touch and deeper strokes made him close his eyes, it gave her another idea. After a brief hesitation, she set aside the comb and used both hands to give him a scalp massage. When Madison had cut Alice's hair, as well as their mother's, she'd always done that as part of the process. She definitely wasn't turning down any justification to bury her fingers in Logan's thick mane.

His resulting grunt of approval amused her. Apparently, everyone loved having their head stroked and rubbed, even a big tough guy. Maybe it went back to early memories of a mother's nurturing care. Of course, she seriously doubted Logan harbored any mommy fantasies. Thank God.

Relationship number two, Phineas, should have come with a pacifier and a blankey, since he basically let her take care of everything for him. With a name like Phineas, she should have known he was an overly coddled mama's boy, looking for a replacement.

And yet, she obviously wasn't it, because he left her, too.

Stop it, Madison. You've got a hot male in your kitchen and you're half naked. Why the hell are you dwelling on things that will fuck everything up?

"All right, no male/male fantasies." She cleared her throat, picked the comb back up. "But I am going to tell you all about the mooning and swooning."

"Mooning and swooning? You're exaggerating."

"One woman said every time she goes into your store, she fantasizes about you coming up behind her while she's looking at merchandise. When you reach forward to pluck whatever she's considering off the wall, you step right up against her. And that means other things would be pressed up against her, and she starts moving her hips, and you cup her breasts . . ."

"She did *not* tell you all of this." He turned his head against the pull of the comb to give her a censorious look. As well as to give her bare breasts another quick appraisal. She tugged his hair.

"You have to keep your head still when I start cutting," she said primly. "Else you really will have that mohawk."

He reached back, felt what she was doing now. "Why are you braiding it?"

"Because the fall is long enough that we can donate it to Locks of Love. That's what Alice and I did when we cut ours. It was all the way to our hips. If it's over a certain length, you can braid it and send it to them, and they'll use it for cancer patients who've lost their hair." Belatedly, she realized she should have found out if he was okay with that, but she needn't have worried. He glanced over his shoulder, giving her a thoughtful look.

"How did you get your customer to tell you her fantasy?"

Uncertain about his shift of topic, she shrugged uncomfortably. "She didn't tell me all that, not at first. I just encouraged her."

Logan snorted. "Figures."

"It increases the rapport, which increases sales," she defended herself. "Alice said people would tell her things they wouldn't even tell their therapist. But it's more than that. It's fun to share. I get as much out of it. You know how much Alice liked to connect with people. I think the way she set it all up—the stock, the music, the colors and lights, the scents—was meant to do that. They all reflected . . . her."

Her gaze slid over the whimsical kitchen witches, the stained glass. She knew most of the places Alice had bought them, had been with her for some of them. When she hadn't been, Alice shared anecdotes about the shopkeepers, tidbits about the adventure that surrounded the find. For Alice, shopping was as much of an adventure as a storybook, and she related it that way in her letters and phone calls, taking Madison on the journey.

She had to stop, fight back the surge of emotion. Oh hell, she was going to fuck up this date anyway. Even though logically she knew several months wasn't that long to grieve, she should be able to control this. At least enough that the timing wasn't so appalling. She put her hand on Logan's shoulder, fingers curling as he tensed. "No, don't turn around. Just give me a moment. I don't want to spoil tonight."

He ignored her, probably because her voice cracked. He turned himself and the chair, settled his big hands at her waist, and lifted her so she straddled him. He slid his arms around her, bringing her close enough she could lay her head alongside his, curl her arms around his shoulders and be held. Her bare breasts were against the cape, which wasn't so intimate, but his arms enfolding her bare back and waist, fingertips curved under her buttocks in the short skirt, were entirely *there*.

He didn't do things in half measures, and she reluctantly appreciated that. She didn't cry. Not outright. Held in the hard grip of loss and grief that made everything so difficult to release, she only managed a sniffle and short sob. Yet as she shattered on the inside, he held together the outside, making sure she didn't crack into a hundred pieces.

"I should have visited more in the last two years," she whispered.

"Why didn't you?" His deep voice vibrated through her as his lips brushed her ear.

"Because I was angry. At the whole world, but especially her, because she had it all figured out and I kept fucking everything up. Then she died with me holding her hand and none of that mattered. It was like a skin that just dropped off, everything I'd built up before unimportant." She sighed, pressed her face hard against the side of his, then pushed back from him, sliding off his lap. When he let her circle behind him, she was glad he didn't ask for more. He even gave her a few moments of silence while she secured the braid at the bottom as she had at the top.

She picked up the scissors. "Last chance."

"Off with all of it."

Wincing on behalf of all womankind, she cut the braid, sliding it into a Ziploc bag she had ready to secure it. His now significantly shortened hair fell loose around his nape and she riffled the ends with her fingertips. "Okay. Now we do the styling part."

"I have faith in my lovely barber."

As she began to snip, he returned to their earlier subject. "Alice asked me once if I did contract hits or knew anyone who did. She wanted to take out your last guy."

"Leroy? Oh, that would have been a waste. Going to prison for stealing a six-pack of beer would be more meaningful than removing his existence from the world."

"Ouch."

His chuckle helped loosen things in her stomach. She moved in front of him to hold a strand straight on either side of his face, determining how much she'd be cutting to put it back at ear level. He indulged in another obvious ogle at her breasts as she leaned forward. It made her smile.

"So when your customers are discussing my tits and ass, do you join in?"

"Yes. We consider them in great detail over morning coffee." His hand snaked out, gave her an admonishing pinch on her thigh, hard enough to send sensation up the inside muscle. "I've merely overheard the conversations, and broken them up with a helpful and pointed question about the store offerings when they get a little too enthusiastic. I haven't shot a nail gun through any of my regular contractors' tender parts for their more crass comments, though restraining myself took an effort."

"I expect the sales you ring up for them helps rein you back."

"Somewhat. But only to a certain point." This time she detected an edge to his countenance. It told her his tolerance in that regard was on the flattering side of possessive . . . and protective.

To shrug away such a romantic fancy, she glanced at her bare upper torso. "Yet you're having me cut your hair like this."

"A private pleasure, shared between you and me alone. You have superior breasts. Gorgeous Cs." He eyed them with a potent heat. "But men should always be respectful, especially when appreciating a woman's body in mixed company. It translates into actual respect when dealing with her privately."

"I think there are some contradictions there." Though only if she dissected the words. In terms of emotions, what he said made perfect sense. When he gazed at her breasts, she felt . . . well, *revered* would be a silly, over-the-top word, but something close to it. Cherished, desired. Lust was there, for certain, but tangled up with other things. Things that made her feel pleasure at his regard, and safe in his care.

She cleared her throat. "When they come into my store to find their wives or girlfriends, they're like scared chickens huddled by the door. I think men have nightmares about lingerie coming to life and smothering them."

He chuckled. However, when she began to snip, he was quiet, and she was okay with that. She wondered if it was deliberate, since it distracted her from the earlier sad emotions and brought her fully into the present. Him sitting in her kitchen while she cut his hair, her wearing nothing but a tiny plaid skirt over a white thong, long white stockings and black shiny shoes. She was glad she'd left her hair loose to brush her bare shoulders. She hadn't worn any jewelry other than the cameo, so anywhere he put his mouth tonight, he'd be tasting only her.

As she moved to his side, worked there, he slid his finger along her thigh, catching the garter, stroking the ribbon and skin beneath it. He gave it an easy, provocative tug. Though he kept his head still, gaze forward, she could well imagine his heated breath bathing her breasts.

Focus, or you'll cut off the tip of his ear. She liked his ears. And everything attached to them.

She cut the back and sides short, sculpting the top so some strands feathered across his forehead, the rest layering back with enviable ease, even with the natural curl to the thickness. Typical man. He favored a left part, which she was relieved to find was the way nature intended it to go. Her dad had always wanted her to cut his hair according to a part opposite from his hair's growth pattern, which made cutting it more of a challenge. After that one touch of her leg, Logan kept his hands to himself, folded beneath the cape, his body relaxed, though she wasn't fooled. He sat with his knees spread, so when she moved in front of him, she had to step between them to get close enough. Now she felt his breath against her skin in reality, only a short distance between her naked breasts and his lips. She was sure her nipples were high and tight points. When he rested his hands on her hips, low enough his fingers slid over her buttocks, she paused, holding her position.

"If you keep doing that, I will scalp you," she said. "It will be an accident, I promise, but it won't save us from an emergency room visit. Or an unsightly bald patch on the side of your head."

"I thought women could multitask." He kneaded her, sending all sorts of nerve endings around her rim into overdrive, telegraphing arousal between her legs.

"Smug insults might turn an accident into an intentional stabbing," she promised. "Changing the subject—deliberately, I might add—I now know why there aren't more topless barbers. Hair clippings get on your skin. And they itch."

"That's when the patron has to help." Leaning forward, he blew softly over her left breast. Her grip on the scissors convulsed, her other hand holding his shoulder for balance. "Better?"

"Loads," she said dryly, and won the sensual pleasure of his chuckle again. With a reproving glance at him, which, given her state of undress, was as effective as him being chastised by a Care Bear, she continued her cutting.

She'd been right. Taking away the length sharpened the alpha look of his profile, those strong features and piercing eyes. When she finished, she removed the cape and towel, brushing the hair off his neck. She resisted the urge to bend close enough to put her lips on his nape, inhale his aftershave up close and personal, but she did comb the hair back from his face with her fingers, enjoying the thick, soft texture. Catching her wrist again, he drew her arm past his shoulder, turned her hand over and kissed it.

She pressed against the chair, wishing the slats weren't between her and his body as he teased the lines of her palm with his tongue. When he moved to her wrist, suckled her pulse, heat shot straight to her core, already simmering for him.

He brought her around him once again, only this time it wasn't for comfort. He pulled her onto his lap, her legs dangling to the floor on either side of his hips as he palmed her buttocks, slid her so her pussy was against the hard length of him. She made a little gasp at that, and his eyes got that dangerous look she was starting to anticipate on both pleasurable and apprehensive levels.

"Put your hands on my shoulders and keep them there," he said.

She obeyed, and closed her eyes when he bracketed her rib cage, palms curved right beneath her arms, the heels of his hands pressed into the sides of her breasts. Lifting her up, he put his mouth over her left nipple. As she dug her fingers into his shoulders, her heels slid around to hook the rungs of the chair, increasing the pressure between their bodies as he suckled. She moaned, rubbing against him.

His hands dropped then, cupping her buttocks beneath the skirt, heated flesh against heated flesh since the thong covered nothing. Taking over, he stroked her against him as his lips squeezed and tongue lashed her nipple, then he sucked it all deeper into his mouth, moist heat against the areola and the skin around it.

"Tell me you want me to fuck you."

"Yes," she breathed. "Yes."

"Call me what you called me earlier."

"Yes . . . Master."

It frightened her, how natural it was to say it. He lifted his head, caught hers in between those big hands. "You'll call me that tonight, unless I say otherwise. You understand?"

"I want to. But I start thinking about it too much. I just met you, Logan." She had to take the risk of breaking the mood with the truth.

He nodded. "Fair enough. You say it when you're ready. But it makes me want to fuck you all the more when you call me that, Madison." His hands gentled, a muscle flexing in his jaw. "I usually don't have a problem with going slow."

She loved hearing that, loved knowing it was an effort to rein himself back. As she'd anticipated, she was already cursing his control. He wanted her to beg him to fuck her, but even when she did, he wouldn't do it. He'd sworn an oath to deny her. To give her a sense of safety and build trust. That, too, was part of how this worked.

"You said something about a movie," she said. "That might help slow things down. Unless you brought porn."

His lips curved at that, his gaze softening like melted chocolate. She could almost feel it sliding over her skin, his tongue licking it away. Okay, not helping.

"I have refreshments," she said desperately. "Popcorn, beer, soda. What can I get you?"

"Popcorn and beer," he decided. He lifted her back to her feet with that impressive upper body strength and nodded toward her shirt. "Put that back on for now. What room will we be in? I want to take a look while you get the popcorn and beer together."

"You don't want to see a mirror?"

He ran a dismissive hand through his hair. "Nope. That feels right."

"I should have put a bowl on your head."

"As I said, I'm confident in my barber's skill."

"Too late." She shrugged on her shirt, giving the knot she tied between her breasts a smart tug to underscore her mock indignation. "You blew your charm score on that one. You'll have to work on recovering your standing for the rest of the evening."

"I'll see what I can do." With a grin, he picked up his tote bag. It didn't make any noises to give her a clue of the contents. He didn't volunteer the information, leaving her with nothing to do but watch him head off toward the living room. With the long hair gone, nothing impeded a view of his wide shoulders, drawing her gaze down the taper of his back to the way denim hugged his ass and strong thighs. He stopped at the archway to the living room and glanced back at her, catching her looking. She would have flushed, but whether he noticed or not, his mind was on other things.

"The refreshments are for me, Madison. None for you right now. I have other things for you to do."

He added to the unsettling statement by giving her a deliberate look from head to toe. As she'd noted, there wasn't a whole lot of difference between wearing the shirt and not wearing it. The shirt was even more titillating, since the white fabric was so thin and stretchy, the difference between the circle of areola and the jutting tip was delineated. The hold of the knot pushed her breasts together, giving her a deep cleavage. Obeying one of those primitive instincts he'd mentioned, she stood still for him until he was done looking. He gave her an approving nod, acknowledging it, and disappeared around the corner. Glancing down, she slid her fingertips along her inner thigh and discovered damp tracks there, evidence of her arousal escaping the saturated thong.

With an erratic breath, she turned to the tasks he'd set for her. Popcorn preparation, beer retrieval. Over the sound of popcorn popping, she could hear furniture being moved, but decided to curb her curiosity. She needed time to collect herself, as much as possible. Retrieving her broom and dustpan, she collected his discarded hair, resisting the urge to keep a lock. That was crazy, moony, girl-stalker stuff.

"Madison?" He called to her, a note of impatience in his tone.

"I'm coming. Just finishing up the popcorn." She dumped it into a bowl, pulled a beer from the fridge and headed for the living room.

He'd retrieved two dining room chairs, straight wooden chairs with velvet seats. A towel from the bathroom had been folded over the cushion of one of them. The two chairs faced one another, one angled toward the television, the other the couch and the wall behind it.

"Put the popcorn and beer on the table here. Then sit down in the chair with the towel." The one facing away from the television had the towel.

"I won't get to see much of the movie this way."

"The movie's for me, not for you. *Force Ten from Navarone.* A personal favorite." He nodded to the chair. "Sit."

She did so, more than a little wary when he removed something from the tote that looked like a control box with wires and clips. He also took out a couple pairs of Velcro cuffs.

"Spread your legs so your feet are on the outside of the front chair legs."

When she complied, he dropped to one knee and removed her shiny shoes, his fingers caressing her ankles. He wrapped the cuff around one ankle, binding it to the chair leg. Then he did the same to the other. The chairs were good-sized, heavy furniture. Alice had always joked that they were meant to accommodate a team of football players. As a result, Madison's legs were splayed wide enough the damp crotch of her panties stretched over her sex. Logan unbuckled his belt, making her eyes widen, but when he stripped it off, he used it around her waist, threading the tongue into the slats of the chair and then buckling it so her backside pressed against them. Her palms were damp again, and she was experiencing that rabbitlike leap of her heart.

"Logan . . ."

"Yes, Madison?"

"I'm . . . this is making me a little afraid."

He was still on one knee, so he put a hand on hers, his fingers wrapping intimately around her thigh. "What kind of fear, Madison? Do you think I'm going to hurt you? Try to frighten you?"

"No." She shook her head. When his expression eased, it helped, seeing that mattered to him. He didn't want her to fear him. At least not that way. "I'm afraid of giving you control like this. Afraid of how it will make me feel. And that something will go wrong and get screwed up."

"That you'll screw something up," he corrected. "Or I'll disappoint you, not be everything you expect?"

That last part made her sound like a total bitch, but he didn't wait for her struggle with an answer. "All you need to do is trust me, Madison. Follow my direction. If something doesn't feel right, you tell me and we'll talk it out. I won't be able to read everything from your mind, any more than you can read everything from mine. Sometimes you have to take a breath, make an adjustment." He cupped her face. "You're under my control, but you're not powerless. Far from it. Understand?"

That was what she feared most. She always either held on too tightly and screwed it up, or let it go and trusted too much, expecting more than any one person should expect from another human being. In the end, giving up on any of it had been the only solution that worked for her.

But the handsome lines on his face and far-too-shrewd eyes told her he'd faced his own obstacles in life. He had a kindness as well as an inflexible strength on which she desperately wanted to rely. She just didn't want Logan to be yet another failed expectation, a memory of cruel apathy.

Well, she was way too far down that path tonight to turn back, right? Hell, she'd dressed up for him in this provocative outfit, had stripped for him, and was letting him tie her up. If she backed away now, it would be rude. Foolish. Yet she was flooded by utter panic, like someone with a paralyzing fear of heights stepping into the elevator of the Space Needle. The door had closed, the button for the top floor pushed, taking her beyond the point of no return.

"Madison, focus on me."

She saw him studying her with that intent look that saw so many things. "Call me Master again. Not for me. Call me that for you. See how it makes you feel."

"Master," she said, and repeated it. "Master."

It did steady her, so much it was ironically a little disturbing. It didn't stop her palms from sweating, but she was able to tune back in to what he was doing.

He squeezed her knee, showing approval, and used two more cuffs to bind her arms behind her, at the small of her back. Another strap bound them to the slats. With her waist bound, the position thrust her breasts out and he sat back on his heels, obviously enjoying that look. She moistened her lips, and his gaze flickered up to her mouth.

"My schoolgirl, all trussed up, hot and bothered, wanting to come. How wet are you, Madison?"

"P-pretty wet. Very."

He retrieved a blindfold from the tote, sitting it next to him. "I'm eventually going to put this on you, to increase your focus on the sensations. This next part will feel good, but it's not much to look at. They haven't figured out a way to make electrodes look sexy."

The word *electrode* caused her to tense up. His hands cupped her knees, then slid up her thighs, thumbs trailing the inner road, drawing her attention to how much more nerve-rich it was than the outsides of her legs. Tiny tadpoles of energy quivered ahead of his touch. When he reached the top of her thighs, he stopped. The skirt didn't cover anything, really, so short her splayed leg position pushed it up to her hipbones. She let out a shaky breath as this thumbs explored that pocket between inner thigh and outer labia. When he allowed one to slide over the crotch of the panties, she made a needy noise.

"Christ, you're soaked. How long has it been since . . ."

She flushed, mortified. It wasn't that. It wasn't. It was him. But if he thought she was some pathetic and horny charity case . . .

"Hey." He touched her chin, but she ducked her face away.

"Let me go. I don't want to do this."

"Yeah, you do. You're just embarrassed because of the way I put it. You're a beautiful, interesting woman, Madison. If you've chosen not to have a man in your bed, it's because you've dealt with too many assholes, not because they wouldn't want to be there. Men. Not assholes."

She shifted, uncertain. "I'm not sure about the electrode thing."

"Don't be afraid. It's not going to hurt, not that way." He returned his touch to her thighs, sliding a finger over the wet crotch panel, then under it. When he met her gaze, slowly pushing a knuckle into her, rotating it, she bit down on a moan.

"I think the panties are going to have to go. I can uncuff your legs, but I'd prefer to cut them off of you."

"You bought the outfit," she managed. "It's yours to do what you want with."

"Just the outfit?" Those brown eyes got darker when he demanded more control, his lips firm in a way that made every part of her shudder.

She'd set herself up for that one, she knew. Even anticipated it. "Maybe not just the outfit."

He nodded. Removing and unzipping a small canvas case from the tote, she saw surgical scissors and a scalpel.

"In case of emergency, this is so I can quickly cut someone out of ropes, fabric, whatever might be restricting them. But they come in handy for other things. Like watching a pretty girl's eyes get wide as saucers when she sees the surgical tools."

"Sadist."

"Part of the job description, more or less." Logan winked. "The same way most subs have more or less of a masochist in them."

"Are you more . . . or less?"

"Depends on what the submissive needs. Whatever you need, Madison, I'll make it happen."

That brought her attention away from the shiny objects, back to his face. "That's pretty ambitious. That could be a million things."

"No. The underlying needs are usually a few simple things. Which you can fulfill in a multitude of marvelous ways." He touched her face again, though this time he stroked her temple, her cheek, slid his hand under her hair to run a fingertip along the point of bone on the back of her skull. He stroked the valley beneath that ran between her neck bones. The entire caress sent a charge through her that made her toes curl as if he'd already turned on the electrodes.

"What . . ."

"Occipital bone. That, and the area all around it, are extremely erogenous. Focusing only on a woman's nipples and pussy is like visiting two cities and ignoring the rest of the country." He dropped his touch back between her legs, ran a finger along the crotch panel once more, the friction making her hips twitch up toward him, pulling against the belt around her waist. "This area is a whole country in itself, not merely a clit and an orifice for a man to shove his dick into."

She blinked as he picked up the scissors. He snipped the straps of the thong over her hipbones, pulled them loose so the air touched the folds between her legs. "Lift your hips as much as you can."

She did, and he leaned forward, bringing his heat and scent close as he slid his hand down her back to pluck the back thong strap free from the crevice between her buttocks. As a result, it didn't chafe when he pulled it free from the front and untangled it from the garters.

He brought the thong to his nose, inhaled her, touched his lips to the moisture. "Did you get the wettest when I was suckling your breast?"

She nodded, unable to speak at the sight of him doing something so intimate. Setting the garment aside, he trailed that magical finger down her belly, teasing her navel, then traversing the plaid skirt until he was beneath the pleats, tracing her smooth mound to her clit. He routed around that, moving down. She bit her lip as he found her moist folds, stroked.

"As I was saying," he continued in a conversational manner, "most men focus only on the clit, but the labia have so many nerves, as does the perineum, the anal rim. A woman's cunt is endlessly responsive, the way she answers to mouth, cock, hand, vibrator . . . My ultimate fantasy is to find a submissive I can give pleasure, over and over and over, until she's my slave in every way."

"You selfish bastard," she said faintly.

She startled a laugh out of him, one that was full of dark, delicious intent. He retrieved the blindfold and slid it over her head, securing it so the world became his voice and touch. She parted her lips to protest, but he anticipated her worry.

"I'm right here, Madison. Even if I'm not touching you, or talking, I won't leave you alone. Not even for a moment. While you're dependent on me like this, nothing in this world has a higher priority to me than your care. Do you understand?"

Understanding and believing were two different things. She was helpless, the blindfold underscoring it. No man had ever been so trustworthy that she'd completely rely on him for her care. But she called on what he'd said would help reassure her. "Yes, Master."

"Good girl." He teased her lips with his thumb, stroked it down her throat. "Say it again."

"Master."

She wasn't sure why it was so calming to say it, but he was right; it was. Maybe the word was a trigger, reminding her of the things she'd filed in her subconscious about him. She'd watched him with Troy, seen Troy's absolute faith when submitting to him. She'd probably been able to come as far as the blindfold without freaking out specifically because of seeing that, proof that he knew what he was doing.

Then there was Alice's letter. *Trust Logan.* She trusted Alice's love for her.

"All right. I'm attaching clips to your labia." He made sure they clamped over the inner and outer area. To do that, he had to grip her securely, and having her legs held open while he handled her with such possessive familiarity resulted in a fluid response he stopped to collect on his fingers.

"You taste like the best kind of sin, Madison."

She went hot all over, thinking of him putting his fingers in his mouth. The wires attached to the clips were light lines of pressure on her thighs. The clips held her firmly, but not in an uncomfortable way. Her fingers curled in her bonds, her palms beginning to moisten again. "You're sure it doesn't hurt?"

"I've done it to myself. On some of my most sensitive parts." His voice held humor. "To be sure. The initial static startles you, but it's because you're anticipating shock. Another day I'll use a violet wand on you. You'll enjoy the way the color plays over your skin."

Her tongue was dry from repeated swallowing. She rubbed her lips together, found no moisture there. A moment later, when he put a wet, folded paper towel to them, a hard twist happened below her breastbone. He'd said he'd pay attention, that her care was the most important thing to her. But those were words. This wasn't.

"Part your lips," he ordered, and when she did, he dripped some cool water onto her tongue, ran the towel over her lips, dampening them. "There you go."

He returned to what he was doing and she listened to him shift, felt him make adjustments to the clips, doing other things she could only imagine.

"When you were talking about your ultimate fantasy . . ." she ventured, "what is it you really want? From . . . a submissive. The one you want to keep. The only one you'll let in your bed."

She shouldn't have put it that way, because it suggested that she was paying way too much attention to everything he said and did. He didn't respond right away, though. She waited, wondering if he would. She also wondered at how she waited on him, what her docility said about her, her acceptance of his total control over her, even this conversation. Before she walked into Logan's store, she'd rejected giving up control of anything. Even now, she was uncomfortably aware that if anyone other than Logan were trying this with her, she'd zap them with one of those wands he mentioned on full voltage. Just sitting here, she'd run this scenario through her mind with every one of her past relationships, even a few fantasy men, acquaintances she'd seen at a distance, as well as some popular actors. Nope, none of them worked.

It was him. Only him. She was smart enough to know that was the scariest thing about all of this, no matter her body's reaction to electrodes or being hung by her heels from the ceiling light. She had no confidence in her judgment. Just because he was living up to everything she wanted from a man, things she hadn't even known she wanted—or yes, maybe she had, deep down, she'd admit that—didn't mean that was what Logan was.

"I'm not going to tell you what I want from a submissive, Madison. All you need to know is that I'm doing exactly what I want to do to you. Your only concern is what I order you to do. You have no other expectations, nothing you need to anticipate. Only the here and now and what I tell you. Understand?"

It could be taken in an offensive way, kind of a *shut up bitch and do what I tell you* response, except everything he'd done so far tonight had brought her pleasure. But she still wanted to know what she could do for him that no other sub could do. Or did she? What if she couldn't do it? Or worse, if she found out any sub compliant enough could fulfill what he wanted?

One minute she was shying away from the idea of this being more than a training session; the next she was wishing she had concrete proof it was. Maybe she needed to say it to herself. *Shut up bitch and let it be what it is.* But her mind didn't obey her the way it did Logan.

"I'm turning on the electrodes now," he interrupted her thoughts. "While I watch the movie, I'm going to enjoy looking at you, all tied up, every part accessible for me to touch, however, whenever I want.

You're helpless and all mine right now. Anything I want to do, I can. Your only job is to let me know if anything hurts the wrong kind of way. All right?"

She bobbed her head, a quick jerk. She didn't have the bravery to call him Master this time, her mind fragmented over her internal worries. She was also kind of stressing about what that electric current was going to be like. Maybe he had a much higher tolerance for pain than she did. Yes, he'd stop if she said it was hurting, but that might be after a hell of a shock.

She heard him go put in his movie choice; then he settled with a creak into the chair facing hers. His calves pressed against her ankles as he stretched out his legs on either side of her chair. The movie company theme music started, the vibration of the volume coming through the thin stockings over the soles of her feet.

She jumped at the first jolt of the electrical current, but he was right; her reaction was caused by anticipation, not discomfort. The low-level sensation sort of stung, but as the pattern built, it also sent tiny squiggles of sensation up the inside of her cunt and into the base of her clit.

"Ohh . . ." She flexed against her bonds, and her movement enhanced the crosscurrent. It was a flowing sensation, across the network of nerves in all those slick tissues.

"Yeah, we'll keep it on this program. It goes through a whole routine of patterns. I want to see the ones that get you worked up the most."

Her legs were spread wide enough they brushed his jeans on either side. He shifted, and she lost that contact, but she didn't have time to be unhappy about it. He bent forward, put gentle, moist lips over her right nipple, the barrier of cloth heated by his breath. As he turned his head to rub his jaw over her other breast, his hair brushed the generously exposed cleavage.

"I like not having that damn hair getting in my way. Yours, though, I like long. Gives me something to wrap my hands around when I fuck you."

The electrical current changed, became more of a stroking, back and forth, skittering among all those nerve endings like a continuous ping-pong game.

She was moaning as he suckled her, so very tenderly, through the thin cloth of the shirt. He moved to the cleavage, running his tongue in the channel between her compressed breasts and playing there, making it impossible not to imagine him doing the same lower down. Then he shifted to the other nipple, got it aching for more, before he sat back, leaving her panting and squirming.

"A little higher intensity, I think."

She let out a cry as the current strengthened. In the first moment it stung, but then she adjusted to it. Her hips jerked with the stimulation, fingers clamping around the slats of the chair.

Yes, in a clinical way, the sheer physical manipulation could arouse her, no different from the solo use of her vibrator, but there were far more elements to this scenario, stoking her to higher levels than she'd experienced with something battery-operated. And it wasn't just the electrodes doing it.

She was wearing an outfit he'd ordered her to wear, was bound to a chair so he could watch her, indulge his own pleasure. The detachment he was demonstrating by watching the movie intensified her reaction, though she couldn't explain why. All of it ostensibly about him, yet in an amazing, confusing way one of the most erotic things she'd ever encountered. He'd been right; it wouldn't have mattered if he'd brought her favorite movie of all time. She wouldn't have heard a word of it.

Her hips couldn't stop twitching, because that electrical current had a gradual, building effect. Her upper body got involved, a sinuous roll. She dropped her head back and brought it back down, all of her as restless as if a tongue was stroking her between her legs, a hugely intense response blooming in her lower body and spreading out.

He'd been eating his popcorn; she could hear him crunching.

Then he set the bowl on the side table. His palms molded around her breasts, his thumbs teasing over her nipples. She cried out, a near scream at that light touch.

"Ssshh. You'll interrupt the movie, baby. Be quiet, or I'll gag you."

She bit back on the moans, the whimpers, but it was so hard. The effort made things even more intense, which she was sure was his plan.

Behind her she heard dialogue, gunfire, seventies theme music . . . it all rolled into one blur of white noise. Her mind became like a video camera mounted in the corner of her living room, imagining what this looked like, a man sprawled out watching a movie, drinking beer—she smelled the faint flavor of hops from where he'd had his mouth on her breast—while she sat there, tied up, vulnerable, so turned on she couldn't stop herself from making these tiny cries and moans, whimpers that sounded a lot like pleas.

"Can't help being a bad girl, can you?"

Though she tried to protest, pull her head away, he coaxed open her mouth with unrelenting fingers, pushing a rubber phallic-shaped object into it. The thick and short gag held down her tongue and stretched her jaw. He buckled it around her head, caressing her jaw with his strong hands, soothing her. Imagining it like his cock in her mouth had her tonguing it, suckling it, her throat working before she was even cognizant of doing such a shameless thing.

"Christ, you can kill a man." His voice was a near growl, yet his hands left her. The gag muffled her wail of protest. He moved out of the chair and she heard him sink down on the nearby couch. Start eating the popcorn again. "There now. Don't want you interrupting the movie at a good part."

She would have called him a bastard, except for the gag and the undisguised rough lust in his voice.

It went on for what seemed like half the movie, well over an hour. She came so close to climax, so many times, but he was always aware of where she was at, that crazy combination of intense attention and seeming disinterest. The electric pulses died down or changed each time she was almost there. She wriggled, squirmed. At a certain point, the pleasurable stress brought forth tears.

When she was whimpering against the gag like a baby, unable to stop her continuous pleading, he turned down the volume, to the point she could hear her ceiling fan rotating. He came back to his chair, his legs against her again. That simple contact was enough to make her shudder. Unbuckling the gag, he slid it free, wiping the saliva around her lips, her chin, with a cloth. He gave her a few sips of water, then rose. She heard his chair scrape the wood floor as he moved it behind her. Her chair adjusted beneath her, and she guessed he'd hooked a foot in the slats beneath to bring her closer. He was sitting right behind her now.

"You asked me about my fantasies, Madison, but what I want to know are yours. Tell me. In your shop all day, surrounded by all those possibilities, what one fantasy belongs to you?" His voice was a mesmerizing purr. "When you're in your bed alone, touching yourself, wanting to give yourself an orgasm, what do you imagine the most often? Pretend you're there now, and my voice is your own mind. There's no wrong answer, no judgment."

Her mind was going in a hundred different directions. She could barely think. As his fingers slid along her nape, teasing that bone, she trembled, hard. Before that touch, her mind gave way, following the track he set for it, no resistance.

"I imagine . . . when I spread my legs, it's someone else spreading them, holding them down while he does . . . oral sex."

He pressed against her back, inner thighs brushing her hips. Sliding an arm around her, he put his knuckle against her pussy again. It interrupted the current with a startling quick shock, a light burn. She was so slick, it was easy to imagine his finger was a tongue. She jerked against the intimate caress, the play of that clever digit.

"Are you in your bedroom or somewhere else?"

"I'm in . . . his bedroom. He . . . bought me." She blurted it out, whispered the rest. "Like at an auction."

"What kind of auction? Present day, or a long time ago? Here, or in a desert somewhere?"

She'd never told anyone about this fantasy. It was shameful, far beyond political correctness, the dictates of feminism . . . It was a deep dark secret, yet she found herself speaking out in the dark, as if telling the devil himself what her greatest temptations were.

"It's . . . here, now. One of those auctions where sheikhs buy virgins, like the *Taken* movie. Only we weren't kidnapped. We were raised, groomed to become someone's sex slave. Like *Story of O.*" She gave a desperate half laugh. "It's like a dream, a mish-mash of things."

"That's fine. It's your fantasy. You can make it fit your own desires. What are you wearing at the auction?"

"Just a thong and a collar, attached by thin chains to nipple clamps, a clamp . . . down there."

"On your clitoris, or labia?"

"Clitoris. The chains are caught in the back . . . with a padlock. Before the auction, men come by, lift you to your knees by the chains, examine you."

"Rough men, men who frighten you, make you worry they'll be the one who buys you."

She nodded.

"So is it a sheikh who buys you?"

She shook her head, then couldn't stop, kept shaking it. She made an inarticulate plea and he had his hand under her hair, digging into a handful of it, holding her fast. "Ssshh," he said firmly. "Be still. Focus. Madison, I'm ordering you to be still. Contain it, hold in the arousal, let it get more intense that way."

It was as difficult as being told she had to do fifty more ab crunches at a fitness class, but she did it, because he'd commanded it.

"You haven't answered my question. Is it a sheikh?"

"It's a soldier. He doesn't fit in. The others look at him, aren't sure why he's there. He's high-ranked, like special ops. I don't know much about the military."

"Again, doesn't matter. Your fantasy. What's he wearing?"

"A dress uniform, very intimidating. He wants his own personal slave. The way he looks at me, I know I'm the one he wants."

"Are you frightened of him?"

"Yes." She shifted. "But during the auction, the way he looks at me . . . I can't imagine belonging to anyone else."

"Like he knows you'll be his, no matter who he has to kill to get you."

She shivered at the very real threat, the determination in the masculine voice. She could hear it in her fantasy.

"How do you feel, when he looks at you that way?"

"Like I'd do anything to please him," she whispered. "He looks stern, a little cruel . . ."

Was she really doing this? Telling it as if it was real, as if she was playing make-believe with Alice and they were teenagers? Only they'd never played make-believe like this. Not together.

"He's making you understand that he's in charge, that you won't manipulate him. That you're his slave; he's not yours. As long as you follow his rules, you're safe, within the structure he's set. There's a big difference between a prison and a fortress. What do you do when they bring you to him, after the auction?"

"I . . . go to my knees while he's holding the chain attached to my collar. It's heavy. It was attached to a concrete ball. We wouldn't run, we were trained for this, but—"

"But everything reinforces that you're not free, your choices are not your own."

Why was she finding this so incredibly arousing? She cried out as he removed his finger and the current went back to the stroking pattern. Another tear leaked out of the corner of her eye as her hips worked. She couldn't come, it wasn't strong enough for that, just enough to drive her even more insane.

Every word she spoke was something she'd never said to anyone. But in darkness, all secrets were kept, right? There was no shame.

"I bend and kiss his foot, and he gives me enough slack to let me do it. That's when I know . . . that I really belong to him. Not just as a piece of property. He wants me, not any slave. Or I hope."

"As I said, the underlying needs are always simple." His breath teased her skin. "Tell me about his shoe."

"Polished, slick. I can smell the shoe polish he uses. Oil and smoke, like a gun."

"When he takes you home, what do you imagine him doing first?"

"He puts me in his tub, scrubs off the hands of all the other men who touched me. He tells me that's why he's doing it, why he's doing it himself."

"You're his prize. His possession. His treasure."

"Yes." She was whispering every word now. Those tears kept coming. "He commands me not to speak. But I'm lost in the way his hands feel. He tells me it's okay for me to look at him. They train us not to lift our gazes except when ordered to do so. So I watch his face, his mouth . . . like I've been given a Christmas present. At one point I forget myself, reach out to touch it. He catches my hand before I can do that, ties my wrists to a bar in the tub until he's done. Then he unties me, carries me to the bed."

"What does he do then?"

She hesitated. Then she shrieked as the current shot up, a quick, hard sting, setting her tissues on fire. "Stop . . . help . . . Logan . . ."

It eased off, leaving her heart racing, her hips still jerking at the sensations. She'd been on the cusp of climax for so long, she knew she couldn't go there, but she'd never been so close and held in such stasis. Imprisoned by his will.

"You'll answer my questions right when I ask them, Madison. No thinking or pausing. What does he do then?"

"He examines all of me, every inch of skin, every crevice. Then he goes down on me."

"He tastes your pussy, licks your clit and you squirm under his hands. But he's much stronger than you, isn't he?"

She nodded. He was in her head, seeing it as she was seeing it. It didn't surprise her to find him there. "He makes me hold on to the bedrails, and then . . . he's chained my wrists there. The manacles are lined inside, soft, but heavy steel on the outside. He says I'll wear them when I sleep or whenever he wants to fuck me. He tells me he's . . . eventually he's going to invite the men in his unit in to watch and . . . if I come too soon, it will prove I want . . . all of them."

"He'll give you to them, won't he?" His mouth was at her ear again, voice now with a touch of a growl to it. "What does he say?"

"He has his mouth on me and he says . . . this is my c-cunt, and I can do whatever I want with it, can't I? I say, 'Yes sir,' because I want to do whatever he wants me to do, even fuck his friends. I know he'll punish me for getting wet when that happens, but I'll be wet because of him watching. Because I'm serving him."

"Do you imagine it, with his friends?"

She whimpered again as his finger trailed down her carotid. "Different sizes, pushing into me. Different hands on my body, different ways of touching me. Then they get impatient, and it's more than one at once . . . one is sucking on my nipples, leaning over my face, as another is inside me. Another . . . they get cruel, one slides a knife down my stomach, nicks me with the blade and tells me I have to stay still, no matter what they do to me . . . He's not touching me, my Master, but I know he's watching. I want to please him."

"Can you see, or have they blindfolded you, like this?" He touched the mask over her eyes, stroking it so she felt the pressure of his fingers.

"Yes. They keep me gagged, except when one of them is straddling my face, making me take his cock in my mouth."

"While another is fucking you?"

She took a shuddering breath. "Yes."

"What do you smell, Madison?"

"Them. Different men. They're burning candles, so they can drip wax on me, bring the flame close to my skin, make me think they're

going to burn me. I hear the clink of their dog tags as they're pushing into me, feel their bodies against me. Ohh . . ."

She dropped her head back on her shoulders, panted harder.
Logan's hands closed over her straining shoulders. "God . . ." Now,
no matter how she moved her hips, it seemed to be increasing the
sensations. And still the climax was out of reach. She wanted to be
touched. She could imagine her soldier's fingers thrusting into her,
his tongue . . . after it was all over, his cock slamming inside her,
his harsh command for her to spread wider, take him deep, so he
could . . .

". . . brand the others away with his come." Holy crap, she'd said
it aloud.

"What happens when it's all over?" Logan's voice was stern, like
she'd imagine her soldier's to be.

"He's back again, and they're all gone. I know his scent. He's
holding me, calling me . . ." She was still too aware of her surroundings and self to say it out loud, but then Logan wrapped his fingers
around her throat, tilting her head back to caress her windpipe, put
his mouth against that churning artery.

"Tell me, Madison. Speak the words. Tell me what you want me
to call you."

"His. His sweet cunt, his devoted slave, his treasure."

"You never doubt his care for you, the fact you belong to him.
There's no uncertainty, no loneliness, no fear. That ownership is the
ultimate sense of security, isn't it?"

She closed her eyes under the blindfold as he stroked her throat
some more. She made a sound of intense pleasure as he released her
arms, loosened the belt around her waist. He drew her to her feet,
which set off a whole other level of stimulation through the clips,
such that she was a puppet with no coordination, driven by the current coming through those lines. It didn't matter. He had her, the
belt replaced by his strong arm as he put himself behind her in the
chair, bringing her back down on his lap, with her still facing out-

ward. His other hand settled on her forehead, pushing her head back on his shoulder. All the way back so if the blindfold were gone she'd be staring at the ceiling, held by him like a doll.

"Logan . . ." she gasped. She couldn't control anything. "Help . . ."

"Let it happen. Give it all to me. You don't get to hold anything back. It's all mine."

He broke the current, reaching down to press into her pussy once more, collect that fluid on a finger, withdraw it. When he painted it on her lips, she smelled herself.

"Lick yourself off of me."

She did, tiny, frantic motions of her tongue, then he cupped her jaw, turned her head and took over with a full, openmouthed kiss, plunging his tongue deep as she quivered and convulsed from all the stimulation he was throwing at her.

The climax started building like a wave in her lower belly, like before, only this time it went so high, it scared her. It was going to make her head explode. It was crazy, she wanted it like she'd never wanted anything, but she was afraid to go over alone. She was calling his name, and he answered.

In those final few escalations, before the wave crashed over her, he had his hands on her face, her waist, his mouth against her cheekbone, breathing the words she needed to hear.

"I'm here, Madison. Go over, baby. I'll hold on to you."

She screamed herself hoarse, fought the climax because that was the nature of it, so excruciating there was no choice but to struggle against it, a base survival instinct that only fueled it to greater levels. At a certain point, he cut the connection, because his hand was there instead, rubbing her, giving her a critical human contact that had her twining all her emotions around that one touch, binding herself to him in every way she could, to give her something to hold on to during the fall.

It was ruthless and powerful, much like him, but he held her through all of it, gave her the last ounce of sensation. When she was done, she was limp in the bonds, her vocal cords raw, her body weak as if she'd been drained of every ounce of energy. She wanted free, needed to be free, but only so she could crawl into him, be held in a different kind of binding. One made of flesh. He understood, for when he removed the clips and freed her legs, he scooped her up, rose and took them to the couch, settling down into the deep cushions with her in his lap. He tugged the blindfold loose, though she kept her eyes closed. He let her wrap her arms around his neck, bury her face in his chest and sob for breath, her body trembling as he murmured to her, stroked her, rocked her.

"Easy. I have you. I'm right here."

It took a while for everything to settle. She might even have dozed off, because when she surfaced, she realized the TV volume was higher. He was taking a sip of his beer, holding her in one arm as her body lay against his, molded against every plane. When he put down the beer, he stroked her hip, the length of her thigh, a pleasurably possessive gesture.

"You've thought a lot about that fantasy," he said. "Developed the story over time."

"Yes." She'd crafted the whole scenario over a variety of lonely masturbation sessions. She wasn't going to share that, but she supposed he'd already guessed it. "Sometimes I fell asleep thinking about . . . less sexual things. He marries me, and yet I'm always his slave behind closed doors. Caring for his house, his clothes . . . but not like . . ."

She obviously was still too caught up in sensation, for her to say such foolish, easy-to-misinterpret things. But Logan didn't laugh at her.

"Not like some asshole who expects you to pick up after him," he finished. "That's different."

She nodded, relieved that he understood. He kept holding her, soothing her. Caring for her. "Why did you . . ."

"Hmm?"

"Why did you sit behind me? I was still blindfolded."

"Sitting where you're aware of me but I'm out of your line of sight, whether blindfolded or not, makes you more comfortable about speaking the deepest things in your head." He dropped a kiss on her temple. "Your body language becomes less self-conscious as well. Non-verbal cues give me as much as your words."

He wasn't the only one who could read non-verbal cues. One of the sensations adding to the pleasurable aftershocks was the enormous erection against her ass. Even now, it was still substantially hard enough to catch her attention. He'd just given her the climax of her life. She wanted to give back. If only she could find the energy to move.

His arm banded around her as she started to shift. "Sssshh. Stay still, Madison. We're at one of the best parts of the movie."

"How would you like to watch the best part while I'm going down on you?"

When he stilled, she put her mouth at the base of his throat, teasing the pocket between his collarbones with her tongue. A bit lethargically, but her motive was clear.

Tangling his hand in her hair, he tipped her head back. She'd finally opened her eyes, but when she looked into his face, saw the heat of lust there, his undeniable, total absorption in her, she remembered what she'd said in her fantasy—gazing upon his face was like being given a Christmas present.

"Getting sucked off by your sweet mouth while I'm enjoying my favorite movie and beer is a guy fantasy come true. But not tonight. Tonight is about something different. Don't ask me what. Just stay quiet and be still."

"But what if I want that? What . . ."

She couldn't believe she could be this forward, but after that climax, was there really any physical realm that she could be shy about? When she pulled out of this weird post-climactic state where Logan had convinced her she could be as open and vulnerable as she wanted, she'd no doubt be mortified, trying to re-craft all her shields. She wanted to take advantage of this state while she could hold on to it.

She curled her fingers around his hand, brought it down her body until it was between her legs, against all that slick moisture from her climax, but more than that. When she pressed his fingers against her, her clit was still flush and full. Through the pressure, he should be able to feel what she felt, the urgent pulse. Yes, she'd just had a climax over the moon, but she was still orbiting. She wanted, needed more.

She met his gaze. "Let me do it. Please."

She wanted to be on her knees for him. She couldn't believe how strong the desire was. When she pushed up out of his lap this time, he let her. Fortunately for her wobbly legs, it wasn't far to go to slide into the opening between his legs and kneel on the rug below. Her fingers clasped his splayed thighs for balance, but she stopped there, waiting, staring up at him. He hadn't said yes yet. She would beg, coax, but there was a line she wouldn't cross to push her suit. A true sign of what she'd revealed about herself tonight, wasn't it?

Recognizing it, diabolically willing to impregnate the moment with even more sexual tension, he'd laid a deceptively casual hand on his inner thigh. Now he lifted the beer in the other, taking a swallow, his attention on the TV screen. She remembered how he'd made Troy wait while he touched her face, and her body responded as Troy had at the anticipation, a low-level coil of need.

She put her mouth on the hand he had on his thigh, tiny touches of her tongue to his knuckles, kissing and tasting his skin. When he turned his fingers over, pushed his thumb into her mouth, she sucked on it, making it clear what she could do for him. His other fingers stroked her throat, a light touch like meadow grass against skin.

Then, victory. He put the beer down, and moved to open his jeans. He slipped the top button, pushed down the zipper and reached in to free himself from the garment beneath. Her lips parted, breath shallow as he revealed his cock, stretching it out full length before her. It had a nice thick steak-and-potatoes meatiness to it. Saliva pooled in her mouth, telling her she wanted that organ stretching her mouth, pushing into the back of her throat. She'd savor every excruciating inch of it.

Curling his fingers in her hair, he guided her to it. As she opened her mouth further to take his girth and length, he pushed her down on it slow. She'd put both her hands on his thighs, but now she shifted them to grip his base, her thumbs resting on the heavy nest of testicles still inside his jeans. He wasn't going to strip them off, give her every inch of his flesh the way he'd compelled her to offer hers. Not tonight. But for now, this was enough.

She remembered her earlier thoughts, about loving to give head, the way it made her feel, as though she was servicing a lover. Servicing . . . her Master. She let herself say it in her head, accept how much she wanted to think of it that way. For the first time in her life, there were no questions or doubts, no games to play that would drain her energy. Logan accepted this side of her, cultivated it, drew it out. He was in charge. She wasn't trying to talk him into something he didn't want to do, or worried what he'd think of this side of her. He'd loosened the grip of her control-freak claws and made her believe that, at least tonight, this might turn out okay.

As a result, the need to submit was surging up far stronger than she'd ever allowed herself to experience it before. It was the difference between a high school crush and first mature relationship. A sad thought, given her age and track record of relationships, but right now the truth didn't hurt as much. There was no room for the sting of failure or embarrassment when her mind was committed to one purpose. Pleasing her Master.

She enjoyed having him in her mouth, and devoted every scrap of energy she had left to giving him as much pleasure as she could. His thighs flexed, his hips pushing up to shove deeper into her mouth as his movements began to simulate the act that had her own hips shifting restlessly against her calves. Sex was so casual now, something people often decided to do on a first date. But nothing felt casual with Logan. He'd even said that wasn't going to happen tonight, no matter what she did, underscoring that it had significance. It had to be earned.

As a result, she put all her effort into teasing him into a higher and higher state of arousal, reveling in the bruising grip of his hand as it became even more aggressive, pushing her down on him. His breath rasped, his body jerking as he started to tip over that edge. She made an encouraging plea against his cock and closed her eyes, triumphant, when that vein pumped under her grip, a harsh groan tearing from his lips.

He came, jetting to the back of her throat, and she sucked, licked, swallowed, not allowing herself to flag, stimulating him to the very end. Until his grip tightened for different reasons, telling her to ease off.

As she obeyed, slowing her pace, he released her hair to stroke it. There was an initial clumsiness to his movements as he had to find coordination again. It felt good that way, more balanced. It also felt good when, after tucking himself back into his jeans, he lifted her under the arms and put her back into his lap. He pressed his jaw against her temple as she curled her hands in his shirt. Picking up the remote, he made a grumbling noise at her.

"Now I'm going to have to go back three scenes. I lost my place, thanks to you."

She snuffled a laugh against him, and he squeezed her. Quiet ensued as they both recovered, as she listened to the thunder of his heart go back to a steady thump, thump and she tasted him on her lips, in her throat.

"I was jealous of her," she said softly.

The room went quiet as he hit mute. He didn't say anything, though, just kept stroking her hair. Giving her the courage to say out loud what she'd only said to herself.

"I was hurting, and jealous, and I couldn't be around someone so loving when all the love had dried up inside me. I don't think I'll ever stop regretting that. Two years passed in a blink, like no time at all. I thought there'd be time, you know. If I'd been here more often . . ." The hard truth was bitter in her mouth. "I'm eaten up by the idea of her dealing with this without me, when I should have been here. Sometimes I'm so angry at her, as if she hid the truth from me to get back at me for withdrawing from her. Isn't that the most petty thing ever? Because she never stopped being Alice during those months. She sent me birthday gifts, e-mails, texts, called faithfully every week, no matter how bitchy I was with her. That made me angry, too. God . . . sometimes I wished she would stop contacting me at all so it wouldn't all feel so one-sided. I was so fucking stupid."

That horrible sense of inadequacy welled up like the sticky frustration of a hot, humid day, regret that could never be purged. She was too vulnerable to its power right now, and yet when she tried to push away, give herself some space, Logan merely flexed his arms around her, keeping her in place.

"Ssh," he said. "No. You're not going into that spot in your head. There'll be a time and place to clean out that room, but it's not tonight. Let it go for now, Madison. She loved you, and you loved her, and sometimes love is difficult. That's all. Breathe. Breathe. Focus on what I want from you right now. Tell me what you told me a few minutes ago. Tell me how you saw yourself."

She breathed, twitched, breathed some more. For a moment, that wave of tangled, angry emotions surged back up again, making her struggle once more, but his arms, his inflexible will, were stronger than hers. She found it was a relief beyond measure.

"I was yours," she said at last. A bare whisper.

"Yeah." He eased his hold as she let herself relax, one tense muscle at a time. "It quieted the voices, didn't it? The bad emotions, the good, it all evened out, like a boat going from chop to a smooth current?"

It was a good description. "How . . . does it do that?"

"A lot of subs are worriers. OCD types, overly analytical. They get mired in their emotions. You ever try to meditate?"

She made a face. "Alice would meditate like she was on the moon, floating through space, and I'd peek at her through my lashes, wondering how she could do that. All while wishing I could move so my knees and back would stop their primal screaming."

His lips curved at that. "For someone with your personality, subspace is your form of meditation."

When her brow creased, he shifted beneath her, adjusting her position on his lap so they were both more comfortable. "When I was in the Army, we went into a lot of hairy situations. Saw things that were hard to see. Afterward, each guy had to figure out a way to deal with it. Everyone copes differently, but the common theme is finding a way to still the voices. There are good ways and bad ways to do that. I found that, no matter where I was, there would always be some quiet place, even if it didn't seem that way. The middle of a mall can be a quiet place. The cushion around you is the key, whether that cushion is anonymity or someone's arms."

He tightened them again, a reminder. "I'd find a patch of woods behind a shack where we were holing up. Or it would be first thing in the morning in the desert, that twilight moment right before the sun starts coming up to heat the sand. I could stand in those places, those moments, shut everything else down and feel how the world was so much vaster than my petty shit or even what had us all there.

Whatever big Thing is out there, knows all of it. And it's okay, because when you find that quiet place, you know it's okay, too. Or how to make it better."

He touched her face. "Alice knew, Madison. She hurt for you, prayed for you. The one thing she wanted me to make absolutely sure you knew was that she *never* doubted your love for her. Never. Sometimes she was mad at you, too, for not pulling your head out of your ass. And at herself, for not being able to figure out how best to help you. That's the bitch about getting trapped in our own pain. We tend to forget other people are dealing with their day-to-day shit at the same time. On first look, maybe that makes you feel like crap, but I'm thinking it might make it a little better, too, when you think about it from the right place. She never lost that connection, but more importantly, she never thought you had, either. She knew you loved her. She had no doubt at all when she called you that you would come."

"Crap." She tried to brush away the tears that escaped from her eyes, but he beat her to it, his fingertips gentle on her face. "But I was too late."

"No. Because here you are, reconnecting with her again. She's as close as the nearest memory."

Madison swallowed. "I'm so glad she had you, Logan. But I also hate you for it in a way. A kind of projected self-loathing, if that makes sense."

"Yeah." He rubbed her back. "You have a lot of regret. Guilt. Things that weigh you down, make it hard for you to trust yourself. It makes it difficult for you to let go, except when you're pushed. Hard."

She sighed, gave him a rueful look. "Is that how you're justifying your sadistic side, Mr. Scott?"

"Mr. Scott. I like that." He gave her a wicked grin, but he stroked her jaw. "That night with Troy, I showed you what it's like to watch another give up control. You were so eager and absorbed, I couldn't resist pulling you into it. Tonight I showed you how it feels with no intermediary, when you give me your trust. But you haven't learned about pain. Where it can take you, what it can show you, about yourself. What it can open up."

When Logan had been whipping Troy with the strap, the young man had shuddered against her, his cock hard and eager against her thigh, his eyes glazed, as if he'd been catapulted to a perfect place. Being bound and blindfolded tonight had stilled those voices, as Logan said. Could she trust him enough to take her to such an extreme step? Maybe not, but she trusted him enough to ask the next question, tentatively crack the door.

"I'm afraid to ask, but what did you have in mind?"

"I think you know what I have in mind, just as I think it's best for me not to give you all the details of it."

"Do I get a safe word? Like *Stop that, you fucking bastard?*"

His eyes sparkled. "That's a mouthful. Maybe something simpler. *Stop* isn't useful, because people in the throes of pleasure tend to say things like *Stop, Help, God Help Me, Save Me, God, God, God . . .* etc."

"So *God* isn't a great safe word. Check." She thought about it. "Okay. *Alice.*"

He lifted his hand to trace the valley between her breasts, hooking the knot of the thin white shirt. "All right. *Alice* it is. Next Friday."

"You like Fridays."

"We're wired to be more open to new experiences at the end of the typical workweek, even if that's not the end of our unique work week. We carry a higher level of adrenaline on Friday nights. A larger sense of adventure."

She considered it. "Can we hold off setting a date for it, for now? I want to think about it some more."

"Sometimes thinking too much isn't a good thing."

"Neither is bullying."

He lifted both hands, giving her a wink. "I wouldn't dream of it."

She gave him a disparaging look. "You know exactly how intimidating you are. You aren't afraid to throw your weight around."

"And you're not afraid to stand up to it. I approve of that." He sobered, giving the tail of the knot on her shirt a little tug. "A healthy sub—hell, a healthy *person*—is one who can stand up for herself when the moment calls for it. Even if my top responsibility is to protect you while you're under my care, you never give up the responsibility to care for yourself. When you assert yourself to me, you're verifying that you have that capacity. That actually helps a Dom, relieves some of the pressure. A submissive who will let you kill her just to please you is a lot of damn work to protect."

"Are there ones like that? Is that healthy?"

"It depends. If they're like that even in a day-to-day, nonsession state, yeah, it can be a problem with self-esteem and identity. If they get like that in subspace, that's a different matter. Every sub has the ability to lose herself during that part. Depending on her frame of mind and the ability of the Dom."

A couple weeks ago, she might not have been able to comprehend such a thing. But the way she'd found herself tied to Troy, the point to which Logan had taken her tonight, where there was nothing in her mind at all but his demands, her own desires . . . it was way easier to imagine and understand. It was also very unsettling.

"I really want to think about the pain thing longer," she said firmly. "I think it would help if . . ."

No, don't go down that road. "Never mind."

She looked down at her hands, but he gripped her chin, drew her face up. He had a way of knowing when she didn't want to meet his gaze, and always pushed her to do so. Damn Dom. She almost smiled, wondered at the wistful twist in her chest at the thought, at using Alice's name as the safe word. At all of it.

"I want to know more about you," she said. "To torture myself, apparently. Where you live, what you do when you're not tying up people in your back room, or doing whip demos. I don't want you to be larger than life, Logan." Even though he obviously was.

"Why would that torture you?"

She'd known he was going to ask, which was why she shouldn't have brought it up. When she looked down this time, he let her, probably realizing it was the only way she was going to get the words out.

"Because you're a fantasy. That's the way I've been treating all this. That's why it's all going so well. We're both getting off from it, and why can't I leave it at that? I'm never happy walking on the street. I always want to know what lies below it, and it's always a sewer."

He blinked. "Wow. We really need that pain session. I'm tempted to start on it right now, whacking your ass until you cry."

She would have chuckled, but he wasn't smiling. He caught her chin in his fingers, a much stronger grip this time. "If I want to get off, I can go home and watch porn. The best fantasy is grounded in reality, Madison. I don't want any other kind."

"I'm not sure if I'm that brave. Or mature enough."

"Yes, you are. Ask me one question about myself, just one. And no, I do not have a tattoo on my ass."

She summoned a smile, but her fingers curled in his shirtfront. One slipped beneath the opening between buttons and tangled in chest hair. The more she tried to think of a question, the more her fingers dug into him, the bigger the knot in her throat became. She'd brought up the subject herself, and now she couldn't follow it through, even with his encouragement. What a coward she was.

"I don't think I can, Logan." She literally couldn't. "I'm not trying to be insulting. I'm just not ready. Let's . . . let's keep it a fantasy awhile longer, okay? Please?"

He studied her for a long time, enough to make her worried he would try to push her, but then he shifted her so she was straddling him in the long white stockings and little plaid skirt, which put her breasts in the thin white top right in front of his face. He cupped them, running his fingers over the nipples. Her thigh muscles tightened, the ache in her throat turning to something else.

"All right. But if we're sticking with fantasies tonight, we're going with one of mine."

She moistened her lips at the look in his eye. Remarkably, she could feel him hardening beneath her. The man had stamina, though it seemed to be calling the same response from her, because she had to suppress the desire to rub her bare pussy against that tempting iron. "I'm here to serve, Master."

What she'd intended as a tease didn't feel that way at all under that penetrating look. "I want my schoolgirl to take off her top. I'm going to suck on her nipples until she's squirming her cute ass on my lap and begging me for my cock. Until I'm so hard I've got to fuck her or die, and she's so wet, she'd slide onto me like melted butter. When she begs me for my cock, though, I'm going to make her rub harder, until she comes against my jeans. Does that fantasy work for you?"

"No objections," she said in a thick voice. She saw no censure in his gaze, but she did have a peculiar emptiness, now that he'd turned away from the other, at her behest. The vagaries of the female mind, disappointed when she was given exactly what she requested.

"Then open your top, Madison. Show me my fantasy."

She tried to unknot it, and fumbled. He took over for her, undoing it, sliding the cloth out of the way, but leaving it on her shoulders. Giving her an enigmatic look, he put his arm around her, his palm on her buttock, and slid her much closer. It fitted her solidly over his length, making her shudder. He nuzzled both breasts with his mouth, his stubbled jaw, his heated breath, and her hands landed on his shoulders.

"Please . . . will you take off your shirt?"

He'd refused her earlier, but she hoped he wouldn't this time.

She was starting to understand the power of denial, how it could drive things higher, but maybe he understood it was a first step to what she'd talked about. Though she might not have the courage to ask him questions about himself, she wanted closer to him, at least physically.

He let go of her to open the shirt, shrug out of it. As he did, he had to lean forward to pull it loose from the back of his jeans. When he did, the cloth was already off of one broad shoulder. She placed her lips there, then her cheek, rubbing. He stilled, his other arm going around her back to hold her in the intimate pose as he wrestled the rest of the shirt loose, then it was both arms holding her, bare skin to bare skin. She let out a little sigh of painful joy. "Thank you."

His chest hair was rough against her breasts, but she liked that. When she drew back at last, her gaze slid down the pectorals, flat nipples and hard abs to the waist of his jeans, where he'd left the top button undone. He had no tattoos, either, at least not where she could see.

"Put your hands back on my shoulders, Madison."

She obeyed, though her fingers whispered down to his biceps as that powerful arm cinched around her waist. His hand palmed her buttock, drawing her closer to his mouth once more.

He didn't go after her aggressively this time, as he had before. Instead, when he wrapped his lips around her right nipple, it was a gentle nursing. It pulled things from her heart, from low in her belly. She slid her hands into the hair she'd cut, held on to him, working her hips in slow circles against him, an unconscious natural rhythm. She hummed and sighed, lost herself in the lovely liquid flow of it. He kneaded her backside, stroking beneath the plaid, and when he turned his head to rub his jaw against her soft flesh again, her knuckles drifted along his cheek. He captured a finger in his teeth, flicking it playfully before releasing it to return his attention to her breasts.

"Logan," she breathed, and he made a deep male noise in response. If only . . .

She'd always sought the reality that was a mirror image of the fantasy. But this was a reality that was a window to a different kind of fantasy, one perhaps better than what she'd imagined. In an entirely different, unexpected way. She wondered if that was why he'd chosen this tactic, to prove that to her. She wouldn't put it past him.

He lifted her, rising from the chair with his arm around her waist, holding her without any apparent effort as she curled her legs around him. He helped, holding her thighs at his hips as he took them around the coffee table to the large area rug.

When he laid her down on her back there, she met his eyes.

"I did the cards here. I fanned them out around me and then . . . I lay on them and masturbated. I thought about you."

The muscle in his jaw flexed. He cupped the side of her face, her turning her head to put her mouth on him, teasing his fingers with her tongue, wanting to suck a finger into her mouth again, but he didn't let her take control to that extent. He drew the hand away, with enough reluctance to please her.

"Put your hands over your head, Madison," he said, his eyes glowing in the dim light. The movie had ended and reverted back to cable, a music channel she'd had on earlier in the day. Children's lullabies, of all things, a channel mothers or fathers could use to help rock the baby to sleep.

She obeyed, and trembled at the look in his eyes. Never in her life had she been with a male who had the confidence to command her, who made her feel as if obeying him was to her benefit. That he could take care of her, that her submission would be a gift to him, not a self-destructive course. She'd been with men for several years, several months, it didn't matter. From the first moment, Logan had given her something none of them ever had.

He knelt between her spread thighs, his fingertips tented on either one, and then he traced them, down to the knee and then back up, slow, until he was under the skirt. "So wet," he said, tsking. "Such a bad girl."

He stretched out on his stomach, his powerful form long enough that his legs extended past the rug. Sliding his hands beneath her thighs, he cupped her bare buttocks beneath the plaid skirt, gripping her under the garter straps. Then he nosed up the skirt and put his mouth right on her cunt.

She arched into that mouth, a gasp escaping her lips. He started with her inner walls, proving what he'd mentioned earlier, that there were so many potential stimulation points beyond the clit. His slow licks progressed deep into those crevices like a kid licking furrows into a dish of ice cream. His nose nuzzled her clit, making her squirm, but he held her still as he continued to worry the inner and outer labia, then his tongue pushed into her, swirling around. She cried out, lifting up so his face was even deeper into her pussy, and he took full advantage of that.

She had to admit, even with her own vibrator, she'd focused on clit manipulation. It was fast, efficient. She'd never realized how sensitive to arousal the labia walls were, but Logan was educating her quickly. She was writhing under his touch, the unusual but not at all unpleasant feelings making it impossible to stay still. Logan stopped, sliding up her body, bracing himself on both elbows, his hard abdomen against her throbbing clit as he gathered up the tails of her shirt. He tied them under her breasts, not over them, so they were displayed in a frame of stretched white fabric. He squeezed them, played his tongue in between them, then left the nipples aching in the cool air as he returned his attention and his mouth between her legs.

When he closed over her clit this time, she nearly came up off the floor. Her fingers curled helplessly above her head, her arms limp because he'd commanded them to be there, to allow herself to be ravished by his mouth with no interference from her. He lifted her hips off the ground, his fingers digging into her buttocks, two of them teasing deep into that crevice, rubbing her anus as she began to beg. She'd already figured out he liked that, but it wouldn't have mattered. She didn't know how not to do so.

"Please . . . please . . ."

He lifted his mouth, glistening with her juices, eyed her down the length of her body. "Please what, Madison? You want the fantasy or the reality?"

She panted at that, tears stinging her eyes. "Both," she whispered. "Both." She'd always wanted both, and that was why she'd always been disappointed. She wanted too much. But he wanted her to reach for it, take the risk once more. He demanded it.

He lowered his mouth to her again. She screamed at the sensations that bombarded her, at how much he could give her with the flick of his tongue, the suckling of his lips, the heat of his breath.

Then he was up on his knees, and flipping her over so her hindquarters were in the air, knees spread, her elbows on the ground. He put his hand on the back of her neck to hold her there and then he gave her bare ass a smack, an unexpected, startling blow that made her cry out.

"Too tempting," he muttered. "We're saving pain for later. Everything in its own time."

Obviously an admonition directed at himself, since she thought she was up for anything at the moment. Then she stopped thinking at all when he put his mouth on her rim, parting her buttocks to tease her there with his mouth.

She made odd babylike cries while he was doing that, short bursts of sound, her fingers clawing the carpet. His fingers slid back into the mix to delve deep in her channel, coming back out to smear that thick arousal over her clit, stroke her there, and then she was pushing herself against his face, responding to the pumping of his fingers, the teasing of his mouth.

"Logan . . . Master . . ."

"Go over for me again."

She did, another long-drawn-out orgasm that had her screaming against the carpet, trying to muffle the sound so the neighbors wouldn't think she was being murdered. He worked her through all of it, until she was begging for mercy, until she couldn't do anything more than whimper under his touch. Only then did he draw his fingers from her, ease her to her side, then her back, so he could collect her in his arms, lift her.

He took her back to the couch. She loved all of it, but she especially loved this part, which probably made it the most dangerous, because it wasn't sexual as much as it was intimate, encouraging pointless imaginings. He hadn't yet put his cock inside her, yet she'd had two of the most intense orgasms she'd ever experienced at his hands—and mouth—alone. But Logan involved her mind in it in a way she'd never imagined possible.

As she lay in his arms in that numb haze, the thought took her back to earlier, to when he'd walked her through her auction fantasy. She knew she was going to be having a serious *WTF* moment tomorrow, thinking about how she'd shared that with him. What kind of woman fantasized about being a slave?

Based on the number of female role-playing costumes of that ilk in her shop, plenty. Logan understood that. It was his world. Her sharing it with him was like a doctor–patient thing, confiding a fantasy to her fantasy. It was all safe, limited and not real.

"What are you thinking about?" he murmured.

"You're out of beer. I should go get you one."

"Not unless you can do it without leaving my lap." He tightened his arms around her. Now that she had some self-awareness returning, she realized how enormous his erection was beneath her buttocks. Again.

"I didn't do anything . . . you said you wanted me to rub—"

"No. Not tonight."

"You said you don't change your mind." She put the smile in her voice, and he chuckled, a grim, strained sound.

"Not about the terms you set up front. But I can change my own game plan as much as I want. I've worked you hard and I want you to rest. But you'll tell me what you were thinking first."

She sighed. "About my stupid fantasy. I was being embarrassed about it, but then I thought about how many of the costumes in the shop seem to focus on . . . servile roles. Maid, belly dancer, palace slave . . . So maybe I'm not as twisted as I thought."

"You're not twisted at all," he reproved her, giving her hip a little pat that was one step below a slap.

"Yeah, but you're this über-Dom, neck-deep in BDSM. So you can't be objective."

He gave her an amused look. "Are you saying *I'm* twisted?"

"Maybe. But in a good way. I like it. Which makes me wonder if thinking something's twisted is more about what you like or don't like than what's actually wrong or right." She frowned. "Can't wrap my mind around it. Gets morely confusing. Morally confusing, I mean." He might be right about the tired thing. Her tongue was clumsy, large in her mouth. It was a good thing he hadn't wanted that beer. She had the coordination of a rag doll.

He pressed her head back down to his shoulder, held her there for a while as they watched the music selections on the TV flicker with trivia about the artists. She had her fingers curled into the arm lying over her hip, his large palm on her buttock holding her secure. She was nearly in a doze when she felt the need to speak again, a quiet mumble.

"I don't think you're twisted. I think you're too perfect. It scares me. You scare me, Logan. A lot."

He dropped a kiss on her head, rubbed slow circles down her back until the wave of somnolent anxiety passed.

"I'm going to take care of you, Madison. You just have to trust me. And trust yourself."

Yeah, good trick, that last one. Trust her own judgment, when it had led her down so many disastrous relationship paths she could audition for Hell's GPS. She let out a little sigh, nestling farther into the cradle of his lap. He would probably decide to leave at some point, unless his tote had a toothbrush. She was fine with him staying the night. She was ready to sleep here in his lap, let dreams carry her away. After all that had happened this evening, they would be very nice dreams. She hoped.

"By the way . . . I have a dress uniform, Madison. And I think you've given me a reason to use it."

The words were a generous contribution to those very nice dreams. Except they were equally capable of waking her back up. In a lot of exciting—and terrifying—ways.

PART III

Bound to Please

"How sweet it is . . . to be loved by you . . ."

Madison belted out lyrics, doing the stroll across the front of the store. As she twirled around her current customer, putting a lot of loose hip action into the movement, the heat from the front window slid across her shoulders, as if the sun was a partner in the dance.

"You just gotta dance when Marvin Gaye sings that one," she said as the music died away. "It's a requirement."

"I'm doing this instead of my step class from now on," Helen Christian said, coming to a laughing, breathless stop. "Wow. That was fun."

When she entered the store, Helen had looked like she needed some fun in her life. She'd been a bit stiff and unsure, until Marvin Gaye came to the rescue and Madison pulled her into an impromptu booty-shaking session.

Madison propped her arms on a rounder of lacy bras and arched a brow. "Okay, now that you're loose, let's try that first question again. Have you talked to your husband about his fantasies?"

Helen grimaced. "Not in a while. I mean, he hates his job. Most of the time when he gets home, he wants to eat dinner and go straight to his gaming."

"What does he play?"

Helen described a computer game that involved warriors, dragons and a lot of maiming and explosions, using swords and spells. Serving the will of the Wrath Queen or the Grey Queen, depending on the character he chose, was the driving force of the game.

As Helen looked through more lingerie choices, Madison gave her a frank and critical look. Helen was a strong-boned, handsome woman, inspiring Madison to make a subtle shift to the role-playing rack and consider the choices there.

She was extra careful not to let her current BDSM explorations direct her customers' desires. Not everyone was interested in Domination and submission fantasies. Just this morning, she'd spent a very enjoyable couple hours helping customers enhance and spice up their relationships with the right type of lingerie, warming oils, body paints, vibrators. Neither restraints nor floggers had been necessary or appropriate to meet their needs. But when Helen explained the game, some inner intuition tingled, and Madison decided to trust it. *What the hell.*

Plucking a Xena-warrior-princess-type outfit off the rack, she gestured at Helen with it. "This would look incredible on you. Imagine if the Wrath Queen showed up in your bedroom and told your husband she was very disappointed by how he'd been neglecting his duties, but Her Majesty had several ideas on how he could gain back her royal favor."

Helen laughed, then realized Madison was serious. While she was intrigued enough to come over and touch the breastplate, her fingers curled into an uncertain ball. "Oh, I don't know. It would be right out of the blue. He'd probably start laughing and I'd be mortified back into neck-high flannel in the middle of summer."

"It's amazing how the right visual can direct the male mind. The fun part—well, the fun part before the *really* fun part—is the setup and presentation. First you need to talk to him about his fantasies, see if he's ever imagined a woman taking charge. You know him better than anyone, so you'll know how to ease it into the conversation."

She saw that sink in; the reminder that, if everything was as it should be, Helen was the most important person in her husband's life. The one whose needs and opinions mattered most to him, and meshed with his own. Enough that they'd said "'til death do us part'" to one another. Madison cleared her throat, thinking of warm brown eyes and Logan's touch on her body. *Don't confuse your desires with hers.* But they could overlap, couldn't they?

"Get him thinking about it, and telegraph your own interest. That will get him speculating on what you might be planning. Then, when you do dress up like this, it will be a special surprise, but it won't come out of the blue. Timing's everything."

"I don't know. I'm not sure I'm the dominatrix type."

"It's just a role, not an identity change. Like playing dress-up when we're small. We all have a bit of the warrior queen or harem girl slave in us, and a lot of versions in between. It's just a way to have fun with the person we love. Show him you're willing to explore different adventures with him. The most critical question is do *you* like the idea? Because as important as it is to figure out if it's one of his fantasies, seeing if it can intertwine with your own is equally important. Then you can tailor it, make it unique to your own relationship."

Since she could see Helen mulling it over, Madison tucked her tongue into her cheek. "Imagine him kneeling before you. You order him to remove his shirt, because you want to trail your fingers over those scars he's gotten in your service, scratch them a bit with your nails. You order him into your bed, commanding him to pleasure you . . . and the rest is all about the two of you getting lost in it."

Helen had a pleasant face, her blond hair pulled back so it emphasized the impact of her direct green eyes. In addition to the strong bones, she was a buxom thirty-something with generous breasts and hips. As she absorbed the words, tried them out in her own head,

Madison had the satisfaction of watching her body language shift. The back straightened, the chin tilting, a sharper look coming to her gaze. All things the woman was probably oblivious to doing, but envisioning the fantasy enough to change her stance was a good sign.

"Yeah," she said slowly. "I kind of like the idea. When I was in college, I had a boyfriend who liked being tied up. I passed it off as a Houdini thing, him trying to get out of restraints, but when I was tying him, I remember the way he watched me, like . . ." She shrugged, gave Madison a smile. "I enjoyed it."

"So there's potential there."

"Maybe." Her gaze slid over Madison's outfit. "You make it look like so much fun. I know wearing your outfits is probably a great way to sell your merchandise, but you look like you get into it."

Today, Madison had chosen the severe librarian look, a crisp but formfitting white shirt tucked into a tailored skirt that hugged her curves. She wore sensible black pumps, and a pair of black-framed glasses perched on her nose. She'd worked her unruly hair into a prim bun and stuck a couple writing pens in it, just to augment the librarian image. To add the sexy, she wore a lacy white bra under the shirt, unbuttoned enough to catch a glimpse of cleavage, enhanced by a gold necklace with "#1 Librarian" scrolled on the locket pendant.

Madison struck a pose, staring down her nose through the glasses. "Nothing like a book applied to a bare backside to catch someone's attention," she said. "No gaming until you have fully satisfied my needs, young man."

Helen grinned. "Maybe I'll start with something like that and work up to Xena."

"Always good to go in stages," Madison approved. "But first things first. Remember to talk to him, get the wheels turning. It's the hardest part, but it will be good for both of you. It's like fantasy foreplay."

She sent Helen on her way with a bra-and-panty purchase and a head full of ideas. As the woman crossed the street to her car, she stopped, her attention caught by something out of view. Madison suspected she'd gotten a whiff of the pastry place a few stores down. More than once, when she was resolved to do an extra workout, she herself snagged a giant cinnamon bun from them. It was worth every sweaty minute.

She smiled as she saw Helen leave the car and head that way. Indulging herself.

Returning to her cash register, Madison caught her reflection in one of the mirror panels. Helen's observation had surprised her, but she had to admit she did look at home in the persona she'd chosen for today.

From the moment she'd decided to honor her sister's dying wish that she take over Naughty Bits, her transformation, inside and out, had hit snags, but now it was a smooth evolution, gaining more ground every day. Especially since the grand opening, several weeks ago. Though Madison had opened the doors of Naughty Bits again well before that, the event had been her official kickoff.

It had gone well, and she'd had the opportunity to draw back more of the loyal customer base Alice had harvested. Many might have attended the grand opening out of sentiment, but that wasn't what had them coming back now.

As her mind traveled back to that day, she knew she was revisiting it not so much because of the event itself, but what had happened after. Another indication of how her confidence, her trust in herself, was improving. As well as her belief that there might just be someone in the world she could trust to catch her when she fell . . .

As the attendees volunteered their stories of how Alice had guided them in their sexual adventures and deepened their emotional bonds with their partners, she listened with a smile on her lips. She laughed when they talked about her sister's quirky and wise insights, her friendship and generosity.

"What a pleasure it was just being around her" . . . "Madison, you look so much like her . . ." . . . "I wish you every success . . ." "I'm so happy I can tell my friends the doors are open again . . ."

Alice hadn't wanted a funeral. She'd told Madison to host a celebration of life whenever it felt like a good time. Unwittingly, the grand opening had become that service. Since she'd placed a picture of Alice on the counter for the event, she saw plenty of people go by, touch her sister's face.

After it was all over, the final person—a tall woman in a multi-hued gauzy dress that smelled of fragrant sage, a scent Alice had loved—gave Madison one last hug and another genuine wish for all good things. Madison nodded, smiled again. Then, once that patron was across the street, Madison took a breath and locked the door, turning over the CLOSED sign.

Cleanup was fairly quick, though collecting the things she needed to take home took extra time. Some of them had brought little gifts, surprisingly. A tribute to her sister, to what she had meant to them.

Madison put the items into one of her store bags and shouldered her purse. As she moved through the storeroom and put her hand on the back door latch, she was struck suddenly by how numb she was, almost as if nothing around her was real, substantial. Then a cramp hit her stomach, a tightness squeezing her chest, taking away her breath.

Dropping her purse, she sank to her knees on the concrete floor, staring sightlessly at the door.

Alice was gone. Truly gone. And she wasn't coming back. No matter how successful Madison made Naughty Bits, no matter how much she talked aloud to her, Alice wasn't here. The sister who'd loved her, helped raise her, who'd always been there. Her family.

Her mind turned to Logan and Troy, and the desperate wish that they were here. They were the closest thing to a family she had now.

Given how short a time she'd known them, that thought should be absurd, but given their connection to Alice, and the intense things they'd shared in that short time, it didn't seem absurd at all.

They'd come to the opening earlier, but hadn't stayed for the whole thing since they had the hardware store next door to run. She understood that. Yet some part of her wanted to get up, run through that connecting backroom door and find them. Fortunately, her weak knees and that terrible pain in her middle kept her from embarrassing herself.

She rocked herself, keening. She expected it to ease off, a few hard waves followed by an ebbing that would allow her to breathe, but it didn't happen. It got worse. She couldn't stop crying.

Even though she wasn't expecting any company, somehow she wasn't surprised when a hand touched her shoulder. "I can't . . . stop . . ." she managed, gasping.

Maybe Troy had come into their storage room and heard her, no matter that she was trying to strangle back the sounds. But it didn't matter how he'd gotten here. The important thing was that he was. Sliding down the wall to take a seat next to her, he folded her in his arms. Her own went around him, clinging as she sobbed. Barely a minute later, her heart broke open all the way, because Logan joined them as well.

When he knelt by her other side, she released Troy to turn toward him, pressing her face into his chest. She was suddenly quite certain she'd be ripped in two if he wasn't there to hold her. As Logan's arms went all the way around her, she let out a sound she expected she'd make if he caught her before she fell over a cliff. Troy stayed at her back, rubbing it until she could breathe again.

Logan wiped her eyes with a handkerchief and Troy found her tissues to blow her nose. They didn't ask her to talk. But she still managed to stammer out the words. "It was wonderful . . . and so hard. So hard."

Logan nodded against her temple, holding her tighter. Troy put

206 Joey W. Hill

his lips to her shoulder, leaned against her back. They surrounded her, and she didn't have to explain. They understood.

Revisiting her sister's memory with those who loved her *had* been wonderful, yet she still stood apart, alone. Her bond to Alice was singular, a blood connection. And Alice was gone, that connection severed, casting Madison adrift. Yet here they were, holding her, keeping her anchored. Somehow, knowing she wasn't alone made it seem that Alice was still present, the tether to her still there.

The first day Madison had met Logan, he'd said Alice had given her to him. At the time, she'd reacted the way she expected anyone would react to such an astounding statement from a stranger. Now she was both paralyzed and suffused with hope that her sister had known what she was doing.

Coming back to the present, Madison remembered how Logan had taken her home, tucked her into her bed with a cup of tea. He'd stayed with her until morning, leaving her with a vague awareness of his lips brushing her brow before she was lost again to a dreamless, exhausted slumber. In her more or less lucid moments, depending on her mood, she found it unsettling, how easily she let him past any emotional shielding or barrier she had. She wanted to believe it was evidence of positive growth in their relationship, rather than her following the same track she always had, trusting too much of herself, too soon, opening herself to being shattered.

Stop it. Trying to distract herself now, she picked up a wooden paddle and slapped it against her hand, giving herself a suitably disapproving look in the mirror. She was finding she could really get into the different ideas she created for her clients, but when it came to punishment, she was still playing around the edges. Logan had given her a brief taste with that one smack on her ass at her house during movie night, but she didn't have a firsthand understanding of the connection between pleasure and pain.

As soon as she gave the word, he would address that deficit of understanding. Every day she came closer to telling Logan yes, she wanted another session. As a result, that coil of anxiety in her lower belly about it was becoming ever more intense. Anticipation and anxiety mixed together, like most things that involved Logan.

Despite all her attempts to stay rational, detached, she was all too aware Logan hadn't mentioned going to his preferred BDSM club since that night at her house. He also found a reason to check in on her every day. No, that described her, not him. She never went next door without a justifiable, somewhat business-related reason to explain her visit. Whereas he didn't present a reason at all when he came over to her store, beyond simply wanting to see her.

This morning he'd brought her a cup of his coffee and asked her how she'd slept last night, engaging in warm chitchat. Then he'd slid behind her counter, gathered her up to him and put his mouth on hers, leaving her with a kiss that was like a straight shot of caffeine, waking her up head to toe.

He was treating her like a love interest. A lover. He wanted to be around her, wanted to see her. It was always nice to be wanted—for however long it lasted.

Did she always have to add those depressing caveats? This time the disapproving librarian face she made really was at herself, not an imaginary late-book offender. She wanted to see him right now, for no other reason than that. It had been too long since that morning kiss.

She waffled over it. She should be as brave and open about it as he was, but she wasn't there. She had to protect herself, no matter how flimsy the shield. Picking up a stack of the new coupons she'd printed up last night on colored paper, as well as the small shopping bag she'd packed up a little while ago with treats for the two men, she put her clock sign out, indicating she'd be back in ten minutes, and locked the door. She was proud that she moved with a brisk, casual stride toward the front of his store, rather than skipping like an infatuated schoolgirl.

Logan was discussing a floor nailer with a customer, the two of them analyzing the different possibilities. She leaned against his counter, watching him and listening to the rise and fall of his voice. If she wasn't careful, she'd just close her eyes and ride that timbre like a boat on a smooth current. To avoid embarrassing herself that way, she focused on what they were discussing. His sales approach wasn't much different from her own. His primary concern was ensuring the customer got the right tool for the job, even if it was only available at Home Depot.

Remarkably, she'd found such an approach still fulfilled her bottom line. From the account history, it was clear Alice had succeeded more because of repeat business and referrals than impulse buys.

Troy emerged from the center aisle. He'd been unloading a truck: he was sweaty, his shirt clinging to his upper body. When he saw her, he headed her way, wiping his neck and face with a bandanna. "Hey, Madison. Wow. I like the outfit. Librarian?"

She peered over her glasses at him with a stern look. "That's Miss Fine to you. Didn't I tell you what would happen if you brought your books back late again, Troy?"

In his flash of surprise at her teasing, she caught an unguarded reaction, a short but very sweet taste of what it must be like to be his Mistress, to have those blue eyes look at her with aroused yearning, an eager desire to please her with every inch of his muscular young body. It made for a nice, quick fantasy.

He recovered in a blink, gave her his slow smile. She was amused when he changed the subject. "We're having a sale on lawn art today. Can I interest you in a concrete frog? You'll be saving a life, because Logan swears he's going to take them all out for target practice if he doesn't get them out from underfoot."

He ducked into the appropriate aisle and retrieved one. The impossibly cute small concrete frog fit into the palm of his hand. She decided it would look lovely sitting on her counter, right next to the basket of hopping genitalia.

"I'll be happy to take one. How much will it set me back?"

"Three dollars. I'd slip it to you for free, but you know how he is." He winked at her. "Just as cost conscious as you are."

"That's how it is when you're the one who pays the bills," she said reprovingly. Then she cocked her head. "You're in a good mood, for a man who just unloaded a truckful of heavy things."

"It just means he isn't working hard enough," Logan said, joining them. His thorough perusal made her blush.

"Stop it. You saw me a couple hours ago."

"Doesn't mean I don't enjoy the hell out of the experience every time. Or can only Troy stammer and blush around you?"

"You haven't stammered or blushed since you were born."

At Troy's emphatic nod of agreement, Logan turned his eye on him. "Don't think I won't tell Shale about that blushing."

"Hey, I was just moving the merchandise. Madison agreed to buy a frog."

"If you want to impress me, tell me she agreed to buy a dozen."

"I was intending to give a touch of whimsy to my cash register, not start a plague in Egypt," she retorted. She lifted the coupons. "We're having a sale. Buy two panties or two bras, get one for free. If you'd put these on your counter or throw one in the bags, that would be great. The first ten men who come over to buy something for their wives will get a free piece of lemon cake."

Troy brightened. "You brought cake today? Like Alice's cake?"

"Yes. It was our mother's recipe." Reaching into the bag she had on her arm, she withdrew the two containers. "I brought some for you two before it's all gone."

"A bribe for sharing your coupons," Logan observed.

"Compensation," she said primly. "Which puts me one up on you, because I've been putting your sales fliers in my customers' bags for no compensation at all." *So to speak.* That kiss went through her mind, his knowing gaze making her suppress a smile. "I've also spoken very highly of your charms, such as they are. Fair's fair."

Troy was eying the cake like a hungry dog, but when she began to hand him one of the containers, Logan laid a casual hand on her wrist, stopping her. "Madison, do you offer a pet a treat without checking with his owner first?"

In deference to their surroundings, he spoke low, but in his usual way, just that tone and look could command her attention. He was asking her to respect Troy's training, but beyond that, he was requiring a certain behavior from her. Bemused, she noticed she and Troy had the same reaction to him, both of them getting still and entirely focused on what he wanted, what he'd require.

"You're right, I'm sorry. May Troy have a piece of cake?"

Logan's mouth quirked. "He'll be salivating all over the shop floor if I don't say yes." He glanced at Troy. "Put it in the back. You can have it on your break."

"Yes sir. Thanks, Madison. Miss Fine." Troy corrected himself with a twinkle in his eyes. After another mischievous leer at her outfit, he disappeared down the main aisle. Madison heard him stop to answer a question about pliers.

Logan lifted a brow. "What did you say to him to make him blush?"

"I was just warning him to return his books on time. He's pretty easy to play with. Should I not tease him like that?" No matter how her instincts gravitated toward submission, she realized there were a lot of rules she didn't know.

"It's not a problem. You're doing it with affection and fun, not to jerk his chain." He glanced down at the coupons. "You reserve that behavior for me, because you want to know what will happen if you jerk hard enough."

Now it was her turn to swallow and change the subject. "Why is he in such a good mood? Not that he isn't normally, but he seems particularly effusive."

"His training will be completed by the end of the week, which means I deliver him back to Shale. He'll get to show her all he's learned. And she'll get the project she commissioned," he added.

Madison had a quick, provocative vision of the beautifully crafted wooden chest that actually converted to a cage, in a size to accommodate a lean, tall Troy. Logan had showed it to Madison the first night they met, and while a part of her had been taken aback, another part of her had wondered what it would be like, to trust a Master enough to submit to the confinement.

"He hasn't seen her all these weeks?" She brought herself back to the topic at hand. As devoted as Troy seemed to be to his Mistress, she couldn't imagine a prolonged separation had been easy.

"That's part of the deal." Logan shrugged. "It amps up the motivation, not that he ever really needed it. He's not a brat or a bottom topper. He's like a fierce golden retriever, worth his weight in gold to a Dom."

"So you don't care much for a brat?"

She won an amused look from him. "It depends," he responded. "There's bratting, and there's being a brat. In a very cute, sexy, begging-for-punishment kind of way." He put his hand over hers on the counter, where she'd put the coupons. "Time for you to go away. You're making me think of closing the store early, something I never do."

"What would you do, if you closed early?" She blinked, all innocence, which just made him narrow those brown eyes.

"Bully you into that session you're almost ready to agree to do. The sooner the better. That's three dollars for the frog. Unless you want to slip it down your shirt and let me catch you shoplifting."

She snorted at that, mainly to cover the nervous quiver his first comment had elicited. Reaching into the open neck of the white shirt, she removed several folded bills from where they'd been tucked into her lacy bra. "I'd intended to buy another coffee, but I'll buy a frog instead and cut down on my caffeine."

She started to put the money on the counter, but instead he put his hand out, taking it from her, caressing her fingers before closing his own over the bills warm from sitting against her breast. With his eyes trained on her, it was clear where his mind was. She ducked her head, slipping the frog into the bag she'd used to bring them cake. "When and if I decide . . . to do that session, where would we do it?"

She should be making chatty conversation, but it was the only topic in her head, especially with him giving her that look that sent anxiety and arousal coursing through her.

"In my back room."

"Would I wear anything special?"

"Whatever you think might bribe me to punish you less. It won't work, but I'll enjoy the attempt."

"Pig."

He winked at her. "Go grab yourself a cup of coffee from behind the counter. I'll take it out in trade."

At that provocative statement, he turned, responding to the call of a customer. Truth, thinking about it, having him talk point-blank about it, anxiety took the lead on anticipation. It was clear Troy wouldn't be there. Or would he? She wasn't sure if she felt safer with Troy present, or if she preferred to evolve the intense cycle of emotions that seemed to happen when it was just her and Logan together. But this time it wouldn't be in her home. It would be in that room with the unfinished concrete floor, naked lights and a wall full of floggers, switches and metal things she couldn't identify.

She'd gone on the Internet to refresh her memory about how this all worked and shut it down just as hastily, horrified by pictures of women tied up like pretzels, tearstained expressions of seeming anguish on their faces while large, fierce men stood behind them with raised whips or cattle prods. *Jesus.* She knew how the Internet could be. He'd been in her home, and it hadn't been like that. Far from it. But then . . . there was an undercurrent when Logan was in full-on Dom mode, something unpredictable and dangerous, and there was some of that in those pictures.

She didn't have to do any of it. The choice was hers. She could take her time, talk to Logan about it. He was as much a teacher as a practitioner when it came to BDSM. Yet he'd warned her more than once that overthinking it wouldn't really help. It might make her more apprehensive than when she was just following her feelings, and those feelings said she longed to be around him, wanted him to take control again.

Just tell him you'll do it, Madison. What are you waiting for?

Returning to her store, she put the frog out on the counter. Surely a man who sold cute, whimsical frogs wouldn't do something too terrible to her.

Fortunately, she was distracted by her post-lunch customer surge. She had a steady flow until late afternoon, including some of the men next door, buying for their wives and seeking cake. Just when she thought she had a lull to go check the Dungeon Room and see if the cake was all gone, a woman slipped in the door, barely opening it enough to trigger the music that played whenever a customer entered or exited.

Prior to taking ownership of Naughty Bits, Madison had held a variety of sales positions, and that experience had given her a radar for hustlers. When she sold cars, shabbily dressed people pretended to be homeless, wandering onto the car lot to hit up browsing clientele for handouts. When she worked in the appliance section of a department store, other undesirables tried to scratch the merchandise unseen to secure a discounted price, or worked scams with the generous return policy.

While her newest customer didn't give her the hustler vibe, the shift of her dull eyes, the nervous movements of her hands, put Madison on alert for shoplifting, perhaps to fuel a drug addiction. She was too thin, which made her look younger than Madison suspected she was. Her hair was pulled back from her face, enhancing her strained countenance.

Then Madison noted her only jewelry. The girl wore a steel collar with a small padlock threaded through the screw holes, and the heavy metal had abraded her skin.

She'd met collared subs who had a decorative collar, something that passed as jewelry in public. It gave them the personal pleasure of wearing a subtle statement of their Dom's ownership. This one was overstated, a la Planet of the Apes, to look exactly like what it was. If worn by someone in Goth or punk garb, it might have blended better, but the woman wore plain jeans and a red knit shirt that hung on her sparse frame.

She could be here to steal, but since she was the only customer in the store, she had Madison's full attention. If she was a shoplifter, she wasn't a very sensible one.

Madison came out from behind the counter with her usual warm smile, though she suspected her gaze was sharper than usual. "Hi, I'm Madison. Can I help you?"

"Um . . . yeah. Yes." The customer fingered one of the peignoirs. "This is so beautiful."

"Yes, it is." If the girl had more meat on her bones, it would look wonderful on her. Her eyes were focused, so she wasn't using. At least not right now. "What's your name?"

"Veronica."

"Veronica, would you like some lemon cake? I baked it this morning." She hoped she had some left. If not, she'd find her a pack of crackers.

"Uh, no. But thank you." However, the girl's eyes latched on to the direction Madison had pointed. Then they stayed there, studying the archway of the Dungeon Room. "I thought you were just a lingerie store." Relief crossed her face, and her attention came back to Madison. "I'm not allowed to eat unless my Master says I can."

So her trepidation might be about going into a store unaccepting of the BDSM lifestyle. It didn't seem to abate, however. Though Veronica kept her gaze on Madison, it was as if she was being forced to look at her. She swallowed noisily.

"He sent me in here to . . . he told me to tell you . . . to ask . . . what's the best outfit you sell for whores, because that's what I am."

Humiliation could be part of BDSM, if that was what a sub enjoyed, though the Dom or sub that pulled a third party into it without permission or forewarning was showing poor manners, at the least. Beyond that, Madison thought of how Troy had responded to her stern teasing this morning, with a blush and a bright, healthy light in his eyes. He was demonstrably eager to be back with his Mistress, even to try out the *cage* she'd had built for him. Compared to this poor thing in front of her, the difference was black and white.

"Let's get you some cake," Madison said firmly. "It will be a good way to talk about what you really want."

She took her arm, but Veronica flinched. As she pulled away, the sleeve of her knit shirt shifted, giving Madison a glimpse of healing cuts, as well as bruising around the wrists. Perhaps from steel manacles that matched the uncomfortable weight and cut of the collar?

In the next blink, a red haze had covered Madison's eyes. Though they'd had their differences on many things, on one thing she and Alice had never disagreed. They had no tolerance for abuse. As teenagers, they'd joined forces to kidnap more than one neglected dog from a terrible life on a short chain in a backyard. When they'd stumbled on two boys behind the school beating up a kid with Down syndrome, Madison had hesitated, not sure whether they should go get help or do something to stop it. Then Alice jumped in and she joined her, the two of them beating the ever-loving crap out of the bullies.

Madison remembered later that same day of the time she'd put peroxide on an abrasion on her sister's arm. The scrape had come from rolling around in the gravel, grappling with one of the boys. Alice would stand for Veronica without thought, making sure she was protected in whatever way necessary. Madison led with that feeling.

"Where is your Master?" She headed for the door, but this time it was Veronica who reached out, held her back.

"Please don't," she said plaintively. "If you get mad at him, he'll get mad at me."

"He's abusing you."

"No." She shook her head. "I'm bad. I'm really bad. He has to punish me and make me do these things to remind me how bad I am."

"No, he . . ."

"What's taking so long?"

Alice's spirit must have been influencing the music selection, because it was the first time Madison had heard "Ride of the Valkyries" fill the store when the door opened. It took over for the poignant "Somewhere in Time" Veronica's arrival had set off.

This had to be Veronica's Master. Wearing khakis and golf shirt, he was tall and husky, with the cocky look the football coach at her high school had possessed. Not always a bad trait in that profession, but arrogance could pave the road to indifferent cruelty. He was about twenty years older than Veronica. At his pointed tone, the girl cringed and tried to scurry toward him, but Madison snagged her arm, taking a firmer hold this time while trying not to aggravate the bruises beneath her grip.

"We were discussing what you wanted her to buy," she said through gritted teeth.

"Sorry," he said. He'd registered her tone, his own saying he wasn't sorry at all. He gave her an easy, feral smile. "It's just a game we're playing. I thought this kind of store, you'd be used to it."

"Role-playing and fantasies are part of what this store is about, yes," Madison said evenly. "Not abuse and malnourishment."

His eyes narrowed. "You better get your hand off my slave."

"You better join the current century and realize she doesn't belong to anyone but herself."

Veronica was shaking. Madison tucked her farther behind her. "Get the hell out of my store, before I call the cops."

"She'll be home by suppertime."

"That will be her choice. You won't be around to help her make it."

"Sanctimonious bitch. I don't have any problems teaching you both a lesson. You're all by yourself in here." He took a step into the store and Madison took a step back, already thinking about the .38 Alice kept under the counter. Unfortunately, he took it as a fearful retreat, not a calculated one. Light kindled in his eyes.

"How about we teach you a lesson instead?"

She bit back a sigh of relief, glancing over her shoulder to see Logan step out from behind her storeroom curtain, Troy on his heels. The two of them shifted apart, shoulder to shoulder, and she saw nothing submissive about Troy now. His eyes were cool flint. A direct contrast to Logan's, which held hellfire.

"You heard her," he said, taking another step forward. "Get out of her store. Now. And don't come back."

Logan's expression left no doubt what would happen if he didn't listen. Madison remembered how dangerous he'd appeared when making erotic threats to Troy, but the difference between sensual intimidation and genuine menace was dangerously clear. Clear enough to penetrate the thick head of the man in the doorway. With a sneer, he turned and left, giving the door a kick that could have broken the glass, if he hadn't missed and hit the frame.

"I really should go with him," the girl quavered. "He's my Master."

"No, he's not." Logan's tone was everything a Master's should be. Authoritative, assured, decisive. Protective. It drew Veronica's attention to him like a magnet. Madison's, too, for that matter. She wanted to kiss him, right then and there.

"He doesn't know the first thing about being a Dom. We're going to get you a meal, take you to a place that will help you figure things out. If you still want to go to him after that, one of us will take you. But you'll give it twenty-four hours. Understand?"

The question was obviously rhetorical. Logan could dial up that Dominant attitude full force, and it had the desired effect on Veronica, underscored by her next stammered words.

"Y-yes sir."

His jaw eased, but not the fury in his gaze. Still, he touched the girl gently, guiding her to Troy, who exercised his usual calming presence to shepherd her behind the curtain and into their adjoining storeroom. When Logan turned his attention to Madison, she realized she was shaking herself, but it wasn't fear. His touch, hands closing on her upper arms, helped calm her.

"You all right?"

"I'd be better if I could blow up his Lincoln Continental with him in it. You don't have any explosives in your store, do you?"

The spirited response eased some of the fire in his visage. Realizing some of that had been on her behalf, a territorial male's desire to protect her, gave her a flutter.

"It's never supposed to be like that," he said, turning his attention to the street, where the Continental was leaving its parking place, the tires squealing as the owner vented his frustration on his exit. "You do know that, don't you, Madison?"

He wasn't looking at her, but she sensed how significant the question was to him, how vital her answer. When his gaze shifted to her, what she saw there confirmed it.

"Right before Veronica got here, I was thinking about the pain session and being a little afraid," she admitted. She lifted her hands to his face before he could say anything to that. "Now I know I picked the right Dom to show me the ropes, so to speak."

He blinked, covered her hands with his own, a light hold on her wrists. "So you've decided."

"You know I have." She took a breath, looked toward her back room. "Will she go back to him?"

"Maybe. It's not the first time a criminal sadist has used our world to cover his sickness. Most Doms have a sadistic side, but it's one they use for mutual pleasure, for them and their subs. Unfortunately, a woman with low self-esteem like that will fall into the wrong kind of Dom's lap like candy. But we'll do our best to make sure she doesn't end up there again."

"How did you know I had a problem?" she asked.

"The security cameras in my store include the entrances and exits to yours. We watch out for our neighbors, and the situation gave me a wrong feeling. I came through the back so if it wasn't anything, I could leave without interrupting you. Troy insisted on coming, too. He's become quite fond of you." Stroking a wisp of hair from her brow, he tapped the librarian glasses lightly. "That makes two of us."

"Well, that's good, because I was going to trade on your affections to draft you and Troy for a fashion show I'm planning. I need some handsome escorts for the models, and someone to show off the male outfits. You know, pirate outfits, the studded leather harnesses and thongs . . ."

"Uh-huh." He snorted. "Good luck with that. That's my cue to get back to my store, talk to Veronica about where she'll be staying tonight."

"And that will be?"

"There's a shelter in the area. It's run by a woman who's been in the lifestyle. Becky was with an asshole like that for three years too long. She handles not only the standard abuse cases, but those that get outed by the BDSM community. We take care of our own there, too. A guy like that gives us all a bad name."

That fierce light flickered again. While she'd wanted to blow up his car, it was obvious he would have preferred to beat Veronica's Master to a pulp with his fists. Logan was a very hands-on type of male, after all.

"If I can convince Veronica to stay there a night," he continued, "long enough to find out there are better, healthier ways to exercise submissive tendencies—and determine if she actually has them, rather than just being a woman with a bad self-image—things will be more in our favor that she'll stay another day, and another, and get her life back on track."

"Would it be okay if I stopped in and visited her tonight?"

He squeezed her hand. "You've got a good heart. I'll ask Becky. The location of the shelter is secret, for obvious reasons, but I know she won't object to you coming as long as she feels it's the right time. She'll likely want to spend the first few hours just feeding her and doing some one-on-one work. But after that, I expect it would be good for Veronica to talk to as many women as possible who know how it's really supposed to work."

She liked that he included her in that number, and was kind of amazed at her personal pride and ownership of that. *I am a submissive.* "Whatever Becky and you think is best. Anything I can do to help, just let me know."

He bent forward, dropping an unexpected kiss to her forehead. Then he slid an arm around her, held her closer. "I'm glad you're all right. But next time anyone gives you wrong vibes, you get your pretty ass back behind your counter and have that gun within reach."

"You know about the gun?"

"Yep. Alice would go to the range with me sometimes to stay in practice. I gave her a few tips to improve her aim." He leaned back, gave her a sharp look. "You know how to use one?"

"Yep. Our daddy taught us both when we were kids. I haven't used one in a while, but he said I was a natural. We'll go to the range sometime and I'll smoke *your* pretty ass on target rounds."

He grinned at that. Leaning down again, he put his mouth on hers. It was reassuring and promising, all at once. Her toes curled in her shoes as he slid his fingertips into her hair, his other arm banding around her waist to hold her even more securely to him. When he lifted his head, she saw a rare instance of sheepishness in his gaze.

"Sorry. I needed that."

"Anything I can do to help," she repeated, a little breathlessly this time. "You know, I still wonder if that whole pain-can-help-heal-and-deal-with-guilt thing is just an excuse to spank me."

The set of his jaw eased, his lips curving. "I have half a mind to do it right now, purely for my own enjoyment."

"See? I knew it was more than a selfless desire to help me."

He sobered. "Madison, you're joking about it, but I want to say it. Remember what I told you from the beginning. There is absolutely *nothing* more important to a Dominant than the care of his or her sub. We might use pain for mutual pleasure, and that mutual pleasure may not be how other people define it. But what he's doing to her, manipulating her emotions, taking advantage of her weaknesses, that's so far from what BDSM is supposed to be about, it's like a dirty cop versus a good one. There is no comparison, even if they look the same at times. You understand that, right?"

"You look nothing like him," she said, meeting his gaze. "And I don't mean physically. From the first moment I met you, I knew I could trust you. Even when I've been afraid, that comes from me, not anything you've done. My sister told me I could trust you with anything." She swallowed. "Even my soul. You haven't done a thing yet to make me feel differently."

It was the truth, she knew it. All her fears about Logan came from her own history, her lack of faith in herself, her certainty that fate or her own actions were going to destroy what seemed to be a growing bond between them, because they always did.

Since Logan had been Alice's primary caregiver until three days before her death, Madison had assumed he'd seen Alice's final letter to her, the part where she'd said Madison could trust Logan more than anyone. Yet his reaction now told her otherwise. He wasn't a man to show softer emotions easily, so she reached out, closed her hand over his arm, reinforcing her belief.

"Thank you," he said quietly. He put his hand over hers for another brief squeeze, and then he moved toward the back room. He needed to go, she knew he did. She wasn't sure if Troy could hold Veronica there indefinitely the way Logan could, though Troy was far more resourceful and determined than it had first appeared. She'd jumped to some pretty stereotypical assumptions about a man who wanted to belong fully to a Mistress.

But what about herself? When she'd thought *I am a submissive*, she'd felt that was true. Yet she was running a business, had just held her own against an asshole who outweighed her and got through life by bullying others. "Submissive" didn't equal "timid" or "doormat." It seemed the more she embraced that side of herself, the better opinion she had of herself.

Even so, she hadn't really explored the other side of things, had she? Logan had assumed from the beginning she would embrace a submissive's role. While so far nothing had said differently—*boy howdy*—she wondered if that was because Logan was a hetero Dom who naturally drew out submissive cravings in a woman as part of his skills, or because it had never occurred to him to look for anything different from her. Well, she could look for it from herself, couldn't she?

"How did you recognize it . . . in me? That I'd be open to the submission thing?" She asked it abruptly, bringing him to a halt.

"It's a feeling I get. For instance, I'm not so sure Veronica is a sub. She might have a dysfunctional family history that made her prey for the likes of that asshole. Until she gets clear of that, there's too much storm debris to know what her soul really looks like. But you . . ."

He inclined his head. "I'm not sure how good an idea it is to say this, but it shines from you like a beacon. You're not her. You're healthy and strong, you feel and you grieve cleanly. You also want and need with such power, it's irresistible. I don't know about those shit-for-brains men you've been with, Madison, and I wish I could have spared you the pain they caused you, but I won't regret a minute of it if it brought you to me as the person you are."

What would seem like bullshit charm or stalker craziness from anyone else always received an answering tone inside her chest when the words came from him. But she wasn't ready to be boxed into something when she wasn't sure about all the other possible boxes in the room. He'd said he liked her assertive side, right?

"What if I wanted to give it a try? The shoe-on-the-other-foot thing?"

"You want to try being a Domme?" The genuine surprise in his gaze was gratifying, proof that she could do something he didn't expect.

"Yes. I think . . . yes. At least once. But I don't think I could do it with a stranger. It wouldn't be a real test. I'd be too divided between not knowing him and what I was trying to figure out about myself." She gave him a hopeful look. "Care to change sides for one night?"

He chuckled. "As tempting and terrifying as it sounds to be at your mercy, I'm a Dom down to the bone, and it would skew your test results. How about Troy?"

She remembered Troy's body against her, his lips in her hair. The way he'd responded to Logan. "Oh . . . well, yes," she said. Cleared her throat.

He grinned. "I'll try not to let that blush and eager light in your eye aggravate me. Much. Let me talk to his Mistress about it. She'd have to clear anything like that."

"And Troy. I wouldn't want to compromise his friendship in any way."

"Part of their contract is that she can share him if she desires. He trusts her to know him well enough to care for him. She might want to be present, though. No Dominant in their right mind allows their sub to be shared without overseeing his well-being, unless they know the Master or Mistress well enough, like Shale knows me. But even with me supervising, she might still want to be there." He gave her an amused look. "That's as much for her to remind Troy who his Mistress is as to protect him. She doesn't worry about Troy transferring his affections to me. Boy's pretty straight, though he'll take it up the ass for her without a blink."

After that bald statement, and a wink, he disappeared behind her curtain, leaving her whirling over a whole new set of possibilities. Her gaze moved to the wall, where a pair of thigh-high boots and a black corset were displayed against the backdrop of a two-dimensional silhouette of a woman's body. Imagining herself in such an outfit, slapping a paddle against a gloved hand, she blanched. What the hell was she thinking?

Though another set of customers kept her busy, she saw Logan pull out of their shared alley in his truck. He had Veronica with him and lifted his hand to Madison as he went by. She assumed he'd left the store in Troy's hands.

He didn't return until late afternoon. When the truck passed by her display window, she caught a glimpse of his face. He looked tired. Perhaps the day's events had left him dispirited. It made sense, given how important a part of his life this was. She expected it was the same thing a social service or humane society worker felt every time they encountered an abuse case, the evil of fellow men sapping their soul.

When she checked her rear security camera, she saw he'd put down the tailgate of his truck and was sitting on it. Not doing anything, really, just staring into space. Maybe he'd prefer his privacy, but it twisted her heart and she couldn't stop herself from wanting to help. Late afternoon was a slow period for her, so she put the clock sign on a thirty-minute return and went out through the back storeroom, taking him out a coffee and her last piece of cake.

He eyed her as she emerged. "Trying to make me fat, woman?"

"I think you can absorb a calorie or two, as busy as you and Troy stay all day long in that store. Want some company? I can just leave the cake and coffee if you don't."

"You're kind," he said quietly. "I can't imagine a moment when your company wouldn't brighten my day." He offered her a hand to help her onto the tailgate.

"Charmer." But she settled next to him, swinging her feet next to his, planted solidly in his work shoes on the ground thanks to his greater height. "How's Veronica?"

"Safe with Becky for the time being. She's pretty docile, all in all, but that can be deceptive. Because it was such a destructive relationship, almost like a drug addiction, later tonight is when she'll start to deal with withdrawal, from being away from him. If she's still there three days from now, her odds of staying will be much higher."

He leaned back, bracing himself with one arm, sipped his coffee. "How did you know I like coffee on a hot day?"

"I've seen you with a steaming cup by the cash register when it was ninety outside. True sign of a caffeine addict, and a purist. You don't do iced coffees, Frappuccinos . . ."

He snorted. "No. But I can do your lemon cake all day long. Yours is a little different from Alice's, but just as good."

"We make it the same way."

"It's the flavor of the hands that make it," he said. "You emphasize the density of it, the weight. Alice focused on making it as light as air. You're the earth, she's the sky."

"Are you a shaman in your spare time?"

He smiled, put his arm around her and slid her closer, so they were hip to hip, then braced his arm again so she could lean inside the triangle of it and his broad shoulder.

She nudged his knee with hers. "What do you do, besides this? Run the store, make BDSM furniture? Train subs and do whip demonstrations. Watch movies with me." Her nose crinkled. "Come to think of it, that's a pretty full schedule, if you add in eating and sleeping."

"It is. But I find time for things. My house is on the outskirts of Matthews. It was a small farm at one time, about thirty acres with a pond, but now I just maintain the property. I have a bigger furniture workshop in the barn. Most of what I have at this location are showroom pieces, though I always keep a couple in process for when I prefer to work here."

"Why'd we watch the movie at my place, instead of there?"

The corner of his mouth tugged up. "I figured you'd be more comfortable in your own surroundings until we got to know each other better. My place is fairly isolated."

She smiled. "Plus, as a bachelor, you'd have to clean the place up with a shovel if I was coming over."

He looked pained. "That makes me sound like a typically lazy male, averse to domestic chores. Which, while wildly true, is stereotyping."

She chuckled. "What do you do out there?"

"Float around in a boat on the pond, read. Bushhog about twice a year. Mow the lawn right around the house. Do basic maintenance when needed. Watch cable. I have a berm I've created so I can practice my shooting, stay up with that. Chase deer away from the bird feeders."

"You shoot at the deer?"

"No. I shoot at the berm. I chase the deer."

She laughed outright as he made motions with his fingers like running. "You have bird feeders?"

"Of course. I like watching them. And the squirrels. It's a very manly pursuit. I have a shirt from the Humane Society that says Real Men Love Animals, so there's your proof. Besides, animals are the ultimate example of purely dominant/submissive relationships. I learn a lot, watching them."

It sounded like a nice existence, a complex man with simple tastes. And she realized she'd asked him more about himself, outside of being a Dom, something she'd been reluctant to do in the past. More progress. As she was mulling that over, he nudged her. "So, Ms. Librarian, what do you want to do to Troy? I talked to Shale on the way back, and she's game. No sex."

"Of course." Madison started. "I hadn't even considered it."

"Good." His obvious emphasis made her glance up at him through her lashes. He gave her a disparaging look. "Don't look smug. We'll have the session in my back room, since I have all the tools and equipment you'll need. If that suits you."

"Yes. Hmm." She noticed Logan was waiting her out, not guiding her as he usually seemed to do. Maybe he was patiently respecting her need to gather her thoughts. Waiting for her to voice what she needed. She'd said she wanted to try the other side of things, and that meant taking charge.

"I'd like to restrain him. Something simple, since I don't really have any rope-tying skills. I may also want to use a blindfold, so I can touch him without him looking at me. Is it about what I want, or about what he wants? Do I need to talk to him first about limits, safe words?"

"Usually, yes, but I know him so well, he'll rely on me to keep you guided so you don't have to get bogged down in all that. His safe word is *goddess*."

Amusement surged through her. "How clever of him. To gasp out an appeal to a goddess when he needs relief."

"Yeah. One of many reasons Shale's as besotted with him as he is with her. They're both young."

"Versus you." She swept her gaze over his powerful torso. "Positively doddering and feeble."

"Keep it up. You still have that pain session coming."

"Unless I choose not to do it."

"Yep," he said, unruffled. She eyed him.

"You don't seem worried."

"It's not that." His gaze became more serious. "It is your choice, Madison. Always. But yes, I think you want the session, so no, I'm not too worried about you backing out. Though you may get some stage fright right before. That's normal. And I reserve the right to use all methods at my disposal to bully or seduce you onto the stage."

"Not coax, plead or beg?"

"I'm not the begging type."

No, he certainly wasn't. She settled back against his arm, still wanting to rile him a little. "So how about using a strap-on with Troy? Does that count as sex?"

"It's a gray area." She bit back a smile at the clipped tone. "I can ask Shale."

"So how big a . . . thing . . . could he take comfortably?"

"Maybe you should stick to the basics the first time out. Restraints, mild flogging, psychological domination. He can also perform oral sex on you, bring you to climax, that kind of thing."

"You'd prefer that to the strap-on."

"This isn't about me."

"Isn't it?"

He straightened then, putting the coffee aside. "Don't play games with me, Madison."

"I'm not." She slid off the tailgate, suddenly uncomfortable. He caught her arm, standing up as well.

"I get your desire to explore this from all sides," he said firmly, "but that doesn't alter what's developing between us. You know where a session ends and a relationship begins. I don't have an on/off switch. My expertise in this area doesn't replace my emotions. You push me, I will push back. No, I don't like the idea of you doing this with Troy. That first time, when you were watching me conduct a session with Troy, how would you have felt if I'd been working with a woman instead? Tying her up, touching her, bringing her to orgasm?"

"I . . . well, you hardly knew me then, and . . ."

"How would you feel about it now?"

She recoiled, and his eyes flickered. "At some point you have to decide which side of the line you're on," he said. "You have to close the door behind you and stay awhile, settle in and see where this takes us. We're still close enough to the beginning stages we can have fun with it, but I don't think there's any question we're headed down a more serious path. So this thing with Troy, is it a true desire, a desire to explore more about yourself, or is it a way to hold me at arm's length, keep me as the ringmaster of your personal circus?"

She didn't care to have a mirror shined so fully on her internal machinations, but that was part and parcel with Logan. He'd dropped his grip on her arm so she stood before him of her own volition. She wasn't backing away, but she didn't really know where to go, either.

"I've stepped wrong so many times, Logan," she said at last. "I've known what it is to feel a man lose interest, to realize he'd never loved me as much as I thought he did. Not once, but seven times, as if I'm some kind of dysfunctional half-wit who can't get a clue."

He made a noise of protest, because he never let her get away with self-deprecation, but this time she pressed on, needing to make the point. "It's *really* hard to take that leap again. Particularly because of how you are. With time, I could see the weaknesses in the guys I was involved with, weaknesses you don't have. You're a decent, amazing man, and you affect me in a way no one else has. We've only known each other for a short time, but if I saw that loss of interest in your eyes, it would break me in a way none of the others did. I'd be done, finished. This time for good, because I don't think another miracle like you would show up to help convince me otherwise."

When he stepped forward, this time she did back away, shaking her head. He stopped, extended a hand. "Come here, Madison."

She did. He clasped her hand but didn't close the distance, letting her breathe. "I'm sorry," he said. "I let my temper get the best of me. I wasn't as impartial about this as I'd intended to be. The day took kind of a shitty turn."

"I know. I'm sorry," she said, meaning it. "I came out to offer support and friendship, not give you something else to be angry about. I really hate that my baggage fucks things up so often, makes things about me, especially when it's not supposed to be about me at all."

He tightened his hand on hers. "I'll accept your apology if you'll accept mine."

"Done." She swung their hands back and forth, making his lips quirk. "Actually, it's kind of nice to see you lose your cool now and then. You're scary calm sometimes."

"You should see me when a vendor screws up an order." He smiled, but then considered her thoughtfully. "Did you ever choose the men you were with, Madison? Or did they choose you?"

She thought about that, about the mutual flirtation that heralded the beginning of a relationship. She'd never approached a man; he'd always approached her. Sometimes she'd have an interest in someone else, perhaps the man's friend or someone else in the same department or club where they met, but once a man showed interest in her, she would abandon any thought of pursuing another.

"They chose me."

That muscle flexed in Logan's jaw. "So your desires and wants never really entered into it. You're the type of person who takes the ingredients you're given and turns it into a cake. But you never put yourself into the ingredients, your choice or will. I am a choice for you, Madison. A submissive has power. She makes the choice of whom to hand her leash. Look at what you want for yourself. Whether we end up finding something worth keeping or we have to part ways when all's said and done, make sure your will and desires are part of it. Then neither one of us will have regrets."

Madison's surprised gaze lifted to his face, but he wasn't finished. "On top of that, you are an amazing, special miracle in your own right. If you see good qualities in me, I appreciate that, but you have to give credit where it's due. I'd like to think we're bringing out the best in each other, because that's what a good relationship does."

Giving her fingers a final caress, he let her go. "Think about that, and I'll see you Friday. It might be good to think about what you want there as well. As far as whether this is about what he wants or what you want, the answer is both. Troy will be yours for the night. You're responsible for his pleasure, as much as seeking your own."

He returned the coffee cup to her, took the cake. As he moved to the back entrance of his storeroom, she turned the cup over in her hand. "Logan? Will you help me? Help me make sure I do that for him?"

He turned at the door, gave her a tired look that twisted her heart. "I'll do anything you need, Madison. Except be something you settle for."

"Before you asked . . . you seemed like you knew that they chose me," she said slowly. "In my other relationships. Why is that?"

He held her gaze, a clasp as intimate as his hand curled around hers. "Because of what I told you earlier. I knew you were that type of submissive from the beginning. There are a lot of people who enjoy the role, who even have the orientation, but they aren't that way down to heart and soul. You are. Which means I'm going to make damn sure you *choose* me. I don't want you any other way."

She wasn't sure how to interpret that statement, but she did know being classified and tagged wasn't something she necessarily accepted. Maybe with the thing with Troy, she'd show him a different side. She'd show herself a different side.

Or make herself see what he was saying . . . in a different way.

She was having a lot of wardrobe issues lately. Deciding what to wear to help a Dom train a sub, now how to dress like a Domme. But she wasn't really one, was she? She had the full regalia at her store; stilettos, corset, lots of leather, but it felt wrong. Ironically, in this instance, it felt like too much of a costume.

Fortunately, UPS came to her rescue on Friday. She was starting to think of Clarence as a fairy godmother in brown shorts and a roaring, gold-and-brown coach. Or her fairy godmother's shipping service. She snickered at the thought of Logan in a fairy costume.

Clarence offered his serious smile and asked after her day. He took a cup of coffee and a cookie from her and left her with a box on her counter. As she studied it, she admitted she particularly liked the suspense right before she opened these packages and saw what magical thing Logan had sent her to make her feel better about whatever challenge she was facing. A fairy godmother in truth.

Using her scissors to slit open the box, she folded back the top and took a breath, closing her eyes briefly in quiet anticipation before she opened them to take a look.

232 Joey W. Hill

The first time he'd given her a gift, it had been an eye-opening
card game and a set of cuffs. Another time it had been a sexy Catholic school girl costume. This time he'd sent her . . . school supplies.

The box held several rulers, an eraser, a box of colored chalk, and
two books. One was a hardback, Charles Dickens' *Oliver Twist*, and
the other was a large, flexible book. *Discipline for Dummies*, a primer
to help obtuse parents. She choked on a snort that became a full-
throated laugh when she reached the item at the bottom. It was a
quilted tote bag, the type of thing teachers carried, complete with
felt appliqués of an apple, the 2+2 equation, and a colorful stack of
books next to the declaration "World's Best Teacher." Logan was
reminding her this could be playful as well as serious.

While there was no obvious sexual purpose to the items, she
recognized their potential after only a moment's reflection. Logan
didn't miss details, and it was obvious he'd noticed the way Troy's
eyes lit up at her librarian outfit. Maybe he'd asked Troy why that
intrigued him, and the answer had resulted in this. Apparently, Troy
had teacher fantasies. That could explain why Logan did so well as
his training Master, given she herself had imagined him as a stern
schoolmaster more than once. Mentor, friend . . . lover. Master.

"I think I'm falling in love with you."

She'd said it aloud, the words echoing in the quiet of the store.
Her heart leaped into her throat, her brain telling her it was way too
soon to feel that way. Way, way, *way* too soon. But it was okay. It
was her secret. It didn't mean anything if she just said it to herself.
Or to the store. Though it seemed to have a life of its own, it tended
to keep secrets well.

Shaking her head at herself, Madison brought her mind back to
the matter at hand. Wardrobe and props. She had plenty of blindfolds
here and, as far as a teacher outfit, she had a plethora of options. He
hadn't addressed her strap-on question, but she knew she wasn't going
to do that. He probably knew it, too. She could let it rankle her, but

remembering their near-argument, she decided to let it go. It was time to close up the store, go home and get dressed.

She prepared herself in Wonderland, the upstairs bedroom where Alice had kept her vast personal collection of role-playing outfits and dress-up options. Sexy teacher was merely a modification of librarian, only Madison decided to make the skirt a little tighter and shorter, the blouse open an extra button to show more cleavage. After all, it was important to tempt her student into bad behavior. Inappropriate staring at the teacher's ass or down her blouse would certainly be grounds for punishment. She added the thick glasses, pulled her hair back up in a bun and slipped into the same sensible pumps.

Madison surveyed herself in the full length mirror with satisfaction. Maybe it was because she'd had to wear the same neutral business clothes every day at her former job as an investment manager in Boston. Now that she was letting herself play dress-up again, she was finding she really liked it, maybe even more than she had as a little girl, and she'd liked it a lot then. Logan apparently liked it when she played dress-up, too. When she thought about how he might like this outfit, she realized she was dressing for him as much as for Troy. Maybe more.

Alice's picture was stuck in the corner of the mirror's frame. It was one Madison had taken when they were at a Western bar out in Arizona. Her sister was grinning, her eyes dancing as she raised her beer in salute. Madison took it as a blessing on her night and smiled back.

"Here goes nothing. I bet you're laughing, thinking of me playing Mistress to some young, hot guy. And wishing you could be there to see it. I wish you could, too."

She switched off the light, then stopped. Pressing a kiss to her

234 Joey W. Hill

palm, she put it against the picture in the semidarkness, closing her eyes. "Love you, sis."

If she believed in some of the fantasy stories she'd read as a child, heaven was perhaps only on the other side of that mirror, and Alice was pressing her palm to hers there. She held an extra minute, just in case, and then she left the room, closing the door behind her.

On the way to the store, she listened to some of her favorite upbeat music selections, refusing to let herself get bogged down in anxieties or doubts. Logan had sent her a good message. She was going to have fun with this, damn it. She wasn't going to overthink it.

Letting herself in through the back, she headed toward Logan's special room. As she went through his furniture workshop and approached the open door, she saw he'd moved some of his finished pieces in there, arranged them in an inviting display so they were available to her, or adding to the ambiance, even if she didn't actually use them.

Three people waited for her. She'd kind of hoped Shale would change her mind about coming. Knowing that hadn't happened, her nervousness returned, showing just how close beneath the surface it rode. The Mistress would witness her missteps, have to intervene to keep her from causing Troy permanent harm.

No. She wasn't going to chicken out now. As an asset manager, she'd met her share of intimidating clients, proving within the first ten minutes she could handle their assets with care and beyond their expectations. She did it by not being afraid to ask questions and by showing sensible initiative. Troy's care was the priority. She'd *want* the Mistress to step in if necessary. Everyone understood she was new to this.

Bolstered by that thought, she stepped into the room. Troy was sitting on a stool, Shale resting comfortably between his spread knees, her backside propped against his thigh, her hand on his shoulder as she spoke to Logan. Troy had his hands on his own knees. It was clear he'd been commanded to keep his hands to himself. He was already blindfolded, a solid black eye mask probably intended for BDSM play, not a convenient scrap of cloth like a scarf. He wore jeans and shirt, but his feet were intriguingly bare, one curved around the bottom rung of the stool, the other braced between his Mistress's booted feet.

Shale was an attractive late-twenty-something with streaked blond hair and a good manicure. She wore snug jeans with the heeled boots and a V-neck rock band T-shirt, AC/DC. It wasn't the look Madison would have expected from a woman who wanted a custom-ized cage built for her submissive. But when her gaze turned to Madison, she changed her mind. Logan had said he could tell Mad-ison was a submissive. Seeing Shale and Logan standing so close together, Madison identified a similar sharp attentiveness to their expressions and a self-assured body language hard to ignore. She didn't expect they were all the same like that, but given the level of submissive Troy was, and the type of Master that Logan seemed to be, it made sense that such a close, trusted associate would share his stamp of interest or drive in the Dominant side of things.

Her attention was also caught by the body language between Troy and Shale. Their reunion early in the week had obviously been welcome and intense. Even now, blindfolded, the way Troy tilted his head and canted his body toward his Mistress, and how her hands barely left him for even a second before they were drawn back as if magnetized to the heat of his skin, told Madison how closely bonded they were. Despite her attempt to play dress-up and fun rock music to set a light mood, seeing that one significant thing, evidence of a Dom/sub relationship that was hitting all the right notes, set off an ache inside her.

"There she is." Logan straightened from where he'd been leaning against the workbench in a relaxed, conversational pose. "Right on time. Shale, this is Madison. Madison, Shale."

Shale extended a hand and Madison met it with a firm grip. "It's a pleasure to meet you. Thank you . . . for agreeing to do this."

She wasn't sure if that was the right thing to say, but apparently she didn't commit any faux pas, because Shale smiled. Her gaze swept Madison, a quick assessment. "He was a little too eager to do this, which earned him a healthy punishment. I expect that's *my* reward for agreeing to it."

She flicked Troy's ear with her long nails, and he tilted his head in deference to her, a faint smile on his face. He kept his head bowed, obviously ordered not to speak.

"Any particular setup you need, Madison?" This from Logan, all warm and neutral courtesy. "We're here to observe and help you with props. We'll intervene if you go into unhealthy territory, but don't take that as a slap down. I know you don't want to hurt Troy from a misstep."

"Definitely." While all the equipment was rather exciting, what she wanted was fairly simple. "Those old-timey wooden chairs you have in the store. The ones for children? Can they take a man's weight?"

"They're built to double as footstools, so yeah. You need one?"

"Two, please."

"All right." He strode from the room, leaving her there with Shale. She needn't have worried about an empty silence.

"What should Troy call you tonight?" the woman asked.

"Miss Fine."

Shale glanced over her outfit, taking in the bag when Madison lifted it for her inspection. She grinned, a conspiratorial gesture that made Madison feel less anxious. Somewhat. "Very appropriate."

"Troy, I'm dropping you off at school." The woman's tone changed. Charged with authority, it made Madison wonder if Shale was a cop, because she had an immediate vision of her asking a tipsy motorist to walk a straight line. "You'll behave for Miss Fine. I don't want to get any more bad reports. Answer me."

"Yes, ma'am." When Troy swallowed, Madison enjoyed a prick of pure anticipation. Her fingers curled into the fabric of her bag.

Slipping her hand off Troy's shoulder, Shale drew Madison a few steps away, dropping her tone to a whisper. "Logan said you know Troy's safe word. He's got a fairly high tolerance for pain, if you warm him up enough first. He strained his right shoulder the other day, helping Logan unload a truck, so if you're going to cuff him, no extreme angles or stress."

Madison nodded. "I really don't want to hurt him," she said. "So please don't hesitate to interrupt if I do anything wrong."

Shale's eyes warmed in approval, even as she gave Madison a look she knew all too well from Logan. "Don't worry. I won't."

The Mistress moved back to her sub. Her fingers slipped over Troy's ear, to his neck, and then down to rest on the right shoulder, testing the tautness there. "Too bad we went ahead and took your cage home," Shale said. "I could have put you in it until Miss Fine was ready to play with you."

Though Troy kept his eyes down, Madison saw his fingers press into his knees, the restless shift of his body. She imagined Shale commanding him to bring his naked body flush up against the bars, push his cock between them so she could grip it, perhaps even bind it there while she tormented it in various ways. Madison took a steadying breath, wondering if Shale might consider sharing webcam footage. Not likely.

She thought of herself in that cage, Logan stroking her body through the bars, sliding her forward and then putting clamps and a connecting chain on her nipples on the outside to hold her there in a similar way. She imagined waiting on him to release her, let her out to play . . .

"Here you go." Logan had returned, holding the two small wooden chairs in his large hands. "Where do you want them?"

"Center of the floor, please. Thank you." Madison looked toward Shale. "Are you okay with us getting started?"

"Yes. No need for excess chitchat before a scene, especially when your mind's already getting into it." Shale glanced toward Logan.

"Can we spotlight the chairs, put everything else in shadows, including you and me? It's hard to concentrate the first time, when there are a lot of distractions. I think she'll do better if it feels like it's just the two of them, right?"

Wow. She was really starting to like this woman. Shale had made it clear that Troy was hers with that *I won't hesitate* remark, but she was facilitating, helping Madison to be more comfortable. Which was sensible because, with fewer distractions, Madison was more likely to focus on doing the right thing, building the rapport with Troy. She wouldn't be as self-conscious and awkward, a less-than-optimal situation for everyone. Veronica's Master had proven that all Doms weren't so professional and intuitive, but Logan wouldn't expose her to someone he didn't trust just as much as himself in such a scenario.

"I think it's time to let Troy have a look at you," Shale said. "To help him center as well. What do you think, Miss Fine?"

"It's only a minute until the bell rings," Madison nodded, warming up to it. "It's time for him to get to class."

Logan had dimmed the lights as Shale suggested, and was in the shadows by the workbench, though Madison felt his attentive gaze. She didn't look toward him, not sure what expression she would see, but feeling it might unsettle her, whatever it was, right before she reached out to interact sexually with another male. As it was, she had to swallow a couple times, take a steadying breath.

Shale stepped behind Troy, loosened the blindfold. "You're now Miss Fine's, Troy. You obey her as you would obey me." With a mischievous twinkle to her eye, blended with a great deal of terrifying Mistress, she brushed her mouth on the back of his neck. "Play nice."

She stepped back to join Logan in the shadows.

Now Madison was in a world of her own creation, with a male waiting to do her bidding. Troy lifted his head.

As he raised his gaze all the way to her face, he covered the terrain starting from her feet. The look in his eyes was different from what she'd seen, even with Logan. It was vibrant, strong. She knew intuitively he wanted to stand up, move toward her, and only a thin veneer of self-restraint held him back. He'd test her, she realized with surprise, make his submission a challenge. Not bratting, not like Logan had described. Troy was just underscoring he was an individual, a male individual, and she'd have to earn his submission.

Anyone who thought a male submissive turned in his man card had never been on the receiving end of such a look. *Wow.* She suspected this was a taste of what Shale felt every time she met those absorbing cerulean eyes, full of power and strength, life. In turn, she experienced a flood of her own power, fueled by how much he wanted her to meet the challenge, how much he wanted the fantasy she could give him, where he'd be held back by her slightest desire or command. The fact this was definitely Troy's choice, not some sick manipulation like what was between Veronica and her Master, made it even more potent.

"Troy, the bell has rung. Why aren't you in your seat?" She pointed to one of the two chairs Logan had left.

Troy moved to it obediently, even as he gave her a sidelong second look, lingering on the curve of her hips in the tight skirt, the deep plunge the button-down blouse revealed. She could tell he was straining his eyes to see the lace edge of her push-up bra. His gaze also hitched over the wooden ruler she'd withdrawn from her bag and held in one hand. When he took a seat in the small chair, his knees came up to his chest, and he had to balance himself carefully on the seat meant for a six-year-old.

Now it was her turn to take pleasure in his choice of outfit. Likely selected by his Mistress, his incredibly snug black T-shirt defined the lean strength of his gorgeous upper body, including the bare curves of biceps. The dark blue jeans he wore rode low on his hips, but they weren't baggy. The shirt was tucked in so she could follow the trim musculature of his waist to the belted waistband. Until he sat down, she could slide her gaze over the impressive imprint of an aroused cock beneath the denim, but his bent-knee position compensated her for the loss of that view with the curve of his buttocks flattened into the chair, the long lengths of his thighs folded up to accommodate the awkward seating.

His full attention still rested on her, and when she met that look this time, she knew the course she'd take.

Before this moment, Madison had had some vague ideas of what she might do, but Shale had been right. Setting the stage helped. She and Alice had done all sorts of skits growing up, impromptu things just for the two of them, and now that flair for drama kicked in.

Crossing her arms over her breasts, she gave him a critical perusal, sweeping her gaze over him from head to toe. Making a tsking noise, she stalked around him, viewing him from every delicious angle. "That shirt is far too tight, Troy," she said abruptly. "It's against school regulations, and you know it. Take it off."

The soft female chuckle from the shadows was a bolstering vote of confidence. "Keep your eyes on the floor," Madison snapped at him. "You're not allowed to ogle the teacher."

"Your skirt isn't regulation, either, Miss Fine," Troy said in a smug drawl. Those blue eyes sparkled at her beneath the fall of hair over his brow. "Just sayin'. Not complaining. Ma'am."

Madison sighed, her lips thinning. "You have impulse control problems, like all naughty boys. We'll have to take care of that. Shirt off," she repeated sternly.

He rose to comply, pulling it over his head and treating her to a gorgeous display of muscles rippling, though she did notice a slight hesitation on the right side, just as Shale had mentioned.

"Over there, at the whipping bench. Bend over it, put your hands on the posts, and don't let go of them."

It was the piece of equipment with the simplest setup, meaning she was least likely to misuse it. As he rose to comply, she returned to her teacher bag.

She'd added a few other things, including a pack of colored construction paper and scissors. As he put his hands on the posts, turning his back to her, she cut off a few inch-wide strips. She could feel Shale's interested attention, and somewhere close to her, a dense energy field that was Logan. Moving to Troy, Madison wrapped a strip around each of his wrists and the adjacent posts, holding him to them with the type of paper cuffs they made in school to decorate Christmas trees.

He still had his eyes down, but he moved a finger, a small caress of her wrist. If she were Shale, he'd be doing it to earn more punishment, but since her hands had trembled a little as she affixed the strips, she had a feeling he was sending her a reassuring message. It helped settle the butterflies—her underlying anxiety that she might truly misstep and harm a friend—a little further.

Acknowledging the message, she let her hand slide over his shoulder and down the curve of his bare back. The jeans were low enough they showed the brand his Mistress had put upon him, the S initial in the small of his back. Madison traced a heart around it, a silent message and accord, one that she saw made Troy's lips curve in a wistful smile, even as his skin shivered under her touch.

She stepped back, returned to her role. "Now, if you flinch during your punishment and break the paper cuffs, you'll double the punishment. Do you understand?"

"Yes, Miss Fine."

Once behind him again, she let out another sigh. "I see your jeans are a violation of regulation as well. Below your hipbones. I can practically see the crack of your ass. What are you wearing under these, Troy? Absolutely nothing, am I correct?"

He nodded. She didn't think, just reacted, slapping him across the broadest part of his bare back with the wooden ruler. He jumped, not expecting the sting, and one of the cuffs ripped. He froze.

At the look in Troy's eyes, Madison felt a surge of something . . . she couldn't really describe it. Triumph, pleasure. He was genuinely dismayed at messing up so early, when he expected so much from himself, but right on the heels of that, she saw an anticipatory spark in his gaze, anticipating what she might do as a result. It was a heady duality. She wondered what she might do in his place, what punishment she would earn from Logan.

She pushed that away. "You don't nod or shake your head to me. Use your words."

"Yes, Miss Fine."

"Open your jeans with your one free hand, push them down. In fact, take them off. You better not break the other cuff while you're doing it."

Though he was already barefoot, it didn't make the task much easier, requiring a lot of careful movement, which she enjoyed thoroughly. The first time Logan had invited her to a session with Troy, Madison had seen him naked—hell, she'd been tied fully clothed against him—but with his Mistress present, Madison was surprised at how she hadn't hesitated to demand he strip. But it wasn't the first time she'd been startled by how easy it was for her to become a part of this world.

Seeing Troy strip was a gift that never lost its luster. Aware of the gleam of Shale's eyes in the darkness, she had a feeling she wasn't alone in that, and Shale had had the privilege of seeing him naked far more often. The shift of those muscular haunches, the pale marble smoothness that made the fingers itch to touch, the ripple of musculature pretty much everywhere as he stretched with unconscious male grace, held Madison rapt until he was done.

Pulling herself out of that, she stepped forward. She trailed her hand down his back again, over that red mark she'd made. Then lower, to the upper rise of his buttocks. Touching him intimately like this, when he was bound by her words and will, not able to interfere or reciprocate until she commanded it, was yet another exotic land. She let her knuckles glide over one cheek, smiling when he shivered, proving he was ticklish. It also made him flex those superior *gluteus maximus* muscles. She thought of him pushing into Shale, her legs locked over him as she ordered him to fuck her deeper, harder . . .

During their movie night, she'd begged to go down on Logan, seeking the deep contentment that had come from that. How she'd wanted him to press her into her mattress, spread her legs and claim her fully, tangling his hands in her hair, eyes pinning her to the bed as much as his body . . .

She brought herself back to the present again, realizing her hand had stilled. "What am I going to do with you?" She wasn't sure if she was talking to herself or Troy.

Returning to the tote bag, she withdrew the two books, the rigid *Oliver Twist*, the flexible *Discipline for Dummies*. As she stepped back up behind him, she tried a couple experimental smacks with the hardback. If she came up at an angle, it gave even Troy's tight ass a nice recoil wobble. But she found the ruler easier to handle, so she set the books aside and gave him another whack with it, this time across the point of his buttocks. Though he twitched from the blow, he held still, working so hard to obey. His head was bent, exposing the tender nape. She flicked the ruler over it, teasing his hair.

"Your hair needs cutting. I'm afraid only military school will help you, Troy. You need a drill sergeant to hammer you with discipline."

"I prefer a woman's discipline, Miss Fine."

"I expect you do. It makes you hard, doesn't it, these little taps with my ruler?" She gave him another, and it wasn't a tap. She was following Shale's direction, ramping up the pain as she went. His fingers dug into the posts, one wrist held by a paper cuff, the other held by her will. Though an erratic breath escaped him, she could see his cock was hard and high. "Look at that disgusting erection. You're having all sorts of nasty thoughts about your teacher. We'll wash your mouth out with soap and maybe it will clean your mind."

"Yes, Miss Fine."

She cut another circle around him. As she did, her gaze lifted and inadvertently locked with Logan's. That was either a mistake, or the absolute right thing to do. Those brown depths captured her, steadied her, guided her. She cleared her throat. "I see Superintendent Scott is here to observe my class today. What would you suggest to handle such an unruly pupil, sir?"

"You have an excellent technique, Miss Fine." His gaze glittered in the shadows, making her heart stutter. "But someone that head-strong, so determined to go his own way, needs the plastic ruler."

She nodded. On quivering legs she moved to her bag and swapped out the rulers. Coming back to Troy, she noticed he'd tensed, perhaps anticipating the greater pain the more flexible ruler would deliver. It hadn't diminished the stiffness of his cock in the least.

Shale caught her eye then. The woman had a condom packet in thumb and forefinger, and waggled it at her with an amused look. Of course. There was no plastic tarp on the floor tonight. When Madison stepped over to her, Shale helpfully ripped the packet open. Madison took it with a nod, and sidled back up to Troy. Enjoying the moment, she pressed herself up against his backside, savoring his indrawn breath as she brought the ruler in front of his face. "Hold this while I make sure you don't mess up my classroom. Dirty boy."

Opening his mouth, he closed his teeth on the plastic shaft. Since her finger was in the way, his bite was gentle—but not too gentle. When she made a noise of mock reproof, he eased up enough so she could remove her finger, then he bit back down on the ruler. She took her time rolling the condom over him, caressing him and delighting at the twitch of his body, the muffled groan.

Everything she was making him do was arousing him further, and she knew just how he felt. God, she knew. She was supposed to be Miss Fine, but part of her wanted to lay her cheek on his back, wrap her arms around his body and melt inside him, become him so she could be as at home in her own submission as he was in his. The longing was suddenly as sharp and needy as his arousal.

She made herself step back, take the ruler from his mouth, but cut another circle around him, trying to refocus. Despite being so aware of Logan, of the way he watched her, she was going to do this. She'd said she was going to see it through. Stopping behind Troy, she eyed that delicious backside. Yeah, she could do this.

Even though she'd already warmed him up as Shale directed, since it was a new weapon she made the first slap light, gauging his reaction. When he seemed to handle that well enough, she gathered up her confidence, gave him a more determined strike. That earned a jump, his breath whistling in between his teeth. A muttered "Fuck."

"Excuse me? Cursing? That will just earn you more punishment."

After several more blows, she'd left a pattern of faint red impressions. She never struck his Mistress's brand, following some intuitive etiquette in that regard, but she ran her nails over it, making him quiver harder.

Every blow Madison gave him resonated in her own nerve endings, in the sensations strumming up her inner thighs. Every move she made, every time she touched him, she was cognizant of the two Doms behind her, tracking all she was doing, how Troy was reacting. But her own awareness was narrowing, zeroing in on the man standing in the shadows behind her.

When she touched Troy's nape, she imagined Logan's fingers trailing along her own. As she marked Troy's ass, the heated regard behind her made her buttocks tense, as if she could feel Logan contemplating doing the same to her, punishing her in all sorts of dark, memorable ways for putting him through this.

It made her hunger grow . . . but not for more of this. She wanted Logan. Her Master.

She stared at Troy's naked back, marked with the ruler, the way his head was bowed. The whipping post faced Shale's direction. Troy's bowed head acknowledged that. He did this all under his Mistress's command. And while Madison had no doubt he had a man's reaction to Miss Fine's provocative behavior and outfit, she was suddenly certain that submitting to Madison at the direction of his Mistress was the strongest source of his arousal.

She was as sure of that as she was that her earlier conversation with Logan about this hadn't been so much about asserting her own will as seeking his permission to do it. He'd granted it, helped her reach this point, but he sure as hell hadn't ordered her to do this. On top of all the other things that were starting to be quite clear, the fire radiating from him told her in no uncertain terms he preferred her *not* to be handling another man intimately front of him. Submissive or otherwise.

She stopped, turned to meet his gaze again. Logan tended to be honest in expression and communication, but his face right now was dispassionate, neutral. He was there to protect and guide her. Yet what had he said earlier? *A submissive has power. She makes the choice of whom to hand her leash. Look at what you want for yourself.*

Glancing toward Shale, Madison registered the avid way the woman was gazing at her submissive. Madison had enjoyed the surge of power, a temporary roller coaster ride, a change of pace. Yet for Shale, the ride never lost its pleasure. Maybe at a certain level, BDSM was a fun, healthy way to achieve extra spice in a relationship, the way she'd indicated to Helen earlier in the day. Playacting to get that zing like when she first took command of Troy. But then there were those who had a deep, abiding desire to serve a Master.

Like herself.

For so long, she'd avoided her fascination with BDSM, period, denying that her craving might be an actual sexual orientation. Probably because of her past relationships' negative reaction to that, when she dared to reveal it. Probably even more because of her own fear of losing control of herself. But Logan had taken her hand, walked her into those waters, and while she'd sometimes stalled at different depths, she'd ultimately kept going forward, because she trusted his lead. And the more she trusted his lead, the more she trusted and let herself face the truth of her own desires.

What she'd done that first night when he tied her to Troy, how quickly she'd gotten caught up in it, yes, at one level it was play, but there was a reality to it at the emotional level she couldn't shake. She'd come closer to admitting it when Logan had come to her house to watch a movie. She wanted to take a closer step toward what it was she was craving, what had lacked definition, but was quickly taking undeniable shape and form.

In short, she'd wanted to try this, and wasn't sorry she had. But it was time to change gears. After she had just a little more fun with it.

Shifting out of Troy's view, she withdrew the heavy wooden paddle she'd bought out of her own stock. She'd sketched and colored in three red shiny apples across the expanse to make it more teacherly. Catching Shale's grin at the design, she smiled back. The Mistress pantomimed a swing, a reminder to come up from a lower position. Pivoting, she ran her knuckles and glossy nails along the small of her own back, the rise of her buttocks, and shook her head, a silent instruction.

Right. Not a good thing to hit higher, where pelvic bones, spine and kidneys could get affected if her swing was too strong. Grateful for the guidance, Madison acknowledged it with a nod, and turned her attention to the unsuspecting Troy, likely braced for another swat with the plastic ruler.

It worked as beautifully as it had last time. Once again, not expecting it, especially with her being an unknown quantity to him in the Mistress role, he jumped . . . and ripped the other cuff. Truth, she'd bound them so close to the post, made them small enough, it was almost impossible for him not to rip them with the least little pull.

His muttered curse, the irritated jerk of his shoulders, were a pure pleasure. She had to quell the desire to plant a kiss on the nape of his sweaty neck. She sighed heavily. "Tsk, tsk. Troy, I'm afraid you're far beyond what I can appropriately address in my classroom. Principal Shale is going to take you personally in hand. She has far more effective methods."

Shale's lips curved with a feral pleasure that told Madison she'd made the right decision, not just for herself, but for Troy. In her wildest dreams, she didn't think she could summon a countenance so full of diabolical promise. As Shale moved forward, the Mistress extended her hand. "Sometimes the most effective tools to handle a stubborn boy are the simplest ones," she said. "If you don't mind sharing your paddle, Ms. Fine, I'll start with that. If that doesn't penetrate his hard head, a baseball bat shoved up his ass should do it."

No doubt. Madison blinked, placed the paddle in Shale's palm. As her fingers closed over it, she met the woman's eyes and mouthed *thank you.* Shale nodded absently, already moving into that zone Logan did, her eyes all for her sub. Troy's shoulders had given an anticipatory twitch when Madison declared her intent to turn him over to "the principal." Now his skin shuddered when Shale ran her nails down his back, following the same track as Madison, only with a little more pressure, the furrows deeper.

His body language shifted. It was subtle but significant, the contrast between visiting a different place, something new and interesting, and coming home. Despite the fact Shale was undoubtedly going to inflict far greater pain on him than Madison could conceive of doing, Troy relaxed even further under his Mistress's touch. He trusted Shale to use pain to take him somewhere beyond every doubt or insecurity he had. In return he would embrace the pain to the point it became intense pleasure for them both.

Wow. Madison was using that word a lot lately, but she was also starting to understand the Marcel Proust quote Alice had kept in her kitchen window. *"The real voyage of discovery consists not in seeking new landscapes, but in having new eyes."*

Speaking of which . . . She faced Logan. Now that she'd officially turned over responsibility for her charge, she had one goal. As she covered the few steps between them, she removed the glasses and unclipped her hair, so it fell to her shoulders. She also stepped out of the pumps so she was barefoot.

When she reached Logan, leaning against his workbench, arms crossed over his chest, she didn't consider any other options. She sank to her knees.

The movement brought an uncanny sense of what she'd seen in Troy when he was turned over to his Mistress. Relief, comfort. A feeling that only increased when Logan put his hand on her head, stroked her hair, as if her kneeling before him was as natural to him as it had felt to her. She didn't want to wait for that pain session. She craved it now. She didn't want to wait for tomorrow when all her ridiculous doubts and insecurities might return, her baggage. Though Logan might be right, that the baggage was what had brought her to him, it was still a pain in the ass.

She wanted to let him know all that in a language he understood, a language she wanted to understand more fully.

"I've misbehaved, sir," she murmured.

His russet eyes kindled in that way that made her want to sigh happily. He understood and agreed. He wasn't going to deny her. She savored the reaction, since she had a feeling it might turn to terror in short order.

"You sure as hell have. The consequences will be severe."

Pulling a cushion from the bottom shelf of the workbench, he dropped it on the floor next to him. "Sit there. Watch Troy's punishment, while I think of the best kind for you."

She shifted to comply, putting her knees on the cushion and sitting back on her heels. As she did so, he caught her loose hair in his fist and jerked her back up onto her knees. She had no time to gasp at the rough movement before he'd claimed her mouth, his tongue tangled with hers, the heat telling her all he'd been hiding behind that façade. When she started to grab hold of his thighs for balance, he growled in her mouth, forcing her to lower her hands, rely on that pull on her scalp for balance. His act of pure possession wrapped like invisible bonds around her body, making the dampness between her thighs become gushing wetness. It was her body's primal response, readying herself for him and him alone.

When he at last released her, he lowered her inch by inch back to the cushion so she was sitting on her heels again. Once there, his burning eyes lingered on her face, his mouth hard. She knew she was trembling. "Watch the Mistress work," he said softly.

It was difficult to watch Shale when all she wanted to do was look at Logan. Especially when she saw he was sporting a sizeable, mouth-watering erection under his jeans. She didn't know if it had been provoked by the kiss, her decision to abandon her Mistress experiment, or because she'd been touching Troy and it was some kind of primitive, chest-beating, testosterone reaction that shouldn't thrill her modern female mind but absolutely did. Whatever the reason for his impressive response, she appreciated the results to the point it was hard to tear her gaze away.

But he'd commanded her to watch Shale and Troy, so she did. She curled her hand around his calf, though, hoping he wouldn't tell her she couldn't touch him. He didn't.

During the kiss, she'd been vaguely aware of the harsh clap of the paddle, Troy's grunts of pain. When she turned her attention back to them now, Shale had set the weapon aside and reclaimed the plastic ruler. Picking up the other children's chair and giving it an artful twirl in one hand, she pointed to the floor with the other. "Lie down, face up."

Troy complied, and Madison had a glimpse of the red marks Shale had left on his buttocks, painful-looking strikes with the paddle that made Madison wince but which she saw hadn't diminished Troy's aroused response at all. Though she hadn't yet experienced it herself, she was getting a good idea of why it could make a certain kind of submissive even needier, craving more. As her ass rested against her heels, she wondered if, before night's end, she'd have her own marks to show. The crazy thing was, she was pretty sure she wanted that. And she wanted Logan's hand to be the one wielding the blows.

Shale put the chair over his head, the front legs planted on either side of his neck, the back ones just clearing his crown. The crosspiece that stabilized the bottom of the chair was over the bridge of his nose, effectively holding his head in place, especially when Shale took a seat on it. Madison noticed that she paused before she did so, looking toward Logan. Glancing up, Madison saw her Master give the Domme an imperceptible nod. He'd said the chair could hold an adult, but Shale was likely confirming.

Safety always came first. It was a tribute to their confidence in their roles that it didn't dilute the thrilling, anxious feel of being under their control. It simply kept the not-erotic feelings of true fear out of it. Madison's analytical mind worked on that, even as her subconscious used it as all the more reason to fall under Logan's spell. A win-win, right?

Taking a seat on the chair, Shale planted one booted foot on Troy's upper abdomen, such that Madison saw a red impression gather around the pointed heel. Shale leaned forward, her hair falling over her shoulder as she stroked his chest. "Look at that hard-on. Shameful. All for Miss Fine. I think we'll be homeschooling you from now on."

"No, not for her, Mistress. For you. Because you were watching."

"I didn't give you permission to talk." Shale brought the ruler down in a sharp slap on his lower abdomen. He jerked, his hands flexing at his sides, a breath whistling out between his teeth.

"Spread your legs. Stretch out your arms as well."

He did it without hesitation, exposing his testicles and sheathed cock to her. When she brought the ruler down, hard, it slapped his inner thigh about five inches below that area. He flinched but didn't move otherwise, his arms out to his sides, palms open.

Shale did it again, and Madison was impressed with her control, because she never came closer than a hand's span to his genitals, though she managed to hit the same spots a few times. Madison expected his mind registered it as much closer, since he couldn't see anything but the bottom of the chair.

Shale looked stern, far more punitive than Miss Fine. Madison glanced up at Logan. His face was expressionless again, but she didn't sense any concern for Troy. She shifted her attention back to the tableau before them because, no matter the uncertain roiling in her stomach at how Troy took his punishment, she couldn't deny she was captivated, and by far more than the sexual component. Though he couldn't see her, it was as if Troy's gaze was fixed on his Mistress. The look on his face matched something Madison understood deep inside. Yet his look took it to a more profound level, because he was further along that road than Madison. He would truly do anything Shale desired. He trusted her with everything. He had utter faith in her control over him.

It was something she'd rarely seen reflected on any adult face, including her own. How long had it taken Shale and Troy to reach that point together? What would happen if it ever turned in the wrong direction, the relationship ending? Troy and Shale were relatively young. How did one recover from such a loss? Trust her to think of that.

Shale stood up, removing the chair, but laying it on its side. "Step into this space."

The supporting pieces beneath the chair formed an open square. Troy rose and stepped in one foot at a time, the opening small enough he had to work first one foot and then the other under the slats, so the chair was a wooden manacle around both his ankles. If Shale wanted him to move forward, he'd have to do it with a very short shuffle, several inches at a time.

"Spread your feet as far as you can, then bend over and grab the sides."

Madison noticed that Shale kept her hand on his back throughout. She was positioned to steady him if he lost his balance. This, despite the fact that cruel expression on her lovely features never altered. When he bent over, spreading his thighs the few inches possible, she reached between them and gripped his testicles, squeezing hard enough to earn a groan from him. She brushed her knuckles over those reddened rectangular areas where she'd slapped him with the paddle.

"Tonight, I'll lock you in your new cage. You can listen to me bring myself to climax with my vibrator. If you stay still and quiet, you might earn the right to lick me clean afterward. Or maybe not. You were too eager to play with your little friend. I'm going to fuck you with my strap-on before I go to work in the morning, so when Logan sees you, he'll know you have a sore ass, because you had to be reminded who owns it." She released him. "Straighten up."

She had the sultry voice of a siren, purring out the dire threats. When she caught his hair, yanked him up by it, Troy's face showed the same emotions Madison had seen when he was underneath the chair. Total acceptance and devotion, but now it was coupled with aggressive desire. His eyes sparked at her. "It's always your ass, Mistress."

She gave his hair another rough tug. "Talking without permission. You never learn. One more word, and I'll be plugging your mouth and ass for the duration of the night."

Gripping his buttock, she must have probed deeper, because a ripple of reaction went through his body, his thighs tensing, stomach contracting.

"You greased yourself up for your little teacher, just in case." Her gaze locked with his. "And now you'll pay the price for that."

Whatever she did had Troy's facial features constricting. Shale put her hand on his stomach, a steadying force, and Madison heard her soft whisper. "Hold on to my shoulder, Troy."

The tender order in the midst of a humiliating punishment had a lump coming to Madison's throat as Troy's face contorted. He grabbed Shale's shoulder as her stimulation forced the climax that made his thighs tremble violently, his hips jerk. If he hadn't been wearing a condom, the semen would have fountained out of his cock. As it was, Madison saw it fill the tip, spread out over the head. He groaned, chin dropping down to his chest as Shale wrested the last drop from him, ruthless in her intent, while her hand stayed firm and steady on his upper abdomen. She'd shifted closer so he was leaning against her, a loose embrace that looked anything but ruthless.

When he was done, his breathing labored, she held him, the two of them swaying together. Madison could tell even in his post-climactic stupor, Troy was trying to keep his whole weight off her, as cognizant of her care as she was of his. It was beautiful, in a way she realized most people wouldn't recognize, seeing only the graphic representation of sex, not all the complex interplay of trust and intimacy.

In time, he was able to straighten. "All right," Shale said quietly. "Let's get you out of this chair. Then I want you to clean up and get dressed."

His minute shifting during the climax had pushed the chair back against his ankles. He'd need help adjusting it to get free, but when Shale started to bend, his arms tightened around her.

Madison glanced up at Logan. "May I help?"

He gave her a significant look. "That would be appropriate."

Troy didn't want his Mistress bending before him. And Madison had recognized it, volunteered to help. Which not only bemused her but also explained that potent look from Logan. Her insight had pleased him, which gave her a ridiculous glow.

Was this the track that Troy and Shale had followed to get to where they were? Learning to embrace all the permutations of Dominant and submissive in themselves, until it was just an instinct one followed, like breathing? Instincts that twined together into the tightly knit relationship, give-and-take, she'd just seen?

As she moved in Troy's direction, Madison kept following that instinct. She lowered her gaze and addressed Shale. "May I help, Mistress?"

"Yes, you may. Hold the chair steady while I hold him. No argument," she said sharply.

Madison realized that last was directed at Troy. Shale latched on to his arm, the other hand on his hip. "You're shaking," she said. "I'm not going to let my property get damaged because of some misguided I-can-do-it-myself testosterone surge."

Troy's lips twisted in a rebellious moue, those eyes flashing again, but he complied, letting Madison hold the chair steady as he stepped out of it, his Mistress's balancing hand on him until he was free. Then she gave him a little push toward his clothes and turned toward Logan.

"An enjoyable evening. Shorter than I'd expected, but not you, I think."

Logan gave Shale a look that suggested he would have preferred her not to say that. From the curve of Shale's lips, she knew it. The Mistress glanced down at Madison. "Don't make it too easy on him. Isn't a woman alive who doesn't enjoy seeing him break a sweat."

She moved toward Troy. He'd hiked his jeans back on and was about to don the T-shirt. She took it away from him, reaching up to caress his jaw before she leaned in to him for a kiss. Madison watched how Troy caught her waist. His arm banded around her as the kiss deepened. All his male strength was unleashed in a moment that was now more about the two of them as lovers, not just Dom/sub.

When Shale at last eased back, her eyes full of Troy, Madison realized she was aching all the way down to the bottom of her scarred heart.

"I love you," Shale whispered. "Always."

"Same goes, Mistress," he responded. Madison thought he was oblivious to anyone else in the room. Though the session was technically ended, it was clear he was fully hers.

Shale gave him a tap, tilted her head toward Logan, a reminder. Troy's eyes cleared and he turned toward the other Dom, though his arm remained around Shale. "Thank you for my training, Master

Logan," Troy said formally. Then his gaze shifted to Madison, still folded on her knees on the floor by the child's chair. "And thank you for your discipline, Miss Fine."

A tiny smile played around his lips, telling her he'd probably tease her about that next time they saw each other. Shale had mentioned him seeing Logan tomorrow. Madison hoped that meant Troy would still be working at the hardware store, that it hadn't been only about his training. Since he'd told her he was buried under student loans, she figured it likely.

The couple left them, their departure covered by the air-conditioning. The fan turned on like a windy sigh, the building vibrating as it always did when the unit engaged.

The spotlight highlighted the chairs where she knelt next to them, Logan still in the shadows. He pulled a tall stool away from the workbench, slid a hip on it and pointed to that cushion beside him.

Rising to her feet, she made it there on unsteady legs, sank back down, looking up at him. "At times, I thought she was really mad at him. But she wasn't, was she?"

"No." He reached down, caressed her face. It felt right, sitting at his knee, him touching her. "A responsible Dominant would never discipline her sub physically when she's truly angry." A smile touched his mouth. "Being female, Shale has far more potent ways of punishing Troy when she's actually pissed at him. Passive-aggressive sarcasm, silent treatment, the use of those dreaded two words, 'I'm fine.' Believe it or not, the boy has a bit of a temper on him as well. He can hold his own with her when they disagree."

She did believe it. She'd seen it in the stubborn set of his lips, that quick flash in the eyes. A couple weeks ago, that wouldn't have made sense to her, hard to reconcile with his eagerness to be treated as a submissive, willing to play a naughty schoolboy and be spanked, but after tonight it did. She just wasn't sure she could put the comprehension of it into actual words. Any more than she could the feelings inside herself.

"Shale is a very good Mistress," Logan continued. "The cage and strap-on, she'll do. She won't put in the gag and plug all night. That was mind play only. That's too long to have something up his ass, given how sensitive those tissues are, and no Dominant would gag a sub and go to sleep, because she can't monitor his breathing."

That smile reached his eyes. "At some point tonight, Troy will beg enough that she'll let him into the bed with her, and then she'll ride him into complete dehydration. Beyond being his Mistress, she's wildly in love with him."

"It's obvious," she said. "Being around them is like watching a dream come true. It hurts some."

She wasn't sure she should have put it that way, but it was true enough. Except for the "some" part. It actually hurt a lot, especially injected with the painful, irresistible hope she couldn't seem to quell inside herself, thanks to the man beside her.

His fingers curved over the line of her jaw, his eyes becoming softer, twisting the knife such that she swallowed, dipped her head into his touch. "It's a game, Madison," he murmured. "A very serious, very real game about the things we need deep down inside ourselves."

"She said you expected this session to be short." She frowned. "Did you think I'd chicken out, or not have the stomach for it?"

"The latter, but not in the way you're thinking. It's not a failing or shortcoming, Madison. Some switches are as much identified with both sides of the whip as I'm a Dom or Troy's a sub, but a great many more of them are merely sexually adventurous. They don't need to be only one or the other to find soul-deep fulfillment with someone."

"But you do." That much was clear. It shed a different light on their earlier discussion about where this might be headed. If she wanted to be with him, if she wasn't as much into the submissive side of things as he was a Dominant, could it work?

"Do you remember what I said about bringing your choices and preferences into the decision of where we're going?" he asked.

She nodded.

"You wanted to try the other side, and you enjoyed it." A rueful look crossed his face. "I won't say it was enjoyable for me to watch you touch another man, though I did enjoy watching how you had fun with it, the revelations you made. But at a certain point, you crossed the line between fun and something deeper. I saw the click. You not only picked up on the deeper layer of what this means to Troy, but what it means to you. If it was just all fun and games, just a sexual adventure, you could have seen it through to a different end, but you sensed there was something more there. And that was what you wanted, wasn't it?"

At her silence, he touched her chin. "I know you feel like I'm infringing on your sense of choice when I state something like that, so I'll make it a question."

"Versus a statement of the obvious?" She gave him a narrow look, and he chuckled.

"Let's pretend I'm asking it as a question, to save me from a possible dose of female silent treatment. You made your choice, didn't you?"

As she wrestled with her answer, he slid a finger along her collarbone, hooked her bra strap. With gentle pressure, he brought her back up onto her knees, bent and put an arm around her waist, sliding her and the cushion closer so she was between his knees, one of those effortless shifts using his upper body strength that made her stomach tilt pleasantly. In this position, she could settle her palms on his thighs to balance herself there, and she did so.

"When you made that decision and came to me, wanting to kneel at my feet, it took all I could do not to send them packing right then. Everything in me said *mine*."

The look in his eyes, the way her heart leaped at his words, told her the only thing she was struggling with was her pride. Yet the possible truth made her want to skitter away like a rabbit. He laid a hand over hers on his knee, holding her in place.

"I don't want it to scare you away, Madison. Until you say it back, and truly mean it, want it with all your heart, then it's not any obligation on you, you understand? We're each responsible for our own feelings, no matter how much they overlap or tangle."

"I want to believe you. I just have a deficit of trust in . . . everything."

"Do you want me to help you with that?"

She swallowed at what she saw in his gaze. Promise, threat. Change. "Yes. But I'm scared. A little bit in some ways, a lot in others."

His expression became tender, making that twist in her chest even tauter. She expected it was a unique look for him, one he didn't often bestow on a woman. Else he'd have a line of groupies outside his front door every morning. "I know the feeling."

"Nothing scares you."

"Spiders make me scream like a girl when they jump out from between the boxes in the storeroom. Troy has to do the catch and release."

"Liar." She aimed a punch at his midriff, which he blocked, capturing both her hands and bringing her to her feet. Molding his palms over her buttocks, he drew her up against him.

"Why, Miss Fine. You're wearing a thong. That's as much against school regulations as Troy not wearing any underwear at all. When an authority figure breaks the rules, their punishment is twice as severe."

Fun and games. He would start her off with fun and games, understanding how she liked to role-play. All she had to do was take the bait, with full knowledge that he'd ultimately take her far beyond the amusement park, into the dark workings beneath it.

She held his gaze, the two of them caught in that stasis, waiting for her decision. Then she lowered her gaze, plucked at a button of his shirt as she gave him a coy glance through her lashes. "Is there anything I can do to get out of it . . . Superintendent?"

"Are you offering me a bribe, Miss Fine?" His disapproving look made her toes curl. He was really good at this. She wondered if he'd done role-playing as a child as well. Pirates, Captain Kirk, cowboys.

"A sexual favor, actually." She moistened her lips, glanced down significantly. "I have excellent oral communication skills. I've heard you have a rather large . . . need in that department."

"Rumors get exaggerated." His eyes danced, but then they lost all humor, his mouth firming. "But as tempting as your favors might be, your behavior requires punishment. You won't manipulate me, Miss Fine."

Rising from the chair, he took her arm, accentuating the difference in height and weight with that one shift. He drew her over to something that looked like a wooden pup tent. The six-inch-wide padded spine was flanked and supported by polished planks. Buckled cuffs were mounted on tracks, spaced horizontally along the planks.

The potential of such a piece filled her mind as he turned her to face him. Yet when she glimpsed his face, she realized he'd turned her back to the equipment to make it clear she had only one focus in this room. Him. Her Master.

Before she expected or could brace herself against the act, he'd laid hold of the neckline of her shirt and jerked. One strong movement ripped it open down the front, sending buttons scattering. She choked on a gasp but he didn't even pause, smoothly pulling it off her shoulders and down to her elbows, so her arms were caught against her body.

He could become intimidating in such a breathtaking way, so quickly. His gaze coursed over the lace bra, the way her breasts were displayed in the cups. When he caressed them, a plea hummed in her throat, but he wasn't done undressing her. He stripped away the skirt and thong beneath so she was standing before him, her lower half naked. With him fully dressed, it only highlighted the power difference. She'd had a sense of that in the Catholic schoolgirl uniform on movie night, him in his sports coat and jeans, but after everything else tonight, the feeling was even more pronounced.

He lifted her, making her straddle the beam. The slick vinyl cover pressed against wet, swollen tissues. Rows of golden tacks held down the vinyl, their rounded heads providing bumps of friction against her pussy, her clit.

Capturing her throat with one strong hand, he held her immobile for a demanding, heated invasion of her mouth with his. When she automatically reached for him, trying to clutch his arms for balance, he broke the kiss.

"Hands behind your back. You haven't earned the right to touch me."

She did it, arms trembling as her fingers clung to one another. He resumed the kiss, taking his time with it, but there was nothing leisurely about it. He lashed at her tongue, demanded she open even wider with the pressure of his lips. If she'd been standing, her knees would have buckled. He put his other palm against her back, and he'd placed her close enough to the end of the sawhorse her breasts were against his chest. Her legs weren't long enough to reach to the bottom of the tent piece, so they dangled, her calves brushing the empty cuffs.

As he kissed her, he found the back fastener of her bra under the torn shirt and released it. Then he pushed the shirt off her arms, took the bra away, all without breaking that hot, wet connection. He lifted her again, his arm a line of heat against her bare skin as he slid her back on the beam, pressing her down on her stomach. Her body lay along its length, her cheek resting against the six-inch expanse of vinyl. He reached beneath her, making her wetter as he gripped her breasts and adjusted them so her cleavage was widened, the inside curves of her breasts against the planks on either side.

He cuffed her ankles and just above each of her calves so her legs were drawn up into a bent angle against the surface of the planks. Pulling her hips to the back edge of the beam put her pussy in a highly exposed—and accessible—position. He adjusted her wrists and elbows like he had her knees and ankles, only in the opposite direction, so her upper arms were clear of her breasts, giving him clear access to them. She realized she looked somewhat like a jockey riding a racehorse running full out. Her heart was racing like one.

Being vulnerable and helpless to Logan shot her arousal up to a level that eclipsed even the most intense climax she'd had before she'd met him. When he took advantage of her helpless position, bending over her to take a solid grip of her breasts on either side, she gasped and moaned as he fondled her nipples, squeezed the curves. He pushed himself against her exposed cunt, rubbing his steel cock beneath his jeans over the moist lips, making her twitch and squirm, trying to rub back. He drew back before she could get any measure of pleasure out of that.

"Already hot and slick. I think it's a good thing I recognized you as a discipline problem, Miss Fine. Your shameless teasing corrupts innocent, hormonal boys like Troy."

Because she couldn't resist the impudent eye roll, she won a firm, sharp slap that made her buttocks wobble and her hands ball in the cuffs. "Every time I strike," he said, "I expect you to say 'I'm a bad girl, sir.' If I don't feel certain you mean it, I'm going to use something that hurts more."

He struck again, harder, and she yelped. "I'm a bad girl, sir."

And again. "I'm a bad girl, sir."

And again.

"You're just not repentant enough, Miss Fine." He moved to his workbench, rummaged through it, came forth with a wooden dowel. "This should help."

"Please . . ."

"Not one of the words we discussed." He brought the dowel against her hindquarters again, and fuck, it definitely hurt more. She wondered if the ruler she'd used on Troy's flesh was comparable to this. Then Logan hit her again and she realized she hadn't obeyed his command.

"I'm a bad girl, sir!"

He kept doing it, and she kept saying it. It was supposed to be a game, right? So why was it, every time she said it, every time he made it more painful, more emphatic, a lump grew thicker in her throat? And she didn't want him to stop, even though it hurt like hell. There was a moment of *Oh, fuck, please stop,* followed by *No, don't stop. Don't stop . . .* Then the really crazy one: *Make it hurt more.* Until she was begging for mercy.

Somewhere along the way, she wasn't saying she was a bad girl. Not exactly.

"I'm a bad . . . I'm bad . . . bad . . ."

Things started to unfold in her mind. Alice dying. Leroy leaving. Every time a man had walked away because she'd failed him. Actually not so much him at all. Herself. She'd failed herself. Over and over and over again. Because she couldn't figure out how to get it right.

I'm so bad . . . I failed . . . I was wrong . . . I'm sorry. Sorry . . .

She was saying the words whether he was striking her or not. When he switched from the dowel back to his hand, every impact resounded through her like the bell of a church. It vibrated through her feet, her chest, a call to salvation, to redemption, to damnation, regret and unforgivable sin.

"I'm so sorry. I'm so, so sorry . . ."

She remembered holding her sister's thin hand as life slipped from her, and now Madison was crying, her fingers clutched into fists in the cuffs. Her heart clenched up the same way. And yet, as he punished her, her sex was as wet as her eyes. If he were a magician and had sawed her in half, she couldn't be more divided.

She was lifting into his strikes, because she craved his hand more than the dowel, his heated palm smarting against her flesh. He paused, and she heard his belt being unbuckled. Was he going to hit her with his belt? Given the power and strength he had in his hand, the idea made her quake . . . and yearn. She could use her safe word. She could, even if saying Alice's name right now might literally tear her heart open to bleed out inside the rest of her body. But she wanted this, wanted all the punishment he could dish out. She wanted to immerse herself in the pain of redemption and paying for her sins, for the hope that on the other side of it she could come out clean. Deserving of love.

He didn't use his belt, but a weapon far more potent. He leaned over her, rough jaw brushing her cheek. "You aren't bad, Madison. Just lost. We all get lost."

A sob choked her, and he pressed his jaw harder against her, making an incoherent, soothing noise. "I'm going to fuck you now, make it all better. Would you like that?"

She nodded, feeling the scratch of his five-o'clock shadow against her fairer skin. She needed him to make it all better.

"Then ask me."

"Please . . ." She swallowed, tasted the salt of her tears. "Please, Master. I need you . . . I need you."

She was supposed to say "Please fuck me," but that was all she could get out. Fortunately, Logan seemed to realize it meant the same thing.

She was vaguely aware of the ripping noise of a condom. Then the head of his cock was against her cunt, spread and flushed for him, the juices sucking him in so that she let out a deep, shuddering sigh as he slid into her, worked his way deeper, all the way to the hilt, so his thighs were pressing against the back of hers. He hadn't taken his jeans all the way off. He was still wearing everything, underscoring her nakedness, his total control of her and the situation.

She dug her fingers into the polished wood beneath her, her eyes closing so her wet lashes fanned her cheeks. He didn't move, didn't start to thrust as her quivering tissues anticipated. Instead, he laid his body over hers and gripped her wrists above the cuffs, his fingers tangling with hers. With a muffled sob, she clung to them so hard she was afraid she might hurt him, but he didn't draw back. Instead, he placed a long kiss on her nape, bared because her hair had slipped down over either side of her neck. Then another kiss on the top bump of her spine. Each touch of his mouth was full of quiet meaning that broke her open further.

"Logan . . ."

"Sssh. I'm here, Madison. I'll always be here. Long as you want and need me."

At this entirely raw moment, she couldn't imagine needing anyone more. The depth of her feelings frightened her. She'd thought herself head over heels in love before, had torn herself open for lovers, removed all shields so she'd had no defenses when a lover thrust the steel of rejection through her. She'd *sworn* she'd never do that again. Sworn it in heart's blood. Meant it so much she'd sacrificed her relationship with the one person she'd always loved soul-deep. Alice.

She trembled. "Please start moving, Logan. Make the thoughts go away."

"You don't have to be afraid of them." He surrounded her, held her. "I won't let them tear you apart."

"I'm afraid they'll ruin this. Please?"

"Beg, and maybe I will." He shifted, a push deeper, and her tissues convulsed around him, making her moan. His fingers were still tangled with hers, and she was able to move her head, put her mouth on them, her lips parted so her teeth cut against his knuckles.

"Please, Master. Please . . . fuck me. Make me forget."

"I'd rather make you forgive. But one step at a time." Slowly, he straightened above her, moving his hands from her wrists to her back, sliding down either side of her spine so she didn't feel the loss of his weight, his heat, so keenly. Putting both hands on her hips, he withdrew just as gradually, then pushed back in the same way.

Just like that, every thought went away, her body's responses taking up all her energy to laser in on the wealth of sensations he created. He was a nice, thick size that rubbed the right ways, inside and outside. As he thrust into her more firmly, his testicles pressed into her clit, sending a pleasurable little spasm through her.

"Oh," she whispered. "Yessss."

He did it again. Her backside was sore from his punishment, but the impact of his body against that tender flesh just added to the spiraling feelings. He held to the same pace, though from the clutch of his fingers, the rasp of his breath, she could tell he was like a bow being drawn, close to loosing the arrow. She was right with him. She couldn't control any of it, except for lifting her hips to every thrust, trying to push back against him, inspire him to increase his pace, but he was stubborn as hell, holding on to all control, making sure the buildup was excruciating. She gasped at each stroke, then moaned, then pleaded.

"Please . . . Master . . ."

He caught a fistful of her hair, pulling her head up and back, emphasizing her bondage, the imposition of his will. She cried out as her clit and the walls inside began to spasm, a precursor to climax. With every stroke, her clit was rubbed against those smooth tacks.

"Ask me to come, Madison. You don't come until I say so."

"Please, Master. Please let me come. And you come, too. Please." She wanted to feel it, wished he would tear away the condom.

"You don't want it bad enough, Miss Fine. You aren't really begging." Sliding his hand beneath her, he lifted her hips, denying her the bumpy stimulation of the golden tack heads as he continued to thrust.

By the time he let them both go, she was begging in ways that creatures tormented by hellfire would. She was crying out his name, calling him Master, pleading for his permission. When at last he let her have that contact with the beam, gripped both hips anew and started thrusting hard enough he was smacking his testicles against her with every stroke, she was screaming. She couldn't hold off any more.

"Please . . . Master . . ."

"Come now, Madison. Let me hear you."

The sound that ripped from her throat was like the dying shriek of a civilization, long and drawn out, laden with the emotions she was releasing along with the climax. New tears bathed her face when the intense spasms started to ease, and then he set her off again by releasing at last. A paroxysm of aftershocks gripped her, goaded by his groans of male pleasure, the bruising grip of his fingers. He slammed into her, not holding back, letting her feel the sheer, rutting animal demand, his mastery unleashed fully in the ultimate act of control, fucking her into insensibility.

Every second of this would haunt her dreams. He hadn't climaxed until she did everything he commanded, holding control over her pleasure and his own until the very end. The significance of that alone would give those dreams an erotic, liquid turn. She anticipated waking in an intense state of arousal every morning for the foreseeable future.

She bet he knew that. He'd said most Doms had a sadistic side, after all. But the real surprise was finding she was more of a masochist than she'd known. His brand of sensual cruelty only made her want one thing—more.

When he released her, there was no choice but to be carried. She was boneless. He readjusted his clothes and lifted her off the structure, then put her feet on the floor only the second needed to scoop her up in his arms. He took her to a curtained opening she'd assumed held more tools, but instead she saw it was a small office, complete with couch, flat screen and desk. He settled on the couch, holding her in his arms, keeping her warm with his body. She was perspiring, but shivering as well, as much nerves as anything, but the cooling sweat was part of it. Pulling a throw off the top of the couch, he put it around her, though she threaded her arms under his and stayed against his body so nothing interfered with her connection to his heat, the warmth she needed most of all.

He made her drink water, eat a couple of crackers. Even on top of the trembling, occasionally her body would jerk in a new set of spasms. Tears kept spilling out of her eyes, no rhyme or reason. He wiped them with tissues, even wiped her nose because she couldn't let go of him. If he shifted, her grip only tightened. She was broken down so thoroughly she had no restraint or filter for her emotions.

He stroked his hand over her hair, cupped her skull, rocked her, spoke quietly to her. She had no idea what he was saying. His voice was the important anchor, not the content. He could have been reciting a bus schedule to her.

"Oh, God, Logan." Those were her first three words, when some rational thought returned. Her voice was high and thin. "Is it always like that?"

"No. The first time you crack open your soul, it has to bleed out all the pus and pain. It might take a few sessions, but eventually it starts to run more clean. You reach a different kind of subspace. Just as powerful, but different."

She turned that idea over in her head in a drifting, hazy way, then gave up any in-depth analysis tonight. She'd have as much chance of discovering a cure for cancer with peanut butter and bananas. "Okay."

His jaw tensed against her, probably a smile. But when she tipped her head up, she found his gaze roving her face in a way that felt . . . overwhelming. He touched her mouth, tracing it, then cupped the side of her throat, his thumb sliding over her windpipe. "That was remarkable for me, too. You were extraordinary."

"Don't," she said softly, feeling the first shard of fear. "Please don't say anything more."

He tucked her head back under his chin, increased his hold around her. "I am going to beat those fears out of you," he promised.

She snorted on a weak, hysteria-induced chuckle. Anyone else might say such a thing as a joke, a teasing threat. Her Master meant it. Meant every word. It made her stomach flip in anticipation.

Her Master.

She told herself the same thing she'd just told him. *Don't.*

"I want you to think about something, Madison."

"When I can think again, I'll get right on that."

He gave her a little admonishing shake, a nip of her ear. She squirmed halfheartedly. "What do you want me to think about?"

"The difference between falling in love and wanting to be loved."

Her lashes lifted. When he looked at her and seemed to see things in herself she couldn't see, that was when it was hardest to hold his gaze. She looked back down at his chest.

He didn't say anything else for awhile. She was the one who broke the silence, changing topic when she thought she could talk. "So I guess we found out I'm not a Mistress."

"Not with me, no. But we aren't, any of us, just one thing. Look at your shop. You're like a Mistress there. You take your customers' desires, push them that last step, give them permission to be who they want to be."

"That might be a stretch," she demurred, but she hadn't really thought about it that way. She traced his forearm, the layer of hair there. "I think it's the control-freak thing that sometimes makes people think . . . I always want to be in control."

"It can be a gray line. Most Doms are control freaks." He brushed his lips over her forehead. "Not me."

"Of course not."

He gave her a light pinch. "Ironically, I've found a lot of female subs *are* control freaks. Our society demands that women succeed at so many things. The only time you let go of that is with the right Dominant personality. Maybe that kind of sub recognizes a control freak bigger and badder than herself and, like a strong alpha female in a wolf pack, she's willing to let him or her Dominate her."

She didn't have the brain function to know exactly where he was going with this, but the words resonated. Rolling her head back on his shoulder, she turned her nose to his shirt, inhaling his scent. She hoped it would imprint itself on her, just like an animal. She was in a very odd place, for sure.

He dipped his head, touched her lips with his, once, twice, then settled back a few inches. There were flecks of gold in his eyes, just like she imagined a wolf would have. "Alice said that the biggest thing you and I had in common is we never followed her relationship advice."

"She tried to give *you* relationship advice?"

"All the time." He grinned. "I needed it, but that didn't mean I listened, any more than you did. The relationships I tried to have outside club sessions never worked. I had a knack for picking the wrong mix. Alice called it a case of the prophet being blind to his own humanity."

"Sounds like her."

In the wry twist of his lips, she saw an echo of the exasperation she'd often exhibited when her sister tried to impose her will upon her. At least that was the way it had felt at the time. She had a different perspective of it now. Alice had wanted her to be happy, and whether or not she had the right or wrong advice for that, the desire to put her on that path would have been driven by love, not a need to run Madison's life, as she'd resentfully assumed. The thought sent a hard shot of longing through her, a couple more tears seeping out.

He kissed the tears away, held her close, started that light rocking again. "Tell me the rest?" she asked in a whisper. He nodded.

"Every time I hit that brick wall, failed again, she didn't say 'I told you so.' She didn't seem smug about it at all."

"I know. That's part of what made it so infuriating."

"Yeah." He paused, and he swallowed against her temple. "She was a true friend. I don't think I've ever met someone so self-assured and yet devoid of ego. She was afraid of true intimacy with a lover; that was her kryptonite. Yet she had infallible judgment when it came to enhancing that quality between others."

He coiled his fingers in her hair, cradling her head in his palm so she met his gaze once more. "And before you even think it again, once and for all, now and forever, you are not, and never will be, a surrogate for your sister to me. What you are is my last promise to her."

Her brow furrowed at a hitch in his voice. He gave her a quick, strained smile. "She made me swear to give being with you a try. 'Even if it doesn't work out, please take care of her, Logan. Watch over her. If it doesn't work out, being lovers, promise me you'll still be her best friend. She's going to need one of those.'"

"Oh, Alice . . ." Emotions swelled back up, clogging her throat. Again Logan held her close, but this time she held him in return, the two of them comforting each other for the loss of family, of deep friendship. Of a powerful connection that had made life seem better in so many ways.

When she at last lifted her face, she saw he hadn't cried, big, tough guy that he was, but his eyes were suspiciously bright. Sliding her fingers over his cheek and jaw, his lips, she offered more comfort. In return, he looked at her in that intent way that made everything inside of her turn to goo. Honestly, she'd never had a man like this look at her like that. It was either the most miraculous or the most terrifying thing she'd ever experienced. She coughed.

"So, at this point, where do you think you are on that? Best friends, lovers, soul mates, friends with benefits, friends with no benefits?"

"You're trying to get me to smack you again. Friends with no benefits is already off the table, don't you think?"

"Probably. Being your friend has definite benefits. Troy, for one thing."

She let out a little shriek as he made an attempt to flip her in his lap, a threat of another spanking. She clung to him like a cat, protesting. "All right, I'm sorry, I'm sorry."

Sobering, she reached up to touch his face again. "You looked so sad. I wanted to make you laugh again."

He caressed her tearstained cheek. "Same goes, Madison. Do you want a serious answer to the question?"

"I'm not sure. But I have a feeling you're going to be your usual tyrannical self and give me one."

"I tend to be a selfish bastard. If there's a potential for any of those—lover, best friend, Master"—his gaze suddenly got far more intense, washing heat over her—"I want all. What do you think?"

She pressed her lips together. Despite her worries, that heat turned into a steady warmth inside her heart. "I think that was Alice's intent all along. She used to say the best love stories are based on friendship."

"All right. Let's leave it there for now."

Grateful for that, she settled back in the span of his arm, pleased when he hummed to her, a tuneless ballad nevertheless soothing in his deep timbre. While he stroked her hip, she teased the gleaming light layer of chest hair available to her from the open neck of his shirt.

It was a lot to think about, but she wasn't up to thinking about much of it, so mostly she just drifted. Eventually, though, a question swam up from her subconscious. "Why does it work that way? The punishment bit? Everything I was ever sorry for came to the top, every time I said the 'bad girl' thing."

"For most of us, our earliest memories of forgiveness and redemption come from punishment at the hand of a parent, the first person we love and trust, whether or not they end up deserving that in the long run. For certain types of discipline, a deep part of us reverts to those feelings. Because we're adults, sexual stimulation can take it to even higher levels. You have the capacity to crave more pain than you'd desire as a child. You connect pure cathartic release with the proper application of restraint and pain. And you trust me to apply it properly to take you to that space. The space you're still in now, a little bit."

"Does anyone ever call you 'Professor'?"

He chuckled. "Sometimes they do at the club, yes."

"You've been in this so long. It makes me feel like a first grader. I'm not sure I like that feeling."

"I'm not a financial wiz like you," he offered. "My accountant has a voodoo doll of me and sticks pins into it whenever she has to wade through my files for tax preparation."

Madison looked at him incredulously. "How can you be so successful at running a business and not be good at accounting?"

"Because I let her handle the complicated stuff, and I stick to the two most important tenets of running a business. Don't spend more than you earn or can pay back within six months, and always treat your customers well." He gave her buttock a light pinch. "But long and short of it, I'm a first grader when it comes to spreadsheets. Should I feel bad about that?"

"You know why it's different."

"No. I don't. I know how to bring a submissive pleasure, how to break down her shields to maximize that, but I know nothing about actually being a submissive. Though Alice told me a lot about you secondhand, I've only recently met you. We're on a journey together. I love seeing you discover this side of yourself and giving you guidance, but every step together is a new one for us both."

She gave him a grumpy look. "I'm going to find a way to win an argument with you. Even if it requires a heavy skillet."

He chuckled. "I'll look forward to that. Are you hungry?"

She was, actually. Starving. But still she hesitated, putting her hand on his forearm. "I really haven't made any hard or fast decisions about any of this. You know that, right?"

"I'd know you were lying to me or yourself if you said otherwise." He brushed a kiss over her forehead. "Why don't we get you dressed and eat some Mexican food? The restaurant's only a short walk from here."

"You just want me to sit on my sore bottom and know I'm squirming because of you."

"There is that perk, yes." His eyes glinted. "But I'm also hungry. Come on. I'm buying."

She got a plate of burritos and a pretty lime green margarita. In contrast to the amazing twists and turns of their relationship thus far, this had the feeling of a regular date. Logan asked her questions about her life in Boston, her childhood with Alice. She asked him about his military service and his life before the hardware store. Being female, she couldn't resist asking about previous relationships. For that, she earned a quirked brow and rolled eyes.

"Why do women always want to know that? Men have no interest at all in a woman's previous lovers unless one of them happens to be her current husband."

"That's because men are so territorial. When they take over a pride, sometimes male lions kill off cubs that come from another male lion."

"Ouch." He winced. "Glad you have such a high opinion of us. How about we talk about your previous relationships, since I think they have a more significant impact on our current one?"

That did make her squirm, but he reached out, touched her hand. "I'd like to know what you're comfortable sharing, Madison. And don't give me sex details unless you want to see me go after some lion cubs."

That made her chuckle, as she was sure he intended. Actually, she was quite happy not to talk about the sex side of her failed relationships. The whole mediocre history was just embarrassing next to the sizzling heat that Logan could evoke in her with barely a glance. "There's honestly not a whole lot to say about them. They made me freakishly gun-shy when it comes to falling in love, because I don't trust my judgment. It is what it is. You're trying to distract me." She pointed a finger at him. "Previous lovers. At least tell me you've been married once."

He broke a chip in half, dipped it in the bowl of salsa between them. "Why?"

"Because you're forty, or nearly there. If you've never been married, that means there's something hinky about you. Dead body in the basement, mommy issues, pick your dysfunction. Maybe you're unwilling to compromise anything about yourself, which is problematic when it comes to meshing two people together in a relationship."

"Wow. All right. I've been married three times, and adapted wonderfully to every wife's quirks and foibles."

She blinked. "Three times? You're lying."

"Absolutely. You just said if I told the truth, that I've never been married, you'd assume I'm a lost cause."

She gave him an exasperated look, but when he caught her hand across the table, linked fingers, she couldn't find it in herself to pull free. "Whether you've had seven failed relationships or never had a single truly committed one," he said, "it all boils down to the same thing, Madison. We didn't find the right match."

"Do you think you and I are?" she asked. "Seriously. I know it's not a fair question, but . . ."

"On the contrary, it's pretty fair at this juncture." He held on to her hand as he picked up his beer, took another swallow from it. "I think we both see the potential. Are you willing to give it a try with me, or are you still pretending this is a fantasy fling you'll walk away from in a year?"

Alice's final letter to her had requested that Madison give running the store a year before deciding whether to keep or sell it. She withdrew her hand. "She told you about that?"

"I had to help her with the will, coordinate with the attorney. I saw the provisions."

She rubbed her forehead. "See, there you go again. Always a step ahead of me, waiting for me to play catch-up. It makes me feel like a child, like I'm being handled. That was how it felt with Alice, and what aggravated me so much. I mean, she fucking waits to tell me she's going to die, three days ahead of time . . ."

She bit back the words as the waiter came back to offer Logan another beer and top off the ice water she'd ordered with her drink. When he departed, she shook her head. "Christ. I'm sorry."

"You know she didn't intend it that way, Madison. I don't either." A look of frustration crossed his face, a rare enough occurrence that it sharpened her attention, drew her out of her resentment. "Here's the truth of it. I've never been able to sustain a relationship that's more than the Dom/sub thing, as you call it. I tend to get to know them first as submissives, inside that environment, and when we get out of it, it doesn't translate well. But it's such an important component to what I want with a woman, it's hard for me to go the opposite way. Imagine me picking up a woman at church. 'Hey, that was a great sermon on loving thy neighbor today. How would you feel about being tied up and spanked?'"

A smile wreathed her face. "You go to church?"

"Certainly. My mother raised me as a good, God-respecting, little-white-church-on-the-corner-of-Fifth-and-Main-whose-denomination-I-don't-know member. The ladies make great cookies for Sunday school," he added, as she choked on a laugh. Then he gave her a speculative look. "I know Alice ranged all the way between fiery Old Testament and New Age Goddess worship."

"Don't forget the Buddhist influence. She shaved her head when she was ten and went around for a week swathed in a harvest orange tablecloth our mother had from the seventies."

"What did you do?"

"Who do you think shaved her head? I made her shave mine, too. Only I didn't want anyone to think I was copycatting, so I wore a brown robe and told everyone I was Gandhi. It's a wonder our mother didn't just throw herself off a cliff, all the things the two of us did."

Logan burst into laughter. The pleasure of the sound, what it did to his handsome face, eased the tension. To hell with it. Enough crazy emotional shit for one night. As if he'd come to the same conclusion, he caught her hand, tugged. "Come over and sit next to me. I want you closer."

When she obliged, she liked leaning against that large, warm body, his arm on the booth behind her. She laid her hand on his thigh, looked up at him as he took another draw at his beer, his upper torso turned toward her so he surrounded her in an altogether pleasant way.

"What if I can't be all you need me to be, in the Dom/sub department?" she asked.

"What if I can't be all you need to be happy?" he countered. "That's the risk of every relationship, Madison. That we'll both fall short of the mark. The question is whether we both think there's enough here to give it a serious go. The whole 'I'd-rather-just-keep-you-a-fantasy' thing isn't going to fly this time." He gave her a mildly threatening look over the top of his beer. "If those words come out of your mouth, I will dedicate myself to being the antithesis of your fantasy. I'll stop bathing, belch loudly in your store and make crude comments about women in crotchless panties."

She rolled her eyes, but took a healthy sip of her margarita, thinking. Then she put it down next to his beer bottle, nudged it close enough that they clinked together. "I let you cuff and beat me tonight, and that's still tons less scary than considering us in a serious relationship. Why is that?"

"You already know the answer to that. There's a detachment to pure BDSM play. You can walk away from every session, and keep treating me as the friendly store owner next door. Get involved with me, it becomes harder to do that."

He fell silent, gave her a look. Waiting. His finger slid along the side of his beer bottle and back up, leaving a slick track in the condensation. She hadn't answered his challenge, and he wasn't letting her get away with it. Sighing, she laid a tentative fingertip on top of his hand, staring at it rather than speaking to him directly.

"My mother is dead and my father is pretty much a non-entity in my life. Alice was my family. Even when we had our two-year separation, so to speak, we spoke by phone every week, and she e-mailed me practically every day. She was my one constant. I can't really describe . . ." She stopped, collected herself, tried again. "I put so much into every one of my relationships. I really believed, every time, that I'd found the right guy. Leroy was the one that . . . he broke something in me."

How could anyone understand unless they'd experienced it? Give someone everything, then have it rejected, like it was a tacky, inappropriate gift? Treating her like she could never imagine treating them.

"I couldn't process his indifference, the sheer cruelty at the end. The same way I can't process ugly divorces. How can you watch a couple's wedding video, see that time when there was nothing that was ever too much to ask of each other, and then, in the end, they can't even give each other basic civility, let alone compassion?"

She sighed. "After Leroy left me, it was like him and all six of my other serious relationships rolled up together into this big, messy ball of string sitting inside my gut. When I'm in a session with you, it's like I can let that go. Who I am, really me, is all there, without all those knots and tangles. As much as it sometimes freaks me out a little, it's the best I've felt about myself in a while. I'm afraid if I take it outside of that . . ."

"The ball of string will take over, and you'll lose sight of that woman again. The one seven idiots never saw, even though she was right in front of them. Though part of it was your fault, wasn't it?"

She drew back a little. "What?"

"You've thought about it yourself." He met her gaze. "Once or twice, it could be them. But seven? There's only one common denominator, right?"

She wanted to move back to her side of the booth, but he merely held on to her, kept her still. "I'm not insulting you, Madison. You're an intelligent, fascinating woman. Remember, you're talking to a guy who has repeatedly failed at relationships outside the scene. I've faced the same thing in myself."

He was right. He'd just ruffled her pride, and she'd reacted in that typically perverse human way. It was one thing to say something critical about yourself; another entirely to hear the same thing from a lover. "Yes, I've thought it."

"Did you come up with any explanation?"

"Did you?" she asked defensively. When he gave her a look, she sighed.

"No. That's what's so frustrating. I thought I did everything they wanted, everything to make them happy."

"Were you happy?"

"I didn't . . . I never really thought about it."

"Bingo. You were a chameleon. You became everything they wanted you to be, except it wasn't you. You know why things feel so different between us, Madison? It's not the D/s stuff. It's that you reached the point you've said the hell with it and you're reaching for what *you* want. Plus, I don't *want* you to become everything I think I want. We both have the track record that proves we suck at that."

At her startled laugh, he nodded, a wry acknowledgment. But the whole conversation was making her antsy. This time when she slid away, really needing to retreat to her side of the booth, he let her. She stared moodily at the basket of chips. "Knowing what we did wrong doesn't really change much, does it?"

"It can. It can keep us from going down the same path."

"And then, yay, we kiss against a magical sunset and say happily-ever-after. It's not right," she snapped abruptly. "To go through all that heartache and pain, every horrible moment, then say, 'Oh gee, it was always as simple as taking Path B instead of Path A. Be yourself, and all will be well.' People in relationships don't want you to be yourself."

"The wrong people don't." His gaze sharpened. "A lot of people assume a Dom is a misogynist who wants a woman who says 'Yes sir' and 'No sir,' no mind of her own. I'm a strong Master, I don't deny it. I demand absolute obedience as part of the charge for us both, when the time is right, but you've already proven you have the intuition to know when I don't want that. There's a lot of room inside that circle between us. I don't want a brainless robot."

When she said nothing, a note of impatience entered his voice. "Do you want *me* to be any different? You might say 'Put down the toilet lid' or 'I wish you'd watch a chick flick instead of football,' but would you really want me to be that all the time? Don't the edges make the shape more interesting?"

She heard him, but it was a murmur behind her memories, playing out on the reflection of her margarita glass. Her fingers played with the damp coaster. When she heard him sigh, she looked up in time to see the ironic twist of his lips. "It's funny, isn't it?" he said. "My problem was finding a woman I wanted to be with outside of the scene as much as in it, and here you are; a woman who only wants me inside the scene because you're afraid of being hurt again. It would be perfect, except it isn't. We were both meant to reach for more."

"But you just said it. You really don't know anything about me, except what Alice told you."

"Bullshit," he said mildly. "That wasn't what I meant, and you know it. What if I said you don't know anything about me? How would you feel about that?"

"*Do* I know much about you?"

"Yeah, I think you do, in an intuitive sort of way. We play off each other's sense of humor pretty well, and you've already taken a lot of steps toward trusting me. You don't do that if you don't feel like you know someone."

"Unless I'm just one of those people with crappy judgment. Didn't I mention that?"

He smiled. "Come on back over here. Let me tell you what I know about you."

When she balked, he put his foot over hers under the table. She slid it away, he followed, then trapped one foot between both of his. She tried to pull free, grimaced at him. "Let go, bully. Fine. I'll come over there."

She didn't want to fight. She really didn't. She just wished . . . she just wished she was back in that session, where everything was clear and still in her head. Where it was all much simpler.

This time when she came back to his side of the booth, he pulled her close. With a sigh, she wrapped her arms around him, put her head down on his chest, closing her eyes briefly when he dropped a kiss on the top of her head. "I didn't intend to hurt you," he said.

"I know. I didn't mean to be bitchy. This is just hard stuff. Tell me all this great knowledge you have about me, so I can tell you you're full of it."

He chuckled, a soothing vibration through his chest. She forced herself to sit up, sip at her margarita, give him a reserved look. Pulling it together.

"You've grown into a really good shopkeeper in an astonishingly short period of time," he said, considering her. "Which tells me everything you needed for that was already there, and Alice knew it. You just needed the venue and the confidence. I also know you like playing dress-up. You like baking for Troy. When his eyes light up over it, you feel better about your day. You like doing nice things for people, you like making them happy. It makes you genuinely happy, the sign of a good person, and a good shopkeeper. I know you watch me a lot, a puzzle you're trying to solve for yourself."

His expression was the one that called forth emotions she couldn't control, but when she looked back down at her glass, he put his hand over hers.

"You're a woman who had a heart big enough to give all of it seven times. There are people out there who get burned once, Madison, and who never try again. I have to believe a woman who believes in true love enough to go for it seven times might just have an eighth inside of her." He slid the beer bottle in a circle around her margarita, bemusing her. "As for me, even when you're not on your knees to me, I want more."

She lifted her head, surprised by the fervor injected into the last sentence. His lips hovered just above hers, giving her the flavor of hops and salsa on his breath, the heat of it on her cheek. He'd left his arm curved around her, his hand resting possessively on her hip, fingers stroking the top of her thigh, keeping her body on a low hum, a separate reaction from her spiraling thoughts.

"That means I want both the day-to-day and the Dom/sub moments," he added. "When two people in a relationship are Master and submissive, there are a lot of possibilities for overlap in both settings. For instance, I love watching you talk about anything, but seeing you get pensive, knowing you're getting tangled up in your head, I want to distract you, make you feel better. So I'm going to put my hand up your skirt and play with your pussy."

She started underneath his hands. He was entirely serious. What was crazier was her body responded as if a switch was flipped, registering the serious set to his mouth, the glint in his gaze. He lowered his voice, sending a shiver up her spine.

"Spread your legs, Madison."

The hum in her body shot straight into a higher gear. Even as she held his gaze for another bated breath, her mind uncertain, her thighs were already loosening. Perhaps because, in the few sessions they'd had, he was already conditioning her to respond to his Master side, regardless of setting. Or maybe that was her own strong craving, unable to be denied.

He'd made the shift from casual date to Master in a heartbeat, certifiable proof he could merge the two. As he removed his arm from around her, brought it down between them, she slowly parted her legs. Casual as picking up his fork, he slid his hand beneath the mid-thigh skirt she'd worn to play Miss Fine, pushing it up enough he could reach the crotch of her thong. They were in a shadowed corner booth, and now she suspected that had been a deliberate choice. They faced a mirrored wall, so though their backs were to the other diners, he'd know if the waiter was coming.

"I should have told you to leave this off," he grumbled about the underwear. "I'll remember next time."

She bit down on a sound as his fingers stroked the damp cotton crotch. "Still wet from earlier," he mused. "What if I got you so wet your honey was trickling down your legs, and you'd have to walk out like that?"

"How would you feel about it?" she asked, breathless.

His brown eyes ignited with mesmerizing fire. "I'd fucking love it. Especially if people noticed. I want them to know I made you cream for me, right here out in public."

He pushed a finger inside of her as she bit back another whimper. "Logan . . ."

"Be still. Just feel," he ordered. "You asked what's next on the agenda. You're going to be that slave you fantasized about, sold at auction."

He'd made her tell him about that fantasy during their movie night. He'd not only refused to let her feel shameful about it, but had coaxed all the vivid details from her. It was a fantasy that had been built over countless lonely nights before she met him, when she'd had only her imagination and her vibrator to help her construct the story in her head.

"A soldier is going to buy you and share you with his friends," he added, confirming he had far too good of a memory. Her cheeks were burning, but that wasn't the only heated part of her. Her pussy contracted on his hand, and he brushed parted lips over hers. "Just the thought is making you hot, isn't it, Madison?"

She couldn't deny it, her voice rasping with desire. "It won't . . . really involve other men?"

"Lucky for you, I can tell you're asking because you don't really want that." He pushed in deeper and she gasped. "It will be a guided fantasy. That means I'm going to make you believe your fantasy is happening, using different props and sensations. Like hypnosis, it helps a sub lose herself in it in a safe way. I might have an assistant or two, but the only cock you're ever going to feel in that eager pussy of yours, now and going forward, is mine. Got it?"

"Oh . . ." She gripped the table as he pushed in a second finger. He started moving them in a coital rhythm, his thumb teasing her clit. "Logan, please don't . . ."

"Hearing you beg me not to do something your body is begging for is like waving fresh meat in front of a shark." Leaning down, he nuzzled her ear, took a sharp nip that made her shudder. "I can be ruthless when circumstances call for it, so if you don't want me to make you come right here, make you scream in this nice restaurant in front of these families, you're going to tell me you're willing to have a real relationship with me. Starting with taking me home with you tonight."

"What? No. I'm not ready—"

God, what had he just done with his fingers? Her hand clamped on his leg like a vise, holding on as she leaned forward against the wave of sensation, so strong she had to fight back the climax. Her change in position made it worse, because it altered the angle of his penetration.

"I'm going to sleep in your bed with you, Madison. I'm not going to fuck you. We'll brush our teeth, kiss each other good night . . ."

The scissoring of his fingers, the rub of his thumb over her clit, was taking her to the edge. "Logan . . ." she pleaded.

"I'm not finished. You'll wear this thong, nothing else, and fall asleep in my arms. I'll nurse a hard-on the size of Florida for being the dumbass who decided dealing with your intimacy issues was more important than sex."

"Okay," she gasped. He cocked a brow.

"I'm sorry? I'm not sure what you're saying okay to."

"I promise to try . . . to have a real relationship with you. Please, Master." She caught his forearm then, trying to bring him to a stop, and those eyes became dark and still.

"Move your hand, Madison. I decide when I stop, unless you're using a safe word."

She should strangle it out, but that dark, pleasurable craving his Mastery triggered made her take her hand away, set her jaw, try her best to hold out against him. When he at last eased his fingers from her, he ran a fingertip over the edge of her margarita glass, collecting some of the salt. Bringing it to his lips, he tasted it and her with a look of feral satisfaction.

"That's my baby."

• • •

She didn't care for the fact he was right, that him sleeping in her bed was far more frightening to her than anything else they'd done yet. If he'd suggested taking her to a PTA meeting and publicly fucking her in front of a bevy of appalled parents, she would have jumped at it faster.

She'd cleaned the day before, which just proved her earlier point about why bachelors preferred going to the woman's house. When she made that acid observation, he just smiled. She was tense as a board when he took the keys from her and unlocked Alice's door, shepherding her through it with a firm hand on her lower back. She put her purse away in the front closet and tried to figure out how not to freak out.

"Board games." He was standing behind her, looking up at the top shelf, where Alice had kept a collection of their childhood favorites. "Perfect."

Nonplused, she watched him reach up and withdraw the tic-tac-toe beanbag toss, keeping her between him and his goal, so that he brushed against her back, a casually affectionate contact. Then he took her hand. "Let's go play in the yard."

The insane man challenged her to a marathon of the game. At first he gallantly attributed her abysmal aim to her nerves, but even after he had her laughing and teasing him right back, she didn't improve. Most of her beanbags ended up in the flower beds. One even plopped into the man-made pond. At that point, he magnanimously gave her what he called a ladies' tee, half the distance he was tossing.

"Good thing we aren't playing for stakes," she observed.

"If we were, what would we bet?"

"What would you bet?" She lifted a brow. "Let me guess. Something related to sex or female nakedity."

"That's not a word. It's also profiling. If you insisted on sexual stakes, I wouldn't hold it against your gender."

She laughed. "I'll bet. No pun intended. There. Hit two in a row. I'm getting better." Of course only one turned up her *O*; the other tipped the cube in favor of his *X*.

"Feeling confident enough to wager?"

She snorted, rolled her eyes. "Why not? Something within reason," she said hastily, seeing his speculative look.

"Chicken. I win the next round, you give me a foot massage. While kneeling, while naked. Just for the aesthetics. Nothing sexual about it."

"Of course," she agreed. "If I win, you vacuum my house. Shirtless, in your jeans. Again, all aesthetics. Not sexual. Though if I decide to get excited watching you and want to occupy myself with a battery-operated boyfriend, you have to stick to your appliance while I enjoy mine."

He narrowed those appealing brown eyes at her. "Not feeling performance pressure, are we?" she asked.

"Not hardly."

"First one to win her toss?"

"Nice try." He grinned at that. "But I'll still give you an edge up. First one to knock over three consecutive blocks. Doesn't matter if it comes up *X* or *O*. I'll even let you go first, so if you win straight off, you win the bet."

"Pretty fair. Also insultingly confident, thank you very much." She sniffed, joining him at his spot on the grass. "It seems only fair I do it on the same mark as you, since you're giving me such an advantage."

At his shrug, she studied the board. Tossing the beanbag up a couple times like a pitcher on the mound won a grin from him. Then she did it in quick succession, no hesitation.

One *O*, two *O*, three *O*. Straight across the center.

She burst out laughing at the look on his face, the closest she'd ever come to seeing Logan Scott taken off guard. "Sorry. I couldn't resist. You were playing the big, strong man to the hilt. It was just too easy a mark."

He eyed her. "How many years did you and Alice play this game to make you a world champion hustler?"

"Quite a few. I was also good at baseball. The boys on the street always had me pitch for their team, because I was that good. Until my mother told me I was too old to play with boys anymore." She grimaced.

"Alice never told me that."

"Good. I was feeling like there was no mystery left to me."

"She could have told me everything she ever knew about you, Madison, and you'd still be a chest of wonders to me." He snagged her around the waist, then, hiking her up his body so she curled her legs around his waist, her arms around his shoulders. "You are really tall," she observed, as he walked her up her back steps. "And really strong."

"Trying to salve my male ego?"

"How am I doing?"

"Keep going. I'll let you know."

She curled her arms around his shoulders, rested her head against the side of his, gratified when he increased the strength of his embrace. "I won't hold you to the bet. It was kind of cheating. But it would be really nice to see you vacuum my house in your jeans. Or nothing at all."

"I might just do it for you. The jeans idea. I have an aversion to being around loud, sucking appliances with my tender parts dangling."

When she chuckled at that, his arms tightened around her again. "I like making you happy, Madison. There's nothing I wouldn't do to make you smile, and to hear you laugh the way you do when you're playing and not worrying, or being sad about things." As he took them into the kitchen and let her feet down, he held on to her waist. She looked up at him, putting her hand on his face.

"I'm bad at this part. It scares me."

"I know. But you don't have to be scared of anything. As long as you're being honest with yourself and with me, there's nothing you can do wrong."

"I didn't admit to it, but you're right. The one common denom-inator was me." She shook her head before he could say anything. "I'm not fishing for reassurance. I thought a lot about it, about the things I did do wrong, but I guess I didn't put it together until you said the thing about choice. And not just tonight. You've been hitting that point in different ways, intentional or not. I tried the sub thing with some of them, but I ended up feeling like a freak, or they took advantage of it in the wrong ways. For the last few relationships, I just kept it inside. I figured I could be submissive in ways that fed my need and didn't ask for anything active from them in that way."

"Anything where you had to trust them to care for you," he said, with that shrewdness that was both one of his most appealing qual-ities and one of the most difficult, when it came to facing this part of herself.

"I thought if I did all the right things, tried to figure out how to make them happy, that's all it would take," she said softly. "Like paint by numbers, just fill in the colors. I never really thought about what I wanted, if I loved them, if I would have picked them out of a crowd and said, 'That's the one I want.'"

She offered him a painful smile. "Alice tried to tell me once. She said, 'Madison, when you go to buy a pair of shoes, do you buy the first one the sales clerk thrusts at you? No, you don't. You shop. You look at the colors and styles, and wait to see which one tickles your fancy. You choose. You pick them out.' I ignored her, the way I tuned out so many things she said."

"She was your older sister. It's a given that we ignore family advice."

She nodded, but then she drew in a deep breath. Even so, the words still came out quiet, so quiet he had to bend his head and she had to repeat them.

"I pick you, Logan. Whatever happens, for however long we get . . . I pick you. You're *my* choice."

He raised his head, but not far, so their eyes were very close. Mouths, bodies, that aura that Alice said vibrated around everything close enough to merge. "Okay," he said. "And I get no choice in this at all?"

Trust him to know the right thing to say, to help her not feel so terrified, so exposed. "None at all," she said staunchly. "I'm sorry, but that's just the way it is. Do you think . . ."

When she trailed off, he touched her jaw, that way he had of making her say whatever foolish thing that came to mind. "Can you be just Logan tonight, and make love to me? Does it always have to be the Dom/sub thing? Is there an off switch?"

She really was an idiot. It came out so wrong, she expected him to step back and close down. She'd just told him she didn't want him to be something he was 120 percent of the time. "I'm sorry," she added hastily, "I didn't mean it quite like that. It's just—"

"Madison, look at me."

When she lifted her gaze to him, his brown eyes were as attentive as ever. She didn't see anger, hurt or anything she'd feared. "Do you stop being a woman if you wear pants instead of a skirt?"

"Not to my knowledge."

"Exactly. You enjoy wearing both, right?"

She nodded. His warm look loosened the band around her chest. "I am a sexual Dominant, yes," he said. "I'm also a man who is developing strong feelings for you, and those feelings aren't contained in one box. I wasn't going to have sex with you tonight, because I don't want you keeping us in that one box, avoiding the things that a fully fleshed-out relationship entails. You've just told me you don't want to avoid that."

"So?" A different kind of feeling took hold of her as a wicked grin crossed his face.

"So that means all bets are off."

He caught her arm, dipped beneath it and slung her over his shoulder as she laughed outright, though that reaction was quickly turned into something else as he took her to the stairs, but not up to the bedroom. Instead he put her down on the stairs, turned her over onto her knees and covered her with his body, pulling up the skirt so he had one thigh inserted firmly between her legs. He put the other arm across her chest, held her there down beneath him as he put his mouth to her throat and bit. She moaned as he pushed her back against that thigh, working her against it.

Yes, he could make love to her as Logan. But Logan, with or without the Master honorific, was a take-charge, overwhelming alpha lover, and he proved it now by making her utterly helpless to anything he desired in a matter of seconds. Reaching beneath her, he unzipped the skirt, pulled it off her hips, stripping her down to her thong. She'd borrowed one of his hardware store baby-doll tees to replace the one he'd ripped off of her, and now he worked his way beneath it, unhooking her bra.

"Take it off. Leave the shirt on."

She worked the straps off through the sleeves. When she remembered what she'd told Troy during their first session, that she thought Logan's preferred lingerie on a woman would be a T-shirt and thong, she would have smiled, if other things weren't taking precedence.

Taking the bra from her, he set it aside. His hand on her back told her she was right where he wanted her as he backed down a couple steps. It was the perfect position to grip her thighs, spread them wider and tease her cunt through the crotch of the thong—with his heated mouth.

She clawed the carpet on the stairs, moaning, driven wild by the way he suckled her clit, traced her labia with the firm pressure of his tongue, rubbed his face in her scent, marking himself with it. She pushed her hips up against him, arching her back, making it clear she was his for the taking in the way she expected female animals had done since the beginning of time. She was wild, suffused with the pleasure of the moment. No fear or worries.

He pulled her panties to her knees and then she heard him opening his jeans. She could barely breathe. When he dropped the belt on the stairs next to her, her fingers curled over the strap, felt the bite of the buckle. His chest pressed into her shoulder blades, his breath at her ear.

"I'll have you in your bed tonight, too. But I can't wait. I want you here first."

To be wanted, desired so keenly he wouldn't deny himself . . . it was a gift she couldn't describe, a balm on every rejection that had ever battered her self-esteem into nothingness. "Can you do it . . . without the condom?"

His arm cinched around her waist, so her bare ass was against his groin, still frustratingly behind fabric, though the jeans were open. Rubbing herself against the ridged friction of his glans, she made needy noises he answered with a growl.

"I don't know, Madison. Can I?"

He was saying he was safe. He was asking her the same, trusting her to be truthful with him. She doubted anyone short of God could lie to Logan Scott when he asked them a direct question.

"Yes." She was protected from pregnancy, and the last man had been Leroy, well over two years and two annual physicals ago. "Please."

He slid one finger along her wrist. "Madison, look down at your hands."

It was hard to focus on anything beyond the throbbing need between her legs, but she obeyed. She saw she'd twisted his belt around her wrists, clasping the ends in her hands so it was as if she'd bound herself. When he'd stripped himself of the belt, her mind had been seized with the image of him binding her wrists with it, hooking it to the banister, holding her there as he fucked her mercilessly on the stairs. She'd acted on her own desires to see it happen, all within the turbulent heat of her subconscious.

"It's not my switch you need to worry about turning off." He gave a dangerous chuckle, his hand closing over her wrists, tightening the hold of the belt and making her heart beat faster. Holding her like that with the one hand, he adjusted his clothes out of the way with the other and put his cock against her slick lips. "Push yourself back against me, Madison. I want to feel you impale yourself on my cock, and I want you to do it slow."

Easier said than done. All she wanted was to slam back into him, alleviate this aching need but, by following his orders, that need grew to a greater intensity that shuddered through her with every inch she gained. When she was finally seated on him, her fingers were trembling and those delicate slick tissues were spasming, on the cusp of climax. She whimpered again as he reached beneath her with both hands, cradled her breasts. She arched, her hard nipples stabbing into his palms. "You stay still," he ordered. "Not a single move until I command it."

With him tweaking her nipples, that was almost impossible, her hips jerking. She put her head down, trying to freeze her muscles, keep herself from reacting, but he made her lift it again, staying open to everything he did to her. Until her self-restraint was shattered, her hips grinding against his, body sinuously moving with the manipulation of his hands, a helpless dance.

"Logan . . ."

He pushed deeper into her, and his heavy testicle sac caressed her clit. She put her face down on the carpet again and this time he was rougher about it, tangling his fist in her hair to yank her head back up. He began to thrust in earnest, the other hand moving to her hip to hold her steady as he pumped into her. His cock stretched her, plowed deep, and she was crying out, near screaming at the pleasure of it.

Just when she thought he was about to go over himself, he brought them to an abrupt halt. Before she could wail a protest, he'd pulled out of her. Swinging her up into his arms, he carried her up the stairs, the belt still wound around her wrists. In her bedroom, he crossed the room, put her down on her back and removed the belt, dropping it to the floor with a clink of metal.

Her gaze clung to him as he straightened and shed all of his clothes. She wished he'd turned on the light so she could devour with her eyes every curve and plane, every muscled ridge, the hard, stiff cock curving up over his testicles, but she shared and savored his urgency, wanting to feel even more than she wanted to see.

Kneeling on the bed, he stripped off her T-shirt and thong. Holding her gaze still, he lay down upon her, body to body, flush against each other with nothing between but the emotions that saturated the air. She closed her eyes, absorbing the heat and strength of him, his weight pressing her into her mattress, his big body spreading her thighs as his hands guided her legs up and around his hips.

A gasp and moan together broke from her lips as he slid back into her. Her hips undulated, accommodating his size and length again, taking him all the way. She made a different noise then, a quiet, feminine note of question and need both. Bracing his elbows on the outside of her shoulders, he cradled her face in his hands.

"Put your hands on my arms, Madison. Hold on to me. Look in my face and know it's about way the hell more than restraints or commands."

She could barely think at this point, but she found some part of her able to latch on to the words as if they were the most important ones ever spoken to her, even as she wasn't in a frame of mind to analyze them. She jumped from rationality to faith in his arms, and knew no fear. At least not in this moment.

She lifted her chin as he stroked deep inside of her, bent to touch his lips to the line of her jaw. Sighing against his flesh, she gripped his incredible biceps. "I love the way you feel."

"Same goes."

The rhythm he set had her rising up to meet him, her teeth biting her lip, her legs locking over his hips, feeling the flex of his ass under her calves, the ripple of his thigh muscles under her ankles hooked over them. The friction of his chest hair against her nipples was just one searing pleasure among many. That feeling between her legs was growing even more concentrated, and she breathed his name against his skin, rearing up to bite his chest. One hand cupped her head, held her there. He braced their weights with one arm, increased the piston of his strokes. So close, so very close . . .

He plunged in deep, making her cry out, but then he stopped there, lodged to the hilt, and spoke against her hair. "Do you love me, Madison?"

He released his hold on her head, lowered it back to the pillow so that she saw him through the gray darkness of her bedroom, illumination provided by the light they'd left on over the hallway steps. She'd given up anticipating anything this man would say to her or ask of her, and this was no exception.

"I want to. I want you to love me . . . back."

His eyes softened then. He held them both on that cusp as her nails raked his shoulders, her hips working against his in tiny, insistent movements, but he pushed down, pinning them. "Ssshh. Be still, love. Be still. Calm down for me."

She stared at him, panting, but gradually, painstakingly, things slowed down, until it seemed they were balanced on some still point in the universe, where they had stopped as everything else passed around them. He waited until he saw her reach that still point with him.

"I will, Madison. I do. You understand me?"

She nodded. Tears trickled over her cheeks, probably baptizing his thumbs. "I want to love you, too, Logan. Really love you. My choice. I want to get there."

"Go over for me," he whispered. "Let me see it happen. Come for me, Madison."

This was the easiest thing of all, given that the stroke of his cock, his skill in rousing her beyond anything she'd ever experienced, took the choice out of her hands. She climaxed, cunt spasming over him, nails biting into his flesh, her body straining up in that crazed rigor during which the human body could do anything. He put his mouth

on her sternum, right between her breasts, holding it there, continuing to pump into her body, work her to the full measure of her
release.

Only when she was starting to come down did he speed up, seek
his own finish. She held on for the ride, loving the feel of his body
shuddering against hers, the male grunts of release and the heat of
him searing her inside. She clung to him for all she was worth, tilting up her hips to give him back as much pleasure as he gave her.
Though she wasn't sure that was possible, she would do her best
to try.

When he at last stopped, brought them both to earth, he lowered
himself so his weight held her down in a pleasurable way, then he
propped some of it on an elbow, keeping his jaw against her temple.
She held him to her, all her limbs still wound around him. It was
perfection. If only the moment never had to stop.

But Logan was the type of man who kept a wheel turning. He
wouldn't let her stop the ride for fear it would go in the wrong direction. And the next stop was going to be one of her deepest fantasies.
The auction, the soldier . . .

He'd been helping her explore her submission fantasies all along,
but with every step along the way, he'd also somehow kept the focus
on the reality of their relationship as well. Like tonight. He would
deliver on her fantasy, like a candy man delivering the most delicious
chocolate, but what happened after?

"Stop thinking," he rumbled against her. "Just sleep with me.
Find good dreams."

Leave it to him to order a woman to have good dreams. Her smile
was a painful one, though. Did he understand how afraid she was of
the other shoe dropping? How did a vessel that had been broken over
and over withstand something as strong as his will? She knew her
heart was safer on the shelf, not subjected to any undue stress on
those cracks, but she hadn't yet been able to deny him.

As he turned them and tucked her against his body, she clasped his forearm, pressed under her breasts. Tightening her hold on him was a reflex, as natural as breathing. She sighed deeply, burrowed into him and prepared for sleep, making a quiet noise as he kissed her neck.

Closing her eyes, she hoped she'd find the best kind of dream in slumber. The one that would still be there when she woke up.

PART IV

The Highest Bid

As the door to Naughty Bits opened, Gloria Estefan's "Wrapped" started up on the music system, the sultry intro earning a startled look from the woman who'd entered.

"It's like having your own theme music, announcing your arrival. Pretty cool, right?" Madison gave her newest customer a smile. She did it from a kneeling position, because she was working on her newest display. The antique lingerie chest, a piece she'd picked up cheap at a consignment store and re-finished with Logan's help, was perfect to display an array of lace panties, bras and corsets, draped over the half-opened drawers and hung on the knobs.

The woman offered her a tentative smile. She was middle-aged, with attractive auburn-tinted hair and brown eyes. Her manicured nails and tailored clothing weren't polished enough to suggest executive management, but likely the strata that kept the wheels running in the office. Perhaps executive assistant. The type of person who would ask for what she needed, when she needed it.

It gave Madison a fleeting thought of herself, working as an investment manager all those years, polished up and always looking the same outside, no matter what might be brewing beneath the surface.

"If you need help with anything, just holler," Madison said, holding eye contact to tell the woman she meant it, not just a store employee offering a rote response to a customer.

The woman nodded. "Do you have . . . costumes?"

"We do." Giving a demi-cup bra one more quick adjustment, Madison rose to her feet. "A variety of them. Which one are you planning to use to dazzle your lover?"

"Oh . . ." The customer chuckled. "Ah, maid?"

"A classic." Madison took her to the rack on the wall and showed her a traditional black-and-white outfit, complete with frilly apron and very low-cut blouse, matched by the high cut of the miniskirt. As the woman fingered the fabric, her expression reminded Madison of the disastrous times she'd sought out lingerie to bandage her own failing relationships. The look in the woman's eyes wasn't a true mesh with the desires she was harboring. Confirming it, she spoke.

"I'm not sure. I really don't know if he'd even like this sort of thing."

"Do *you* like the idea?"

"Maybe. I just remember years ago when we saw a movie that had a sexy maid in it, and how he liked that. Maybe I'm being foolish. It seems to take more to get him interested these days since he turned fifty, and I thought maybe something . . ."

What can I do to get him to pay attention again? To look at me the way he did at first? It was as clear as if she'd said it aloud, but the silence said it was too painful to be voiced.

Not more than a couple months ago, tangled up in her own baggage, Madison would have been unable to help, beyond offering the woman the number to a good divorce attorney. Since then, she'd connected with her own desires, thanks to Logan's direction. As such, Madison could step back and look at the situation from the woman's perspective, sympathizing with it, but not getting it confused with her own. This woman was dealing with middle-age libido issues with her husband. A simple thing that wasn't so simple when dealing with the heart. "Would you mind telling me your name?"

"Nancy."

"Nancy. I'm Madison. And if you don't mind a couple suggestions, I think you may be focusing on the wrong person here. There's a good kind of selfishness, the kind that helps everyone involved. We have to be able to turn ourselves on before we can turn on a lover. As obtuse as guys can be, nothing centers their radar like a woman who's getting hot and bothered. It also sounds to me like rather than taking him on a wild rapids ride, you need to take him to a secluded lagoon."

At Nancy's blank look, Madison drew her to the bookshelf. "Does he like to read?"

"He'll spend a whole day with a book on the weekends and he reads at bedtime every night. He's even read my romances when he has nothing else." Nancy gave a little laugh. "Wasn't self-conscious about it at all. Said he liked a couple of the historical ones."

"Wonderful. Who gets home from work first?"

Nancy shrugged. "He does, usually."

"Okay. How would you feel if you came home from work and he met you at the door, naked and ready to go at it like rabbits?"

Nancy put her hand over her mouth, stifling a surprised giggle. Then, seeing Madison wanted her to consider the question, she did, and whatever went through her mind sobered her. "Well, I expect I'd feel a little pressured. I mean, I'd be glad he was interested, but—"

Madison waved a hand, accepting that. "Of course you'd feel pressured. My point is that maybe that's his problem. When we're in our twenties or, God help us, our teens, it's all about our hormones. At fifty, it's about his boss, about the job stresses, the jerk who cuts him off in traffic on the way home. Whether there will be enough money for the kids' college, retirement, the vacation you've both always wanted to take to Europe. You have to help him change gears when he comes home."

As Nancy digested that, Madison picked up a book selection. "How about one Friday night, you suggest reading to him? He can put his head in your lap, close his eyes."

She put the book in Nancy's hands. "This one is a ménage a trois, with one man and two women, written with both genders in mind. Plenty of things to intrigue him, as well as you. There are sketches in it as well."

Nancy flipped open the book and blanched. "Wow . . ." She gave it a closer look while Madison suppressed a smile. "That's actually very . . . nicely done."

"Yes. There's some erotic photography in there too. Again, things that will appeal to him visually and you emotionally, the best of both worlds." Letting her hold on to the book, Madison took her to a different section of the store and picked up a remote control panty with bullet vibrator in the crotch. She made a mental note to order more, since she'd sold about half a dozen of them this week.

"Encourage him to be interactive. When you're reading, switch this on, show him what you're doing. Get yourself worked up, and draw him into the spell. Then turn the remote and the reins over to him, so he feels like a man, like he's taking the lead. I bet things will take a good turn."

She took a breath. "If they don't, then maybe you need to dial it down further—or shoot him in the head and bury him in the backyard—but what's most important is getting in touch with what you want, Nancy. Pleasure yourself and invite him to take the journey with you. That's the key to reconnecting to him. If he's worth anything at all."

A few minutes later, as she was checking Nancy out with a generous purchase that included a couple of the books and the panty, she saw Clarence's UPS truck turning into the alley. Today was Friday, and not just any Friday. It was one of those Fridays where he might be bringing her something from Logan. When she heard the motor idle outside her back door, then Clarence turning the back room door latch, delight surged through her.

Nancy flicked a glance at her as she swiped her credit card. "You must have ordered something nice. You look like a pony just arrived at your birthday party."

She hadn't ordered anything at all, which was exactly why she had that look on her face. A week ago, Logan had told her it was time to give her the guided fantasy he'd promised her, a tantalizing erotic threat. She expected whatever Clarence was delivering would officially kick that off.

That same night, Logan had taken her for an after-dark walk in a park near her neighborhood. He'd done nothing more than hold her hand, flirt, and let her talk about a hundred different things. Then he'd backed her against a tree and given her long, hot kisses that made her feel like a teenager out necking past curfew. She'd had a stubble burn on her throat the next day she'd caressed with her fingers when she discovered it.

He'd refused to take things further that night, but he left her reeling with the possibilities, thanks to his parting words.

"Can you clear your Sunday next weekend?" At her nod, those brown eyes had kindled with heat. *"Then do it. I have plans for my sub."*

She still leaned toward keeping their relationship a chain of erotic sessions, nervous about moving too fast into deeper territory. However, the obvious care Logan put into making those sessions special and unique perversely transferred those qualities to their relationship as a whole. The man was far too clever.

Nancy took her leave with a smile and a nervous look, but nervous in the right kind of way. Madison well understood the feeling. While she engaged Clarence in pleasant conversation, she had to quell her impatience to shoo him out of the store before more customers arrived and she'd have to wait to find out what was in the package he left on her counter.

As he was leaving, though, he paused at the curtain to the back storeroom and looked back at her. Like most UPS drivers, he was fit. Not very old, maybe a couple years younger than Madison, but she'd often wondered about his story, because there were lines around his eyes, and a look in them that said he'd had some interesting journeys in his life.

"I bet Alice smiles every time she looks down from Heaven and sees you behind that counter, ma'am," he said. "You fit here. You really do. Not like you're her, but like you were the best person to honor this place. To honor what she made of it. I think that's why she gave it to you."

It was the most she'd ever heard the quiet man say, and it left her staring after him as he beat a hasty retreat. He lifted a hand before he disappeared out the door, though, and she automatically raised her hand in answer, giving him a warm smile again so he didn't feel awkward about it. After the door shut behind him, she thought about it, though. And smiled.

"I really didn't fuck this up after all, did I, Alice?"

Each person walking through her doors was a potential story or desire to realize, just as Logan had said. As Alice had said. Madison wondered why she'd spent five years of her life doing something that didn't speak to her heart the way this job did. And pursuing relationships so different from the one she was in now.

The answer to that was pretty simple. She'd been looking for love, a relationship, instead of actualizing herself. Moving to a new place, realizing how much she enjoyed doing this, gave her a different sense of who she was, almost as if she was becoming a more evolved Madison. One who was involved in . . . something . . . with an extraordinary man. A Master.

As she picked up the box, she knew she might be about to evolve even further—if she could hold on to her courage with both hands.

The box wasn't as small as the last one, but too small to hold a full costume. Shaking it, she heard what sounded like several loose items.

"Why do you shake a present before you open it?" She remembered her eight-year-old self asking Alice. *"You're going to open it anyway."*

"Why do you smell chocolate before you bite into it?" her sister had rebounded. *"It's the same thing."*

Lately, Madison had been shaking packages as well as savoring her chocolate. Good changes.

When she opened the box, the first thing she saw was an embossed invitation on heavy, cream-colored paper. When she opened it, the handwriting looked like a woman's script.

Novitiate, your training is complete. It's time for you to be claimed by a Master. At six p.m. this coming Sunday, you will wait in a kneeling position inside the door of your quarters, leaving the door unlocked. A servant will retrieve you for the auction. It will be the last time you see your home. Wear and bring nothing but what is contained in this box. Prepare yourself exactly in accordance with the instructions.—Training Mistress

What Logan had coaxed from the deepest, most shameful corners of her mind was her recurring desire to play out a fantasy where she was a female sex slave, trained to serve a Master. The pinnacle of the fantasy was an auction where the highest bidder would take possession of her. A particular bidder—a soldier. Quelling a little quiver in her lower vitals, she looked deeper into the box.

She lifted out a utilitarian collar, no more than a buckled strap with several D-rings placed around its circumference. There were chains attached to it. A diagram showed her how it fit. The chains ran to a set of nipple clamps, and then continued around back to be reconnected to the collar. As she registered the weight of the chain, imagining the pull, her nipples gave a twinge.

At the bottom of the box was a thong like she'd sold Nancy, a bullet vibrator inserted into the crotch panel. There was no obvious way to turn it on, suggesting it was remote-controlled, but that piece wasn't included. Her heart fluttered as she thought of the control in Logan's hands. The thong's back strap had a metal ring sewn into it. Glancing at the bottom of the box, she found out why. She also found she was starting to breathe a little more shallowly. The room had become even more silent, the air dense, pressing on her exposed skin.

She pulled out a butt plug. It was about three inches long, but thick as a man's cock. As Logan's cock. Opening the folded sheet included with the announcement, the referenced "instructions," she started to read. The quiver of the paper told her she was shaking.

From here forward, you are not allowed to pleasure yourself in any way. Or be pleasured. A single infraction will incur severe punishment. Twenty-five strikes with a switch.

You will not speak to anyone about your preparations or the auction. For eight hours before you are picked up, you will not eat, or drink anything but water. You will not watch television, read or do anything to occupy your time except think of how you will serve your new Master.

Four hours before the auction, you will do the following:

You will use the cleansing products included and flush out your vagina and anus thoroughly, purging away the leavings of other males you endured as part of your training. You come to your Master clean and pure, never again to be touched by anyone except him and whom he designates.

"Whom he designates." Logan had said he would give her a guided fantasy, that other men wouldn't really be touching her. He would just make her believe it "might" be happening. He was doing a good job, because she was already wondering if she'd misunderstood, or if she needed to reinforce the message with him.

Take an hour-long bath, soaking in the oils included in this package. Wash your hair, braid it and put it in a tight topknot on your head. Use the sculpting clay so not a single strand is loose. Put on the collar.

A half hour before the pickup time, attach the chain and nipple clamps. Put on the thong, making sure the bullet is positioned against your clit and the plug is pushed all the way inside you. The back ring will hold it in place.

A webcam was included in the box, with a separate note attached to it.

As you prepare yourself, you will keep this webcam turned toward you at all times. The footage will be a live feed to the individuals interested in bidding on you. They will view the property they wish to purchase, and verify your obedience. As you learned at the training center where you have spent the last six months, you have no right to privacy of any kind with your Master.

Wow. Had she bitten off more than she could chew?

At ten minutes before six, while kneeling by the door, you will put on the blindfold. Remember Alice.

"Remember Alice"? What did that mean? Unsettled, she folded the paper and sifted through all the items. Maybe she needed to talk to Logan about this. But she knew enough about how he planned things to know the note's wording was carefully chosen, like "you will not speak to anyone about your preparations." In the fantasy, she wasn't the Madison who ran this store and he wasn't the store owner next door. But she still wanted to see him. Needed to see him. *Remember Alice?*

Brownstone's sultry "If You Love Me" started up as three black women came in, lively and in full-blown shopping mode. She closed the box and slid it under the counter, hoping her cheeks weren't scarlet, as if she'd been caught doing something illicit. In this store, that would probably just be considered one of the perks of the job. Taking a deep breath, she moved out from behind her counter to engage.

Fortunately, the women were too involved in their own banter to pay close attention to her, at least initially, and by the time they did, she had herself under better control.

Sally, Nell and Diana were all in their thirties, divorced and deep in the dating pool, so they plunged right into a delightful evaluation of her different vibrator options and how they compared to their current boyfriends, a purely female discussion that had them all howling with laughter in no time, including Madison.

It was when the ladies were narrowing down their purchase options that she noticed Logan had come out of her back room. He was leaning against the curtained opening, watching them all with an amused twist to his handsome lips, arms crossed over his broad chest.

Nell noticed him then as well, and her brows lifted. In the uninhibited mood that now reigned, Madison wasn't at all surprised to see her give Logan a thorough, blatant appraisal, pursing her glossed lips.

"Well, you're a cool drink of water, followed by a hot bubble bath." She nudged her friends to draw their attention. Holding up one of the more sizeable dildos in a nice chocolate color—it came with a chocolate syrup dipping sauce as well—she waggled it at Logan. "How do you think you'd measure up to this one, honey?"

Madison tucked her tongue in her cheek. A lesser man would cut and run, but Logan offered an easy smile. "Well, ma'am, I'm taken, but otherwise I'd prove to you size doesn't matter. It's how good you make her feel."

That brought a fervent "Amen" from Sally, and a "That's the damn truth" from Diana. Nell sighed dramatically. "Honey, I wish more men knew that."

Logan sent a wicked look toward Madison. "As far as the size department, I can hold my own. Just ask her."

The women hooted, especially when Madison flushed to the roots of her hair. She swore vengeance in her mock glare at him.

"So is he telling tales?" Nell demanded.

"Actually . . ." Madison gave him her own appraising look, just as bald as her customers'. His brows lifted, eyes dancing with amusement. "He's understating it."

"Oh, don't tell us that. Nell has a weak heart. She might just pass right out."

"I can handle three men to your one any day, you silly bitch."

More of the same banter followed, but fortunately they were ready to check out. It only took about five minutes to ring them up and give them a friendly wave, an invitation to come back soon. But with Logan leaning in the doorway behind her, engaging the women in casual conversation as she handled their purchases, the thrum of sexual tension between her and him built in a way that made those five minutes feel much longer.

Soon as they left the store, she turned, not surprised to find him less than a foot away. She could actually feel his heat envelop her before she turned. She would have lunged at him, then and there, but his gaze adjusted downward, deliberately focusing on that box beneath the counter.

Not allowed to pleasure yourself in any way. Surely that didn't mean even a single kiss, a stolen touch . . .

She met his gaze. Shit, it did. Her only consolation was seeing regret in his eyes, a banked frustration that probably mirrored her own, but she knew he'd hold firm. How bad could twenty-five switches be? Pretty bad. She'd been switched by her mother a couple times as a child. A switch in Logan's hand would be *Ouchy* to the nth degree of Band-Aids.

"Taken, hmm?" she said, with a casualness she didn't feel.

"In my mind, yes. Still working on the lady's feelings on the matter."

"Does something bring you here?" *Other than the desire to torment me?*

"I'm out of fives and wondered if you could save me a trip to the

bank by loaning me a few. I have more cash customers than most."
He held up three twenty-dollar bills.

"I thought Logan Scott was always prepared for every contingency."

"I am," he said comfortably. "I knew you'd have some."

She sniffed at that, but counted him out a dozen fives and
exchanged. As they did, his hand closed over hers and stayed there.
"You're trembling," he observed.

"A little." She didn't have to talk about why, thereby breaking the
rule in the note. He knew why she was trembling, since he was behind
all of it. He drew her to him, and she decided she wasn't going to
interpret comfort as pleasure, even though it was definitely a favorite
memory of the day, to be held against that broad chest, his strong
arms wrapped around her. Plus, he'd initiated it, right? She laid her
head on his shoulder and closed her eyes as he stroked her hair.

"We chose your safe word, but we really didn't talk about what
it means, did we? Not directly."

Of course. The note hadn't been telling her to remember her sister.
He was reminding her of her safe word. *Alice.* One mystery solved.

"It's more than a functional word, telling a Master to stop," he
continued against her hair. "Having that word is a diamond in your
pocket, a constant reminder that your care is more important to your
Master than anything else."

"You've told me that before."

"You looked like you needed the reminder."

She thought of Veronica, the abused woman who had come into
her shop a few weeks ago with a cruel asshole pretending to know
what a Master truly was. Logan had convinced Veronica to go to a
battered women's shelter and the woman had chosen to stay. Since
then she'd been taking steps toward reclaiming her life.

Madison also thought about the barely controlled fury Logan had
demonstrated toward the way Veronica's "Master" had treated her. Still,
he'd switched gears in a blink and handled Veronica with gentle firmness, the way a Master—and a man—should handle such a situation.

That, and everything else Madison knew about him, told her that Logan wouldn't let any harm come to her. But with his fancy invitations and his sets of rules, he'd made her as nervous as if she was going to be auctioned off in truth. Even after this hug, she bet when she reread that invitation, she'd feel it again. That was his skill and the point, wasn't it? He'd said the intent of a guided fantasy was to help a sub suspend disbelief, get completely lost in it so that she accepted the fantasy as real. Like a day at Disneyland, where everyone but the most cynical bought into that magic. It was all about the props, right? The cherry on top of the sundae would be Logan himself, becoming the center of her fantasy.

She had no doubt he could pull it off. His reality was already close enough to it. Her fantasy was about a masterful soldier; Logan was an Army veteran as well as a Dom with a damn super capital *D*. In the sessions he'd done with her, at their pinnacle, she had to admit she'd felt literally owned by him. She'd wanted nothing less. At least in the session, at that moment.

All she had to do was trust him. It would be impossible to immerse herself in such a complex, volatile fantasy, unless she did . . . at all levels. And such trust would start to make her trust his other ideas. Pain for pleasure, him in her life, in her home . . . in her, forever.

"Bastard," she muttered.

He smiled against her hair, though he couldn't know why she was calling him names. She guessed it didn't really matter, since she was clinging to him like he was her last hope in the world.

"Troy and I were going to grab some pizza down the street after closing tonight," he said, lifting his head and tugging her hair so she'd look up at him. "Want to meet us? Shale's coming after work and we can make it a foursome."

"Sure. What does she do for a living? Cop? MP? MMA instructor?"

"Close. She's a geriatric floor nurse over at the hospital. Has no problem at all keeping her patients in line." He gave her a wink.

"I'll bet."

Dinner was . . . normal. A little Italian bistro with good wine, tiramisu and no talk of Dom/sub things. Troy and Shale teased and flirted like any other young couple, and planned to go out dancing afterward. Madison and Logan were invited. After a glance at him to see his thoughts on it, she agreed. She hadn't been dancing since the last time she'd done it with Alice. The club they visited had a good DJ, ample floor space and dollar beer. She wasn't surprised to see Troy was an excellent dancer. He and Shale made a striking couple, as much because of their obvious close rapport as the fact they were also good dance partners.

"How do they turn it on and off? Or is that part of why it works? The defined limits? And is that why some BDSM people have a relationship like that with more than one person?"

She and Logan were taking a breather in a booth. It felt entirely right to be leaning against his chest, her leg guided over his thigh so she was half on his lap as he kept an arm around her waist, the two of them watching Troy, Shale and the other dancers. His chest rose and fell against her shoulder. The position allowed them both to be heard over the loud music, because when she lifted her face, her lips brushed his jaw. As she spoke now, she stayed there, nuzzling beneath his ear, against his throat. Keeping it soft, easy. Not taking pleasure. Sort of. Maybe skirting around the lines. His arm tightened around her, a warning, and she eased back.

"Do you do that?" she asked. "Go to your club and have sessions with subs, and then come to me?"

It was the first time she'd asked it right out. Maybe in his world it was considered acceptable. Dating was full of so many gray areas, the boundaries unclear, whereas in D/s, maybe the deal was: *When you're with me, in this room, it's only about us, and this time belongs exclusively to you.* The trade-off was what happened when they were out of it. It made sense some people might prefer that to the stress of wondering what their significant other was doing when not with them.

Logan still hadn't spoken, probably because she couldn't seem to stop, now that she was on the topic. "Gerald told me that he had sex with other women to serve a different need, something that had nothing to do with me. He was loser number five."

Logan brushed his lips against her temple. "Progress. You're calling *them* losers now. Not yourself."

"I'm an equal-opportunity judgmental bitch," she said. "Able to criticize others as scathingly as myself."

"Stop it." He gave her a harder squeeze.

"You haven't answered the question. You don't have to, I mean . . ."

"Yes, I do." He put his mouth to her ear, his breath teasing her neck. She hoped they kept playing loud music all night long, because it gave them an excuse to be this close, stay in their own intimate world.

"Yeah, there are people with vanilla spouses who aren't interested in playing Dom or sub. So they come to the club, rather than taking it home. They see it as therapy. They want to be married to the person they have; their spouse just can't satisfy that urge. Some of them know about it, some don't."

"I wouldn't want that. I couldn't do it." That might be the final answer about their future together, mightn't it? He'd said he could just be Logan with her sometimes, but how could she, a person exploring submissive feelings, be enough for a man who was obviously pure Dom?

Her body had telegraphed her sudden tension. His tongue took a teasing lick along the outer shell of her ear, sending pleasurable tingles down her spine. "Your biggest problem is you always anticipate the worst," he said. "You sabotage the relationship before you can see how it unfolds. People aren't tab A and slot B, you know."

He directed her attention back to Shale and Troy. They were now doing a slow dance, even though the DJ was still playing a fast number. Moving to a beat all their own, they seemed to have wrapped a cocoon around themselves, oblivious to anything but each other. "Watch. See her soften as he draws her closer, almost yielding, as it were . . ."

Troy dipped his head to kiss her, and yes, it looked like he was taking the lead in their dance, holding Shale securely in his strong arms, her body melted into his, swaying in rhythm.

"But now watch . . . see her hand . . ."

Her fingers, gripping his biceps, tightened, her nails biting into his skin, a clear order. Troy's head lifted, his lips wet, his eyes fastened on hers. Madison had seen that switch happen in his gaze before, like the day she'd played the role of stern librarian at Naughty Bits and teased him about being late with his books. She'd also seen it when Logan spoke to him a certain way. Troy was in control of this moment, but would hand Shale that control the way he'd hand her a whip to strike his flesh. With anticipation and the pleasure of serving both their needs.

"There are well-defined D/s relationships, Madison," Logan said. "With clear boundaries. They serve the needs of those involved in them. There might be affection there, trust, a form of caring and partnership that's highly valued. But then there's the wild card. Love. It can change the rules, destroy them, rebuild them, in accordance with the people involved, not fitting any set of rules or etiquette, or bullshit terminology. That's why being in love is the scariest relationship. It risks the soul, but it's the one thing in the whole universe worth that risk. That's why Alice said you were the braver of the two of you. You've risked yours over and over."

"But what if I'm not like Troy? What if—"

"You're not like Troy." He tipped up her chin, held it, his hand a light collar on her throat that riveted all her attention on him. "You're Madison. All you need to be is who you are."

It was then she realized the trust he kept talking about in D/s was something far more harrowing than restraints and spankings. It was believing what he was telling her and acting accordingly. She had a monument to self-doubt built up inside of her, augmented by every failed relationship. He was telling her she could destroy it, sweep the pieces out of her subconscious entirely.

"You still didn't answer the question," she said at last, swallowing. "About yourself."

"I think the answer will scare you."

"Everything about you scares me."

His eyes darkened with regret, compassion, and something else, something that really made her wish they'd done this before she'd received that package. His body was so firm beneath her, his scent in her nose. All she wanted to do was immerse herself in him. As if he picked up on the thought, he traced her lips with a finger, and she bit him, an act of pure sexual and emotional frustration. He gave her an exasperated look, but then he answered her.

"I haven't had a session with anyone at the club or outside of it, other than Troy or an instructional demo, since you arrived in town."

That would have been during Alice's last few days, which meant weeks before she and Logan had actually met. Her gaze snapped up to him, searching his face for the truth. He was right. Seeing the truth there scared her.

"Why?"

He held her gaze. "My promise to Alice. She gave you to me, and I knew you needed a man who was faithful to you in all ways."

"How am I supposed to even respond to that? It makes me feel like I'm obligated—"

"To do nothing." His tone was sharp enough to cut through the music, draw brief attention from other booths. It startled her, but it was highly effective. She pressed her lips together, unsure, but he shook his head. "I told you before. There is no obligation on your part, Madison. Only to follow where your feelings take you. C'mon. Stop this. Dance with me some more."

He dragged her out of the booth, whirled her back onto the floor. She was stiff at first, but he wasn't going to let her brood on it. When Troy and Shale engaged them in a four-way marathon of spinning and gyrating, she had to let go of her worries and hold on to Logan instead unless she wanted broken ankles. He was a relaxed dancer, not as accomplished and loose-hipped as Troy, but one who enjoyed the music and could move well with his partner, as he proved by holding her securely as they pivoted and turned together, his hands on her waist, grasping her fingers or sometimes bringing her back full against him with a large hand cupped on the side of her neck, the other on her hip as she wrapped her arms around his upper torso and enjoyed just moving with him.

Shale and Troy eventually wove themselves back into their choreography, switching partners so she danced with Troy and Logan with Shale. Another turn brought her and Shale together. Shale gave her a conspiratorial wink and turned Madison in her arms, wrapping both arms low on Madison's waist as they faced the two men and Shale took at nip at her throat.

The act caused about half the males on the dance floor to trip over their tongues. Troy's eyes sparkled at his Mistress's teasing. Logan gave them his slow grin, though he captured Madison's hand and pulled her firmly back to his side with a stern finger pointing at Shale. She crossed her eyes at him.

It was pure, sexy fun, from beginning to end. By the time they were ready to call it a night, Madison was doing exactly what he'd suggested. Being who she was, as well as having the pleasure of discovering more of what that meant. She'd been doing it since the day she'd taken over Naughty Bits. Though she realized he'd been her facilitator throughout, she wasn't entirely passive in the process. Not at all. And that helped her take a sledgehammer to that monument of self-doubt a little more enthusiastically. Maybe a lot more.

Troy left with Shale in her car, and Logan drove Madison back to hers at the store. Logan walked her to it, took her keys and opened it, looking inside before handing them back. It was the act of a courteous Southern gentleman, but there was that additional component to it as well, him taking charge in a way that kept her nerves humming pleasurably from the close proximity. The rules could be bent, right? Yes, but with consequences. She thought about those twenty-five switches. She had no doubt Logan would carry through with them. Then she thought of that look Troy had given his Mistress when her nails dug into his biceps. That was part of it for them, wasn't it? The line between misbehavior that was improper, unwelcome, and stepping across the line to give his Mistress the opportunity to administer punishment. Two needs being met. It was a delicate dance, but one that didn't require much thought at all on her part. Just being who she was.

Logan bent to brush her lips with his, an obviously restrained gesture with so much more vibrating beneath it. "See you Monday," he said.

She played along, wanting to goad him a little. "So what are you doing with your weekend?"

"Making some renovations at the house. I'm preparing for a new tenant and I want to make sure everything is in place to keep her there for a good long time."

He gave her a wink while her stomach fluttered. When he started to step back, she curled her fingers into the spaces between the buttons of his shirt, holding on. He paused, eyes finding hers.

"Please kiss me, Master," she whispered. "Really kiss me. I'd rather take a punishment later than not have that now."

He put his hands on her shoulders, and she sighed into his mouth as his lips sealed over hers. Slow, but not restrained. It was a thorough, overwhelming kiss that had her sliding her arms under his so she could get even closer. He let go of her shoulders to frame her jaw and throat with both hands, hold her there as her lips parted and his tongue mated with hers. Then he had her against her car, his body trapping her there, so she dug her fingers into his back and made a needy sound in her throat.

She'd loved dancing with him, loved talking with him. She teased him about being the all-knowing guru of BDSM, but she clung to every word as he taught her about it, secure in his knowledge about a world that was both so new and yet instinctively familiar to her.

He didn't talk to her the way he talked to Troy. It was like he was her personal guide, her partner, not just a temporary teacher. It was different, the same way it was different for Troy and Shale.

She stopped thinking. She let go of everything but being kissed by Logan Scott, thinking of him as hers. Her Master and no one else's.

When he lifted his head at last, they stared at each other. Nothing needed to be said, but so many possibilities whirled in the air between them. He gestured toward her car door. "Get in so I can make sure you're safe and on your way before I go back into my shop."

"Will you work late tonight?"

"I have a piece I'm finishing."

"I'd like to stay and watch. May I?"

"I'm not much of a conversationalist when I'm working. It's important to focus, to be sure I'm creating what the person is wanting."

"I just want to watch." She tilted her head, giving him a look intended to be humorous, but instead she stayed serious. "I'll only speak if spoken to."

She loved those sparks that ignited in his brown eyes. He had triggers for his Master cravings, the same as she had for her submissive ones. Maybe she wasn't a full-octane sub like Troy, but maybe worrying that she wouldn't be as much of a sub as Logan wanted was inhibiting her getting in touch with just how much of a submissive she really was. She could already imagine the ways he might let her "watch" if she fully embraced her desires in that regard.

"Your pulse just increased and I can feel your nipples becoming harder. If I reached under your skirt, you'd be wet, wouldn't you?"

"I've been that way since I first saw you today," she said. Right after she'd received the box.

The look in his eyes speared longing right to her core. "But something made you even wetter just now. Tell me what it was."

She amazed herself by doing just that. "I imagined you letting me watch you work, but you put a collar on me. Attached it with a long chain to the leg of the couch in your workshop area. Like I'm a . . . pet waiting for your attention. And I'm naked."

When he finished creating, he'd come to her, sawdust still on his hands, that fresh, sweet smell. He'd part her bare thighs and sheathe himself. She'd be so wet, no foreplay would be needed. He'd slide right into her body, available to her Master whenever he wanted it.

She said all that in a whisper, her gaze dropping to his throat. He tilted her face up, fingers pressing hard into her tender flesh, his eyes on fire. "I like that idea," he growled. His grip eased, somewhat, as he caressed her face. "But tonight, clothes stay on. You'd be too distracting for your Master otherwise."

When she closed her eyes, he tapped her cheek. "What?"

"I . . . like it when you call yourself that." *Her Master.*

"Good. Because that's what I am, Madison. You're starting to realize that, aren't you?"

Hoping. Terrified, thrilled. But hoping.

She felt as still as a bird in a box when they went into his workshop area. He nodded toward the small restroom facility, suggesting she use it before he got started. While she was in there, she heard a noise that drew things tighter in her lower belly. The clank of chains.

When she came out, he'd added a couple pillows to the couch and some magazines, making her space more comfortable. Perhaps it was self-interest to give her a distraction, since having a chained girl staring at him while he was working might be a little distracting. She was a mass of butterflies. She was going to let him collar her, make her lie quietly at his command and watch him work. Wait on his pleasure, his attention. The fact she'd asked to be in such a position and he'd agreed was a significant step forward in their journey together. She knew he was as aware of that as she was, else he wouldn't have reacted with that piercing regard, the possessive growl in his voice that had made her even wetter.

He turned from the piece she assumed was his project for the evening and came to her, his gaze passing over her in that assessing way he had. Taking her arm in a firm grasp, he guided her to the couch. She'd borrowed from her stock and changed for the club into a pair of dance heels, a short skirt and a sexy silky blouse through which she'd felt the heat of his hands quite a few times tonight. His eyes had often dipped into the low-cut, gathered neckline to catch a glimpse of the barely there lace bra beneath. She'd put up her hair for the dancing, which exposed her neck.

Now, as she kept her gaze on him, he picked up a collar he'd left on the couch arm. It was a serviceable collar, like one she'd seen him put on Troy, though this had a more slender strap, one he buckled around her neck snugly, but it wasn't too tight. He let her see the next piece as well, a heart-shaped lock about a square inch in size. When he hooked it into the buckling piece of the collar, she realized it meant the collar couldn't be removed without opening the lock. Suddenly that small weight seemed much more substantial.

He bent again, picked up the chain she'd heard clanking. He'd attached it to the leg of the sofa, just as she'd described. Threading the padlock into the end link of the chain, he attached it to the collar and snapped the lock closed. Now neither chain nor collar could be removed without him providing the key.

He wasn't done, however. As he sat her down on the couch, her pulse had speeded up even more. He guided her legs so she was reclined on a hip, then he moved down to the opposite end. Taking another chain and attaching the end of it to the opposite sofa leg, he looped the slack around her ankle and beneath the sole of the shoe before using another small padlock to secure the chain at her ankle. It held her foot securely to the other end of the couch with just enough length she could keep her foot up on the cushions.

If he'd left her attached only at one point, the collar, she could have slipped off the couch, moved around. Even lifted the end of the sofa if it wasn't too heavy and slipped the chain attached to her collar out from under its anchor. Now, stretched between the two points, that was impossible. Not uncomfortably so. She could partially sit up, even stretch out on her back, but she wasn't getting away from the couch without his help, and the psychology of that elicited a potent reaction.

His fingers slid up her inner thigh. Without any command from him, she parted her legs. Reaching beneath the short skirt, Logan stroked her through the thin barrier of the panties.

"Christ, you're as soaked as if you climaxed." He gave her a mock-stern look, pinched her clit, making her jump, gasp. "Did you masturbate while you were in the bathroom?"

"No, Master." She shook her head. "You know I didn't. It's just . . . you make me this way."

Those licks of fire in his eyes were going to make her burst into flame. He bent, put his lips on her thigh, his nostrils flaring as he obviously inhaled her scent. Then he straightened. "If I didn't have to concentrate, I'd put a vibrator on you and watch you come again and again," he said. "But I think this will be enough to inspire me. My client's going to get my best work tonight, thanks to you."

How could any rational woman explain why it turned her into a pool of lust to be collared and chained by such a man? Such feelings only increased as he moved to do his work, leaving her there as his possession, to be enjoyed and used by him at his leisure, not her own. Knowing he did it *because* it made her so intensely aroused, her helpless pleasure driving his? It was indescribable.

Yes, she could see herself during a night out with the women she'd worked with at her former job in Boston. "Oh, Doris, I'm so glad to hear you aced your recent board meeting and sent that bunch of sexist assholes home with their tails between their legs. Last weekend, I was chained to a sofa like a sex slave by a man I've started to call Master." *And I've never felt so cherished . . . or felt so loved . . . in all my life.*

She stared at him, her pulse pounding high and hard now for a different reason. It was the truth, and she found no fault with it, no instant scream for therapy from her rational mind. He picked up his tools. "Read your magazines," he ordered. "Let me know if you get uncomfortable or if you need anything. Anything important," he amended, that familiar gleam coming to his eye. "Else I'll have to gag you."

He worked for a solid two hours. With no access to a clock, she thought it could have been two minutes or two eternities. Time was both irrelevant and excruciating. She did page through one of the magazines, but in the end, she just watched him. She folded her hands beneath her head, fingers idly playing in the links of the chain attached to the collar. Her legs were bent enough she could feel the pull of the other chain on her ankle.

He chiseled out curves in the wood as sweet as a woman's. He bored holes, biceps flexing as he put pressure on the tool, and attached pieces with carefully placed fasteners.

As his work took shape, she saw it was fashioned after the stocks placed in a public square to punish and humiliate someone. It had the usual three holes for head and wrists, but he had it designed so the height could be adjusted, the servant bent at angles according to the desires of the Dominant. He had an additional panel that could be slotted and locked into the top of the stocks. Studying it, she realized the spaced holes were intended for a woman's breasts. Just like the bench piece he'd shown her the first time she'd toured his workshop, it gave the Master the ability to run a chain between nipple clamps or piercings, so the captive couldn't pull back, free herself.

The way he carefully checked the dimensions suggested the woman in question had been measured, probably by her Master. She imagined Logan doing that to her, so he could design furniture to hold her according to his desires. She wondered what he might make, what he'd like to do to her.

Though he was absorbed in his work, he did glance her way now and then. He didn't speak, but she thought he might be checking on how she was doing, or perhaps gaining more inspiration, because his gaze would course over the chains holding her, linger on her collar. Once, when he did that, she found herself lifting her chin to display it more prominently. The flicker in his eyes made her fingers curl into the sofa cushions. When he returned his attention to his work, she was nearly breathless.

She wondered if all craftsmen were as beautiful as the objects they created. He'd shed his shirt, revealing the white undershirt he wore beneath it, and had pulled that free from his jeans. When he squatted to peer up at something from a different angle, denim stretched deliciously over his thighs, his taut ass, his shoulders flexing as he tented his fingers on the ground, holding his balance. Later, when he finished coaxing out the shape of the wood, he began to use the hand sander, smoothing the wood while tiny shavings frosted his forearms. His arm muscles rolled like ocean surf as he performed every step needed to perfect his work.

She wanted him to come to her, push her back on the sofa, still chained, and take her like she'd imagined. Leave her wet with his seed, and then go back to what he was doing, making her feel used and needed. Though he appeared to be fully engrossed in what he was doing, she'd never felt so noticed, at an intense level she'd never imagined it possible for a man to notice a woman. He was as aware of her as he was his own breath or heart beating. Most people thought they didn't think about those things, but in fact they were more aware of them than anything else, an integral part of their existence, a constant reminder they were alive.

At length, he was done for the night. He wiped down his tools, put them away. Sweeping up the sawdust, he dumped it in a bin, hung the dustpan and broom back on the wall, then moved to the utility sink to wash his hands and forearms. She watched him dry his hands, run a wet cloth over his face and neck before he turned to her.

Her lips were parted, her throat dry. She hadn't thought to drink any of the bottled water he'd left within reach, her focus all on him. He leaned against the sink and picked up his own bottle, taking a deep swig from it. As he wiped his mouth with a casual forearm, his eyes stayed on her.

"Are you still wet for me, Madison?"

When she nodded, his gaze sharpened like the tools he was using. He didn't have to say anything; he was a teacher adept at giving his students precise nonverbal cues.

"Yes sir." *Yes, Master.* She wanted to call him that, write it on a chalkboard over and over like a punishment and reward both.

"Show me you're ready to be fucked. Put your fingers inside yourself, move them around so I can hear your cunt suck on them."

It was amazing how vulgarity became poetry in the right circumstances. She shifted, hearing the sound of her chains as she put her hands beneath the skirt.

"Pull it up. I want to see."

She wriggled so the short skirt was up at her hips and he could see the swatch of panties she wore. He raised a finger, stilling her.

He took another sip of the water, studying what she was revealing, probably the crotch panel of her panties, so soaked the silk would be transparent. "Spread your legs wider."

She trembled at his tone. She'd refuse him nothing. The note had said *From here forward, you are not allowed to pleasure yourself in any way. Or be pleasured. A single infraction will incur severe punishment. Twenty-five strikes with a switch.*

But he was her Master, here in the flesh, and she wouldn't resist him. Wouldn't deny him. Would he still, in whatever role he played for her this weekend, punish her for not following the instructions? Of course he would. That was part of the game, right? It made her tremble harder, knowing the punishment would be harsh, and yet whatever happened here would be worth it.

"Proceed."

She pulled aside the crotch panel and dipped two fingers inside herself. Her lips parted farther, her throat working on a noisy swallow at the brief contact between her fingers and the sensitive internal and external tissues. Under his gaze, her pussy contracted, and she did hear it, that greedy suck on her fingers as her sex begged for that for which her fingers could only be a poor substitute. She pushed deeper inside herself, pulled out enough to repeat the noise, and a moan slipped from her lips. A plea.

He watched her, his lips firm and unyielding, eyes fastened on what she was doing. He'd stopped drinking from the bottle, however, and when he shifted his thighs so his feet were planted at a wider angle, she wished the hem of the shirt wasn't hiding his reaction beneath the jeans. She wanted to see his erection growing, wanted to know just how much effort it was taking to deny himself. She also wanted to drop her head back, close her eyes, immerse herself in the feeling, but watching him was such an essential part of that, she didn't want to lose the visual input.

"Stop. Remove your fingers from yourself and hold them out toward me."

She did it, seeing her knuckles glistening with her juices. When he moved toward her at last, the quivering of her body increased. He moved with such purpose, such focus, it was as if he pulled in everything around him, including her, increasing the density of the very air.

Grasping her wrist, he tugged her upright until the chain pulled at her collar, indicating she'd come up as far as her bonds allowed. He dipped his head, smelled her fingers, his nostrils flaring. Then his tongue came out and he licked, a light tracing of her knuckle, sampling. When at last he sucked one finger in fully, the chains jangled as she jerked in sensual reaction.

He raised his head. "Lie back and spread your legs again. Both arms above your head, fingers holding on to the arm of the couch. Stay that way."

She obeyed, and she couldn't stop shaking, needing. He took off his shirt, revealing fine, furred muscle. He opened his jeans, a quick slip of the button, a tugging of the zipper, the denim pushed down just enough to suit his intent. From the sinuous roll of his hips, the way he reached in to stretch out what was beneath, she anticipated and was not disappointed to see he was fully erect, thick and hard, the tip already damp with viscous fluid.

As he knelt between her legs, he gave her that implacable look. "You're my obedient slave," he murmured. "You don't move, except in whatever way I move you."

"Yes, Master." There was no hesitation, no sense that she was playing a game. She'd called him what he was, and he'd just as clearly told her what she was in this moment. Nothing in her objected or disagreed with it.

He slid his hands beneath her thighs to cradle her buttocks, and then he tilted her hips up. He had one knee on the couch, the other foot planted on the floor, in between her chained foot and the sofa so her ankle rubbed against his pants leg, the chain making its soft metallic music as she twitched, involuntary movements she couldn't control.

He pushed into her, holding her still as a doll, and she gave a tremulous sigh, a tiny pleading sound captured in the breath. He held her gaze, binding her to his will as he eased in all the way, lifting her higher and adjusting his own hips to navigate her channel, moving slow to protect her from pain, even as his size stretched her in a pleasurably less comfortable way. Then he stayed that way, deep inside her, his fingers kneading her buttocks. It made a swirl of sensation spin from the delicate anal region to her cunt, spreading out through her stomach, up to her breasts. He hadn't had her remove her blouse, but now, when his eyes finally moved to it, she anticipated his next order.

"Take it off."

She unbuttoned it and had to arch her body to shrug out of it, which impaled her further upon him. She let the fabric slide to the floor. His gaze rested on the bra she'd chosen tonight. It was all thin lace, not intended to conceal or cushion the shape of the nipples at all, so beneath the dark blue lace the circles of her areolae, the hard points of her nipples, were visible. The bra had a front clasp.

"Open it."

When the cups slid away, revealing her breasts, his gaze devoured them. He moistened his lips, and she jolted as if he'd put his mouth there with just the implication.

"Grip them as if you're offering them to me. Squeeze them and hold that tension on them so they'll swell out of your hands."

She obeyed, and his brown eyes glinted. "Keep that pose, and don't move." Then he began to thrust.

"Aahhh." The noise couldn't be contained, not that one, nor the ones she uttered afterward. The other night he'd been gentle, building up to fast. Tonight, with her pose, with his orders, he was making it clear this was about his pleasure. Which, diabolically, made her even crazier with lust. Her pussy spasmed with each impact. He was going to make her come, disobey the instructions entirely, because she could take nothing but pleasure from this. But she lacked any will to stop him, to protect herself from anything he might do to her, and somewhere in her lust-fogged brain, she understood that was the point.

It was impossible not to move during an orgasm, but she fought hard to obey. As the waves started to build, about to crash over her, she was pushed over by his own hard, fast release, his cock convulsing inside her, spewing hot seed over her cervix and channel, making her cry out, her body bow up impossibly as she still held her breasts on display for him, fingers leaving pressure marks in her soft skin.

As she went over her own crest, his other arm snaked under her waist and, still pumping, he bent and captured her right nipple in his mouth, making her scream as he bit down, lashed at it, licked at her tight fingers. She worked her hips on him, her other leg coming up to hook his hip, but he shoved it down, held it pinned in the position he proscribed. It made the orgasm a long, never-ending toss in the surf, where she kept surfacing for air and then was pushed down again, drowning in the pleasure, rolled over and over.

When she was at last done, floating, her body jerking with tiny movements as if recovering from a seizure, he guided her hands from her breasts, letting her arms fall limp as they needed to do. He kept kissing her breasts, teasing nips, then he caught his fingers in the chain, tugging against the collar so she opened her eyes, focused on him. She was utterly lost, with him her only chance of rescue from this vast sea of nothingness, a place she would dwell forever at his behest.

"Logan . . ." Her voice was barely a whisper.

"It's all right, love. Ssshhh." He fingered the lock, keeping his weight on her without inhibiting her breath, as if he knew she needed the anchor of his body holding her to the couch. "I've half a mind to keep you like this for the next week or so, but I don't think I'd get any work done, knowing you were back here, waiting for me to do whatever I want to you. And Troy would swallow his tongue if he saw you."

She trembled harder, and felt an odd reaction: tears. "What's wrong with me?"

"Not a thing. Not a fucking thing in the whole world. You're perfect." He stroked back her hair, and his words just made the tears come spilling right out of her eyes. "It's like I told you that first night at your house. You're still working through things. This is still new to you, completely opening yourself up like that. This is the way it feels."

"Did you cry the first time it happened to you, on the Dom side of things?"

His eyes crinkled at her. "I think a Master feels it a little differently."

"Oh."

"Not less intensely. Different. For that one moment, when you gave yourself fully to me . . ." He paused and she latched on to his expression, the inward focus that told her he was genuinely attempting to explain something that was difficult to put into words. She knew the feeling. "I would have killed anyone who tried to hurt you. I wanted to protect you, possess you, cherish you, with everything I am. And I thanked God for the gift of you."

Never in her life had a man spoken to her so simply, honestly, with such genuine feeling. She lifted her hand, touched his face, traced his jaw, his lips. He kissed it. "I can still smell your honey on your fingers," he said. "I like it."

He withdrew with a regretful look, tucked himself back in and refastened his jeans before fishing out the key. She put her hand over the lock, a move she made before she even thought about why she did it, but she knew she didn't want him to remove it. The world was far more confusing and painful without it, and she was loath to return to that reality.

His countenance gentled, though he put firm fingers over hers, pulled hers away. "It won't be the last time I put a collar on you, Madison. I promise you that. If you decide you genuinely want it there," his gaze met hers, "It will be there, all the time. You'll feel my ownership no matter what you're wearing, or not wearing. Do you understand?"

She didn't, but she wanted to. However, his words were helping to ground her some, bring her back to reality, making her a little abashed at herself, at the intense, uninhibited way she was feeling and expressing herself.

He touched her face. "The way you're feeling right now, it's called subspace. It's like a high, the good kind. But sometimes, afterward, you can experience a crash, especially if you're still resolving a lot of emotional issues, if it's happening too fast, which this is, in some ways. So I want you to promise me something. If you get home tonight, and things feel wrong or sad, you call me. Even if it's just to hear me breathing on the other side of the phone, neither of us saying anything, that's okay. All right?"

She nodded. "Can you . . . would you leave the collar on for a while?"

In answer, he slipped off the padlock, removed the chain but left the collar and then shifted onto the couch, pulling her into his lap. From that position he unlocked the chain around her foot, let it fall to the floor. Then he gathered her more securely in his lap, her knees bent up against her body so she was almost in a ball against his chest, her bottom nestled into his lap. Wrapping those strong arms around her, rocking her gently, dropping kisses along her hair, he said nothing more, just held her. She had her hands folded against herself, her fingers playing with the D-link of the collar, the buckle on it. Laying her head on his shoulder, she pressed her face into his neck and let her mind float.

When he slipped off her shoes, rubbed her arches with his other hand, she moaned softly at the pleasure of it. "You're a hell of a dancer," he said.

"You're a pretty good one."

He chuckled at that. "You're coming down. Else you would have told me I was utterly perfect in all ways."

"So subspace makes a woman completely lose her mind." She was glad to see her lips were no longer quite as numb, though it was still an effort to form words, let alone smile. The dampness of his seed was on her thighs, against her pussy, where he'd readjusted the panties. Warm semen had trickled out of her, making her glad the panties would absorb some of it, so she'd smell that masculine scent later when she undressed.

"Do you know what I'm thinking?"

"You're a woman. I couldn't even begin to guess. It's like predicting which of the flying balls will be the winning bingo number."

She ignored that. "Clarence always delivers after ten o'clock in the morning. I'm thinking that first package on my first day here was put there by you, to get me to come over to your store. You sent Troy over to make sure I'd found it."

"That's pretty manipulative. Doesn't sound like me at all."

She smiled against his flesh, then sobered. She wanted him to come home with her like he had the other night, but she already had a sense he wouldn't do that, not unless it was clear she wasn't oriented enough to go home alone. While she thought about faking it just to get him there, she was pretty sure he'd see through the ruse. Plus, the sad reality was, when this feeling went away, she'd probably need space to think about what had happened tonight, what egg had been cracked open and whether what had been released had been ready to be born.

"You dance with your whole body," he said. "Arms, legs . . . hips, breasts, ass, your gorgeous hair." His fingers stroked through it. At some point she'd released it from the barrette that held it off her neck. "If you decide to do one of those strip dancing classes respectable women take to arouse their husbands, I won't object."

"I'll let you know when you're my husband."

Clearly, she wasn't evaluating what was coming out of her mouth. When she stiffened, he merely stroked his knuckles along her jaw. "Sounds like a hell of an incentive to propose. But only if you promise to do the dance at the reception, instead of the traditional first waltz."

Just like that, he took them back to safer footing, somewhat. She imagined him sitting in a chair in the center of a ballroom while she started the provocative dance in front of a faceless crowd. Circling him, peeling away clothes as his gaze got hotter and hotter . . .

"If you have any living parents attending, deal's off. Completely. Waltz only."

He chuckled. "Just as well. My dad has a bad heart. It might finish him off, though he'd argue it was a hell of a way to go. Even if he had to explain to my late mother how he got to her in the afterlife."

As if sensing she was starting to feel a little hemmed in, he eased her onto the sofa cushion next to him. He unbuckled the collar, their gazes holding. When he set the collar aside but rested his hands briefly on either side of her neck, a flesh-and-blood collar, her lips parted at his touch there. She thought again of what he'd said. *You'll feel my ownership, no matter what you're wearing.*

He glanced toward the bathroom. "You can clean up to go home, if you're ready for that."

She felt his eyes on her as she rose, moved unsteadily in that direction. He seemed to anticipate her so well, but that was what he did, wasn't it? What made her different from any other woman he'd initiated into this world? They'd probably all been overwhelmed by it.

She cleaned herself up, put her blouse back on, adjusted her skirt and balled up the wet panties, tucking them in her purse. While it seemed decadent not to be wearing any under a short skirt, she was going straight home. In the aftermath, cold wet panties against one's crotch was not the best feeling, a reality check of its own.

When she emerged, he was sitting on the arm of the couch. He'd been studying the stocks he'd worked on tonight, but as she opened the door, he looked in her direction, gaze sweeping over her.

"I'm not sure . . . about this weekend."

He nodded. "Any time you want to call anything to a halt, Madison, all you have to do is remember your safe word." He extended a hand to her. "Come here."

She balked at the door, fingering the molding on the threshold. "It's too much, Logan." She said it to that inanimate object, rather than to him. "You're like a tsunami. I can't hold on to anything when you sweep over me, and eventually I'm going to hit something. Like a car or a building, some immovable object, and I'll be bashed to bits. Please don't say I'm taking this all too seriously, that I should think of it as fun and games."

"I wouldn't. That's usually your line, remember?" He said it mildly, with no censure. He still had the hand out. "Come here. Now."

She dragged her feet, but she came. When his hand closed over hers, she let it lie limp in his grasp. She just wanted to go home. "It can't be real."

"Why not, Madison? Because so often what you thought was real hasn't been, and you're wanting to fold the cards before the house can call?"

"It feels like the only control I have with you."

That crash he was talking about had her in a solid grip, but she hadn't lost her self-awareness, not entirely. She was lashing out at him for no good reason. Even so, when he caught her chin, she tried to pull back. He only tightened his grip, forcing her to look at him.

"Think about what we just did, Madison. How you felt. It all felt right, didn't it? Don't be defensive, Goddamn it. Just answer honestly."

When she gave him a startled look, he shook his head at her, dropped his hand. "It's never occurred to you you're not all alone in this relationship, has it? Maybe in the past you thought you were alone in your feelings. But you're *not* alone this time."

She crossed her arms over herself. "I don't know where to go from here."

"How about we finish the night the way we started? Like a regular date. I walk you to your car, kiss you good night. Tell you I had a wonderful time, because I did. You could do the same if you feel merciful."

She shook her head at the grim humor in his voice. "You don't need reassurance. You're the most secure man I've ever met."

"Doesn't have to do with that. I've just reached the point in my life that when I know what I want, how I want it, I put it out there. If it comes to pass, it was meant to be. If it doesn't, I just work harder at it. It takes a hell of a lot to defeat me, Madison. So you can get afraid and retreat as often as you wish. It just means every line you back across, I'll follow you, until I'm so deep inside of you, you'll never get rid of me."

He tugged her closer, bringing her between his long thighs. He gripped her waist, then dropped lower, under the skirt to stroke her bare buttocks. "I'd bend you over my knee and give you a proper spanking to center your mind, make you stop this shit, but if I do it right now, I'll use my temper. Trust me, that wouldn't be what either of us wants."

She made a face at him, even as her stomach quaked a little at the real threat she heard in the words. "What *do* you want, Logan?"

He'd pulled her so close she had no choice but to put her hands on his shoulders, dig her fingers into that solid wall. "I want your trust, Madison," he said. "I want into your heart and soul, so we can see where that will take us. I want you."

She stared at his throat, closed her eyes. Shook her head. Not a negation. Just an inability to speak to the issue right now. A weighted moment passed where she thought he was going to torment her further, but then he pushed her back and stood. He held on to her, though, adjusting her skirt, smoothing it down over the curve of her backside before he gave her a smart smack. She jumped, and he gave her an easy smile that didn't dilute the intensity in his eyes. It made her wonder if that spanking might have done them both some good, exorcising his temper and her fears a little bit. But her fears kept coming back, didn't they?

He took her through their joined storerooms. She kept her gaze trained on his broad shoulders, following in his footsteps in the near darkness since he knew this area better than she did. As they passed through the lockout door between the two areas, her gaze went to the wall where he'd held and kissed her, that night he'd tied her to Troy.

Then they'd passed that point and he had her out her back door, where her car was waiting. He opened it for her, handed her the keys and gestured to her to get in. When she paused, he gave her a look, his brow quirking.

"You promised me a good night kiss," she said. "If you're feeling merciful."

His face eased into a more natural smile this time, making her feel better. He drew her to him, hands on her waist, and bent to put his mouth on hers. She melted into him, heard him mutter an oath before he pulled her close, holding her tight against his body. Despite their conflict, he kissed her with spine-tingling thoroughness. She gave back just as good on that this time, teasing his tongue, rubbing her body against him, unable to keep herself from responding to the limitless desire that he seemed to stoke inside her.

When he put her away from him, she was pleased to see he was just as aroused as she was. He maneuvered her into the car, closed the door firmly. As she lowered the window, he gave her a heated look.

"You're going to have an interesting weekend," he promised. "Start the car."

She complied, but she held his gaze as she did it. The next time she saw him, they'd be playing different roles. What would it be like, to see him as a fantasy? To see herself that way? And could it resolve the problems in their reality, or would it just enhance them? Damn it.

Putting her hand on the box in her passenger seat, the one that contained those items and instructions, she drove out of the alley, cognizant of him watching her depart and wondering if his mind was as full of the possibilities and pitfalls as hers was.

She'd been worried about the scattered nature of her mind when she left him that night, but as she started following the directions on that note Sunday morning, doubt transformed into nervous anticipation, helped along by a hard-core state of arousal that made any emotional debris a distraction at best.

But she was starting to understand. If she could stay in that submissive role, where her mind quieted and nothing else mattered, all was okay. It was in the sane moments that reality stole her joy. Was she indulging in a drug that kept her from facing reality, or was this a spiritual exercise that might eventually help her heal? She had no idea, but for this it didn't matter. Logan was making one of her deepest, most shameful fantasies a reality, and the man had proven he was damn capable in this department. She'd be insane not to see it through.

His skill at such things told her how well practiced he was at this stuff. Sheer female perversity had her appreciating that yet not wanting to dwell on how he'd acquired it. Maybe that was the female version of what he'd said, about most men not really wanting to know about a woman's former lovers. Women did want to know about men's former lovers, but not the sexual side of it. They wanted to dissect the emotional landscape of that relationship, see how it could work better with them, but they didn't want to hear how good that woman was in bed or how hot she was. No way, no how.

That was okay. As the day progressed, by following those instructions to the letter, she moved out of the realm of such issues. It was like the pretend dress-up, the skits she and Alice had created, on a far more adult and serious level, because there was no doubt that tonight was about more than some spirited role-playing. She moved away from the reality of herself, Madison, a thirty-something shopkeeper and former financial manager. She was a slave given to the training center on her eighteenth birthday to be readied for a Master's ownership. She'd graduated and would be auctioned tonight, would be offered to whomever bid the highest for her, for the talents she'd learned and perfected to serve a Master.

The reasons the instructions specified a bath became clear. She didn't have to draw the curtain to take a bath. She'd mounted the webcam on her tablet, set it on the kitchen counter, and with that little light flickering, she knew he'd be watching. Was he at his house, making his own preparations, keeping an eye on her? But part of a guided fantasy was guiding herself in it as well. She dispelled that thought, closing her eyes and imagining many eyes on her. Male eyes, strangers, watching. Considering how much they'd pay for her to be their slave.

Cleaning herself inside and out before an audience was the biggest hurdle, particularly the inside part. She used the products provided to flush out her most private regions, knowing her face was scarlet during some of it. Refilling the tub afterward, she bathed with the perfumed soaps. When she had to stand up on her knees to reach around and wash between her buttocks, arching her back in a way that tilted up her breasts, she started thinking about her audience. Getting braver, considering how she might drive up the bidding, she rose. Putting her foot on the tub edge, she leaned back against the wall and rubbed between her legs with soapy fingers, then cupped her breasts and tweaked her nipples so her lips parted at the sensations.

It wasn't a self-pleasuring infraction, because her intent wasn't orgasm. She wanted to make the eyes watching her grow intent with lust. She thought of the men's cocks getting hard. They weren't restricted the way she was. They could open their pants, fondle themselves, jack off, imagining how they'd have her down on her knees, doing for them when she was part of their household.

Her soldier. She thought of him, the glimpses she'd seen of him at the training house, the stern eyes and hard mouth with a little cruelty to it. He watched her a lot, telling her with his eyes, his manner, he already considered her claimed. By him. She'd felt that way the first moment he'd looked at her. What if he was outbid? What if one of the others took her? What if she had to spend her life serving a Master who didn't make her pussy cream when he looked at her, who didn't make her heart trip with longing to serve him however he demanded?

She stopped herself, lowering her head and opening her eyes to gaze at the webcam, as if she could send a message to him alone, no matter how many bidders might be staring at her.

A beep, and the screen showed a text message.

Training Mistress: A bidder has paid for a private viewing for the next five minutes. Spread your legs. Place your fingers on either side of your clit. He wants to see how swollen it is.

She braced her foot on the tub edge again and complied, spreading her thighs as wide as she could, and aligning her fingers on either side of her clitoris, pinching it to increase the pouting, flushed look. Just that pressure made her catch her lip in her teeth as the throbbing increased.

Wet your finger in your mouth and put it up your ass.

She hadn't gotten really comfortable with the anal stuff yet, but with that cursor blinking, she moved to obey. Staying in that position, one foot up on the tub edge, she wet her finger in her mouth, slowly, sucking on it until the knuckle was glistening. She rocked herself back and forth as she did it, the playful naughty girl with a lollipop, and then let the finger come free. Lowering her gaze, knowing how hard her soldier would get from the contrast, naughty girl and obedient slave, she reached back and worked the finger into her rectum. Her hips jerked at the sensation, and she had to reach out and steady herself against the wall as she did it, her thighs still in their spread position, so now her breasts were also thrust out and tilted up.

Roll your hips. Show him how much you wish to please him.

She made it a slow, circular motion, lifting up so he had a clear view of her wet, soapy pussy, arching her back so her breasts were even more on display. It pushed her finger in deeper and she let out a moan. Her pussy rippled. She could come, just from the stimulus of exhibiting herself for him.

Stop.

She came to a halt, dizzy, throbbing.

Continue your preparations as instructed. Do not remove any evidence of arousal from now until the auction. The screen went dark again.

She sat down on the tub edge, made sure she was steady enough to step out of it. There'd been two energy bars in the box and a postscript to her instructions that had said she was allowed to eat either or both of those and drink a cup of juice if she became light-headed, but she knew this feeling wasn't from hunger. Plus, she wanted to be light-headed, floating in a euphoria, where she had to focus on simple things really hard, keep anything more complicated out of her head.

Powders, lotions. Drying her hair, brushing it out until it shone and fell past her shoulder blades. She wanted to keep it that way for him, but the directions were clear. She put the sculpting clay in her hair, worked it into a braided topknot, every piece held in place by the style and the clay, leaving her neck fully exposed and her face with nothing to curtain any vulnerability.

At last, she lifted the collar and put it around her throat. When she threaded the buckle, her fingers shook. She pulled it too tight at first, wanting to feel that hold, the brief constriction of her air. Then she buckled it at the proper fit, still savoring the restraint, what it meant. That act alone inspired a contraction between her legs, and more slippery honey slid from her pussy. As it trickled down her leg, she reached for a tissue, then remembered. She wasn't to remove any of it.

Pausing, she straightened, put the tissue back. Then, feeling wicked, she ran her finger up the inside of her leg, collecting some of the fluid. Putting it in her mouth, she lifted her lashes to give the webcam a sultry, come-punish-me-for-it look. He'd bust her ass for that one, wouldn't he? She hoped so. She was caught between a giddy, slightly hysterical laugh and a throbbing need to pant like a sex-starved nymphomaniac. She was losing her mind.

The acceleration of her heart told her how close to six o'clock it was getting. Still, she verified it was five thirty on the dot when she stood in front of the webcam and seated the well-lubricated plug in her rectum, holding it in place with the ring in the back of the thong. The bullet in the crotch pressed against her clit, especially when she altered the ties of the side straps to hold both stimulants in place. The pressure made her sway, the stimulation in her ass only adding to it. She caught the edge of the counter, had to sit down on the commode lid, which only made the desire to rock against the two pieces almost overwhelming. Her clit was so swollen, even more swollen than it had been in the tub. She thought if she rubbed it at all, she might go off, so she locked her legs together, tried to think of broccoli, cigarette smoke, roadkill—the least sexually appealing things possible—until the feeling passed.

She fixed the chains to the collar, attached the nipple clamps, pinching each nipple as she screwed the clamp in place. The sensation made her hum in her throat, made her want to play with them. She closed her eyes, imagining her soldier tugging on that chain.

Ten minutes before she was scheduled to be picked up, she laced the blindfold in place and knelt by her door. She'd placed the webcam by it, so she could still be viewed. As she thought of the picture she made, she was trembling, gooseflesh on her arms, her mind blank. She was a sex slave, waiting to be sold, waiting to find out whom she would spend the rest of her life serving.

She was ready. *Please, let it be him.*

She heard a car turn into her driveway, two doors opening and closing, footsteps. As they reached her porch, and the screen door latch turned, one quick, Madison-near-hysteria thought invaded. She visualized a pair of Jehovah's Witnesses about to confront a kneeling, blindfolded and collared naked woman.

Instead, the door opened, no knock. The air around her moved as someone stood before her, looking at her. It wasn't him. She could tell, but it still made her quiver harder, a stranger seeing her like this. Then the person squatted and a finger caught the edge of her collar, tugging on it. That pressure, as well as how the chains twitched against her nipples, brought forth a needy sigh. She recognized his touch, his scent.

Troy.

He snapped a lead to the collar. "Stand up."

His tone wasn't unkind, but it wasn't injected with the warmth or subtle gentle note always there when he spoke to women, even his Mistress. Did women speak differently to men than they did among themselves as well, as if dealing with another gender required a different tonal language, a different form of music? Just as it had on movie night, the blindfold had her noticing a lot of things.

The firm tension on the lead, Troy's hand at her elbow, had her rising to her feet. Were they going to parade her naked down her front stoop?

"You disobeyed your instructions, slave." Shale's voice was devoid of the friendly tone she'd had the night she and Madison had danced and teased their men together. "You took pleasure for yourself."

Madison's stomach did a nervous somersault. Shale meant the kisses she'd sought from Logan. Or maybe the orgasm she'd experienced at his hands on the couch, an orgasm she'd been helpless to resist.

"Yes, ma'am."

Shale made a disapproving noise. "I told the directors you should be pulled from the auction and forced to repeat the full training regimen, but they disagreed. They said a severe punishment would teach you the necessary lesson. The marks you bear as evidence of your disobedience will drive up your price for those bidders who relish an excuse to punish a slave."

Her voice sharpened. "Now ask for the punishment you deserve."

Madison wet dry lips. She'd known it was coming, hadn't she? It was part of what she could give to her Master, the pleasure of being punished. She thought of the webcam, still focused on her.

"I want to please my Master," she said in a near whisper. "I want to prove I'll . . . incur any punishment that pleases him."

"Then get back on your knees." Shale's stern tone held a note of approbation. "Forehead and palms to the floor, ass in the air. Knees spread shoulder width apart."

Twenty-five strikes with a switch. That was the punishment laid out in the instructions for seeking her own pleasure. Madison suppressed a serious quake of nerves. Logan had spanked her, and while his hand had hurt at a certain point, open-palm-to-bare-buttock had a threshold. She remembered the switch in her mother's hand. Even applied with the restraint appropriate for a six-year-old's punishment, it had hurt like fire.

Something beeped and Shale stepped back. "Yes. I understand. Thank you."

She must be wearing a hands-free earpiece. Madison heard her step forward again, felt the brush of her high heel against the side of her bare foot. Kneeling the way Madison was, the soles of her feet curved up and vulnerable, she had a harrowing vision of Shale pressing a spike heel in the center of one.

"It was deemed that twenty-five is too many, just prior to the auction. We want your best assets displayed, not covered with welts. We don't want whoever buys you to spend his night having to tend you, do we?"

"No, Mistress."

"The sentence is eight."

Seven plus one. Seven failed relationships plus this one. The final one, the one she wanted to work out more than she'd wanted anything in a long time. Had Logan deliberately turned her mind in that direction by choosing eight strikes for punishment? He was so clever, she wouldn't put it past him. Being with him for a lifetime would be a challenge. She'd have to show him she could be pretty clever herself. Though the nice thing was she didn't have to be clever around him. She could be whatever she needed to be.

"Ass up," Shale reminded her. "Keep it off your heels so I can see your pussy, switch it if I want to do so."

She quaked. "Yes, Mistress." She forced herself to lift her hips higher and curled her fingers into balls, pushing her forehead harder into the floor.

"None of that. Breathe, and relax every part of your body. You don't tense up and resist your Master's discipline, do you?"

She made herself relax, one muscle at a time. And, points to Shale for noticing details, she didn't land the first blow until she'd finished, her entire body open to whatever was about to be done to it.

Yep, a switch still hurt like hell, particularly on an ass that was essentially bare. The thong didn't offer much in the way of protection. Madison bit back a cry for the first one and the second one, but on the third one it wrested free. It cut like fire, like her skin was being split, though she reasoned that couldn't be the case. Logan hadn't done a thing to break skin yet. But CIA torturers could reduce someone to a mass of jelly without even so much as a paper cut. She'd read that in a suspense novel.

Tears had gathered on that third stroke, the pain bringing the other emotions to the surface, just as before. What had Logan said? *The first couple of times, it boils things up like pus, until it will run clean and you'll feel other things. Just as good, but different.* Given her past, she wanted to think of it as a way of cleaning out all the other relationships. Was that why the instructions had told herself to clean herself inside and out, removing the touch of other men? That wasn't just the fantasy. This was a true clean slate, first step, and this punishment was just adding to the purging.

"God . . ." She'd lost count and that terrified her, because she needed to look forward to that eighth one, not get lost in the prior ones. That was important. Fortunately, Shale saved her on that.

"This is number five."

Madison cried out again, her thighs quivering. Shale ran her hand over the marks and gave her a little smack over them. "Very pretty. Your Master will be pleased. Three more to go."

"Please . . ." She didn't know what she was begging for, but it wasn't her safe word, so Shale didn't stop. Was Troy watching, wishing it was him, his cock getting hard even as he felt that quake in the lower belly, knowing that bearing the pain was part of it?

"Six."

When she yelped into the carpet, muffling the noise, she thought of her soldier. Standing in front of the camera, feet braced, arms crossed, his steely eyes focused on everything. How she was responding, every bare inch of flesh, every part of her, inside and out, that he intended to claim fully, all the way to her soul. She trembled harder. "Please . . ." she whispered, and now she knew what she was begging for.

"Seven."

"*God.*" She didn't know if Shale was hitting harder, or the pain built with each one. Just one more. One more. The most important one, the one that mattered more than the others.

"Call it out, slave."

"Eight. Please."

It slashed across her hindquarters, low enough that sting burned through her pussy, like an itch she couldn't reach back and satisfy. That wasn't her job, either. She panted, letting the sting turn into throbbing, trying not to wince as Shale ran her hand over the layers of marks, nails scraping across them.

"Nice. An excellent job. Thank you, Troy. Give me back the switch and bring her back to her feet. Clean her up."

That had been Troy? She realized then that both of them flanked her. Troy had been so quiet, and with the blindfold, her senses were disoriented. She'd just assumed Shale was doing the punishment.

His hand was under her arm, drawing her back up to her heels and then to her feet. She swayed, sniffled. "Close your eyes," he said with quiet firmness.

She was wearing a blindfold, so she wasn't sure why that was necessary, but she obeyed. Then he loosened the blindfold and lifted it. A soft handkerchief absorbed the tears that had fallen. Troy also carefully wiped around her mouth where the saliva had gathered from her position and stress. There was a reason the instructions had not included wearing makeup. He replaced the blindfold. "Open your eyes and tell me if you can see anything, even light. Be truthful."

She opened her eyes. "A little, under the left eye. Like candlelight."

He tightened it, and she was back in total darkness again, shaking like a leaf. They were going to take her to the auction, take her out of the house. That worry of being paraded down her stoop was back, trying to pull her out of her fantasy, and she resented it. It was dispelled like magic when a cloak was settled over her shoulders, smoothed by a pair of smaller hands. She recognized Shale's jasmine lotion, remembered her touch from the club, dancing with her arms around Madison, teasing the men.

Troy put his hand on Madison's lower back, clasping the tether now under the cloak and curved around her hip. In that manner, she was guided out the door, halted briefly as it was locked and secured; then they took her to the car.

It was an SUV, because Troy helped her up the step into the back-seat. He sat next to her as Shale went up front to drive. Once the doors were closed and the engine started, Troy unfastened the cape down the front, slid it off her shoulders. She assumed the windows were tinted dark. Knowing she was a slave going to auction, stripped down to mostly full nudity and being transported that way amid an oblivious public, made her inexplicably hotter and more anxious.

"Lift your hips so I can fold it beneath you."

She obeyed, and she was sitting naked next to him, in nothing but collar, tether and thong. And plug, but she supposed in its current position it couldn't count as outerwear. She was grateful for the cushion of the cloak, because those stripes still hurt.

"Open your legs."

He didn't have Logan's commanding delivery, but she didn't sense that was his intent. He was a servant of the auction, here to provide further instruction, an extension of the note. When she complied, his hands went to her thighs. He guided another strap around each, cinched and buckled them, testing the hold with a functional slide of his fingers beneath, though the proximity of his fingers to her wet cunt, the bullet forced more firmly against her from the spread-legged position, kept her breathing erratic. He attached similar straps to her wrists and guided them to her sides. A sound of metal snapping, and her wrists were clipped to the thigh straps.

She had so many things going on in her stomach and chest now. Anticipation, anxiety, restlessness. Arousal. Her nipples were beaded tight. As she shifted her thighs, she knew her folded cloak was absorbing the moisture that kept gathering on her labia, evidence of her readiness for her Master. How far would they drive?

She'd nursed this fantasy for a long time, so it was easy to revisit it, twine past imaginings with present ones in the swirling darkness created by the blindfold. The fantasy had started to build itself in her mind as soon as she'd begun the preparations, and now it continued in that vein, taking on a life of its own.

She knew some of her potential bidders, the way she knew the soldier. They'd all come to the parties the Training Mistress had planned to show off her offerings. The slaves were the servers on those nights, the estate where they trained full of powerful men and women. Glittering chandeliers, lots of dark, polished woods and marble floors, cold and hard where they'd kneel in proscribed positions until they were called to serve drinks and hors d'oeuvres.

Whenever she dared a glance through her lashes, she would see the soldier's dark brown eyes latched on her. His gaze would flicker, an admonishment as if he could already command her as her Master, and her eyes would dart back toward the floor. She wanted to slide across the hard stone and kneel at his feet then and there. But her fate was not hers to decide.

One night, though, he'd answered her wish. While kneeling, waiting to be called to serve again, she'd seen his polished shoe by her knee. He and another Master spoke over her head, talking of general things. His time in Afghanistan, what he thought of the oil situation. He was smart, her Master, speaking of what he knew without elaboration or boast, while being careful of subjects that related to his service, not meant to be revealed casually. When he shifted, the toe of his shoe was nearly beneath her knee. If she leaned forward even from a breath, she might press against it. Before she could do that, he did something different.

Her hands were flat on the floor, spaced six inches out from her knee. When he placed his shoe over her fingers, her instinct was to draw back before he accidentally stepped on her, broke bones. She was supposed to protect the assets of the Training House, and she was one of them. Broken fingers would earn her punishment for her carelessness. But she found herself quelling the instinct, holding still, and then she was caught up in a wondrous bliss.

He didn't put his weight on them. He had his shoe over her fingers, as light and gentle as if he'd covered them with his hand, which said he knew what he was doing, that he was touching her in an incidental way not prohibited during this phase of the evaluation process. It was a test, and she hoped she'd passed it. He put more pressure on it, enough to flatten her fingers, hold them more firmly to the ground, still not causing pain, though, and she forgot to breathe. She wanted to put her forehead to the ground, kneel fully to him, and maybe dare to turn her head, touch her mouth to his shoe. But she didn't.

Madison surfaced slowly from the image, though her current state and surroundings helped her stay caught up in its spell. Tonight was all about her fate. This was the turning point. Like the rituals prevalent in so many secret societies, where a new initiate stepped from the outer circle into the inner one, only the circle she was stepping into was essentially a circle of two. What she was leaving outside was all the others, all the wrong fit, the life she'd had.

She shivered, caught between the fears that overlapped between fantasy and reality. Troy's hand closed briefly over hers on the seat, strong and warm. He would try to comfort her, even if it wasn't allowed. But it would be noticed.

"We'll be arriving at the auction house shortly." Shale spoke sharply, and he withdrew. Her tone was capable of making a man's testicles shrink back into his body. "Remember your training."

348 Joey W. Hill

She wasn't sure to whom Shale was speaking, until she continued. "You don't speak or respond unless ordered to do so. You submit to anything required, whether pain or pleasure. Be a credit to your training. Understand?"

"Yes, Mistress."

"When you are purchased, you will be turned over to your new Master or Mistress. From that moment on, you obey him or her only. You are no longer part of the Training House. Your absolute obedience and loyalty belong to your Master or Mistress."

The car came to a rolling stop. This time, Troy left the cape off. He guided her out of the car with a supporting hand on her elbow and a tug on the leash firm enough that it pulled against the collar. She inhaled oil, metal. Maybe a parking area? As they moved forward, her wearing nothing but the thong and her collar, she felt the touch of open air. She had to trust she was in an isolated place, right? Oddly, though, it mattered even less to her now, as if she was being pulled deeper into the spell. This was the auction site, where other slaves dressed just the same would be on display, paraded across the same open area. She was probably being looked at even now.

A few minutes later, she sensed they'd entered a pavilion area, the air changing as curtains were pulled back, and sounds reflecting the echoing note they had when captured in an enclosed space. She stiffened as she heard voices, felt more air movement, as if her immediate surroundings contained people. Something like this would be held someplace private, unexpected, out of the way. Maybe a warehouse. As she was led farther inside, though she was blindfolded, that darkness seemed to get even darker. Dim, murky. A place where people could move in shadows. A place of dark secrets and sinful desires. The oil and metal smell outside was replaced by an exotic incense, one that teased her nose, made her feel dizzier. Despite her wrists being pinioned to her sides, she stretched out her fingers and found she was able to grasp a tiny inch of the slacks Troy was wearing, a tight hold on that small piece of him.

"Remember Alice?" he murmured, and gave her hip a single, reassuring caress.

The reminder and touch helped. She didn't want to get him in trouble, so she released him and followed his lead, a little steadier. Brighter, artificial light touched the edges of the blindfold, and she was taken up a set of steps, walked across planks. She was on a makeshift stage. The noise of people grew louder, the air movement denser, as if they were packed more closely around that display area. She was naked, in front of a group of strangers, here to assess her for purchase. Her pulse hammered up hard in her throat. Had she lost her mind? If her hands hadn't been bound, she would have ripped the blindfold away, tried to find that cloak.

She'd come to a stop, balked against Troy's hold. There were too many people around, too many voices. She turned, bumped into Troy, pulled against the bindings. She'd freak out if someone she didn't know did touch her. If that happened, she wouldn't know if anything he'd told her could be trusted. She wasn't ready for this. She'd lost her mind. All she had to do was say *Alice*. Right?

"I was very clear when I spoke to the Training Mistress. She's too shy for these coarse surroundings. That's why I paid for a private holding room for her."

The soldier's voice. Stern and commanding, a far harsher tone than he'd used in her presence before, but still very much him. As she lunged in his direction, the collar brought her up short, the tether suddenly wrapped up against Troy's fist, resting on her collarbone.

"Well, she seems to have made *her* choice." Shale's voice was amused, but cool. "We were taking her to the back for your private viewing, sir. The backroom access is through the stage."

"Which gives everyone a chance to see her," the soldier said, his voice like ice. "Driving her price up even higher."

Shale made a polite but noncommittal noise. The soldier placed a hand on Madison's bare shoulder. With a simple shift, he took her away from Troy and she was against him. He was wearing a uniform, and the wool scratched her bare flesh. She burrowed against him anyway, and his arm slid around her waist, hand palming her buttock. When he squeezed, the marks of the switch throbbed and the plug was nudged by his knuckles. The mix of pleasure and discomfort made her breath catch.

"I'll examine her thoroughly in the back. When the auction starts, you can communicate her bids to me via intercom. I will match and exceed them. No one will touch her except by my say-so."

"As you wish, sir." Shale's voice was as satisfied as any commissioned employee of the Training Mistress's would be, knowing she was going to get top dollar for her efforts.

He was guiding her away from the noise, the light. Yes, there might be people here, but he was taking her away from that. No one was going to touch her unless he permitted it. He'd said so. She inhaled his scent. He was near, holding her leash. It was okay.

She passed through another seemingly crowded area and then she was in blissful solitude with him, a quiet room that seemed quite a bit smaller. He unsnapped the tether, leaving her standing there without his support. She heard him moving around her, measured steps in crisp shoes. Military shoes.

"You're as lovely as I remember. Beautiful breasts, soft skin. You were ill-behaved in front of the camera this afternoon, a shameless tease." He pinched her buttock, hard, making her jump. "I see your bottom has already been whipped for an infraction. You'll be punished by me as well. Have you ever felt the bite of a single tail, sweet slave?"

She shook her head, and then yelped as something stung her nipple. Something electric, like a wand. She heard the crackle of the energy. "No sir."

"Better. You will address me as Master or Sergeant Major, at all times."

"Yes, Master." She shook as he moved the wand over her flesh, coming close enough for her to feel that tiny jolt and sting again. Under her nipple, along her hipbone, across her thigh. A thigh tracked with her moisture. His finger traced it and she bit her lip, then gave a yelp as he tugged on the chain to her nipple clamps, a firm hold that also pulled on the collar in a provocative way, reminding her she was wearing it.

"Spread your legs."

This was an entirely different tone from what she'd experienced before. There was no hesitation, no pause to determine what she was thinking, feeling, making sure they were going slow enough, reassuring her. But she was a trained slave. It was assumed she was ready for this, right? And though her heart was pounding rapidly and she was caught between nerves and a flight instinct, she was well aware she was responding to every word from his mouth, every touch. He'd taken her away from the stage, brought her here, just the two of them. She'd spread her legs as he'd commanded. Her fingers fisted in the bonds at her sides as the wand touched her labia, just under the thong, sending the kiss of pain through those sensitive nerve endings. Catching the side strap in one finger, he pulled the garment outward enough to slide the wand down in between it and the bullet, making her hips jerk in rhythm as he kept applying those electrical impulses to her clit.

"Master . . ." She bit back a yelp as he gave her a sharper zap, a reminder she was not allowed to speak unless spoken to. But he caressed her cheek as if her outburst had pleased him.

"The bidding is about to begin for her, sir." Shale's voice, through an intercom. "Would you like to open?"

"Twenty-five thousand."

"Very good, sir."

He put pressure on her shoulder, holding her steady until her knees met the floor since she had no hands to balance her. She heard the rustle of clothing, a zipper opening, then she inhaled the intoxicating musk of his cock. "Now would be the time for you to convince me just how much you want to be mine."

She already had her lips parted. He fed his stiff organ to her, keeping his fist wrapped around it so he gave her a provocative inch at a time, making her lick and suck and tease at his knuckles with her mouth. With the sway of her body and the fervency with which she worked her lips over the portion he gave her, she begged for more. The plug inside her, the rub of the bullet against her clit, all added to her enthusiasm, her arousal.

"Thirty thousand."

Another pause as more bids were taken. Every few moments, the voice came through again, Shale patiently waiting for his next counteroffer. Sometimes he paused, and Madison would renew her efforts, frantic that he might change his mind. This was her reality, fully immersed in the fantasy that had been drawn around her, made impossible to resist by the blindfold she wore, the way he'd submerged her senses in an environment that convinced her she was in an auction house, and he was one of her bidders, this stern man in uniform.

"Fifty-six thousand." He reached down, caught one of those chains and she came off her heels as he tugged at her left nipple, pulling it up higher. She moaned against his cock as he thrust harder, his other hand fisted in her hair. "You're worth a hundred thousand for your mouth alone," he muttered. "But I have to have enough left over to feed you."

She didn't need food. She just needed him. She teased the corona, sucking on the edges, flicking her tongue along the throbbing vein. She wanted to make him come, wanted to hear him make the winning bid in a strangled tone of near release. He chuckled harshly as if he sensed her intent, and then pulled her off of him.

"Forehead to floor, ass in the air. Spread your thighs. Let me see those switch marks."

She obeyed, whimpering. She was so close to coming it was as if she was in aftershocks already. It was hard not to move. He pulled up a chair near her and rested the flat of one shoe against her ass cheek, using her as a footrest. A struck match and she smelled the scent of a clove cigarette, a much more pleasant scent than the tobacco kind.

"We have a competing bid of ninety thousand, sir. I believe you have some competition."

"One hundred and five thousand. I know my competition, and he's about tapped out. He doesn't want her as much as I do. Which will be his eternal loss."

He shifted his foot, rocking her body slightly, almost like she was a cradle to soothe a baby, only she was the occupant being soothed by the movement as well. "I have some friends eager to meet you. You're my gift to them tonight. After I enjoy you myself. I have to be sure you're worth what I've paid for you."

Another silence, and then the intercom crackled. "Congratulations, sir. You have the winning bid. We've completed the transfer from your account. You may take her home."

"I'd like to see them try to stop me." The delicious threat and promise rippled along her spine. Her Master rose, trailing his fingers along that same track, down to the crease of her buttocks, probing between them, making her twitch as he dipped down beneath the thong to collect some moisture from her pussy, paint it around the rim where it was stretched around the plug. "It's good they've stretched you out there, but not too much. Some of the boys will want that pleasure tonight."

He lifted her to her knees, caught his finger beneath the collar. "You've made this too tight, baby. Trying to please your Master." He loosened it a notch, and she realized she could breathe a little easier. "Your handler should have checked that. I'll be sure to take it out on his ass."

She felt a twinge of sympathy for Troy, but she also wondered if she'd have the sadistic pleasure of witnessing it. The soldier gave her a sharp tug with the lead that had her stumbling to her feet, his hand grasping her arm to keep her from falling. Once she was steady, he dropped the lead and she let out a whimper as he unclamped the nipple jewelry, removing the chains that connected them to the collar so she wore just the collar and the thong. He cupped her breasts, massaged her nipples with his thumbs as the painful tingle made her shudder, bite back another whimper.

"They're nice and swollen now. I have an oil at home that, when painted on nipples, makes them stay aroused and stiff for hours. When I rub it onto your pussy, it will keep you so worked up I'll have to gag you to stop you begging to be fucked."

Her lips parted, that whimper turning into a pleading noise. She was almost at that point now. He stepped back, taking his hands away.

"You'll go with the two who brought you here tonight. They'll bring you to my home."

She didn't want him to leave her again, and she made a movement forward before she thought to restrain herself. He touched her face, telling her he wasn't displeased with her show of preference, but his voice was uncompromising.

"You'll behave, or I'll hear of it. You're mine now. You'll be a credit to my ownership, or you'll face punishment."

She swallowed, sinking back down to her knees to convey her obedience. As his footsteps receded, she heard two other sets approaching. Though she stayed in place as she'd been bid, she had an overpowering need to be with her Master again. Was that part of full submission, this swelling anxiety unless her Master was near?

Troy and Shale stood over her, speaking as if indifferent to her presence, a pet patiently sitting at their feet, though Troy did pick up the tether, since she felt the tug on the collar from his direction.

"I was surprised he bid so high," Troy said. "He's not the romantic type."

"He's a Master." Shale's voice reflected cool amusement. "It's not romance like candy and flowers, but something that means even more. When it's the one you want to belong to you, not just the one you're owning for the moment, you'd pay anything for that."

Her voice softened over those words. Madison suspected she'd reached out to touch some part of Troy, the one who belonged to her. The silence suggested Troy was responding to that, probably with one of those scorching looks the two of them liked to exchange.

"It reminds me of the first day he saw her." Troy paused. "I saw this look on his face, like when he's at the club and figuring out if a new member is a sub or Dom, or just vanilla out for a lark. I was pretty sure I knew what she was, because I could feel it, like a kinship, a sub-to-sub thing. But I wanted to be sure he and I were on the same page, so I said outright, 'She's a sub, right?'"

She remembered that first day, coming into their hardware store to bring the UPS package that Clarence had left at the wrong store. She also remembered the weighted feel of Logan's eyes on her as she'd gone back to her own store. This had happened at that moment. Troy's careful wording told Madison he was trying to communicate something about the reality that had led them here, without disrupting the fantasy, and she was hanging onto every word.

"He looked at me as if he was coming out of some dark tunnel," Troy said. "He blinked, then smiled that smile he has."

"Dangerous, make-a-woman's-knees-weak?"

"If you want to put it that way." Troy sounded a little aggrieved.

"Don't be a baby. What did he say when you asked if she was a sub?" Shale's voice was warm, teasing.

"'Oh yeah. Through and through.' I asked him if he was thinking of taking her into training, but he shook his head, said he was interested in something more than that. 'I want to see the spark turn into a fire.' That's what he said. I guess this is our answer. He didn't want to train her. He wanted to own her."

Madison drew in a breath. He already did, didn't he? Alice had given her to him.

Troy twitched the tether attached to her collar, the little tug a silent message of accord and reassurance she welcomed.

Did all guided fantasies work like this, or was it unique to her, what she was feeling, who she was? Yes, Logan had done everything to draw her into the role of Nameless Slave, bound to a Master she desired to serve above everything else in life. He knew so much about her, including her penchant for dress-up, for role-playing with her sister when she was young. He also knew just how far she'd taken herself away from play and make-believe for the past few years, such that she was starving for it now, but starving for it with an adult woman's desires and needs. She didn't even want to think of herself as Madison. She was simply the soldier's property now.

Yet Troy's words pointed out the message that kept replaying itself, whenever she was involved with Logan this way. This wasn't happening just because of Logan's consummate skill at creating the sensory input for a viable fantasy, but also because of her own deep-seated desires and needs that meshed with his. She'd worried about being enough of a sub for him, but he'd said it that night on the stairs, hadn't he?

"It's not my switch you need to worry about turning off."

She thought about how she'd reacted each time he'd led her down this path. Uncertain, one hand tentatively holding on to her perceived reality, but as Logan took her other hand, took command, she let go of that reality without hesitation and let him take her into his.

Into theirs.

A radio chirped, maybe on Troy's belt, because she heard him unclip it. "Sir?"

"I'm done up front. Bring her to my compound. I'll be just ahead of you."

"Yes sir."

Another car ride, again sitting on the cloak. She was getting used to being unclothed. The auction house would have been almost uncomfortably warm if she weren't. The A/C in the SUV gave her goosebumps, but when Troy's fingertip slid along her forearm, detecting them, he must have made some gesture to Shale. The temperature almost immediately modulated, and she was no longer cold.

A few minutes later, another method of warming happened. The bullet started vibrating.

So did the plug.

She hadn't expected the latter to be electronic, but the thick rubber was unmistakably humming against her stretched rim as the bullet was doing the same against her clit and labia. If it hadn't been both at once, she would have assumed she'd shifted or done something to set one off, but then she thought of what he'd said on the radio.

I'll be just ahead of you.

They were following her Master, and of course he had the remote. She shifted, which was a mistake. She was already intensely aroused, her brief interruption of mulling notwithstanding. A rolling feeling like waves of surf, ebbing and surging against her anus and cunt, ratcheted it to a much higher level. She bit down on her lip, tightening her fingers into balls at her side as she sat in the seat and tried not to wriggle or squirm, moan or gasp. Partially because she was self-conscious, partially because she knew the self-restraint was vital. She would not be allowed to come without his permission, and if she gave in to the feeling, she'd be there all the sooner.

But oh God, the stimulation was overwhelming. Feeling that hum against her sensitive anal rim, the buzz against her clit and labia, she had all she could do not to lift her hips in a coital rhythm.

"You better get rid of that hard-on before you get out of the car," Shale advised from the front. "Or he'll use a needle to deflate it. I'll help him."

"Kind of difficult to control," Troy muttered, and she realized his eyes were on her, watching her struggle. Could he see the light perspiration like dew on her skin? She imagined her Master's lips sucking the moisture away, entirely the wrong thought to have.

"Oh . . ." The plea escaped her lips, despite herself. She heard Troy bite back an oath. He'd be trying to obey his Mistress, she was sure of it, and yet this would give Shale a reason to taunt and punish

358 Joey W. Hill

him later. Her Master liked to reward his helpers as diabolically as he knew how to torment his own possession.

His slave. He'd called her that. The vibration's intensity bumped up, and it changed rhythm. No longer concentrated only in the nose of the bullet, it moved over her labia and pattered over her clit. Her hips convulsed, and she thrashed her head, pulling against the hold Troy had on her tether. "No . . . no . . ."

There was no help for it. She couldn't stop herself. She tried to rein the reaction back, but her Master wasn't going to give her any choice at all. He was his to command, his to push over that edge whenever he wished, no matter if it won her a punishment.

"Help . . ." But there was no help being offered for this. The climax took her, squeezing her internal muscles down on the plug, her pussy rippling beneath the vibration of the bullet. She squirmed on the folded cloak, hips jerking, fingers splayed wide in their bindings against her thighs. It got more and more intense and she screamed in the contained space of the vehicle, the sound rebounding and echoing against her like additional vibration and stimulus. Her nipples were throbbing, still tender from the clamps.

She choked it down as soon as she could, cognizant that she'd released without permission, but her hips were still moving with that rhythm, her breath choking in her throat. The vibration didn't abate, such that she jerked and writhed on the seat like a caught fish. She couldn't make it stop. Couldn't control her body. Because it wasn't hers. It was his.

"Yes sir. She's done now."

The bullet and plug eased down to a hum again, like a slow lick over her tissues by a lover's tongue. She moaned in relief and heard Troy shift next to her. There was a click as he let off the radio. She realized he'd been holding it up close to her face as she climaxed, so her new Master could hear her. She thought of him driving ahead of her, thought of how his erection had probably swelled to an impressive length and thickness. Then she thought of her mouth on him there again and licked her lips. She'd just had a climax, but it wasn't enough. She was still throbbing. She wanted him inside her, in every orifice, penetrating heart, soul and mind.

As the car rolled to a stop, she rested her temple against the seat back, trying to catch her breath. She was close to Troy's face, his breath sweet and warm on her forehead. "This is your new home, pretty slave," Shale said from the front. "Serve your Master well."

The car door was opened and she was drawn from the vehicle with another tug against the collar. The smell of mown grass reached her nostrils. Things felt open and quiet, an absence of city noise. She could hear nighttime insects, perhaps some frogs on a nearby pond. Was this the soldier's property? A remote area, where no one would realize her owner had his own personal slave trained to do his bidding, 24/7, naked all the time if that was what he demanded.

Her legs were wobbly, such that Troy was supporting her under her arm and around her waist.

"Sir." He spoke, and she sensed the transfer of the tether to another's hand, one who firmly reeled her in until she stood right before him, his heat overwhelming her own. His fingers gripped her chin. "Did anyone give you permission to come, slave?"

"No, Master." Though he'd made it impossible for any different outcome. She didn't really care that it wasn't fair, though. What did that say about her?

"Then you understand you must pay the consequences."

"Yes sir. My Master wanted me to come to have the opportunity to punish me."

She couldn't resist, which meant her mind wasn't really straight. She thought she heard a muffled chuckle from Troy, right before her Master's hand settled on her throat, just above the collar.

"The Training Mistress warned me about that clever tongue of yours. Another comment like that, and you'll have it strapped down by a gag for the rest of the night, when it's not being used in other ways."

She shivered at that tone he did so well. "Each time you come without permission tonight," he continued, "I'll mark it down. That's how many times my friends will get to fuck you."

"Will you tell me . . . about them?"

"What does that matter?" His tone sharpened, making her jump like the prick of a rose's thick thorn. "You'll serve whomever I wish."

"Yes, Master. I wanted to know more about them . . . to know how best to please them for you."

Silence as he thought that over. She could sense him circling her. She gasped as he caught her hair, jerked her head back, his thumb tracing her mouth. "Open wide."

She complied. As she held her mouth open so wide it made her jaw ache, he kept tracing her lips. "One of them has a very large dick. So large it makes a slave cry, even when she has to take it in her mouth. He likes that, likes feeling her tears fall on his cock. He'll strap you on a table, put your head over the edge so his balls will be against your face as he thrusts into your throat. Two of my friends like suckling a slave's nipples while he does that. They'll put their fingers inside you, make you come again. They'll keep you tied down so you can only cry for mercy. What will you do, slave?"

"I will do as my Master wishes." Her throat was dry, heart pounding so hard he had to hear it. "I will please him and make him proud."

"We'll see."

He jerked on her leash, making her follow him. Hearing the vehicle start behind her, she knew Troy and Shale were leaving. It was just the two of them. Maybe. He was so good at this, she was starting to doubt what he'd said, that he would be the only one to touch her tonight. However, if that assertion was true, what he said earlier suggested her Master would be having anal sex with her tonight. As well as every other kind of sex he wanted to have.

She'd never done that. She had the safe word. But, as scary as some of this was, nothing was scary enough to make her want to use that.

He was so close in front of her, she was guided by his body heat. She was brought up onto a deck, taken inside a screened porch. The heat of flame suggested burning candles. It had to be night at this point. "Keep your eyes closed until I tell you to do otherwise."

"Yes, Sergeant Major." She hadn't tried out that title yet and liked how it came off the tongue. She knew sergeant was an enlisted man's rank, not an officer's. She found that idea fit him perfectly. He was the type of man who preferred to remain directly in charge of those under his command.

The blindfold was removed, the tether snapped off her collar. Her wrists were freed from the thigh cuffs, though he didn't remove either set, indicating they might be used again. She heard him move away from her, the creak as he settled into a chair. The tab of a canned drink popped, so she imagined him drinking a beer while he studied her there, naked, waiting on his will.

"You may lift your gaze."

It reminded her of the provocative scene in *True Lies*, where Arnold sat in a corner of the hotel room and ordered Jamie Lee Curtis to turn and display herself, undress, dance for him. Just like in that scene, she could see Logan's outline, his features, but nothing specific in the semi-darkness. He sipped the beer, the heat of his gaze like the sun. She'd never imagined doing any of this, but her focus wasn't on the macrocosm, but on every unique detail.

Standing before him naked, silent, not allowed to speak, she couldn't create a shield of words to protect her vulnerability. No, she had to merely stand while he thought whatever he wished of her. The nearby candles, heated by the wick of flame, turned soft and molten under the inexorable burn, the fragrance released by the accelerated temperature. A drop of her own wax, so to speak, rolled down her inner thigh, hot and slick. She could hear her breath, slow and yet erratic, like a languid breeze passing through the branches of a tree.

Setting the beer aside, he rose. He came to her, and the shadows resolved themselves into his forbidding, handsome expression. He unbuckled one thigh cuff, slid it around, refastened it, then he did the same to the other. Then he guided her wrists behind her, crossed them. He'd adjusted the D-rings so they were beneath the fullest point of her buttocks, so now her hands were cuffed behind her, the position and crossing of her wrists pulling her shoulders back to a more severe arch of her back.

He hadn't said she had to look down, so she watched him with hungry eyes. She thought the olive-green coat and crisply ironed slacks, the gold buttons and insignia on the sleeve, the braiding and polished shoes, just added to his look of total command.

As did that intent gaze, that Master's absorption that said he was seeing, thinking everything. Her thoughts might have the randomness of autumn leaves spinning in a storm, but in a way it meshed, that submissive chaos orbiting the Master in the center. He had strategic focus, each point on the line to his goal marked with every action.

She'd vaguely registered her surroundings. The screened porch, the chair where he'd sat watching her, but now she detected a different scent. Heated water. He gripped her elbow, turned her, and she saw the hot tub in the corner, steaming. He had the bubbles turned off.

Unbuttoning his coat, he shrugged out of it, hung it up on a coatrack. Then he loosened his tie, removed it, and rolled up his sleeves. Casual movements she found unbelievably sexy, such that when he bent and scooped her up as if she weighed nothing, she wanted to curl her arms around his neck, press her face there, feel the strength of his body against her breasts through the thin shirt. But he had her bound, denying her.

He sat her on one of the benches in the tub, the heated water coming up to her waist. Reaching below the water's surface, he lifted her legs and wrapped two straps around her ankles, spreading and attaching them to the bench across from her, her feet curled over the edge of it. Her thigh straps were hooked to steel clips on the bench she was on, limiting the mobility of her hips. He fastened the chain to her collar to a hook on the side of the hot tub, taking up the slack enough it pulled against the side of her throat, but it was a psychological reminder, not restrictive. Easing her head back against the wide, flat edge behind her, he strapped her forehead down. In this position she was arched back, her breasts thrust up at him, legs spread beneath the water.

Then he turned on the jets.

One hit her on the labia and clit, a direct, solid hit, the force enough to have her gasping and trying to writhe right away.

"You keep yourself positioned right in front of that. No wiggling away."

"Yes, Master," she managed in a desperate rasp.

He loomed above her, watching as the water stimulated her already overwhelmed tissues. She was caught in a permanent state of arousal, almost where she couldn't go higher or lower, just had to stay in this mindless needy mode. Where she'd beg to be fucked, just like he'd said. She kept her eyes latched on his, knowing the plea was in her gaze. He was watching the reactions of her body, those stern, detail-oriented eyes covering every response.

Picking up one of the candles, he brought the flame close enough to her exposed breast that she felt the heat. She quaked but didn't draw back. He put a hand on her shoulder to steady her regardless, and then tipped it over her skin, already glistening from the steam off the water.

She gasped again at the heat of the wax, a fast sear of the flesh that turned to liquid heat, rolling over the crinkled ground of her areola and her nipple before beginning to harden. He did it to the other, and she arched farther toward him, not away. Setting the candle aside, he placed the blindfold back on her, lacing it more tightly than Troy had, so the darkness was absolute. She doubted any light could filter through, even around the edges.

His hands framed her neck, thumbs resting on her collarbone, then they made a slow upward stroke over her windpipe, to the base of the collar. She raised her chin as his mouth touched hers lightly, tongue tracing her lips. She made a soft plea which he answered by tightening his grip, indicating he expected her to stay utterly still, passive. It made things all the more combustible. The water was stroking her, pummeling her, and she cried softly into his mouth. He didn't respond to that, instead taking his time playing with her lips, while she shut her eyes tight behind the blindfold, the contrast helping her keep her mouth slack, which only intensified the sensations.

"Mine," he murmured, leaving her mouth to speak against her ear. "My devoted slave, my treasure. Your sweet cunt is all mine."

Those were the words she'd told Logan she'd imagined her soldier saying, when all this—everything he'd brought to life for her tonight—had been merely a masturbation fantasy to keep her company in her lonely bed.

Before tonight, she would have said she'd been fantasizing about a Master who couldn't possibly exist. But those words Logan spoke against her flesh didn't feel like mere imitation to fit her fantasy. It was as if he'd sent them to her dreams long before she met him. Logan was the Master she'd dreamed about, and he was here, incredibly, overwhelmingly real.

She was going to come. *Oh fuck* . . . She whimpered, conveying the desperation in the plea.

The cry caught in her throat, a near miss. He'd reduced the water pressure, the diabolical man. The water now flowed over her swollen tissues in a languorous stroke that in some ways made it harder to be still. But as Logan moved his mouth back to her cheekbone, the corner of her lips, her lifted jaw, things slowed down, the throb of her body becoming more like a heartbeat, pounding and sure, irrefutable.

Images filled her mind, riding that rhythm. Their first session, where he'd tied her to Troy, her "helping" him train the male sub. Sitting on the tailgate of his truck with her, Logan letting her see his sadness over Veronica's situation, as well as his adamant desire that Madison should never fear him the way the abused sub had feared her Dom. The way he'd backed down Veronica's Master, he and Troy ready to protect them both, with a great deal of violence if necessary. Such things stirred a woman's blood, no matter how barbaric it might seem.

His expression when he made her smile, as if he was the one who'd been given a gift. She thought of the many times she'd visualized Logan at Alice's bedside, caring for her, her primary caregiver, doing what Madison should have been doing. And would have, if her sister had let her know she was sick, or if Madison had paid closer attention to the signs. Except now Madison realized maybe Alice had wanted to go out on her own terms, and part of those terms had included helping Madison find what she'd never been able to find for herself.

Now, in the touch of Logan's hands, in the way she was sure his eyes rested on her, she realized that hadn't been a gift for only one person. If Madison believed Logan, Alice had given him something he hadn't been able to find for himself, either. Just one more time, could she risk her heart? Trust that she'd finally found what she'd always been seeking?

Tears burned in her eyes under the mask. When Logan's thumbs moved over her throat she swallowed beneath his touch, his collar. "I love you," she whispered.

His hands stopped but she shook her head. "Please don't take off the blindfold. I want to be yours . . . I want the fantasy to become the reality."

Would he understand such a strangely worded request, since

keeping the blindfold on would seem to be promoting the fantasy? In the end, he was a Master, wasn't he? He understood that some things became far clearer while within the session, things that escaped when they were outside it. If she stayed within it long enough tonight, she could brand it on her soul, so she never lost it. She hoped. There were truths to be found here, and she'd just stepped over the threshold, saying she was willing to accept them, find them in his ownership.

"When I'm done tonight, you'll feel like you've been fucked by ten men," he said, after a long pause, making her breath sigh out in relief. "But they'll all be me. I'm not going to share you. It will always, only, be me. Say it."

"Only you, Master." Her lips curved in tremulous answer, and his hands dropped to her waist. For one blissful instant, he was up against her, his lips at her temple, telling her he understood. That he knew what this moment meant to them both.

He unhooked the thigh straps. "Hold your breath," he said quietly. "And trust me."

"I do."

He pushed her beneath the water, into a thundering world of bubbles. Her knees bent, the ankle straps holding her feet against the opposite bench. The chain pulled against the collar, reminding her of her connection to the world above, but it had enough slack her head came to rest on that bench where she'd been sitting, her backside now suspended in that open area between the two benches. One second, two seconds . . . He caressed her, hands sliding over her breasts, dislodging the wax, rubbing her nipples. She tried to hold her breath rather than strangling at the incredible sensation. Then, slowly, he brought her back up.

She'd trusted him entirely for that, for holding her underwater, and her response to that was powerful. She'd been shaking for a while, but now the feeling had doubled in intensity. He removed the tether attached to her collar, freed her ankles and pulled off the thigh straps, but left her hands cuffed behind her back. Then he scooped her up and brought her out. As he set her down and drew back, she assumed to find a towel, he had to remove his hands from her, step away.

It was then she realized all these revelations were too unsettling. Her knees buckled, a tree without roots.

She didn't even have a chance to call out. He was back in the space of a heartbeat, his body providing her support. He bent and lifted her again, cradling her back so even with her arms pulled behind her, she felt secure. She was soaking wet and against his dress shirt, but he didn't seem to care. Taking her a few steps across the room, he laid her down on her side on a thinly padded table.

He spread a towel over her, gently dried her, head to toe. The sculpting clay had done its job: even after her dunking, her hair still firmly held in that topknot on her head, but he patted the area above the collar, her face, then all over, careful and thorough as if drying a child. She quivered under his touch and thought thoughts no child ever did.

When he was done, even down to rubbing the soles of her feet dry, he unhooked her wrists and turned her on her back. Her ass was on the table's edge, but then she heard a sliding sound, and her legs were fitted into bendable cool metal brace pieces that came out from beneath the table, like stirrups in the doctor's office, only for a far more sexy use. He strapped her ankles, calves and thighs to those brace pieces. Then he bent her legs to a more severe angle, her knees pushed up toward her body, but spread out so her anus and cunt were completely exposed to him on the edge of the table. She was supported and helpless at once, from the waist down.

Of course he wasn't done. He strapped down her upper body as well, her forehead, hips, and above and below her breasts. They were wider strips, padded, so they didn't cut into her as her weight redistributed. He stretched her arms out on braces as well, held them there like bent angel wings.

He had her completely immobilized, at his mercy. She was a

little teary, and so aroused she could barely speak. Fortunately he wasn't asking her to recite poetry, though she had a feeling by the time he was done, she'd be speaking in tongues.

He moved away from her again, and she heard him open a drawer, remove something. The tear of foil, possibly a condom being rolled on. Then another scent, the squirt of a bottle. Lubricant being added to the condom, to augment what was already there. The sound of something being snapped in place, and then rolled across what had to be a wood floor, based on the sound of his shoes on it earlier and now.

Touching her pussy lips, he pushed an oiled finger into her to tease her channel with tiny caresses that had her trying to lift up to his touch. She could manage some movement, but her restrained legs kept it to a limited wriggling that seemed to please him, because he put another hand on her breast, gently thumbed the nipple.

"That's my gorgeous slave, all wet and eager for me."

His fingers withdrew, but only to replace them with something else. He began to ease a dildo that felt like flesh into her. Thick, very thick flesh. "This is my friend with the sizeable cock. The one that I would have had stretch your mouth, push down into your throat until he made you gag. Looking at you all tied up like this, he can't resist. He wants your pussy, and he's such a good friend, I won't deny him the gift. No, don't you tense up. You keep moving your hips. He's dripping with lube. You can take him."

It was a credit to his skill, that he could use that mesmerizing voice and her subjugated position, the way it scrambled her brain, to revive the fantasy, despite the fact she knew he was alone with her. She heard the murmur of voices, wondered if he'd turned on a recording, but it didn't matter. Like the auction, there were erratic air currents, as if there were more people in the room, and now it was as if he was talking to his friend, not her. "She's trained to do this. You can go balls deep in her. How does that feel? Tight as fuck, right? Look at her face. Lips parted, practically begging to take another cock down her throat. She loves serving her Master."

He bore down, kept working it, working it, as it stretched her impossibly, filled her. When she thought she couldn't take a millimeter more, he stopped, strapped it in place.

"My other friend wants your ass. What do you say to your Master?"

"Yes . . . sir. Please."

She let out a startled breath as the table was elevated, her hips at a higher angle than her head. The reason for the supportive, wider straps was now apparent. Once she was in position, he began to work a plug into her anus. This one was as thick as the one in her pussy, though perhaps it wasn't, because she couldn't imagine taking two of that size without splitting in two.

"Master . . . I'm not sure . . ."

"Are you afraid your Master will let someone hurt you in a way you won't like?"

"Yes sir."

"Have I ever done that before?"

"No sir." She swallowed. "Please . . . I'm sorry. Please, keep going?"

He did, working the other one into her until it was seated and cinched in place. Moving upward, he stroked her temple, then adjusted another hinged piece to tilt her head back, toward the floor. A ring gag was lodged in her mouth to hold it open wide. As he buckled the strap for it around the back of her neck, the ring made her jaw ache, but the idea of a thick cock being thrust between her immobilized lips made her tremble more.

"My friend wants you to suck him off while the other two fuck you. You're being such a good slave. I'm very proud of you."

Her pussy got even wetter, just from her hearing his approval. She adjusted her jaw so she could take the ring gag deeper, make her mouth wider. He growled in response. "Are you pleasing them or your Master?"

"You," she said, despite the ring holding down her tongue. "Only . . . you."

He fit another dildo into that, a firm, fleshlike one with testicles that were so lifelike, it just took her further into the fantasy, the way they squashed against her forehead, the bridge of her nose. She was twitching, so aroused, her nerves so wound up, her emotions started to spiral everywhere, a perverse reaction to being so restrained.

He trailed a hand down her body as he moved back between her legs, a firm caress that reassured. When he moved the two dildos slightly, working them in and out, greasing her up further, she moaned against the gag. There was no direct contact with her clit, but every other erogenous nerve ending was on high alert, including her mind. She could envision the way she looked, spread out and impaled for his pleasure. Because of the pictures he'd painted, she could imagine his three friends there, all military men like himself, with muscles, tattoos and short, shaved hair, eyes intent and serious, filled with lust and need. Wanting to take pleasure from her bound, helpless body. It was her fantasy and more . . . by making it only him, he'd made it the reality she craved as well.

A hum and she let out a cry as the dildos in her anus and pussy started moving in a synchronized way. The rolling and snapping sounds made sense now. The dildos were attached to one of those machines she'd seen in the clubs she and Alice had visited. A fucking machine, one with a dual attachment, adjusted to the right angles. Slow push inward, then withdraw, then repeat. It made the idea of two males fucking her all the more real in her mind. One beneath her, thrusting up as she lay upon him, the other pushing into her pussy, standing between her spread knees and straddling the other man's legs.

The next change nearly shattered her. The dildo in her mouth was removed, as was the ring gag holding it, and instead she got the real thing. Her Master's flesh-and-blood cock between her lips. She sucked him in with all the eagerness and desire she could convey, to the point she was almost a little too enthusiastic. He tightened a hand in her hair, a gentle reproof to tone it down. Oh, but it was so difficult to do so, especially with those other two pushing in, pulling out. His testicles pressed against the bridge of her nose, his scent filling her like his cock.

"There you are. You serve me with your mouth as your ass and cunt are taking care of my friends. My sweet, sweet slave. Worth every dollar I paid for you. I'm going to keep you naked in a pretty gilded cage when I'm not fucking you, let everyone see my gorgeous pet, walk you around the grounds with a leash, remind you who you belong to every day . . ."

God, he was driving her even crazier. She heard the mutter of other male voices now, while the scent of his cock and seed absorbed her, along with the heat and aroma of the candles, making it all come to overwhelming life.

"Damn, Sarge, she's a beauty. She's so bloody tight and wet . . . I could bugger her ass all day long. We'll switch after this and have another go at her. I want to fuck her to death . . ."

A husky Aussie accent, coming from the direction of those fucking machines. Yeah, it was probably a recording, but in her current state it sounded real. Jesus, the man didn't miss a trick. She moaned, kept working him in her mouth, lost in the bliss of it. Her pussy spasmed hard, wanting the climax so much, but the stimulation was so crazy, so intense, it was as if she were paralyzed on a point of arousal that was mindless and infinite, no going forward or back.

Infinite . . . a figure eight symbol . . .

The significance of eight had hit her earlier. Now it flashed in her mind again, lingering at the edges of her consciousness. In this state, she couldn't recite her ABCs, let alone reach out for a nebulous thought. But she wanted to. It was important. Something about that symbol was important, especially now.

A moment later, she was sure of it, because seeing the flash of that symbol in her mind changed something. Though this was all perfect, so perfect, tears were sliding out from beneath the blindfold. She was breaking apart, and making pleading noises. She knew when the tears hit his thumbs, from his rough words, his rough demands.

"You don't like my friends? You won't serve them if I demand it?"

She shook her head, not really clear on what she was conveying until she realized she was indicating a negative response. His voice got harsher.

"You're my slave to loan out as I see fit. If I order you to fuck my friends, you'll refuse me?"

She'd refuse him nothing, but perversely she was nodding, even as she sucked harder on him. *I'm sorry . . . I only want to belong to you. Only you.* "Only you," she pleaded against his flesh. "Only you . . ."

A fantasy couldn't work; not if the reality was so precious that any illusion paled in comparison. Denying herself what she'd always wanted, because of something as pointless as fear—fear of failure, rejection or loneliness—God, that was the bigger mistake, the bigger terror.

Logan paused, his hands resting on her throat. She had her head tilted up toward him. In that charged second, both of them so still, the importance of that infinity symbol came to her. The figure eight, the sign of infinity, of eternity.

Alice had it tattooed on her wrist. She'd explained it to Madison, words that had fallen on mostly deaf ears, but apparently the words had bypassed her consciousness and planted themselves in Madison's soul, coming forth to show her the way now, to make everything else make sense.

It was as if her sister were speaking to her directly from Heaven itself.

• • •

"*Did* you know there are eight parts to reaching Nirvana?" Alice spoke between labored breaths. Madison, lying on the bed next to her, her arm around her waist, felt like she struggled for every breath with her. Her sister lifted a shaking hand, ticking off the points on thin fingers.

"Faith . . . judgment . . . language . . . pure action . . . the right livelihood . . ." Alice paused at that, her eyes twinkling as if at a private joke. "Spirit . . . spiritual application to all aspects of the law . . . the right memory, and the right concentration . . . meditation. Don't make a face. I know you hate meditation. But eight is a very good number, Madison. Remember that. It's the number of infinity, eternity, self-destruction. And sometimes self-destruction isn't a bad thing. It's the final moment, when everything is revealed."

When Alice turned her head on the pillow, Madison couldn't pull herself away from the intensity in her sister's eyes, as if Alice was struggling particularly hard to make this point.

She raised her other hand, showing Madison the tattoo on the inside of her forearm. The figure eight, the symbol of infinity, was surrounded by lovely vines and scrollwork. Madison passed her fingers over it, caressing her sister's fragile skin as Alice's eyes stayed fastened on her face.

"I got this a few months ago, when I realized where my path was headed."

"Oh, Alice." Madison circled her wrist, then bowed her head, her grip slipping away as Alice laid that hand on her hair.

"Don't forget, MadGirl. Eight . . . the sign of infinite possibilities. Promise me."

Madison had, even though she'd thought it ramblings due to illness and medication. Now she knew differently. *Eight.* Logan would be Madison's eighth significant relationship. He'd had Shale and Troy give her eight switch marks. Always before, she'd thought of her seven previous relationships as a map of her failures. But Alice's words suggested they'd been necessary preparation for the most important relationship, the infinite, final one. She just had to have enough faith. One more leap. One more time. After her refusal, her declaration that she only wanted him, Logan had pulled away from her. At her moan of protest, he gave her hair a reproving tug before moving to her legs. Bringing those machines to a halt, he withdrew the dildos slowly from her convulsing body. She moaned again, knowing if he touched her clit, she'd go into mindless, screaming orgasm for an hour. Instead, he raised the table to an upright position, undid the straps. She was woozy, too messed up to sit up on her own, but he slid his arms around her back, brought her up against him.

Had she screwed up? Should she have said *Alice* instead, invoking the safe word? Did it fit, if it was the truth inside the scene as well as out of it? With the dildos gone, she felt how slick she was, how needy for a different kind of penetration.

"Say it again," he demanded, and though she was afraid she would be punished for it, she did.

"Only you, Master. I only want you. In fantasy or reality."

Logan framed her blindfolded face in strong hands. "Good answer," he growled, right before he crushed his lips to hers.

It was like the first taste of food after starvation, every sense heightened, everything he'd denied her now given in one sweeping, overwhelming rush. If ever she could come from a kiss alone, this one would be it. In fact, she did, rubbing herself against him involuntarily. That bare touch of her clit against his body made her explode.

She screamed into his mouth, working herself against him like a pure animal, wishing he hadn't fastened his trousers and tucked himself away, wishing he'd shove balls deep into her. However, he put a firm hand on her ass, holding her against him as she let go against rough wool, rubbing shamelessly, coming endlessly from nothing more than the overwhelming pleasure of him holding her.

Every time she was with Logan, she thought it wasn't possible for him to give her a more emotional and erotic experience than the last one. He kept proving her wrong. And apparently it was only the beginning.

When that climax started to ebb, eons later, he was still holding her just as tight. His lips brushed hers once, again, then he was kissing every inch of flesh exposed around the blindfold. Forehead, cheeks, jawline, down to her throat. Her head fell back into his hands, his fingers tangling in her hair as he worked his way down her throat. She didn't need restraints, only the limp state of her body to show him she was all his.

She remembered how Troy almost went lax in Logan's grip, when he'd held his throat, told him he was helpless, he had him. The message being *I've got you, I have the control, there's nothing you control here, you're completely under my Dominance.* Just like the fantasy she nursed so often, that she'd called to mind the very first time she pulled up to Naughty Bits, trying to find the courage to go inside without Alice.

Now she knew just how potent such a fantasy could really feel, and she was in a far deeper state of relaxation, of total surrender, in his arms. She could sense how Logan fed off of it, how deeply it met what he needed from her.

He picked her up once more, and this time when he settled her, he put her in a deep, comfortable chair, perhaps a recliner. Draping her legs over the arms so she was wide open, he pressed her back flush against the reclined upper part.

"Hands over your head. Hold on to the cushion and don't let go. Don't move a muscle unless I order it."

Sure. And she'd work on that whole water-to-wine thing while she was at it, because a moment later he was kneeling between her legs, his mouth taking over her wet cunt like a man sitting down to a seven-course meal. One he planned to spend all afternoon enjoying. He licked, sucked, nibbled, stroked, swirled . . . it was like she was made of water, all the sinuous ways she twisted in that chair. He stayed with one rhythm only long enough to have her crazed, her fingers digging into the cushions, her body shuddering at the effort not to arch up against him, grind herself against his face; then he'd switch it and build her up all over again.

He left her incoherent, sounds coming from her that meant only one thing. *Mercy. But don't stop.*

He shifted, put his knee against her pussy. She sucked in a breath, not expecting it, and when he wrapped his arm around her waist, pulling her up against him, she rubbed hard against the blissfully bare layers of muscle, the blunt cock pressing insistently against her hip. He was naked.

He took her place in the chair so she was straddling him. With his hands bracketed just beneath her rib cage, steadying her, he barked another order at her.

"Hands laced behind your head."

Oh God, he was trying to destroy her. She obeyed, her arms still twitching like she had a palsy, and he controlled it all, lowering her onto his cock, keeping her swaying body steady with his strength, pushing her all the way down as a sound of guttural need wrenched from her throat. She'd never had anyone strip her so raw emotionally and physically. She had no restraints upon her except the blindfold, but the fact she was obeying his every word said he didn't need them, did he? He was all of it. Every restraint, every device. He was her Master, and she'd do anything he commanded, feeding off of the same energy that was driving him to even crazier, more intent demands of her. He would push and push, because he needed her submission as much as she needed his Dominance. Neither of them ever sated.

He lifted and lowered her, brought his own hip movements into it, making another orgasm threaten in a matter of a few strokes. But he kept it as long and drawn out as a glittering strand of a spider's web, holding her in that net as he ensured she got ever closer to climax, but not to the edge of the cliff. It was like dividing a number by two into infinity.

She kept coming back to that figure eight, didn't she?

"Please . . ." she whispered. "Please, Master."

"Not yet." It sounded like his teeth were gritted, gratifying evidence he was holding on to his own control by that same fragile set of threads. "You have no idea . . . how fucking beautiful you look."

Who knew words could push one beyond the point of no return? She tried her best, but she couldn't hold out, not before the power of the emotion in those words. Possession, reverence, devotion. Need, to the point of pain. Love, a visceral, raw, not beautiful thing, but as miraculous and spellbinding as a naked beating heart.

Why hadn't she ever seen it, what was so clear now? All the wrong guys she'd chosen before, they hadn't been the wrong choices merely for nurturing the Dom/sub side of things. They'd been the wrong choice for all the important parts of a relationship, all those things as interconnected as those eight paths of Nirvana. She was as sure of that as she was that the right man was holding her now.

"Go, love. Go over."

She had to drop her arms, grab hold of him for support. Yes, he had her body, but she had to have the contact through her palms, feel the ripple of muscle as he drove harder into her. As a result, she felt him shudder beneath her fingers as he released with a hard groan. Reaching up to catch the back of her neck, he yanked her down against him, cinching his other arm around her hips, driving into her deeper, the strokes becoming so short there was almost no movement at all, just a straining against each other, trying to crawl inside each other's souls as they both shattered.

Another one of those long ebb periods, where it could have been four minutes or four hundred, like they'd stepped into a magical world where time was merely a passing thought, nothing that could touch their reality. He'd continued to hold her tight like that, and she did the same, her fingers curved over his biceps, her cheek against his throat, forehead against the recliner. She breathed in the heated space between his shoulder and neck. She loved feeling him like this against her, nothing between them, no clothes. She realized the blindfold only enhanced all of it. She had no desire to remove it. She liked relying on him totally in her dark world and wondered if it was somehow a primal return to before birth. When, whether one was held in the womb or the hand of a god, there was naught to do but feel . . . and trust. "This is your house, isn't it?" she asked at long last.

He was stroking her back, teasing the bumps of her spine with his fingertips. "Yes. I want you living here, Madison. Starting tonight. I've already cleared room for your things. We can move them in tomorrow."

That should have startled her, maybe panicked her a little bit, and perhaps it would in the morning. Instead she made a quiet noise, but one that wasn't a refusal. "That doesn't mean you get to order me around all the time. You do know that?"

"Why, no. I assumed one unforgettable orgasm would change God's original plan and turn the female mind into a docile bowl of oatmeal."

She chuckled against his shoulder, giving it a feeble thump. A climax that powerful left no energy at all. Of course, the manly specimen beneath her wasn't acting ready for an Iron Man contest himself.

His arms tightened around her, though. "I do mean it, Madison. I know it's going to take a while for you not to fear intimacy, for every argument we have not to be a rehashing of your past. If I have you here, living with me day to day, from that first brushing of teeth in the morning, to the last kiss at night, I'll prove it to you, every moment."

"Plus you'll have a sex slave within reach of your fingertips."

"There is that."

Another thump, and this time he chuckled as well, shifting her so she was cradled in his lap. He unlaced the blindfold, removed it, stroking her hair away from her face. "Not going to open your eyes for me?" he queried tenderly.

She shook her head. "Not yet."

"Open your eyes, Madison. I need to see them."

The order gave her the strength. She raised her lashes to meet his brown gaze. The intensity of the emotions they'd shared still lingered in his expression, which did a great deal to quell any butterflies in her stomach that were trying to resurrect themselves.

"They say, after people turn thirty, it's really hard for them to change their ways," she said. "Makes it hard to live together."

"Which is why I want to start working on the adjustment period as soon as possible. Because after forty, it's completely impossible. I'm thirty-nine."

Reaching up, she touched his mouth, making his gaze soften. "I felt like I was all yours," she whispered. "I want to always feel that way."

"It's the truth," he promised, his gaze becoming fierce, immutable. "Give me your faith and trust, Madison, and I'll never betray it. I promise."

Faith. One of those eight paths that Alice had mentioned. A way to the infinite power of this, a love that she could believe wouldn't end. A love as strong as her Master's will. And her own.

"How come you never doubted? You were so sure that I was meant to be yours."

Giving her an affectionate look, he traced her throat, the side of her breast. "Alice was good at seeing deep inside of people. I saw her do it for her customers, over and over. You have a lot of her in you, though you have your own lovely style. I learned never to doubt her. When she told me that you'd be mine, I believed her. She also said I'd be yours. Not sure if she told you that, but it's true."

She shook her head. "I want it to be true."

"Then say it, because it is."

His gaze could turn fierce in a blink, his hands on her waist, lifting her. Remarkably, she found he was still hard enough to push inside her, hold her on him, his hands bracketed on her shoulders, thumbs rubbing against the base of her collar, the sensitive part of her throat.

"Say it, Madison. Who does your Master belong to?"

She swallowed, holding his gaze. "Me. You're mine."

"Yeah." Those mesmerizing eyes held her as powerfully as his hands. "Move for me, sweet slave. Stroke my cock."

They both began to move then, slow, easy, like the rise and fall of the tides. She held his gaze, and felt everything that was wrapped into this denouement. Logan and Madison, love, Dominance, submission. It wasn't the labels that defined what they would be to each other . . . it was who they were, deep in their souls. All the rest just tangled with it in a glorious tapestry that would become their love story.

Hopefully a love story that would never end.

Keep reading for an excerpt from

Unrestrained

Available now from Berkley

The first time she stepped into a BDSM club, it felt like home. *Surprised* wasn't the right word for her reaction. Surprise was what one felt toward a party thrown in one's honor, planned on the sly by someone else. When she stepped into that dim environment, inhaled the intangible layers of want and need intertwined with the surface scents of tears and sweat, perfume and leather, her unconscious revealed the secret it had kept for so long. This was where she belonged. It rose up into her chest, an unexpected comfort and validation. Ironic, given that she hadn't been there for herself. Not essentially.

Roy had talked her into giving it a try. He wanted to take the play they did in the privacy of their home into a discreet but more populated world. It had mattered to him, so she'd prepared herself to accept it, no matter how sordid it might end up being.

Everyone knew New Orleans had a seedy side. No one bothered to call it an "underside," since it was broadly displayed in the French Quarter at all hours of the day, and it had worsened since Katrina, when more of the city's criminal element shifted into that section. But then she found there was an actual underworld, and the darkness there was heated, welcoming. Not seedy at all. The perspiration gleaming on marked skin, the cries of pleasure and pain, the glitter of eyes in the dim light, the energy that pulsed in Club Release like its own power source . . . it reminded her of what she'd felt in some of the old churches in the city.

That connection had come much later, when Roy got sick. Occasionally there would be things at the company she had to handle in person, so she'd leave him with his nurse for the bare minimum time necessary. One day, on the way back home, she obeyed an impulse driven by simple weariness of spirit and allowed herself a fifteen-minute detour into a small Catholic church. It had a trio of archways beckoning the faithful, and the smell of stone and wood over a hundred years old. She'd sat in the sanctuary, stilling her mind, letting everything go for those precious few moments. She realized the ambiance that compelled hushed voices, a still soul, was like what she felt in the club. There was also euphoria, a contained joy, the best kind to feel. Things always felt more intense when restrained. She'd seen it in how Roy reacted to it, though she'd never experienced it firsthand.

Though she didn't share why she'd stopped at the church, not wanting him to worry about her, she'd shared that comparison with Roy. He smiled at her, nodded, his eyes still bright in the gaunt face. They remained bright until the last few days, when he slipped into that pre-death, morphine coma so common to cancer patients. At the end, she'd whispered in his ear, commanded him to let go. She told him that she'd be all right, that his Mistress would always love him. He would like her putting it in those terms, she knew. So his Mistress let him go, even as his wife sat at his bedside, clutching his hand, the loneliness closing around her when his breath stopped and he obeyed her.

"Want another one?"

She returned to the present and Jimmy, who ran the bar at Club Release. He'd drawn her back out of herself. Since it was a private club run as a nonprofit membership group, they didn't serve alcohol, but they had a good selection of drinks, everything from chili pepper cocoa to lemonade or O'Doul's. He gave her glass a significant glance. "I can top that to two-thirds, Lady Mistress, so you can slip in a little more of that vodka you don't think I'm seeing."

She gave him a faint smile. "My sleight of hand's out of practice."

"Naw. You just know that I already know. And you're sad tonight." He hesitated, put his hand on the bar next to hers, no contact, but the offer of connection was there. "You know, it's been over two years. Dillon and Seth are easygoing, gentle subs. Either one of them would help you break the dry spell. It's no different for us than it is for a vanilla person going on that first date. It might even be a little easier, because they saw you work with Roy and know how you operate. You can tell me 'shut up, bitch' if I'm way off base, but I can't help but feel you're looking for something."

"Maybe. I'll think about it." It wasn't the first time he'd suggested it, though he hadn't been as blunt in the past. It also wasn't the first time she'd given that noncommittal response.

When she started coming back here, a few months ago, they'd let her lack of participation pass without comment. They'd known her and Roy in a way no one else did, which meant Club Release offered a unique type of sanctuary. However, not only was she no longer playing, she was hardly watching when she showed up. She just closed her eyes and listened, using the club's sounds as the soundtrack to her own personal memory reel. It was bound to invite more pointed comments after a while. Sometimes it could be a pain in the ass, people knowing certain parts of you too well . . . and other parts not at all.

Yes, she'd felt at home here, with Roy. But it was as if she'd lost weight and the mirror showed a core version of herself that other layers had disguised. It made her think it was time to put down the whip and do something different. Be on the other side of the whip. Craving the lash, the pain . . . the release.

The first time that thought crystallized in her mind's eye, refusing to be shrouded, it had startled her. She wasn't used to analyzing and thinking about herself in a solitary way. It was always in relation to something else, someone else. Roy, first and foremost, and then a hundred others lined up after him. Family members, the community, business.

Though this was when she normally would pay her tab and go home, she didn't want Jimmy to pry further, so she would make an effort. She rose, picking up her drink, and wandered into the Fortress of Solitude. In this section of the club, no talking was allowed. A safe gesture replaced a safe word, and submissives were gagged. Their bodies, eyes and faces broadcast what was happening to them. A Master or Mistress ordered them through touch: a hand on their shoulder to guide them to a restraint, a tug of the leash, a pressure to put them on their hands and knees. It was a good place to avoid conversation.

With it being Tuesday night, she'd hoped no one would be in there, that the few members in attendance had gravitated toward the more social rooms, which also had more popular equipment. Her hopes were short-lived.

At least it was only one couple, a Master and his female sub. She didn't recognize the Dom, but she hadn't been to the club in over a month, too busy with other things. He wore a black eyemask and bandanna knotted at his nape. Together, they hid all of his features except his mouth, the line of his jaw. He wore tight black gloves.

Practitioners of BDSM came from all walks of life, many of them average Janes and Joes whose unremarkable facets became polished gems when their true natures sparkled in these rooms. She'd seen it happen with lean Goths, bikers, comfortable middle-class types, military, and then those like her. Her infallibly ladylike demeanor, the old Southern money roots she couldn't and wouldn't try to conceal, had earned her the nickname Jimmy had spoken tonight. Lady Mistress.

Despite the diverse club population, she was fairly certain she'd never seen a Master quite like this one. Unless it was in one of the confusing, erotic dreams that had been teasing the edges of her sleep of late, dreams she didn't feel comfortable sharing even in this venue. Perhaps especially in this venue.

She'd handled fund-raising for the USO charity ball three years running. During that time, she'd become friendly with a variety of military wives. One night she and Roy had the pleasure of hosting a dinner party for them and their spouses. Several of the husbands were Navy SEALs. She'd noted a unique stamp to the way they carried themselves, the look in their eyes. On top of that, each had an impressive physique. It was understandable since, in the SEALs, the body was pushed to the max in terms of endurance, speed and strength. One of the wives told Athena that many of the men, even those who'd never been injured, ended up requiring some disability benefits by the end of their career, due to the punishing demands on joints, muscles, skeletal system.

"They never quit. They just go until the body is completely worn-out." The wife had said it half jokingly, though her eyes had followed her husband with that combination of fierce love and quiet acceptance military wives had to possess for the marriage to last.

This Master had that unique stamp to him. If Athena was right and he was a SEAL, he definitely wasn't at that worn-out point. The black jeans and unmarked black T-shirt defined a body that said he was capable of pretty much any physical demand. She wondered at his age, his hair color. He wore silver-tipped cowboy boots. There was no other ornamentation on him. His concentration was on the woman dependent on his mercy.

If it wasn't a Tuesday, with such sparse attendance, she expected he would have had far more of an audience, but maybe that was why he preferred a quiet weeknight. Maybe he considered her as much of an intrusion as she'd initially considered him. But though Athena sensed his awareness of her presence, he didn't seem distracted by it.

Willow, his submissive, was a regular at the club, one who craved heavy punishment from a Master, hence the pseudonym. A willow bent under any punishment, but didn't break. She was tied spread eagle to an upright metal frame. This room had several frames like that, as well as a pegboard of whips, floggers, paddles, thumpers and uncomplicated restraint options. The Fortress of Solitude tended to attract those who preferred to use the basics and let psychological domination do the rest.

At the moment, this Master was utterly still. He held a cane in one large hand, the end resting in the half-curled palm of the other, while his gaze coursed over his captive's body. Willow was stripped to the skin, which would be a viewing pleasure for anyone watching, but his body language said that was irrelevant to him. Even more importantly, it told Willow she was stripped for his pleasure alone.

He stood with feet evenly braced, T-shirt pulling across his shoulders and chest, his ass and thigh muscles taut beneath the mold of the denim. The tilt of his head, as if he was listening to something no one else could hear, made the rule of silence not a guideline, but a mandate that would incur punishment if broken. Athena wet her lips.

His profile could have been etched from granite, his jaw looked that resilient. She wanted to see the rest of his face. She thought he'd be dark haired, because the scattering of hair on his arms was dark, and his five-o'clock shadow was a blue-black that made a woman think of pirates. Since the shadowing in the room made it impossible to determine his eye color, she imagined them as green, then brown or blue. A dark blue, like a cold ocean, hiding pleasures and dangers both.

He moved then, sweeping the cane across Willow's buttocks, a strike across the widest part. She jerked, biting down on the gag. He did it again, creating an X, and then kept doing it, focusing on her ass and upper thighs.

The girl was a pale-skinned, white-haired blonde with a soft, pretty body. She had the tattoo of a rose on the back of her shoulder, the thorny stem winding its way around her shoulder blade and to the front. When she twisted in pain, reacting to the cane, Athena glimpsed the rest of the tattoo. The stem ended at her left nipple, which was pierced with a barbed barbell.

He stopped. The girl panted behind her gag, her fingers opening and closing in the cuffs that held her to the frame. She wore a blindfold, but Athena saw the tears that had trickled down to the corners of her mouth. Her body was shuddering. Athena's stomach was quivering in response, a sympathetic tingle in her thighs and buttocks where she had them pressed against the wall. She could sit down on the couch in the corner, but she preferred to be here, part of the ungiving and cool cinder-block wall.

The masked man planted a boot between Willow's spread feet. Caressing her biceps, he slid a gloved hand over the tender bend of her elbow before he dropped his touch to her hip. Willow's head turned toward him, the attitude of her body one of yearning, desire for his attention. Wanting to please him.

Was he a consistent sadist, or had he tailored his skill set to Willow's need for pain? He might be the type of Dom who chose a different sub on each visit, enjoying the challenge of exploring various techniques, anticipating the needs of different playmates. Even so, he'd have a personal preference; most Doms did. Athena wondered what it was, wondered what it would be like to be bound to him uniquely, such that he would reveal his own desires and let her be the willing recipient of serving them.

"Her" meaning a special sub, bound to this faceless Master. She didn't mean herself, of course, except in the comfort of her fantasies.

Subs had their own preferences as well. Roy had liked the psychology of being dominated and enjoyed some pain to reinforce it, but the restraints, the sense of helplessness, that was what he truly needed.

Willow shuddered in the man's grip. From the slackness of her mouth, the jerky movements of her body, as well as the flushed look of her swollen clitoris, she was soaring. Teetering on the edge of climax, caught in mindless submission, the state a Dom loved to see.

He put his mouth against her ear. Speaking was permitted if the Master or sub had a safety issue to clarify. He spoke so softly, however, that Athena couldn't hear him. Willow did, her trembling increasing. She shook her head, a whimper escaping her. Though the sound was muffled by the gag, he gave her marked ass a sharp smack, and she stilled, obeying the rules. His touch now became more gentle, though his tone increased enough that Athena caught the rumble. He had a deep voice. She found that pleasing, soothing. Apparently, so did Willow. The girl nodded at last, more tears leaking out from under the blindfold. Anything for you, her body language said. I will give you anything. I will fly for you.

Athena swallowed.

The man moved back, switching out the cane for a six-foot single tail. It took considerable skill to wield one well, but Athena had no doubt he had that skill. When he assumed the proper stance, it was as if the room bent inward toward him like one of the Matrix movies, responding to his focus. Athena was a peripheral, no different from the wall itself. Everything for him would be about Willow's reactions, monitoring them, making sure this went where Master and sub both desired, until it became organic, a spiral where intuition was guiding every action and reaction.

Willow cried out at the pop on her tender flesh. No help for that, and why the sub wore a gag, in case she couldn't hold back involuntary noises. Club Release allowed bloodplay, but Willow's unbroken yet abraded flesh said she preferred the pain but not the injury, and he gave her the former in good measure. As she yanked against the bonds, the pain overcame her control, and she was screaming against the gag with every stinging strike.

Athena closed her eyes, imagining being where Willow stood, feeling that lash. Could such pure agony purge deeper, more emotional pain, bring it all to the surface, let it bleed out, boil forth like a pus? The idea mesmerized her, held her paralyzed against the wall, caught up in the sounds, the tears, the miasma of Domination and surrender.

When Willow went silent, except for more whimpering, Athena brought herself back, though it was like pulling herself out of a womb. The man put the whip aside, came back to Willow.

He gripped her hair, yanked her head back as he slid his hand down her front, covered her clit and labia and began to massage. Two of his fingers pushed inside her wet pussy as his thumb worked her outside. Willow struggled, wailed, and then she came. Athena shifted to the other wall so she could see the girl's climax spurt over his gloved fingers. Her gaze latched on to his forearm, pressed against Willow's abdomen, and she thought about the heat of that arm against her own flesh.

He didn't stop when Willow was done, continuing until she was squirming in discomfort. He gave her another disciplinary smack, forcing her to accept her Master's will in motionless agony, his manipulation of the oversensitized nerves. By the time he chose to stop, she would have been in a puddle on the floor, had her restraints and the arm he had around her waist not been holding her up. He removed his other glove by pulling at the fingers with his teeth, then shook it loose so it dropped to the floor. Stroking her hair with the bare hand, he bent to press a kiss to the crown of her head.

The glove had landed three feet away from Athena. She stared at it as he performed aftercare for his sub. It was a vital process that gave emotional reassurance to Willow, told her she'd done well, that she'd pleased her Master. It also physically grounded her, since a sub could be so disoriented right after an intense session like this that she couldn't even be trusted to walk unaided.

After she'd punished Roy over a spanking bench with a paddle or flogger until he climaxed, Athena would make him stretch out fully on the bench. She'd bring him back down to earth with a slow massage of his broad shoulders and back, his firm buttocks.

Setting her drink on a shelf, she bent to pick up the glove. She told herself she did it so it wouldn't be in the way, so that the Master wouldn't step on it, but as she held it, she couldn't resist slipping it over her hand. The glove had retained the heat of his body. She imagined how it had emanated through the thin outer layer, adding to the burn as he slapped Willow's ass.

The man straightened and looked over his shoulder at her. The SEALs at her dinner party had registered the slightest shift of the other guests in the same way, particularly at the entry and exit points, or if a guest made an unexpected movement, as she'd just done. Now his gaze fell on her hand, covered in his glove.

Her cheeks flushed, but rather than prompting her to pull it off, his look made her fingers curl over it. Vaguely, she thought she should apologize, because she might be disrupting his session, but speaking wasn't allowed. Plus, she wasn't sure if she'd offended him. His body language gave nothing away. The dim light obscured his gaze, but she wondered if she was right, if his eyes were dark blue. Or maybe hazel, that intriguing gray-gold-green color.

At some point, she wasn't simply meeting his gaze; she was caught in it. Wishes, inarticulate needs, things so contained she wasn't sure she could move for fear of eruption, seemed to rise up to a perilous level inside her. She wanted to tell him something, tell him everything, but she had no idea what. Or even how to start.

Some shocking part of her wanted to sink to her knees, wait until his other gloved hand touched her face, lifted her chin. He'd command her to take Willow's place on the frame and send her soaring as well.

Jimmy's jaw would drop at that, for sure.

Retrieving her drink, she turned away, leaving the room. Aftercare was personal, intimate. It had been her favorite part of the sessions with Roy. Even though this Master and Willow were in a public club environment, Athena didn't have a desire to intrude on that. It made too many things hurt.

It wasn't until she'd left the room that she realized she was still wearing the glove. She took it off, left it on a drink table next to the archway leading into the Fortress, where he'd be sure to find it. She had to suppress a strong urge to keep it. She wanted to sleep with it on her pillow, her cheek against it. She wanted to put it back on her hand, rub it between her legs the way he'd massaged Willow, and imagine him whispering in her ear. "*Come for me.*"

When she put her cup on the bar, Jimmy gave her a knowing look. "The new guy's something, isn't he? He's been really popular with the lowercase ladies."

Athena offered a faint smile at his reference to female submissives. When submissives wrote their names on the guest logs, most of them, even those who used their actual first names, wrote them in lowercase. Willow would be willow. Only Masters and Mistresses had capitalized names.

"He won't play with men?"

"No. To the eternal disappointment of those of us with bi or queer tendencies." Jimmy winked. He was bisexual and a switch on top of that, though she knew his preference was submissive. "But I'm not sure I'd call what he does play. He goes at it with a singular intensity, like he's performing a religious rite. You hear about that happening, but rarely see it in action. Not to the level he does it. You should come in one night, see him do it from beginning to end. The way he prepares himself, lays out what he'll use. That's why we've taken to calling him Master Craftsman—MC. He said he thought we were comparing him to a Sears department store. Solid quality but something most folks sadly consider outdated. That part didn't seem to bother him. In fact, I think he took it as a compliment."

Jimmy flashed a grin. "Oh, and on the straight-versus-gay thing, he told me he doesn't mind watching some Mistress-girl action."

Athena made a wry face. "That's every straight man's fantasy, Jimmy. You know that."

"Yeah. Isn't it peculiar, how many religions get worked up over two guys going at it, but they don't say diddly about two women?"

"Just proves men wrote religious texts."

"No argument there." Jimmy chuckled. "I bet MC would have

enjoyed the heck out of that thing you orchestrated for Roy's last birthday."

She'd put Roy on that same frame that Willow was on now. She'd wrapped his arms, legs and torso with multiple bindings so that he could barely move. Then she lay down on a divan several feet in front of him. Marsha, a submissive who liked being commanded to do oral on men or women, had lent Athena her services that night. She'd put her soft lips between Athena's legs, curled her pretty hands around her thighs and made her come while Roy watched. When she was done, Athena ordered Marsha on her knees in front of Roy to service him the same way while Athena watched, standing behind her. After she'd given him permission to come, Roy had gushed into the cherry-chocolate-flavored condom Marsha was sucking.

Marsha had been thanked and dismissed, and then Athena had shifted behind him, laid her cheek on Roy's back. Listening to his breath go in and out, absorbing the shudder of his body through her own, she'd been captivated by what she'd done to him. He'd been hers, but she'd been his, too. Had he realized that? She missed having a man look at her with pure ownership in his eyes. Very much.

"I'm calling it a night, Jimmy. Thanks for the drink."

"Sure thing. Don't stay away so long next time. And hey . . . I mean, if Dillon and Seth don't interest you, I'm another option. Just give me a heads-up and I'll make sure I'm not on shift here."

"Thanks, I appreciate that. You're a good friend." The sudden flash of male interest made her uncomfortable, however. Perhaps sensing it, he waved his hand dismissively. "I'm a guy, Lady Mistress. You know it's a selfish offer. A lot of us would love to experience what Roy did. You're an amazing Domme."

How would he react if he knew she wanted to go to her knees for a Dom she'd just seen for the first time? Jimmy's innocuous and honest proposal made her want to flee. Not wishing to hurt his feelings, she gave him a distant smile, shaking her head to deflect the compliment, then took her leave.

The club was on the second level of a warehouse in an industrial area, so she took a set of stairs down to the first level. They had a volunteer at a table just inside the entrance door. He served as an informal security guard, keeping an eye on the cars in the parking lot. She nodded to him, pushing open the door.

Her dark blue BMW was close to the entrance, and she unlocked it, slipped in behind the wheel, closed the door. Embracing that personal cocoon, a haven from questions and the outside world, she tried to shrug off her confusing emotions. Jimmy's suggestion had stabbed something down deep inside her. Something that rose up with astonishing firmness and proclaimed never again. She'd been a Mistress to Roy alone.

Yet she wasn't done with this, was she? The sense that she belonged in this world kept drawing her back. She just didn't know how to change her role in it, or if she really wanted to change, or if she was just confused. Sometimes the simplest thing was best. Perhaps it was time to cut it out of her life. Bury it as she had her husband. Metaphorically, since he was cremated.

When she keyed the ignition, she saw she had less than a quarter tank of gas left. Enough to get home, but tomorrow she'd be heading to the Garden Club meeting, so it would be more convenient to get gas tonight. She should have thought about it earlier, but lately she'd been more forgetful about those kinds of things. Suppressing a sigh, she glanced across the street. There was a twenty-four-hour, credit-card-only station there. Despite the late hour, since she was across from the club entrance, it should be safe enough to put in a few gallons.

She cut across the quiet street. After she processed her credit card and inserted the pump into the BMW to start fueling, an old Cadillac pulled into the aisle across from hers. The two men driving didn't look particularly reputable, but in New Orleans, that didn't necessarily signify danger.

She was merely annoyed, not alarmed, when the driver approached her. He was probably going to try and bum a few dollars off of her. As she unhooked the gas pump from her tank, put it back in its slot, the other man emerged from the Caddy, circled around to the other side of her car.

In hindsight, she knew she should have jumped in the car at the first sight of them, locked the doors and lay down on the horn. The club volunteer was at the proper angle to view the parking lot, but he wouldn't be looking toward the gas station unless something drew his attention there, like a blaring horn. It might have been an over-reaction if they meant her no harm, but it would have been better than what she was facing now.

Hindsight never really did anyone much good, did it? She should have filled up earlier. She needed to give herself a firm scolding for that. Unbidden, she imagined "MC" giving her that scolding, and received a shiver up her spine at the mere thought.

What was the matter with her? Two men had her hemmed in at her car, and yet she seemed caught in a fog, her natural adrenaline reaction clogged. Her response to their threat was perilously slow. Almost apathetic.

"Give me your credit card and whatever cash you're carrying. As well as that sparkly ring you're wearing." The driver seemed laid-back, almost conversational about it. Not even particularly aggressive, but then, he didn't need to be. The look in his eyes told her he'd done violence before, and wouldn't hesitate to do it again. "C'mon, bitch. Just give 'em to me and you can go back to your fancy life, order a couple hundred more credit cards."

Of course. Because like all rich people, I simply pull money out of my ass by magic, not hard work. She was smart enough not to say it, but she met his gaze squarely. "No."

The punch in the face was unexpected, jarring. As the world reeled, she thought of the masked man smacking Willow's ass. It had been intended to provoke pleasure as much as pain. This was simple violence, the companion to hate and resentment and all the things that made a person not care what they were doing to another. As a result, a matching response boiled up inside her.

She might have screamed in rage, she wasn't sure. All she knew was she flew at the young man with nails and teeth. She was a small woman in her forties with no fighting skills, so it would be nothing for him to beat her into the ground, but she didn't stop pummeling at him, no matter how ineffectually. His second blow caught her on the temple and she staggered. She was vaguely aware of the other one opening her car door to yank out her purse. She lunged at him and the driver shoved her against the gas pump, the handles jamming into her lower back.

"Stop fighting," he snapped impatiently.

He'd caught her hand, was wrenching at her rings. The engagement ring Roy had given her at a soiree with her family and friends. The twenty-year anniversary band. The plain gold wedding band. His mistake was he was trying to work all three off together, and her knuckles were not the same as they'd been at twenty-one, when Roy had placed two of them there. She screamed in rage, for help, to be noticed, to stop him. She also kicked at him, dropping to the ground so he had to follow her, practically roll with her as she curled around the rings like she was protecting a child.

He grabbed hold of her hair. Again she was struck with the contrast, the way the Master had seized Willow's hair to drag her head back. This man was going to smash her face against the raised concrete dais. She'd be another NOLA crime statistic.

Instead, he was yanked off her and slung back over her car. He hit the hood with a resounding thump, fell off. The BMW might need body work. A flurry of violent activity ensued, punctuated by male swearing. A cry followed a sound like breadsticks being snapped. Then there was a scramble, the two men running back to their car, one limping and the other holding his arm against himself. The Caddy sped away, the driver shouting obscenities out the window, his eyes wild, spooked.

She was trying to get up, but a large hand closed over her shoulder, keeping her down. "Easy, let's take this slow. See what's what." When he tried to uncurl her hands from her chest, she was too disoriented. She made a noise between angry protest and pleading.

"It's all right. I'm not going to hurt you or take anything from you, I promise."

It was his rumbling tone that brought things into focus. The man in the Caddy had tried to take her rings, not this man. This man was trying to help her.

He gently manacled her wrist, using his hold on it and the arm he slid behind her shoulders to help her sit up on the concrete island. He unfolded her legs so they were stretched out in front of her. She blinked, bemused when he guided her calf so one ankle was crossed over the other. A ladylike pose, rather than sprawled ignominy. It helped.

"You okay?"

She focused. "Your eyes aren't dark blue."

Maybe it was because she was still fuzzy, but she had an impression of several colors. Green at the bottom of the iris, melding into blue at the top. A center ring of gold around the pupil. She knew it was him, not just because of the black T-shirt and jeans and his build, but because of that unique stamp to him. He barely seemed winded after dispatching the two men.

Her gaze shifted to his hair. It was charcoal-colored, with a handsome peppering of gray. She suspected he was a little older than her, maybe late forties. She really had wanted to see his face, and now that she'd been granted her wish, she was having trouble focusing on it. She locked her attention on that granite jaw. That, and his touch, made good anchor points to help her steady. The heat of his palms on her arms was so much better than what she'd felt when she'd slipped her fingers into his glove. She wanted him to keep them there.

"Answer my question, Athena. Are you okay?"

"Yes. Just bumps and bruises." Her vision had only blurred when she was hit, so she didn't think she had a concussion. Her cheek had hit the cement, not her skull. She'd have quite a story to tell at the Garden Club luncheon. She'd make them laugh by telling them it was due to an unfortunate run-in with her rebellious rosebushes. She didn't think they'd laugh if she told them it was because of an attempted mugging outside her favorite BDSM club. "It was just a shock to be hit that way."

"Yeah. That's usually the first hurdle in combat training. Understanding you're going to get hit in hand-to-hand, and you can't flinch from it. You didn't flinch at all."

"I'd like to say it was bravery, but I simply didn't expect it."

"Most people don't expect someone to do that to them. Not if it's never happened before. If you had some training, I think you'd have kicked that bastard's ass."

"Thank you. A nice way of saying I fight like a girl. Would you mind helping me up?"

He rested his hand on her knee, drawing her attention to the fact that one was knocking against the other. Until he touched it, and then it stilled, with an uncertain quiver. "Let's sit here for another minute or two."

He was sitting next to her, which would ordinarily be pleasant, but the location wasn't.

"I'd like to at least move to my car," she said. "This isn't a very comfortable or aromatic position. The gas smell's a little overpowering."

"Aromatic?" His lips quirked, and they were handsome and firm. "No wonder they call you Lady Mistress. All right, then. Point taken. You're going to lean on me, though. No arguments."

It wasn't the only reason they called her that. She was Athena Francesca Summers, born of old Southern money, married to Roy "Rocket" Summers. She'd been at his side for over twenty years as the two of them expanded and increased the success of the company he started, Summers Industries, which was now a multinational corporation that also employed thousands domestically. On top of that, she was practically a professional volunteer fund-raiser for various high-profile New Orleans charities.

Though most at Club Release hadn't known her true identity in the beginning, it wasn't hard to figure out as time went on, since photographs of her and Roy regularly showed up in the business and social columns. Club Release was known for its exclusive membership and small size, which was one of the reasons Roy had chosen it, despite more upscale fetish club choices in the New Orleans area, like the nearby Club Progeny.

There was no shame in a Southern lady leaning on a handsome male rescuer, but even if there had been, she would have had little choice. Despite the odd calmness of her mind, her legs couldn't support her weight. However, he did more than let her lean. When she expected him to open her driver's side door, instead he bent, slid his arms beneath her and lifted her off her feet. He walked around to the passenger side, letting her down there before he opened the door.

Roy hadn't been a weakling, but she could count on one hand the times he'd carried her. Worried he might throw out his back, she'd insist he put her down, even though she'd hold on to his neck as she fussed. When he did put her down, she'd compliment his show of manly strength, laughing at the mischief in his brown eyes. Lord, she missed that man's sense of humor.

She leaned against the frame of the door, swamped by the feeling. A near mugging could do that, remind a woman of the practicalities she faced when her husband was dead and no close family lived in the area. No one was directly involved in her day-to-day well-being. Had she even updated her emergency contact numbers in her purse or at the house? If she'd been seriously hurt, would the emergency room have tried to find Roy?

Oh, for heaven's sake. She wasn't going to fall into this self-pitying drivel. She'd update it tomorrow, choose one of her many friends to be primary contact. None of those friends knew about this part of her life, though. They'd have no clue why she was pumping gas in the middle of the night in a part of town none of them frequented. It didn't really matter, did it? If she needed an emergency contact, she expected discretion wouldn't be high on her list of priorities.

She noticed her purse was on the edge of the seat, straps dangling to the floorboards, her lipstick a glittering tube of silver on the carpet. It suggested the other man had gotten no further than that in pulling her bag from the car. The one responsible for thwarting him stood at her back, close enough for her to feel his heat. His hand was just above hers on the frame as he waited her out.

She had a sudden desire to slide her hand up over his, hold on tight, feel that human contact. If he turned his hand to clasp hers, she'd experience firsthand the restrained strength he'd used when he brought that cane down on Willow's flanks, and then again when he'd slid his hand down her bare body, fingers decisively capturing her clit, pushing her over the edge. One more small step, and he'd be as close to Athena as he'd been to his bound submissive.

"I'd like to thank you properly," she said, staring at that hand. "May I ask your name? Or do you prefer Master Craftsman?" She knew Jimmy had meant it as a joke, a teasing nickname, but it was all she had.

"Hardly. Do you feel Lady Mistress is a good fit for you?"

"It was, once." She spoke before she thought about the wisdom of saying so, but watching him had brought such thoughts to the surface, hadn't it? Her legs were trembling again, and her grip slipped on the door frame. "Damn it."

"Ease in there." He moved the purse to the floor and folded her firmly into the passenger seat. She'd lost her shoes during the scuffle, but he had them. He placed them neatly by her feet. Her toes curled into the rug, the rougher fibers a contrast with the silk of her nylons.

He shut the door, then came around to the driver's side. He reached beneath the seat to slide it back and accommodate his larger frame before he took the spot. Her purse was still on the console, her keys in the ignition, so he turned the engine over, adjusting the air so a low heat began to fill the car. Though it was a warm enough night in New Orleans, she was shivering. Shock, she supposed, and watched him press the seat warmer for the passenger side. It warmed both the back and backside, and she couldn't help a small sigh of comfort when it responded quickly. German luxury cars were a gift of the gods.

Her dashboard GPS came up, and he glanced at it, pressing the icon programmed for home. Just like that, he had her address. She wasn't that concerned about it, because he didn't feel like a threat. Not that way. Her gaze fastened onto his forearm, that dark sprinkle of hair. Lifting her attention to the silver hair at his temples, she reached out, touched it.

Those intent eyes locked with hers in a way that made her close her hand, lower it with only a brief impression of the soft texture. He held her gaze, unsmiling, until she put the hand back in her lap. She could almost hear the click, the connection made, a mutual understanding of their behavior. His wasn't a surprise to her, not after having watched him in the club. But his reacting that way now told her he wasn't simply a bedroom Dom, one demanding those terms in the boundaries of a defined session, a sexual scenario. Few men had the confidence to pull it off believably outside a structured environment.

That intel, rather than suggesting she might act with more caution around him, gave her far more unwise thoughts and desires.

If her reaction had surprised him, given that she was classified as a Domme, he didn't show it. "I'm taking you home," he said, "and then I'll call a cab to get me back to my place. I came with a friend tonight, so I don't have my truck here. Take a hot shower tonight and a couple aspirin. It'll make you feel better tomorrow."

"Voice of experience?" Her tongue seemed to be too thick in her mouth. "That didn't seem like your first fisticuffs."

His lips quirked again. "Fisticuffs? Really? Are you a librarian?"

"Do I look like one?"

"Depends." His gaze covered her, head to toe, and he took his time about it. "I've had some interesting fantasies about librarians. The kind where I bend them over a stack of books and discipline them with a nice flexible paperback for shushing me one too many times."

Was he trying to steady her with the teasing? Giving him a silly smile, she leaned forward and put her finger to her lips, trying to summon a suitably stern librarian expression. "Shh."

He closed his hand over hers and brought the one finger to his lips, brushing a kiss over the pad. They knew what type of animal they each were, and they'd met through a sexually focused club, so this type of flirtation was meaningless. Two Doms teasing each other with no intent to engage. Except as he continued to hold her wrist, his eyes became more serious, while her fingers loosened, becoming more pliant.

"The name doesn't fit anymore, does it?" he asked. "That's what you were saying."

She swallowed, sat back. As she did, he let her slide free. She looked out the window. She'd been maudlin earlier. Sad, Jimmy had called it, but still dangerously mawkish. Now was not a time to make impetuous decisions. "You don't need to take me home. Use the car to go back to your own place, and by that time I'll be steady enough to drive. No sense in inconveniencing you by trying to get a cab out to my place this time of night."

When he said nothing, she settled deeper into the seat, closed her eyes and crossed her arms over herself. "All right?"

"You're no inconvenience. And I'll see how you're doing when we get to my place. My name is Dale. Dale Rousseau."

"Rousseau." She smiled, eyes still closed. The warmth of the car was making her drowsy. Her trembling had stopped. Things were slowing down again, the fog returning. 'Nothing is less in our power than the heart, and far from commanding, we are forced to obey it.'"

"Intriguing choice. 'To live is not merely to breathe; it is to act; it is to make use of our organs, senses, faculties—of all those parts of ourselves which give us the feeling of existence.'"

"A Master who knows his Rousseau. Thank you, Dale."

She wasn't sure if she was thanking him for knowing Rousseau, for driving her home or for rescuing her from the two thugs, but it didn't matter. A lady always offered her thanks for a kindness, and so far he'd been nothing but kind.

It just showed the depths of her capricious mood that she yearned for the part of him she'd seen earlier in the evening—when he'd been far less kind.

Joey W. Hill is the author of the Knights of the Boardroom series, including *Honor Bound* and *Controlled Response*, the Vampire Queen series, including *Taken by the Vampire*, and the stand-alone novel *Unrestrained*. Having received multiple Top Reviewer Picks from *RT Book Reviews, Night Owl Romance, ParaNormal Romance Reviews, TwoLips* and others, she has also been awarded the *RT Book Reviews* Career Achievement Award in Erotica.